*T*UESDAY HEARD HIM SNORING. LEAVING THE BABY *sleeping on one end of the cot, she headed for the ladder. Slowly she climbed, determined not to make any noise and awaken Jacob. Holding her breath every time the ladder creaked, she kept going. She reached the top of the ladder and crawled into the loft. As she turned and looked down, she saw Patty standing in a circle of candlelight. The flickering firelight shining in Patty's eyes revealed pools of terror.*

She turned back to Jacob who was lying on his left side with his back toward her. Oh, please let the pills be in his right-hand pocket. If not, I can't risk turning him over. She inched closer to Jacob and carefully reached into his pocket. She felt a small plastic pill bottle. I can't believe my luck! She pulled her hand back and there were the sleeping pills. The bottle was one-quarter full.

After she tucked the bottle into her pocket, she backed toward the ladder, afraid to take her eyes off Jacob. As she felt the edge of the loft with her toes, though, she was forced to turn around to find the top rung of the ladder. She turned back and threw her leg over the side and found a rung for her foot. She grabbed the top rung with her left hand, and before she could begin her descent down the ladder, Jacob—quick as a lightning bolt— grabbed her right arm.

Cabin II

Return to
Winding Ridge

To Donna

Enjoy

C J Henderson

Cabin II

Return to Winding Ridge

C. J. Henderson

MICHAEL PUBLISHING

Michael Publishing
P.O. Box 778
Fairmont, WV 26554

Copyright © 2000 by C. J. Henderson
Cover art by Dustin Merrill
Cover layout and pages designed by Beth Oberholtzer
Photo of author by Warner Photography,
    Fairmont, West Virginia

Henderson, C. J., 1942-
        Cabin II, return to Winding Ridge/C.J. Henderson.
    -- 1st ed.
        p. cm. -- (The cabin series ; 2)
        ISBN 0-87012-645-8

        1. West Virginia--Fiction.   I. Title

PS3558.E48243Ca 2000   813'.54
                                QBI00-901697

First Michael Publishing Printing: December 2000

Printed in the U.S.A

Fairmont Printing Company, Fairmont, West Virginia

For Jack,
my husband and best friend

This is a work of fiction. The story is intended for entertainment, and my hope is that each and everyone who reads the story gets much enjoyment from it. Also, I pray that each reader chooses to put reading the Bible first each day before beginning other books or activities.

Do your best to present yourself to God as one approved by him, a worker who has no need to be ashamed, rightly explaining the word of truth.

(2 TIMOTHY 2:15, NRSV)

As a new author, without the support and backing of my friends and family, I could not have kept up the solitary hours of writing and researching required to create The Cabin Series. My son John Michael, who is an avid reader, has taken part in the editing function of this creation. My son Mark Michael and my brother Orval Henderson have believed in me from the very first day I began the series. Other family members who have no idea that they played a part in my success are my nephew Pete Cole, who helped me believe in my storytelling skills; my nephew Harry Henderson, who read the raw manuscript and cheered me on; my sisters, Fran Henderson, Edith Hess, and Karen Leggett; my niece Sherry Clarke, who was an invaluable support on my book-signing tour in Florida; my niece Lea Robinson, who took part in the distribution of the novels; my niece Sherry Leggett, who looked for errors as pages came from my computer; and Travis Leggett, my nephew and spiritual mentor. Those nieces and nephews who have been a great treasure in my life as well are Chuck Hess,

Rick Henderson, Michael Henderson, Tim Henderson, Dean Howerton, Terry Sturdivant, Lisa Polis, and Jennifer Chipps.

My thanks would not be complete if I did not thank the many people who read my first novel, *The Cabin: Misery on the Mountain,* and gave their valuable time to write and let me know that they enjoyed the novel and couldn't wait to read the next one.

Thanks again to Valerie Gittings, who edited this novel, and Dustin Merrill, who created the artwork for the front cover.

1

*T*HE TRUCK IDLED AT THE CURB. SMOKE DRIFTED from the tail pipe, dissipating as it rose toward the sky.

"Seems like that truck's been there for the past three days or so," the bus driver mumbled to himself. He picked up a note pad and recorded the license number and a description of the truck: black with a red "4 x 4" on the side, mud flaps with crimson reflector lights. The children filed down the steps onto the sidewalk and walked toward the truck.

The driver's wrinkled brow, lined as perfectly as a plowed field in early spring, showed his inability to determine the seriousness of the matter. With the children well on the way toward their homes, he moved toward his next stop. He'd get angry complaints from disapproving parents if he didn't keep on schedule.

As soon as the bus's taillights moved from his sight, the man in the truck jumped from his seat. Peering over the cab of the truck, Aubry Moats scanned the street.

On the previous three days he had cased this particular bus stop and had picked out a little girl who on each day stood waiting alone at the corner. On those days, about twenty minutes after the bus had gone, a late-model Mercedes pulled up to the curb, and the girl climbed in.

With no one else in sight, Moats vaulted across the street, heading directly toward the girl. Before she could react, he grabbed her and forced a dirty rag into her mouth. It smelled of gasoline.

She gagged.

Moats scooped her up and ran across the street, carrying her in his strong, athletic arms. As he reached the truck he held her to his side and tightened his hold, giving himself a free hand to open the door. He threw her onto the front seat.

"If ya keep strugglin' I'll have to hurt ya," Moats warned, his rank breath forcing her to turn her head away. He buckled the seat belt and slammed the door. Hurrying around to the driver's side, he scanned the area again and saw no one who might have observed his activities.

Throwing the truck into gear, he maneuvered along the residential street. He took care to keep within the speed limit.

The girl wept.

A few miles beyond the bus stop, Moats reached over and pulled the rag from the girl's mouth. As routine, he pulled off the road nearly three miles out of town. He removed the license plate he'd stolen the week before and replaced it with the one he had swiped that morning.

Then he jumped back in the truck, heading toward the freeway and away from the danger of being caught.

"Boy, wouldn't th' coal miners what's a riskin' their lives in th' coal mines in Windin' Ridge be impressed if they knowed th' money I'm makin'," he gloated aloud.

Next to him the girl flinched at the unexpected sound of his voice. Moats ignored her. They were near the interstate and he would have them out of town before anyone was the wiser.

"Th' coal miners work night an' day diggin' coal for almost nothin'," he said as he shifted gears. "Never goin' to catch me in no coal mine again, no siree, not after th' explosion. If I hadn't gotten so drunk the night of th' explosion that I couldn't make it to work, I'd be buried alive with all th' others on my shift. It's not for me, workin' underground like a mole, no siree. I just pick up a kid here an' there. No work, no sweat. Them mountain men don't knowed what real livin' is.

"Someday soon I'm goin' to pay a visit to my brother, th' big-feelin' Sheriff Ozzie Moats livin' up on th' mountain. Goin' to tell him I'm a big executive with a fancy office."

Aubry Moats was on a mission to transport the girl to Steven Lloyd and get her off his hands. In the past he had sold children to George Cunningham, but for the past eight months George had been doing time, and nobody worked for him now. With both Aubry Moats and Jacob McCallister coming from the same mountain town, it was curious that they never knew that they had simultaneously worked for George Cunningham.

The messages McCallister sent to Aubry Moats through the grapevine, asking Moats to contact him, had gone unanswered. "No siree, law's lookin' for McCallister." The man spoke out loud once again, breaking the silence that had filled the cab since the girl had ceased sobbing. "Don't want no doin's with him. With our trucks bein' just alike, I could be a suspect 'cause he got hisself in trouble.

Admire him, that's why I got a truck like his'n an' all. No siree, though, I'm not goin' to have no doin's with him. Not now."

The broken white lines slid speedily by, putting miles between Aubry Moats and his two latest crime scenes. The first was of the boy he had picked up a few days ago. To kill a couple of hours until school let out, Moats had walked along the Monongahela River bank. It was cold to be out exercising, but he'd been raised in the mountains and was used to extremely cold weather.

Along the edge of the water he spied a young boy fishing alone. "What luck," Moats had smirked. The boy had broken a hole through the ice and was standing with his fishing pole extended over the opening. The water rippled in circles where the line disappeared into the darkness.

Moats took his handkerchief out of his pocket and moved toward the boy, who stood with his back to him. Before the boy could know what was happening, Moats had the rag stuffed into the boy's mouth and was headed for the truck with the child slung over his shoulder.

"I'm tired of this nowhere town," Jacob McCallister said to the attractive woman who lay at his side. "Can't hook up with Aubry Moats. The no-good won't answer the messages I send him. You'd never know he keeps a house in this no man's land by the short amount of time he spends here between jobs."

"He'll come around," Olene said. "Always does when he has a child to pass off. I don't know why you'd want to do business with that no-good anyway."

"It's none of your damn business what I want him for," McCallister said.

"He's got connections," Olene said. "That's why you want to get in touch with him. And you don't need to act like such a jerk when I ask you something."

"I'm just blowing off steam. Takes too damn long to make my own babies, and if I stay here I'm going to run out of money and I'll never get to my number-one mission of going after Tuesday and Patty. Times right now, I'm tired of being stuck in this hillbilly town. I have my fake IDs and if things get too hot, I'll go in disguise so no one will know who I am." He smiled and inspected the photo on one of his fake licenses.

On McCallister's two new IDs his name was Victor Newman, and on one of them the face in the photo did not bear any resemblance to Jacob McCallister. It was an excellent disguise. He'd had the second one made in the alias name without the disguise in the case he got stopped when he was not wearing it. He was covered for any event.

"Yes, Olene, I'm ready to move. I know the perfect place to keep Tuesday and Patty. The key is to take them by surprise."

"When are you leaving?" Olene asked.

"Soon, Olene, soon," McCallister said.

"When are you coming back?"

"Look, Olene, I don't want to have to tell you again! Stifle the questions. I'll tell you what I want you to know."

Jacob McCallister leaned back on a cheap pillow that was covered with a shabby pillowcase. "Bet my life the heat's off me. No one seems to be busting their chops to find out where I am. I don't see anything about Tuesday's 'elusive captor' in the newspaper anymore." Without warning, he threw his legs over the side of the bed. Grabbing his clothes, he strode into the bathroom.

"Where're you going?" Olene asked.

"Pack my things," McCallister said. "I'm out of here. I told you that I'm tired of this nowhere town."

"I'm going with you."

"The hell you are. Do as I said."

A shrill scream shattered the stillness of the night, awakening Tuesday from her deep sleep. She stumbled over her slippers in her haste to get across the hall to Patty's bedroom. Guided by the moonlight shining through the window at the head of the stairs, Tuesday reached the door to Patty's room and threw the door open to darkness. She flipped the switch, bathing the room in light. She saw Patty was sitting up in bed with tears running down her face.

Tuesday crossed the room. She sat on the bed and took the sobbing girl in her arms. "It's okay, Patty. Everything's fine," Tuesday comforted the girl.

This was not the first time Patty had awakened Tuesday with her night screams. She often had nightmares that her father, Jacob McCallister, was coming after them and then forcing them to go with him. His cruel threats of punishing them for running away from the mountain cabin often rang in her ears as she fell asleep at night.

Eight months had passed since Jacob McCallister had taken Tuesday against her will to his remote cabin. On the mountain, trapped in McCallister's macabre world, Tuesday had implored Patty to help her escape from him. Patty had agreed and had expressed her dream of living in the city with Tuesday. Unlike her sister and mothers, she had always dreamed of getting away from the primitive mountain existence.

Patty had told Tuesday about her dreams—dreams that time and again were forecasts of the future—as they sat in the corner room of the remote cabin. Patty had exposed the fact that McCallister had sold a set of twins earlier and had sold his infant daughter just before Tuesday had been abducted. Thus, Tuesday discovered that Jacob's actual business was selling his own children to baby brokers. He had never sold liquor or medical supplies as he'd told her. That was a cover-up for his disgusting crimes.

The cabin in the remote mountains was where the babies were to be sold. He had not sold Patty because of the disfiguring birthmark that covered the side of her pretty face; it covered most of the right side and was shaped like a map of South America done in purple. Tuesday had learned that, when Patty and Sara, her half-sister, were of child-bearing age, their offspring were destined to increase McCallister's illicit income.

McCallister had kept his son, Joe, to do the work that he did not care to do, but Joe's main job was to help keep the younger girls pregnant. This arrangement allowed McCallister to spend more of his time in the city of Wheeling, where he liked to gamble and socialize with beautiful women.

As Tuesday sat and held Patty, whose fourteenth birthday had been just a few days ago, she thought back to the night eight months ago when Sergeant Cliff Moran had found her and Patty hiding in the damp, dark cave where they hid after escaping from the cellar in which McCallister had imprisoned them.

Some time after she and Patty had escaped, Tuesday became aware that she carried a child in her womb, a result of brutal rapes by her captor, Jacob McCallister. She continued to have nightmares of the rapes, forced to relive the humiliation she had had to endure. The child was due, in four more weeks, at the end of January.

Cliff Moran was the one who had been responsible for Tuesday and Patty's rescue. He had arranged for their escort off the mountain to the hospital in the town of Winding Ridge that was nestled at the foot of the mountain.

But Tuesday's first meeting with Cliff Moran was actually a few weeks after she had met McCallister. Her friend, Cora, had the good fortune of having Cliff as the detective who investigated the kidnapping of her daughter, Linda, who had been taken at the age of one. After two years of questioning, probing, and searching, Cliff had found Linda and united her with her grateful parents. Cora had introduced Cliff to Tuesday.

Now Patty had fallen asleep in Tuesday's arms. Tuesday laid the girl on her pillow. *I hope Cliff finds Jacob and puts him in jail where he belongs so we can live in peace*, she prayed.

Jacob had disappeared without a trace, but Tuesday constantly feared that he would come to take Patty and her back to the cabin or some place as vile or worse. Tuesday could not forget Jacob's warning: "You are mine." She knew that he had become obsessed with her. She'd heard of these things happening; all she had to do was turn on a TV talk show and there was another similar story. She was sure in her heart if he was not caught and arrested, McCallister would come for Patty, her unborn child, and her.

Patty's dreams were all too often accurate forecasts of future happenings.

Across the street, a dark shadow, just out of reach of the street light, obscured a dark-colored car from which a man patiently watched the house.

2

*A*NNABELLE STOOD BY THE OLD WOODBURNER AND gazed out the window. "It's a mighty bad winter," she said to no one in particular.

"Yeah," Aggie replied, rocking in the chair beside the potbelly stove. "I felt it in my bones an' I told ya an' I was right, so I was."

The view from the window Annabelle looked from had been spectacular two months before—partly because she ignored the trash and the ugly, weather-beaten outhouse that stood about ten yards from the cabin at the top of a steep bank. The autumn leaves had been orange, yellow, red, and green. Pine trees that grew here and there had given accent to the brilliant contrasts of tones, which set the world aglow with flaming colors.

Now, in late December, Annabelle focused her mind's eye away from her by-gone memories and saw that the trees were bare and looked like marching death. The lush pine trees now served only to make the other, once elegant trees, stripped of their summer foliage, look desolate.

Aggie picked up her snuff-stained spittoon and spit into it. "I'm runnin' low on snuff, so I am."

Annabelle hated Aggie's habit of leaving the dirty can on the table. It was merely a rusty tin that had once contained beans. Brown spittle trickled over the rim and down the sides. And Annabelle was well aware that Aggie did not care in the least that she and Daisy would have preferred that Aggie go back to her own cabin a few miles above them.

Despite what they wanted, Aggie swore to them that she would not leave until McCallister returned.

"What ya doin' jus' standin' there? There's chores to be doin', so there is," Aggie demanded.

In the eight months Aunt Aggie had lived in the cabin with Jacob's wives, she and Annabelle had fought constantly for control. Before Aunt Aggie had moved in, Annabelle had been the one the women looked to for their orders when McCallister was absent. Aunt Aggie and Annabelle disagreed all the time, confusing the others by giving contrary instructions. Annabelle felt that she should be in charge because she was Jacob's first wife; Aunt Aggie insisted that she was boss because she had raised Jacob from a boy.

"Who ya thinkin' ya are, th' pope? I can look out th' window whenever I want. Ya ain't goin' to 'tell me what to do," Annabelle answered with indignation.

Daisy and Rose entered the kitchen by way of the musty curtained doorway.

Daisy was due to give birth and so was Annabelle. They kept no calendar and could only guess how soon they were due.

It was ironic now that McCallister was gone that they could keep their children as they had always wanted, but without him to provide for them the children would surely starve.

Rose, the youngest of the women, was not recovered psychologically from the effects of her husband selling her child and remained enveloped in a world of her own. She simply sat and rocked in the rocking chair beside the potbelly stove all during the day. At the age of sixteen, Rose looked middle-aged. Annabelle worried about her, but was unsure how to handle her, so she did nothing.

Since Jacob had gone away to escape the law, the women, with the exception of Daisy, had grown even more ragged and unkempt. They let any chore go undone if it was not necessary for their bare survival. They worked from dawn to dark as it was. Their feedsack dresses were streaked with food stains and dotted with blood spots from preparing Joe's kills. Doing laundry was an inconvenience that required hanging the wet clothes throughout the cabin to dry.

"Daisy, ya go out to th' cellar an' fetch th' flour. An' see if ya can find a jar of sausage that we'd put up last summer. I'm fixin' to start th' breakfast," Annabelle ordered.

"Don't want to have sausage for breakfast, so I don't," Aunt Aggie said, as Daisy started out the back door. "We can't have it ever' day, so we can't. We're goin' to run out. Today we're goin' to have biscuits and gravy. Daisy, get th' flour an' lard. That's what you're goin' to do, so ya are."

Annabelle knew it was useless to argue. Aunt Aggie would win in the end anyway.

Annabelle hurried into the children's room, her slippers slap, slapping as she went. As usual, strands of hair flew wildly from the bun that she wore high on her head. "Joe, ya get up an' chop th' wood. We're goin' to run out before we can get th' breakfast ready."

Joe jumped up at the sound of Annabelle's voice. After assuring herself that the children were awake, Annabelle turned her attention once again to the women in the kitchen.

Minutes before Annabelle's appearance at their door, Sara had told Joe, "I think I'm goin' to have a baby. I ain't sure, but my breasts are gettin' sore and I ain't been bleedin' every month." In the absence of a calendar, the women used full moons to keep track of their monthly cycles.

After Annabelle left, and without a word, Joe dressed and hurried out to chop wood. Trees he had cut down and dragged to the side of the old barn needed to be split for use in the stoves. In the days and weeks to come, he would chop down many more trees to last the winter, when they would need to keep the old woodburner and pot-belly stove going day and night. In the summer, although it was too hot in the cabin anyway, they had to keep the woodburner going for cooking and for heating water. The stoves both gave them comfort and added to their year-round discomfort—not enough heat in the winter, too much heat in the summer.

Aunt Aggie's dogs began barking and running, kicking up a spray of snow in their wake. They ran to Joe and then back again to the rotting, back porch. Joe stopped swinging the axe. The dogs were making a fuss over something out of the ordinary. It was Frank Dillon, making his way up the hill as he headed toward the cabin.

"Hi, Joe. Want to talk to you for a minute," Dillon said and propped his booted foot on a nearby log.

"Yeah? What ya wantin'?" Joe resumed chopping.

"It's time I told you that I talked to your pa before he left and he asked me to take his wives and children for my own."

Joe continued chopping, his impressive muscles bulging with each powerful swing. "Don't want to move to your place. I like it here. I'm my own boss now."

"Here, you only have Sara. How would you like to have six other women anytime you want? Your father never gave you an opportunity like that."

It was true. Joe's father never gave him any opportunities. And he never treated him like the son that he was. "Sounds interestin'," Joe said and set down his axe.

"If you come to live in my cabin, you can have any of the women you want, anytime you want. I have six women now. The youngest is fourteen and the oldest is twenty-nine. I want more children, but I don't want to be stuck on the mountain. I have business in Wheeling to take care of. You can do the chores that the women can't handle, and keep them under control."

Frank Dillon—like McCallister—did not speak with the mountain brogue. They both prided themselves on their speech. Dillon had been forced to learn proper pronunciation by his father before his death. Dillon's father would take him to the shed and use a horsewhip on his backside if he failed to make progress. At the time, Dillon had not been able to see the good of it, but later in life he had been grateful.

Dillon's teacher, who taught in the one-room school, reinforced his father's training. She had as much pride in Dillon as she'd had in Jacob McCallister before him, never having learned McCallister's immoral reason for desiring to learn. Neither had she learned that her extra effort in helping Dillon had opened the doors for him to follow in Jacob McCallister's footsteps. They both mingled with the city people as if they had never lived and worked among the mountain folk.

Joe leaned on his axe, the majestic mountain range climbing into the deep blue heavens in the

background. He had seen Dillon's women occasionally as he passed by his cabin when hunting for
meat or going to school. There was one whom Joe
had taken a particular liking to. On the occasions
he'd found himself near Dillon's cabin, he went out
of his way for the chance to get a glimpse of her, yet
he never got too close. Mountain folk didn't nose
around where they didn't belong.

Inside the cabin, Annabelle watched the two men
from the window. *What's Frank Dillon talkin' to Joe
about?* she pondered.

Aggie sat rocking in the chair beside Rose, with
the cats leisurely rubbing back and forth against her
legs. "What ya lookin' at? Looks like ya fixin' to stay
there all day, so it does."

"Joe an' Frank look like they're discussin' some
important matter," Annabelle said. "I don't knowed
what Joe'd have to say what'd interest Frank. I don't
have a good feelin' about Frank comin' around."

"Don't like th' sound of 'im hangin' around, so I
don't," Aggie said darkly. "He ain't comin' here out
of th' good of his heart. He's up to no good, so he is."
She spit in her spittoon and set it back on the table.

Sheriff Ozzie Moats sat at his desk reading *Playboy*
magazine as he did every day until some petty
crime or dispute happened to take his attention
from the favored pastime.

"Sheriff," Deputy Jess Willis said as he rushed
into the office, allowing the gusting wind to assault
the warm, comfortable room. "I'd better go check
around McCallister's cabin today. I haven't been on
the mountain this week."

"Go ahead," Sheriff Moats said, "although in my
estimation you're wastin' your time. Wouldn't have
you goin', but the high-flutin' detective from
Wheelin' will be callin' to see if we're checkin'

McCallister's cabin. If we don't do it, he'll come nosin' around hisself, tellin' us how to do our job."

Deputy Willis left the office and immediately ran into Bud Cougar. "Hi, Bud. You comin' to see the sheriff?"

"No, Jess, not today. I'm on my way to the store."

"Have a good one," Jess said.

"You're lookin' mighty pleased with yourself," Bud said, "wearin' that smirk on your face."

"Damn it, it's the sheriff. I can just see his leerin' face as he gets his *Playboy* magazine out when no one's around. It gets to me that he sets behind his desk doin, nothin' but orderin' me to clean the jail and sendin' me here and there on trivial jobs. The sheriff don't mind wastin' taxpayer's money doing nothin', but insists that I constantly keep busy and earn my keep," Willis grumbled.

As Jess Willis left Cougar and continued walking toward the sheriff's Jeep, Andy Hillberry charged up to him. "Looks like you're goin' somewhere," Andy said. "Ya goin' to run the county's Jeep up an' down th' mountain, or ya goin' to take care of business?"

"How about mindin' your own?" Jess said.

"I am mindin' my business. Have ya done anythin' about McCallister yet?" Andy demanded, showing his remaining tobacco-stained teeth. Several lone teeth protruded here and there from an expansion of exposed gums.

"No, we haven't, Andy. Don't know why you're so all fired up about him though. The law ain't none of your affair. So why don't you go about your own business and I'll go about mine." Jess looped his thumb through his holster and with his free hand tipped his cap to the back of his head. He stood in his most authoritative pose, but his skinny, lanky body and high-pitched voice belied it.

"I just don't like it, Jess. And you ain't no big shot. So ya don't need to act like it. You're just th' sheriff's puppy dog, doin' his biddin'. If I'm wantin' to knowed somethin' 'bout what's goin' on in th' county, it's your duty to tell me. You're a public servant after all. Taxpayer's money what's payin' you."

Everyone knew that Andy Hillberry had yet to pay taxes; he'd never held a job in his life. He scraped his meager living off his rocky land, barely managing to feed his wife and children.

Jess stood his ground, rocking back and forth on the balls of his feet. "Well, I told you ain't nothin' happenin'. You're just a nuisance who's always makin' trouble."

"Sheriff's in there readin' his trash," Andy Hillberry informed Jess of what Jess already knew. "He's a no-good just like his brother, Aubry."

"I have to go, Andy. I don't have time to stand out here chattin' with you." Jess shoved past Andy and got into the patrol car and headed toward the mountain and Jacob McCallister's cabin.

Jess continued up the mountain road. Each time that Jess went to check out Jacob's cabin, it was the same: the women had nothing to say; they knew nothing.

*D*ON'T WANT TO GO TO SCHOOL," PATTY PLEADED
with Tuesday. She sat in the sunny kitchen,
picking at her breakfast with a frown on her pretty
face.

"I suppose it's the same old thing."

"Yeah, th' kids laugh at me. They're worse than
th' kids livin' at Windin' Ridge," Patty complained.
"On th' mountain I wasn't th' only one without a
friend. There was th' other mountain kids, and I had
Joe and Sara."

"Patty, as you improve your speech and manners
they'll forget and accept you. They'll realize that they
could learn a great deal from your background."

"That won't help my face," Patty said with tears
streaming down her cheeks.

"As soon as you're settled in school," Tuesday
promised, "I'm going to take you to a plastic surgeon
and see about removing your birthmark. It's done all
the time. Then you'll look like all the other children."

"What's a plastic surgeon?" Patty asked.

"It's a doctor who fixes those kinds of things like
your birthmark," Tuesday said.

"Oh, I knowed what a doctor is," Patty said.

"I know you do," Tuesday said, "but with a plastic surgeon you're not usually sick. Among other things, he takes care of problems like you have. You'll be just like other girls, except prettier because you're a very attractive girl in the first place."

"It would be so wonderful to have a normal face. Sometimes I think other kids are afraid of me 'cause of my face, an' ya said they can learn from me, but I don't feel like I knowed anythin'. I want to learn to talk like them an' then I'll go to school. I want to laugh like they do an' be friends with them. Until I can be like them, I don't want to go to school. I want to stay with you. Please let me," Patty begged.

"Okay, Patty, but don't ever forget we all learn from each other and you have as much to offer as anyone else does."

In an attempt to help Patty fit in, Tuesday had bought dresses, jeans, and other clothing in the styles children liked to wear. Each of the outfits was becoming on Patty's just blossoming figure.

Tuesday had had Patty's hair done in a popular style. The new layered cut framed her face with feathery softness and fell to her shoulders. Patty had flowered into a beautiful girl, and many of the other girls were secretly jealous of her. Even though in appearance there was nothing left of the wild mountain girl, she continued to stand on the outside looking in.

"Patty, maybe a class for special children or a tutor is best for now. If we don't give up, I promise the other children will eventually stop teasing and see you for the sweet girl that you are."

"I'll try t-t-to learn."

"That's good, Patty. It's just a matter of time and exposure to a more sophisticated lifestyle."

Patty looked confused. "What's so'piss'ta'ca'ted mean?"

"I know you don't comprehend all of this," Tuesday laughed at Patty's pronunciation of the word, "but one day you will. To be sophisticated means to be refined, like the difference between the cabin and this house."

"Yeah, I think I understand," Patty said. "Like th' difference between th' way mountain people talk and the way ya talk."

"Yes, that's it," Tuesday smiled. "We'll work on the way you talk too. Instead of me trying to correct you all the time, you'll be going to a speech therapist. If only you had not been down with mono those months, you'd have made enough progress to be comfortable with the other children in your class.

"How would you like to have lunch with Cora and Linda today?" Tuesday asked changing the topic.

"Yeah," Patty replied brightly. Then her face darkened. "When I think of th' lonely life on th' mountain with nothin' fun to do an' nowhere to go, I can't believe my life now. Sometimes I'm afraid I'm goin' to wake up, and all this'll be gone, an' I'll wake up back in th' cabin on my old mat."

Tuesday remembered the first time she took Patty out to eat. Patty's delight at being able to order whatever she wanted was charming. She had not known what to order, as she was unfamiliar with the choices on the menu. Tuesday had ended up choosing for her, and when the waiter set a plate of lasagna in front of Patty, she had no idea what it was.

Patty picked up her fork and tasted the new food. "It's th' best thing I've ever tasted," Patty had said, smiling from ear to ear. Next, she tasted the garlic toast and without another word finished the meal as if she thought she would never get another one.

and Lieutenant Hal Brooks, who worked with Sergeant Cliff Moran, had taken the twins into his home. When it was discovered that they were Jacob McCallister's children, Hal and his wife had started the adoption process. Jacob McCallister's third wife, Daisy, was their mother. After McCallister ran, Daisy could not care for the children and she had consented to the adoption.

The detectives had not forgotten another mountain man, who lived in a larger cabin below McCallister's. While conducting a cabin-to-cabin search for Tuesday, Cliff had knocked at the man's door and had spoken to two women who had let him know that the man would be furious if he found out they had talked to a stranger. The cabin and women had the same feel as McCallister's. One woman had been young and pretty; the other looked much older, and her huge body dwarfed a head of hair that resembled a porcupine.

Cliff was leaving the cabin when he came upon the man, who was just short of being civil. Like McCallister, the man was a bit too polished for the mountain life.

Tuesday and Patty were already seated when Cora and Linda arrived at the restaurant. Linda saw them first and ran to Patty. Even with their age difference the girls had become close friends. "Hi, Cora, Linda," Tuesday greeted them.

"So, Patty, you're skipping school today?" Cora asked.

"Yeah, th' kids don't like me cause I'm different from them. I want to be like them. I don't want to be laughed at. They're always playin' an' havin' fun an' doin' fun things like plannin' for their dances an' ball games an' parties an' stuff."

"Maybe you should send Patty to a school for

special children," Cora winked, "and take her out of public school. She's going to have psychological problems from all this."

"I've already come to that conclusion. It's a constant battle getting Patty to go to school. She always comes home in tears when she does go. If I don't get her settled in a school for children with special needs, she'll never get rid of her mountain brogue. I don't know why I didn't do it in the first place. She's been with me for eight months and has made no progress."

"That's okay, Tuesday. It's not like you've had experience raising a young teenager. There's plenty of time."

"You're right. It's a learning experience, for sure."

"It'll be a class with children who have the same problems as you," Cora explained to Patty. "You'll have a lot in common with them and they'll not tease you. When you're ready, you can go back to public school again.

"With that problem solved," Cora changed subjects, "how're you and Cliff getting along? When's the wedding?"

Tuesday laughed. Cora never minded saying what was on her mind, but Tuesday's laughter faded as her fear of Jacob resurfaced, sharpened by Patty's early morning recounting of her dream of his return. Tuesday knew Jacob would go to great lengths to keep his menacing promises that he would never let them go. Worse yet, he had promised that he would make Tuesday and Patty sorry for running away from him.

After lunch, Tuesday returned to her house. Cora took Patty home with her so that Tuesday and Cliff could dine alone that evening.

Later that day, Tuesday hurried to get ready; Cliff was to arrive in half an hour. She looked at her reflection in the mirror as she turned back and forth. *Oh, I look like a blimp,* she thought. *How can Cliff love me when he knows that I'm carrying another man's child?*

Although Cliff had proven himself to be honest and caring, her experience with Jacob had left deep emotional scars that had made it difficult for her to get close to Cliff.

It had taken time and patience on Cliff's part, but he had stilled her tormenting thoughts that only an idiot would have believed that Jacob McCallister was what he had appeared to be.

When the doorbell rang, Tuesday peered through the peephole. Cliff stood there looking extremely handsome.

"Hi, Cliff," she said as she opened the door.

Cliff kissed Tuesday softly. "Where's Patty? She usually races you to the door to meet me."

"We had lunch with Cora and Linda. Patty went home with them. Cora gets such a kick out of showing Patty something she's never seen before."

"It is fun to watch the wonder in her eyes as she investigates something new."

Tuesday handed Cliff a glass of wine; she had a club soda. "Is there any news about Jacob?" Tuesday asked.

"No, Tuesday, it's as if he disappeared from the face of the earth."

"What about the mountain cabin? You're still checking in case he goes back there?"

"Yes. Sheriff Moats and his deputy check the cabin every week. McCallister has not been back and, frankly, I don't believe that he will be. He's smart enough to stay away."

"But," she asked, "what about returning to the scene of the crime? I hear that all the time. They always return to the scene of the crime."

"We're doing everything possible to find him," Cliff assured her. "I'll see to it that Sheriff Moats keeps a watch out for him in case he does return to Winding Ridge. Tuesday, we'll find McCallister wherever he's gone. Don't worry. But where did all these questions come from. Did something happen that I don't know about?"

"Patty has been having dreams about Jacob coming for us. Last night was the worst yet."

"I wish I could talk you into coming to live with me until we catch McCallister," Cliff said.

"No!" Tuesday said. "I'm not going to let the scumbag run me from my home."

"I'll move in with you," Cliff offered.

"No, not until we're married, and I want to wait until the baby is born before we get married," Tuesday said. "I won't walk down the isle looking like a blimp."

"We can get married in a private ceremony and have a formal wedding later," Cliff said. "That would solve the problem of you and Patty being alone."

"Cliff, even if we're married, you can't be here all the time to protect us," Tuesday said. "Besides, I want our wedding and honeymoon to be special. If we're already married the magic will be ruined."

"Okay, I won't argue the point, Tuesday, but are you careful to keep the doors and windows locked all the time? Even in the daytime?"

"Yes, day and night." She had to smile at the worry lines that ran across his brow below his unruly, wavy hair whenever he thought of her welfare.

"Don't let your guard down, not for a minute," Cliff said, taking Tuesday in his arms.

"Believe me, Cliff, I won't. You know Patty's dreams come true. Remember the twins."

Cliff took Tuesday's face in the palms of his hands and said, "Look at the positive side of Patty's dreams. If we see them as a warning, we can prevent a disastrous situation from happening."

"I hope you're right," Tuesday said. She felt that being forewarned by Patty's dreams was indeed a great advantage. McCallister had no idea they were on alert, but at Cliff's words "disastrous situation," cold chills shot down her spine.

Her face lost its color and Cliff hugged her. "Please try not to worry. It's not good for you in your condition. You know I'll do everything in my power to keep you and Patty safe."

"I know," Tuesday said and hid her face against his shoulder. "If it weren't for the dreams . . ."

"No, Tuesday, we can prevent something from happening because of the dreams. You must remember they are a good thing."

"Oh, I understand that," Tuesday said. "I just mean that I wish she were not dreaming about Jacob. If he weren't planning to come for us, he wouldn't be in her dreams. Then we wouldn't be worrying that he's out there ready to come for us."

"Hang in there," Cliff said. "I know it's rough, but it's best all around if he's found and locked up. You'd never have to worry about him again."

"I know," Tuesday sighed.

"Just remember there's a patrol car cruising by the house on a regular schedule," Cliff reminded her.

4

*J*OE SPOKE TO SARA ABOUT DILLON'S VISIT AS THEY walked home from school. "Frank's wantin' us to move to his cabin. I'm thinkn' I like th' idea."

Sara stopped in her tracks. "No! I don't want to move to Frank's cabin. Ya knowed he's mean. He's even meaner than Pa. Ya knowed he is."

"Don't give me that back-talk." Joe said darkly. "Ya don't knowed nothin' 'bout him."

He gripped her by her shoulders until she dropped her gaze. "As th' man of th' house, I'm in control now that Pa's gone. We're goin' to starve, if we don't go. If Frank hadn't brung us food n'stuff we'd already starved. I knowed if we don't go, he's not goin' to bother with us no more. We're goin'. That's th' end of it."

They continued walking, heads bent to the wind. The path was steep and rocky. Joe's surefooted steps helped him to make a steady climb. As Sara stumbled occasionally, he caught her under the arm to keep her from falling to the ground.

As Joe and Sara neared the cabin, they saw the sheriff's Jeep. "What th' hell's he doin' here again?"

Joe swore. "Gettin' tired of him nosin' around."

They rounded the corner of the cabin and there stood Deputy Willis on the back porch, talking to Aunt Aggie.

"What ya wantin' here?" Joe demanded. "We done told ya a thousand times before we don't knowed where Pa's gone."

Willis turned at the unfriendly tone of Joe's voice, with his hand on his holstered gun, an equalizer to their size difference. He looked like the skinny, timid man he was rather than the tough lawman he always strove to be. "Don't get smart, boy. You're gettin' too big for your britches. I'm obliged to find those who break the law, and I'm not goin' to stop lookin' until your father's found."

"Well Pa ain't here an' I don't expect he'd come back no how. I'd be much obliged if you'd get your skinny ass off my property, before I wipe that smug smile off your face. If you're smart, ya knowed I'm not scared of ya."

Willis kicked a rock out of his way and climbed into his Jeep.

Joe's hostile attitude and muscular frame would intimidate most any man.

The Jeep bounced down the mountain road toward town. The deputy had done his job. He'd checked the cabin for Jacob.

Earlier in the day, Frank Dillon had invited Joe to meet his women. If Joe agreed to Dillon's plan, his mothers, sister, and aunt would have no choice. Daisy and Annabelle were due to give birth anytime and Sara was due a little later. For Dillon, the women were money in the bank, and that was the reason he had agreed to take them in.

At the sound of stomping feet on Dillon's front porch, he opened the door. Joe stepped through the doorway and pulled off his toboggan, unmindful of the snow he was tracking in.

Joe resembled his father, Jacob McCallister, with his thick, dark hair and muscular build. He had the same charisma as his father too, the same appeal that would make women fall unconditionally in love with him, but there was a cold, cruel look in the too-handsome boy's eyes. A look that some women, too charmed to see otherwise, would interpret as strength.

"Come in, Joe. Glad you could make it," Dillon said.

"Yeah, I'm anxious to get started now that we made a deal," Joe said.

"First I want to make sure we understand one another," Dillon said.

"Yeah, I can't fault ya with that," Joe said.

"Boy," Dillon said, "I need you to be hard-nosed with my women. I need to trust that you can handle the women and keep them in line. You must not allow them to charm you into leniency. Control on your part—that's the only way this deal will work. I need things to run smoothly here while I'm spending time in Wheeling."

"I can do that," Joe said. "I'm not goin' to let a woman take charge of me."

"Come closer to the fire, Joe, over there where it's warm." Dillon slapped Joe on the shoulder and led him closer to the potbelly stove. The muscles rippled under Joe's jacket as he moved.

"You're going to be a large man like your father," Dillon said. "How old are you?"

"I just turned sixteen this winter," Joe answered. "We both knowed I need ya for my own welfare now, but someday soon, I'll need no one an' I'll leave to go on my own. Ya need to knowed up front that I only agreed to th' deal because of havin' your women. If ya understand that we'll do fine."

"You just remember your place, Joe," Dillon spat. "Right now, you need me as much as I need you. I expect some loyalty from you. I may not be ready for you to leave when you think you're ready to go. Do you understand?"

"It won't be that'a'way," Joe said, standing his ground. "When I'm ready to go, I'll go."

"It's your funeral," Dillon warned, "but the women stay."

"If she wants, Sara goes with me," Joe said.

"That's no problem for me," Dillon said and turned toward the kitchen area. "First, let me introduce you to my women. Then you can give me your final answer if you stay or not."

"Get 'em out here," Joe said.

"Big Bessie," Dillon called, "gather the girls and come here now!"

Big Bessie hurried to the center of the cabin where she could see up to the loft. The kitchen area was under the loft floor, where she had been cleaning up from dinner. "Get down here. Hurry now," Big Bessie bellowed, her fat face holding a look of importance.

The girls hurried down the ladders. There were four ladders, one to each section of the loft. They were attached all around the square log cabin. The loft was where they all slept, except for the one Frank allowed in the big bed for the night.

Big Bessie was Frank's oldest wife, his first. She had earned the name Big Bessie by giving in to her love for food. Her arms were as large as hams and her hands were big and powerful. She was quick to swing at any of the younger, prettier women. Big Bessie's brown hair was short. She cut it herself with sewing shears. As a result, her hair stood straight up, uneven and unmanageable, causing her fat face to carry a look of surprise.

Big Bessie stood in front of Frank and Joe. The other women stood behind her and waited to be told what to do.

"This is Big Bessie. She thinks she's boss, and I guess she is because when one of the girls doesn't listen to her she'll feel the power behind those huge arms."

Big Bessie beamed at his remark. Anytime Frank gave the women any attention at all they lapped it up like puppies. He was the center of their very existence. Not one of them had ever been off the mountain.

Frank pointed to Melverta, and she stepped forward. "This is Melverta. She's twenty-five."

Melverta stood twisting back and forth with her hands clasped in front of her. Melverta's oily, straight, brown hair was shoulder length. Her ears stuck through her hair, and she vaguely resembled a monkey. Her features were sharp and masculine. She was skinny except for the bulge that the child she carried made in her feedsack dress. She was six months pregnant and was due to give birth in March.

Frank pointed to the next girl in line, and she stepped forward. "This is Eva Belle. She's eighteen."

Eva Belle stood with her head down, her dishwater blonde hair falling over her face.

"Get your head up so we can see you," Frank ordered.

Eva Belle lifted her face and shuffled her feet. The women were not used to strangers, and although they'd seen Joe pass by many times, he was still a stranger to them. Eva Belle was only four-feet-eleven-inches tall. She was tiny and dainty looking; her huge blue eyes were framed with long lashes. Eva Belle was four months pregnant and was due in May.

Frank pointed to the next girl, and she stepped forward. "This is Mary Lou. She's sixteen." She was the girl Joe had hoped to see each time he passed Frank's cabin.

Mary Lou stood looking boldly at Frank and Joe. Her jet-black hair was thick and her natural curls bounced around her pretty face. Unlike the others, Mary Lou's eyes sparkled with life. Mary Lou spent a lot of time poring over the glamorous women pictured in the catalog that was used for toilet tissue in the outhouse. Sitting on the wooden bench, she admired the pictures of the beautiful models for hours. She studied their hairstyles and clothes. Mary Lou often vowed that she would be like them someday. The women pictured in the magazines were proof there was a better way of life. They didn't have the hopeless look in their eyes that her sister wives had.

The next girl, Sally Ann, was fourteen. She was a plain, skinny girl with red hair and freckles.

The last girl was Emma Jean, who was fifteen. Emma Jean's dark brown hair hung in waves and grew down her back to her waist.

"She stutters and won't talk much. She acts like she's afraid of her own shadow," Frank said pointing at Emma Jean.

Frank sent the women back to their work and turned to Joe. "You had time to think it over and now you have seen my women. Do you still want to live here and be my right arm?"

Big Bessie glared at Joe, who was a threat to her authority.

The girls went back to work, keeping their eyes on Joe and Frank as they finished their chores.

HE WINTER SUN SHONE BRIGHTLY THROUGH Tuesday's kitchen window. As Patty sat hungrily eating her breakfast, she listened as Tuesday chatted about the new school.

"Are we goin' today?" Patty asked.

"We're going to look at a couple of schools Cora and I picked out for you. Cora and Linda are going with us."

"After that, can we go to th' mall?" Patty asked. "I like to look at all th' things ya can buy. Th' mall's so big an' grand."

"Sure, it'll be like a treasure hunt. We can explore," Tuesday said. "Actually, I think going to the mall is educational for you. We always find something new that you haven't seen yet."

"I can't imagine that there's somethin' more for me to see," Patty said. "I just can't believe that I was living my life in such hopelessness an' there was this wonderful world out here that I didn't knowed nothin' 'bout. The catalogs I use to look at didn't even come close to showin' me what I was missin'."

C. J. Henderson

"There's much, much more for you to see," Tuesday said, knowing that Patty was a little overwhelmed. "One thing I've noticed is that your vocabulary is growing since you're now living in the city."

"What's that mean?" Patty said, a frown on her pretty face.

"Vocabulary is the variety of words that you know and use," Tuesday answered her. "Your improvement is marvelous." At the questioning look of Patty's face, Tuesday explained that marvelous means good, great, and wonderful.

"Ya knowed, Tuesday, I'm happy living here, an' I don't know how to thank ya for keepin' me with ya when I knowed that I'm so much trouble."

"Patty, you're no trouble," Tuesday said. "I think of you as my daughter now. We're a family. You'll think this strange, but getting you away from that hopeless wilderness was worth the torture I went through. We're family, forever."

"Like Linda? She has a mother. She has love an' a home with everything she needs. Nobody's goin' to sell her. Now, I have those things." Patty got up and hugged Tuesday.

How wonderful it is to have Patty to share my life. She makes what I went through at the hands of Jacob worth it.

"Let me show you something, Patty," Tuesday said and took her hand.

"Okay." Patty got up and went with Tuesday.

"I've been waiting for the right time," Tuesday said. She led Patty through the house to the back stairwell. They went up to the first landing, and Tuesday opened a door that Patty had never paid much attention to. The door seemed unimportant with so many new and amazing things for her to absorb. Beyond the door was another set of narrow steps that led to the attic.

They climbed the stairway, and Tuesday opened a second door. She found the light that hung from a beam on the end of a long cable. Reaching out, Tuesday pulled on the chain at the base of the light fixture. The tug sent the light swinging back and forth, spilling an eerie light across the room that revealed boxes and trunks scattered all over the attic floor. They were spread out amid old, discarded furniture squatting in the darkness, appearing to be evil phantoms lurking in the dim light.

The thick dust and cobwebs, revealed by the dim light as it swayed on the end of the cable, attested to the fact that it had been years since anyone had visited the attic.

"Tuesday, it's scary up here," Patty said, clinging to Tuesday's hand.

"It's just an old, dirty attic," Tuesday said laughing. "There's nothing to be afraid of." She led Patty to the far corner, clearing the cobwebs from their path with her hands as they went. Still, cobwebs collected in their hair and clothes. "Here we are," Tuesday said. Several boxes were marked with Tuesday's name.

"What's in th' boxes?" Patty asked.

"Let's open one and see," Tuesday said. She opened one of the boxes that held many of her treasures from her preteen years.

"What is it?" Patty asked.

"It's a game. We'll take it downstairs and I'll show you how to play. First, let's see what else is in the box. The game will be fun, but it's not what I'm looking for."

Among the many items Patty had never seen before was a make-up mirror. It was electric and

Tuesday was unnerved about Patty's reaction to the doll, but Patty was still very young and Tuesday knew many children used fantasy to help themselves through hard times.

Tuesday was mesmerized as she listened while Patty talked to the doll. *Patty is a little too old for imaginary friends, but she has had a hard life. What an understatement that is! If I put it together with her ability to predict future events—in her dreams—I guess her age has nothing to do with it. Somehow the doll is a part of her unusual gift.*

Later, in her room, Patty sat on her bed with the doll.

"I'm so glad that I can talk to ya anytime I want. Ya knowed I'm afraid that Pa is goin' to come an' take us back to th' cabin. It'll be worse than before."

Patty held the doll to her ear. *Patty, you're right. Your pa is going to come for you.*

"Why, Summer. Why's he wantin' me back on th' dreary old mountain?"

He wants Tuesday. He'll take you too.

"What can we do?" Patty asked the doll.

I don't think you can do anything but watch and listen.

Tuesday heard the murmur of Patty's voice and opened Patty's door. "Patty, it sounded like you were talking to someone."

"Ya, I'm talking to Summer. She told me that Pa's goin' to take us away.

Tuesday did not know what to say. They were talking about a message from a doll. *I guess it's not unusual that Patty believes the doll talks to her,* Tuesday thought. *Isn't that what an imaginary friend is all about? When in need for companionship it's what a child does—invents a friend to communicate with. But that's not the problem. The problem is what she's saying. I can't let that happen. I have no intention of ever seeing Jacob or his cabin again.*

"Patty," Tuesday said, "Cliff won't let that happen."

"I hope you're right," Patty said, "but it's real to me. My dreams always happen."

"They happen because no one tries to stop them like we're going to do now!" Tuesday exclaimed. "Like Cliff said, we will consider your dreams a warning and we can prevent them from happening!"

Cliff and Hal were in Cliff's office going over the newest report on missing children. "I can't keep my mind on this," Cliff said. "Where's McCallister?" He stood up so fast he crashed his chair against the window. Ignoring the possibility of broken glass, he walked around the desk. "Hal, I have to find him before he decides to come back for Tuesday and Patty!" Cliff's outburst was inspired by Tuesday's report of Patty's most recent dream. "I'm sure that's his priority. The elaborate scheme he concocted to take Tuesday to his cabin, and then the way he locked her and Patty in an underground cellar to keep them captive again after they attempted to escape, show just how committed he is to keeping them under his thumb. He'll not give up. I can't guard them twenty-four hours a day and find him too! Where in the hell is he?"

"Calm down, Cliff. We'll find him. He'll grow complacent and do something stupid."

Cliff dragged his fingers through his unruly hair. "But the million dollar question is: will it be in time?"

"Cliff, you know we're doing all we can. We're having her house watched, but we can't have a twenty-four hour guard on it. If we did that, we wouldn't have enough men to go around, not to mention having any men left to conduct an investigation. The men who are cruising the street are keeping a close eye on her house. You can bet on that."

"I know, I know. I just keep seeing Tuesday and Patty huddled in that cold, dark cave." Cliff said. "Remember Patty's dreams. They're not to be ignored."

"We'll find him."

"Yeah, just pray it's in time."

"Anything new on Steven Lloyd?" Hal asked.

"Yes, Judy got her hands on an old carton filled with old files of Lloyd's. They contain files on more than enough unlawful adoptions to hang him."

"I hope Judy's being cautious," Hal worried. "She could get herself into trouble."

"You're right about that," Cliff said. "Steven Lloyd could be dangerous, if he's backed into a corner."

"Talked to Amy and Ralph Thompson?"

"Not yet," Cliff answered. "They're at the hospital with the boy. The doctor tells me he's suffering from malnutrition. He won't talk to anyone. He's going to have psychological problems but will recover physically. I'm due to meet his parents at the hospital cafeteria in a half hour."

Amy and Ralph were the parents of a child who had recently been found after a report of abuse had been made, and he was taken from his adoptive parent. A child welfare agency reported to Cliff and Hal's department that there were two boys who were taken from the home of Simon Leonard and admitted to the hospital. It was suspected that Leonard illegally adopted the boys. One of the boys, Jeff, was traced to Amy and Ralph Thompson, whose son had been kidnapped years earlier.

"By the way, did you see this?" Hal asked. "The girl who was kidnapped in Pennsylvania last week? Let's see, here it is, Ashley Blake. Look at the description of the vehicle reported as being seen at the scene of the crime. Black, Ford truck, 1999 model, red "4 x 4", and crimson reflector lights on the mud flaps. The school bus driver had noticed the truck at the bus stop several days running and took down the license number and description. It's the same description of the truck used in the kidnapping of Todd nine months ago. Remember, we suspected that it was Jacob McCallister because the description of his truck fit. Could be McCallister—he'd have to make money some way. Looks like whoever it is makes a living of it."

"Think he'd take a chance like that?" Cliff asked.

"It certainly fits the description of his truck," Hal said. "We'll check every possibility."

"Have you run a check on the license number?" Cliff asked. "The license was probably stolen. Maybe it's Aubry Moats, the sheriff's brother. Rumor is he has a truck just like his idol McCallister."

"McCoy and his men are pursuing Aubry Moats and the possibility he's involved with McCallister in these abductions."

"They're cut from the same cloth," Cliff said. "My hunch is, if we find Aubry Moats, he'll lead us to McCallister.

"When we get McCallister, it'll answer a lot of questions, I'm sure."

"That's the day I live for," Cliff said.

"You'd better get going or you're going to be late for your meeting with the Thompsons."

"You're right. I'll catch you later." Cliff left for his meeting.

The hospital cafeteria was a bustle of activity. Over the clatter of many dishes and the hum of many voices, Cliff sat talking to Amy and Ralph Thompson. Cliff had had too many sessions like this in the past four and half years with broken-hearted par-

saw Joe and Frank Dillon walking toward the cabin. "What's he wantin' here? Don't like it one bit, so I don't," she grumbled to Rose who sat and rocked, not noticing as the others went about their day. Turning away from the window, Aggie picked up her spittoon and spat. She ran the back of her hand across her mouth to rid herself of the spittle. Now they were on the back porch. She stepped back as they noisily tromped inside.

Annabelle and Daisy hurried into the kitchen to see what the commotion was about. These days someone at the door could only be trouble.

"Sit down," Dillon surveyed the room. "I have something to say to you."

The women did as he said, not taking their eyes off him.

"You will come to live in my cabin," Dillon ordered.

Annabelle was shocked by Frank Dillon's demand. *He's goin' to have a fight on his hands with Aggie,* she thought, *an' I won't blame her one bit 'cause I don't trust Frank as far as I can throw him.* She was accustomed to Jacob and his ability to get his way with others. Although Frank was a handsome man, he lacked the charisma that the overly handsome Jacob possessed.

"Start getting your things together. Bring only what you need and can carry. I want all of you in my cabin before lunch tomorrow." Frank shook hands with Joe and left.

As soon as the door slammed behind Frank, Aunt Aggie found her tongue. "Ain't goin', so I ain't."

"Aggie, I can't believe ya just sat there an' didn't say a word while he was here," Annabelle said. "It just ain't like ya."

"Took me by surprise, so it did," Aggie said. "But I told ya right. I ain't goin', so I ain't."

Joe stood taller and said, "Pa'd told Frank before he left he wanted Frank to take us in." Sara came in as Joe was telling the women what she already knew and dreaded. "Ya all knowed we're goin' to starve here without Pa," Joe continued. "We're all goin' to Frank's, an' that's that."

Annabelle wasn't surprised at the deliberate, calm way Joe spoke to them. Slow and sure, since his father had gone, he had taken over. His association with Frank had only escalated the process. She knew that they would have to obey him—living under a man's authority was their way of life. When the canned goods were gone, without Joe to hunt they would starve. It was a long time until summer and a vegetable garden.

Sara ran to her room and threw herself down on her mat.

Joe had nothing more to say to the women. He followed Sara to their room. Joe sat on the mat beside her and lifted her face in the palm of his hand. "Sara, why're ya cryin'?"

"It won't be th' same with us anymore," Sara sobbed.

"Ya are my sister. Nothin' is goin' to change for us. Ya should knowed that." Joe laid beside Sara and held her until she stopped crying.

In the kitchen Annabelle asked, "What're we goin' to do? I don't want to go live with that man. He's a mean one. I've overheard th' people at th' church sayin' he's a devil!"

Daisy got everyone's attention quickly when she said, "He's a handsome one, though. I won't mind if he takes me into his bed."

Annabelle wanted to slap her. "Don't be stupid. Ya don't knowed what ya talkin' about."

"Ya can't think of anythin'," Aggie spat, "but gettin' in th' bed with a man, so ya can't. As for myself, I'm goin' to wait right here till Jeb comes back, so I am."

"Ya want to starve?" Annabelle switched sides. "Ya knowed we goin' to starve here by ourselves. We've got to think of th' babies me an' Daisy's goin' to have, too. We don't have no choice no how." Annabelle had either changed her mind on the subject of moving or, more likely, wanted to disagree with Aunt Aggie.

Back and forth the chair by the potbelly stove rocked. The old tomcat jumped on Rose's lap, as he often did. He pranced around her lap looking for a warm place to rest. Finding one, he laid down. Rose continued to rock. She neither acknowledged nor seemed to care about the crucial turn their lives would take.

Meanwhile, Randy McCoy and Bert Howard parked in front of the sheriff's office and barged in unannounced.

Sheriff Ozzie Moats, recognizing the men from previous visits, slipped his sexy magazine between the pages of the *Winding Ridge Weekly* as they walked into the room. "What you wantin' now? Guess I'm never goin' to get shed of you people."

"We're looking for your brother, Aubry Moats. We have reason to believe he's involved in several kidnappings."

Ozzie Moats kept a straight face. "I know nothin' about my no-account brother. He left the mountain to find work and I never supposed I'd ever hear from him again."

"Where'd you last see him?" Randy asked. "We've been assigned to find him, and that's exactly what we're going to do."

"I haven't seen my brother since he left Windin' Ridge just after the big mine explosion."

"How long ago was that?" Randy questioned.

"It's none of your business about me and my brother, but since you're so bent on knowin' it's been a few years back that he left. I've never had much time to spend with him, bein' I'm busy enforcing the law and all. I can assure you I know nothin', period."

"When's the last time you checked on the mountain for McCallister?" Bert Howard asked.

"Was yesterday my deputy drove up there. Not a sign of him. Don't expect you'll ever see McCallister on this mountain again anytime soon. He's not dumb. He ain't goin' to come back while this case is hot. Maybe not ever. Man leaves the mountain, he don't want to come back. Just like my brother did. They up and leave and that's the end of it."

"Continue to keep a close watch on McCallister's cabin regardless of what you think," Randy said. "You can't second guess a man like him, and you haven't heard the end of it about your brother, Sheriff."

Later, Randy and Bert drove across town toward the mountain trail that led to McCallister's cabin. They had instructions to interrogate McCallister's women and neighbors about the whereabouts of McCallister and Aubry Moats.

The weather was changing fast. Visibility was almost zero and the wind squalled, swirling loose debris around buildings, cars, and any unfortunate people out on the street. Before they'd entered the sheriff's office there'd been light snow falling, but during the short time they had been talking to the sheriff the wind had kicked up to almost hurricane force and the light snow had turned to heavy snow showers.

"Think we can make it up the mountain in this mess?"

7

*P*ATTY, YOU'RE CHOKING ME," TUESDAY CRIED. Patty loosened her hold a little and whispered, "He's in th' house."

Tuesday thought she heard a scraping noise. Pure, cold terror ran up her spine. *If Patty heard something, too, then I can't count on its being my imagination.*

If Tuesday had had time, she would have said a prayer of thanks for the phone that sat beside Patty's bed. She reached for the phone and, unable to free herself from Patty's stranglehold, dragged her along.

With her free hand, Tuesday picked up the receiver. With it tucked under her chin and Patty tight against her arm clutching her neck, she began punching in Cliff's number.

Suddenly, from behind her, Jacob moved across the room in three strides. He wrenched the receiver from Tuesday and smashed it against the night table before she had finished dialing all the digits.

Patty hid her face against Tuesday's neck and sobbed. Her body went limp in defeat.

Jacob moved out to the hallway and returned with two steaming cups of hot chocolate.

"You are a bastard, Jacob," Tuesday swore. When she saw the laughter in his eyes change to deep anger, she was frightened.

Then abruptly, he laughed aloud. "Where did you learn to swear, Miss Goody Goody? Maybe when you learned to swear you also learned to kidnap children. I don't appreciate you kidnapping my daughter, Tuesday."

"Oh, get real, you pig," Tuesday spat. "You're going to stand there and pretend that you care about your daughter?"

"Let loose of the girl, Tuesday," Jacob ordered. "I want you both to drink this chocolate. Don't give me any more trouble. I'm not in the mood—believe me."

Tuesday tried to pry Patty's arms from around her neck. "Patty, honey," she soothed, "please do as he says. Please! You know he'll hurt us if we don't do as he says." She felt Patty slowly loosen her hold. Tuesday gently pushed Patty back until she sat on her own, trading the comfort in the nearness of Tuesday for the comfort of her doll, Summer.

"Take this, Patty," Jacob ordered. "For you, my darling," he said, handing another cup to Tuesday and sitting next to her. "I see our child will be arriving soon."

"The child is not yours."

"I know you too well, Tuesday, and I know that you're not married. I've been watching your house for some time. If it were up to you, you wouldn't allow yourself to become an unwed mother. But it wasn't up to you. It was me who gave you that child you are carrying."

"It's not your child, and you're not going to get away with this," Tuesday said. "You should have known my house is being watched."

"Is that right?" Jacob said.

"Yes," Tuesday said, "so you'd better leave before you're arrested."

"Isn't that nice?" Jacob leered. "You're concerned about my welfare."

Patty sat sipping her hot chocolate and holding on to her doll. She did not take her eyes off her father. She knew from her dreams that he would take them back to the cabin.

"Drink it!" Jacob demanded.

Tuesday jumped, startled by his barking command. She lifted her cup to her lips and sipped.

"So you thought you could run from me. Why? You know you want me."

Tuesday could not believe her ears. He could not actually believe that she wanted anything to do with him. Did he not remember how she fought off the brutal rapes and all the other indignities he had subjected her and his own daughter Patty to? *He is insane*, she thought.

While they sipped their chocolate, Jacob turned the light off to avoid attracting attention from the street. He sat in the chair beside the bed and watched the street from the window. He had watched the house for a full week and made note of how often the police car cruised by the house.

As Jacob waited and watched, he bragged about his earlier steps. "Just so you'll know I'm smart enough not to leave a trail, I want you to know that I had the foresight to bring a new pain of glass to replace the one I cut to unlock the front door.

"I want Cliff Moran to believe that the two of you were taken from the mall, so there can be no sign of a break in. I used a glasscutter to cut a circle out of the window, and then used a suction cup to remove the glass without breaking it. Without any trouble at all, I reached in and unlocked the door.

"Believe me, I carefully thought out the plan. Last week in the middle of the night while you slept, I measured the window opening and ordered the glass. Yesterday I picked up the new glass and window-glazing compound to repair the window, which I'll fix while you get more sound asleep.

"There's the patrol car. I have an hour to replace the new glass and get the two of you out before the cruiser comes by again."

That's where you made your first mistake, Tuesday thought bitterly. *They're going by more often now.*

Jacob had left his truck at a nearby shopping mall, creeping to the house on foot. Months ago he'd ditched the former one using his fake identification; he had bought the new truck and had it registered in the phony name.

Jacob left the two and found Tuesday's room. Without turning the lights on he found her purse and dumped the contents on the bed, searching for her car keys. Pocketing them, he felt in the closet for her coat by running his hand from left to right. When he felt the heavy material, he removed it.

He found Patty's coat into her closet and, careful not to wake her, pushed her arms into her coat sleeves and zipped it up. In the same manner, he lifted Tuesday and laid her coat behind her. He pushed her arms through the sleeves and buttoned it.

"There you are. You're dressed for traveling," he whispered in Tuesday's ear. "What you have on is all you'll need. Some of your clothes are still at the cabin—they'll do. I know you'd like to take some of your nice things, but if your things are found missing from here it'll kill the theory of the two of you being taken from the mall."

He carried Patty to Tuesday's car.

After his second trip, he settled Tuesday beside Patty in the back seat and he got in the front. "Damn it," he grumbled to the sleeping pair, "I left her purse on the bed with everything scattered. That sure would tip Cliff off. Can't make mistakes."

He went into the house again and scooped the purse's contents back inside.

On the way out, he walked over to the fireplace and put his fingers into the ashes that had fallen onto the hearth. At the door, he lightly ran a smudged finger around the new, too-white compound that he'd used to replace the window. With a clean finger on his left hand, he smudged it again, to soften the effect. The glass no longer stood out as new.

He got into the car where Tuesday and Patty now slept and used the remote control to open the garage door. Without turning the headlights on, he slowly drove out of the garage and remotely closed the door again.

Looking first left then right he drove cautiously onto the street. He drove three blocks before he turned the headlights on. "I have five hours for sure and possibly up to seven," he calculated out loud, "before she's missed."

The clock on the dash read 3 A.M. It had only taken McCallister about forty-five minutes to get in and out and on the road again.

McCallister had lucked out. Cliff's patrol was going by twice each hour now, much more often than McCallister had learned as he cased the house and made his plans to take Tuesday and Patty. Tonight, the patrolmen had gone by fifteen minutes before McCallister had arrived at the house and they drove by as he sat beside Patty's bed. He was pulling in at the mall when they drove by again. It was sheer luck that he wasn't spotted as he broke into the house or drove Tuesday's car away.

The many hours he had spent watching Tuesday's house had taught him that there was no activity at all before 7:00 A.M. The light in her room went on between 7:00 and 7:30 A.M., never earlier. It was barely light around that hour. The days of December were short. Each morning he had watched the house from a different viewpoint and used a different car to assure it would not be remembered later.

One hour had passed from the time he'd entered the house. He'd entered the house only two minutes before Patty's screams woke Tuesday.

The drive to the cabin was four and a half hours, which would get them there at 7:30 A.M. Her friends or neighbors would not know anything was amiss before seven and they would be four hours away by then. It would appear that she was sleeping as usual.

If the neighbors or the men patrolling her street noticed her light was not on at seven or seven thirty as usual and checked and found that she was gone, McCallister figured it would be too late. They would have arrived at Aggie's cabin by then. He was totally unaware that Cliff Moran knew about Aggie's cabin.

He drove Tuesday's car into the mall parking lot and went around to the back. The lot surrounded the mall with a wooded area behind. McCallister's truck was parked in a dark corner where it would attract the least attention.

Jacob pulled up beside his truck. The floodlights were spaced in such a way that there were pools of light surrounded by a total darkness that enveloped his truck. He got out and assessed the area and was reasonably sure no one was there to witness his activity. A few cars were scattered around the parking lot, mostly in the back. It was unlikely his truck or Tuesday's car was noticed. With the mall closed, there were no people around.

One at a time, Jacob quickly carried Tuesday and Patty from the car to the truck. They slept undisturbed after being moved. He drove onto the road and headed east on Interstate 70. "No one will find us," he said to the sleeping pair in his satisfaction at implementing his scheme. "My plan is foolproof. Carrying the two of you from the car to my truck was probably the highest risk I'll be taking."

CHAPTER

8

_S_NOW FELL FROM THE SKY RESEMBLING TINY COTTON
flakes. It had begun the evening before,
swiftly hiding the old, well-used paths, foot tracks,
and trash. It obscured the ugly bare patch of ground
beside the back porch where the women emptied
their dirty dishwater. The snow blanketing the back
porch, which tilted to the ground in disrepair, created a soft white carpet, transforming the scene into
a picture-postcard wonderland.

Annabelle stood looking out the window above
the wood-burning stove. She did not want to move
into Frank's cabin, even though it was larger than
Jacob's was. Most of all, she did not want to relin-
quish her position of power. She loved to exert her
will over the others.

Annabelle sighed, knowing she would have to
make the best of what had happened. She couldn't
do anything about it. She heard Aggie moving
around behind her; she had awakened and was
rolling her mat to be put aside.

It's gettin' light out, Annabelle thought and turned
off the oil lamp.

Aggie reached into her apron pocket and pulled out her last box of snuff. That did it— she would go to Dillon's with the others. Maybe he would get her snuff. With Jacob gone and Joe living at Dillon's cabin, she would have no way to get more. Jacob had always kept her supplied. She dipped her forefinger into the snuffbox and lifted her finger to her mouth. With the finger on her free hand she pulled her lip out and placed the snuff between her lip and her stained teeth.

Annabelle went to the women's bedroom to wake the others.

Aggie bent to the wood-box as she prepared to start the fires in the stoves.

Hearing Aggie at the wood-box, Annabelle left the others to dress and hurried back to the kitchen, angrily pushing the curtains aside as she stepped through the doorway. Although this was the last morning to be spent in the cabin, she was provoked that Aggie was busy starting the fires. She considered building the fires in the stoves her job.

In the bedroom, Daisy shivered as she dressed. Except for the trip to the outhouse, getting out of the big four-poster, where there were two other women to keep her warm, was the hardest time of the day. After helping Rose, who wouldn't bother to dress if she were not directed to, Daisy led her to the kitchen.

Preparing to make her morning trip to the outhouse, Annabelle looked from the window over Aggie's shoulder. When she saw that the snow had continued falling throughout the night, she headed for the chamber pot, telling Rose to use it next.

The climb to the outhouse was difficult anytime, and she was in no mood to make the trip in the newly fallen snow. Before returning to the bedroom, Annabelle threw the cat off the table, knowing that

Aggie would not like it. Quickly, to avoid Aggie's temper, she continued to the bedroom.

Not minding the children beyond the curtained doorway, she lifted the lid from the chamber pot and pulled her dress to her waist. She wore no panties; not one of them owned underwear. She squatted on the pot. She was a large woman and the pot was dwarfed by her size.

The children heard the clang of the lid and the ping of the urine as it sprayed in the pot, and they knew the weather had gotten worse. When they used the pot the smell was rank.

This day it would not matter anyway. They would make the trip to Frank's cabin and would have to leave far earlier than they had planned. The snow fell as if the sky had ruptured from its heavy burden, and soon it would be so deep they would not be able to make it to Frank's cabin safely, if at all.

"Get down here, ya worthless mountain trash," Big Bessie yelled to the girls who were still up in the loft. "Jacob's people're goin' to come today an' ya ain't goin' to use that as an excuse to keep from your chores."

The kitchen in Frank's cabin had two woodburning stoves. They were needed because there were so many people to cook for. Big Bessie was constantly canning in an attempt to keep up with the great amount of food that they consumed.

The kitchen area was under the loft on the back wall. A huge iron bed with a feather-tic mattress sat in the north corner at the front of the cabin. The potbelly stove was opposite the big bed in the south corner at the front of the cabin. The front door stood between them. The interior was an open area, lacking any dividing walls that would separate individual rooms. There were half a dozen wooden rocking chairs scattered around the front of the potbelly stove where the women took their relaxation or rocked their babies.

In the center of the cabin sat an old wooden table with eight wooden chairs arranged around it. The tabletop was rough with deep marks where some-one had been whittling at it with a knife. From this table Big Bessie could see anywhere in the cabin, except for the floor of the loft and the deep loft cor-ners where the light of day did not reach. There was no furniture in the loft. Mats and quilts were scat-tered where the girls slept.

At Big Bessie's command, the girls pulled their feedsack nightgowns over their heads and replaced them with their feedsack dresses. No one, other than the girls, would be able to tell which was the dress and which was the gown.

The girls climbed down the ladders and took their turns going to the outhouse. They wore Frank's old boots and an old hunting jacket, which were kept beside the back door. Both were too large for the girls, except for Big Bessie, and they fit her fine.

The storm had reached blizzard status. Each girl stumbled to the outhouse, looking like a voyager lost at sea in turbulent waters, as the pelting ice and raging wind blinded her. The wind tore at her jacket and the snow sucked up the boots with each step as she walked to the outhouse that sat just ten yards from the back door.

Big Bessie sent Eva Belle to turn off the oil lamps. She wasn't one to waste the oil. They ran out all too often, and they had no other source of light. With no streetlights or lighted windows shining from neighboring cabins, darkness was absolute when night fell.

The smell of food made the girls' mouths water. They were hungry. It had been twelve hours since their last meal. They had their dinner each night at six o'clock, and there was no food for late-night snacks.

Each girl helped Big Bessie with the chores after returning from her trip to the outhouse, knowing which chore was hers.

Big Bessie made the girls toe the line. They were almost as afraid of Big Bessie as they were of Frank. Bessie was quick to slap one of them with the full power of her huge arm.

Dillon, predicting worse weather, had arisen well before daybreak, ready to hunt as it grew light. Having the good fortune to have shot two turkeys for their dinner, he returned in a swirling gale. A flurry of snow followed him inside before he slammed the back door behind him. He had not minded having to hunt that morning; it would be Joe's job in the future.

Dillon threw the turkeys on the table, and puddles of blood spread over the rough wood surface. Unmindful of the mess, he sat on a chair and held his foot out. Melverta ran over to him and pulled his boot off. That was her job. He lifted his other leg, and she removed that boot, too.

All the females had been taught to tend to his needs without question.

Big Bessie had a bald spot on the back of her head from a time when she'd burned Frank's potatoes and eggs. She'd sat them in front of him, and as she moved away, he had reached up and grabbed her hair, yanking her head backward. Her hair came away in his hand, leaving a red, raw spot where hair would never grow again. That was the last time Big Bessie served her husband burned food. It was not easy, though, to cook on the woodburner, because the heat could not be adjusted. Since that time she had set aside any burned food for the girls and prepared another plate for him.

Frank pulled his jacket off and threw it on the floor. Sally Ann ran and picked it up. He sat at the table, and Big Bessie put his plate in front of him. The women would eat after he had finished his meal.

Frank watched Mary Lou as he ate. She was on her knees, leaning over their large round tub, scrubbing clothes on the washboard with her back to him. He watched her work as her arms moved up and down the washboard. "She's the best of the lot, Bessie," Frank said.

"Ya can't take all that stuff, Aunt Aggie," Annabelle said. "We're jus' supposed to take our clothes. Ya can't carry all that stuff down th' mountain path no ways. Ya knowed it's snowin' hard an' we maybe can't make it down anyway."

"I can too. Ya can't tell me what to do, so ya can't. I want to take my cats an' dogs. Can't leave them, so I can't," Aggie complained.

"Both of ya shut your mouth. I'll come back for th' cats an' dogs if Frank says ya can have them. Take what ya can carry. I can't help ya an' ya ain't comin' back here no more." Joe ordered.

"Th' older ya get th' more like your pa ya are, so ya are, bossin' an' such," Annabelle said. "I'm still your mother an' don't ya forget it."

Joe didn't bother to answer. The trip down the mountain with five women was a major challenge for one man. The weather was bad and getting worse. Except for Sara, the others were not used to climbing the trails and two of them were pregnant. Rose was lost in her own world, and Aunt Aggie was too old to be climbing down the snow-covered, slick mountain trail.

They'd managed to make it halfway down the mountain—trudging single file, looking like amateur mountain climbers coming home after failing to make it to the top—before Rose fell.

She had lagged farther and farther behind the other five since leaving the cabin. She had not recognized a cluster of rocks that were covered by the falling snow. She tripped and, sliding headfirst, tumbled to a rock ten feet below. She looked like a ragdoll crumpled at the base of the rocks.

"Oh, no," Joe cried. "Rose fell! Everybody wait!" Joe threw his belongings aside and scrambled to Rose. "Rose, get up," he said as he shook her. "Rose, get up!"

When he realized that she was unconscious, he stashed his sack and mat on a ledge sheltered by an overhanging rock and picked her up. She was so thin that she was lighter than the burden he had put aside. He picked up her bundle. "Let's go," he ordered. "I'll get my things later."

They walked once again, doggedly making their way toward Frank's cabin.

Later, Frank opened the door, having been alerted by the stomping on the front porch. They had arrived—his new wives and Joe. He opened the door and Joe walked in, carrying an unconscious Rose in his arms. The others followed behind.

"What the hell happened to her?" Frank asked.

"She fell comin' down th' mountain," Joe said.

"We need to tend to her, so we do," Aggie said. "Where'd ya want Joe to put her?"

"Take her up on the loft," Frank said. "I didn't expect any sickly women, Joe."

"She's not sickly," Joe said, not revealing that the fall was not her only problem—that she had had an emotional breakdown and was worthless to him. "She just fell and knocked herself out, that's all."

CHAPTER

9

AS MCCALLISTER DROVE THROUGH THE NIGHT, THE closer he got to Winding Ridge the worse the weather got. At first the snow fell lightly, but as he neared the mountain range, the light snow turned to heavy snow showers and the wind became violent. The snow continued to fall relentlessly. By the time McCallister got to Winding Ridge, five inches had fallen, dressing the starkly bare trees in thick white, fur coats. The low visibility and snow-covered roads made driving treacherous. After going through the small town of Winding Ridge, McCallister passed the main road that led to Aggie's and his own cabin and took a logging road that no one used any longer. Although he had four-wheel drive, the truck had its work cut out for it. He was accustomed to the weather; still, he had had a little trouble making it up the more traveled narrow road that led up to the town. The fierce wind had caused small snowdrifts to form on the sharp turns that wound their way up to the Ridge.

Twice he'd been forced to stop his truck and dig the drifting snow out of his way. Mountain dwellers regularly carried tools for road emergencies, such as jumper cables, an extra battery, a can of antifreeze, a toolbox, and, most important to him now, a snow shovel.

As the truck moved up the logging road to Aggie's cabin, the clock on the dash read 7:30 A.M. McCallister's calculations had been that they would arrive at the cabin by that time.

"I've made the trip up and down the mountain many times in the past, and soon even I could not make the trip in this weather," Jacob mumbled aloud to break the unnatural silence of a vehicle filled with three people.

He no longer cared whether Patty and Tuesday woke up. They could wave, scream, and jump from the truck, but there was no one to see or help them. "All this, and I have a beaut of a backup plan. Couldn't be more perfect," he glanced at the woman and girl sleeping on the seat of his truck. "When you see that no one's going to find you, you'll settle into your new lives. I'll see to that."

Suddenly, up ahead all that was visible through the gusting snow was a stark white landscape. Like a bridal veil, a snow slide obscured the narrow road. McCallister stopped the truck. Careless in his displeasure at being detained again, he lost his footing and nearly slid under the truck as he hopped out. He steadied himself by holding on to the truck-bed and groped in the toolbox to find the shovel. The narrow road at that point ran through a valley that was formed by two mountain ridges.

Tuesday awoke as Jacob dug, making a path through the snowdrift. *Where am I? It's freezing cold.* She sat up and saw the barren, snow-covered landscape. *Oh, no.* Tuesday's heart hammered in her chest as she rolled down the window and demanded, "Jacob, what are you doing?"

"What do you think I'm doing? Hell, I'm digging us out of this mess."

"You're a crazy pig, Jacob. I suppose you don't know you're the one who got us into this mess in the first place."

"Look, I don't need your holier-than-thou speeches, and don't you dare call me a pig again!" McCallister said through clenched teeth.

"This is impossible," he declared a short while later, leaning on his shovel. "I'd hate to leave my truck here. That'd mean dealing with getting the two of you up the mountain on foot. No one would see the damn truck if I left it here, though. No one uses this road anymore."

"We can't walk in this blizzard. You can just turn around and take us back," Tuesday demanded, oblivious to the beauty of the swaying curtain of snow flakes—of every size and shape—falling around them.

McCallister laughed and continued digging. "The snow is an advantage to me." He chose not to acknowledge Tuesday's demand. "Very soon no one will be able to get through this passage and not even the more traveled road to the cabin. My ace in the hole is they'll be positive I couldn't have gotten through." He stopped digging and looked at his watch. "It's eight o'clock. Most likely you haven't been missed yet, since you're on leave from your job and you haven't been sending Patty to school everyday."

After a half an hour of digging, he had made a narrow trench through the drift, exposing the old logging road. Satisfied, he threw his shovel into the back of the truck and climbed in. He threw the truck into gear, moving slowly at first. Gaining speed, he plowed through. The truck bucked and bounced its way up the old road.

McCallister stopped and retrieved his shovel from the bed of the truck. He shoveled the snow back over the road. The falling snow did the rest, erasing the truck's passing as if it had never happened at all.

Patty, who was much smaller than Tuesday and had been affected more deeply by the sleeping tablet, slowly awoke to the sound of angry voices. Jacob wrenched the truck door open. Icy air blew in, making goosebumps appear on her skin. She clutched her doll closer to her.

"Good, you're both awake now. We'll be home soon."

"Home! You bastard! Are you crazy?" Tuesday blurted.

"You have spunk after all," he laughed.

Tuesday looked out the window, and there was nothing as far as she could see except the glaring white snow. *It's ironic*, she thought. *It was snowing like this when I first met Jacob. I was on Interstate 70 when my car broke down. I remember thinking how handsome he was. How masculine to stop and help me with my car. I was afraid of freezing. It was cold and snowing like now. I couldn't run my heater and someone I thought was a knight in shining armor stopped to help. What a laugh that was. No, not a laugh. No, the beginning of a very bad nightmare. A nightmare I can't seem to awake from.*

They eased slowly forward. Behind them the falling snow wiped out their tracks. It would be utterly impossible to detect that a vehicle had passed through.

The truck bounced and slid side to side, fishtailing. Abruptly, they came to a stop, jammed in a snow bank.

"Damn, another hang-up, just when we're almost there."

"Where, Jacob? Where are you taking us?"

"I told you. I'm taking you home." He got out of the truck and left it running so they would not get cold.

Tuesday watched as Jacob retrieved the shovel from the back and walked to the slide.

"Are ya okay?" Patty asked.

"Sure I am, Patty. Do you recognize where we are?"

Patty sat up straight and looked out the window. "I'm guessin' that we're goin' up th' back road to Aunt Aggie's cabin. It's hard to tell for sure in this blizzard." They sat huddled together and watched as Jacob dug in the snow, making a path the truck could pass through.

"Is Aunt Aggie's cabin as bad as the one before?" Tuesday asked.

"It's just a cabin like any other. Cold an' bare," Patty answered listlessly. "Ya don't think Pa'll take my doll away from me, do ya?"

Tuesday saw that Patty had her newly acquired doll clutched to her chest. "No, Patty, I don't think he even noticed that you have the doll. I wouldn't stand for it if he did try to take it," Tuesday said.

"Good. I need Summer to talk to," Patty said.

"Patty, you know that you can talk to me about anything, don't you?"

"Yeah, I do. I just need th' doll. Ya knowed I never had one before."

Twenty minuets later, Jacob threw the shovel into the back of the truck and got in. He slowly moved the truck forward. Gradually gaining speed, it bounced and jerked from left to right, moving faster and finally, with a jarring crash, it veered off the trail and slammed into the rocky mountain face.

"Damn it, anyway," Jacob swore. He eased the truck backward, then threw it into low gear, then reverse, thus rocking it back and forth until it rolled back a few feet, clearing the mountain face. Jacob shifted to low gear and eased forward. He moved forward cautiously and was heading up the mountain once again. Jacob kept a steady speed as the truck fishtailed its way up the mountain.

A few minutes later, the truck suddenly began skidding from side to side, totally out of control. It slid backward down the steep incline. Abruptly, the cab of the truck slid around in a half-circle and they were speeding down the steep slope sideways. Shrieking, Tuesday fell against Patty, and Patty hit her head against the window of the passenger door as the truck came to a heart-stopping standstill.

*W*HERE IS SHE?" CORA ASKED BILL. "DID SHE forget that we were going to enroll Patty in her new school?" Cora looked at the clock that hung over the mantel: 9:30 A.M. She placed the phone back in its cradle. "Maybe she had to run to the market. I'll try again in a half hour."

"You're worrying over nothing. Something came up, and she had to take care of it," Bill said.

At ten o'clock Cora let the phone ring fifteen times before she gave up. "If Tuesday had gone out, why didn't she turn on her answering machine?" Cora worried.

"I suppose she forgot," Bill said. "Try her cell phone."

Cora had started for the stairs and stopped. "I have. There's no answer. It's either turned off or out of range. I should call Cliff. Even if nothing's wrong, it's best not to take chances with the threat of Jacob McCallister hanging over our heads. Maybe it's the baby." She shrugged and walked back to the phone to dial Cliff's private number.

"Hello. Sergeant Cliff Moran here."

"Cliff, this is Cora."

"Hi, Cora. What's up?" Cliff asked.

"I've been trying to call Tuesday for an hour. Her answering machine isn't turned on and she doesn't pick up the phone. Also, there's no answer on her cell phone. We were going to check out schools for Patty today and I can't imagine she forgot something that important to her. I was hoping that you might know where she is."

"Tuesday told me she was going to meet you this morning. She should be home as far as I know, since she's not with you," Cliff said.

"I'm worried. If something had come up, she would've let me know," Cora said. "I'm going to her house. Maybe her phone is out of order."

"Do you have a key?"

"Yes," Cora answered.

"Take your cell phone so if her phone's out of order you can still call me when you get there. Whatever you do, don't touch anything, just in case McCallister's been there. In the meantime, I'll call the officers who were on patrol last night and this morning. I'll call her neighbors, too. If anything happened one of them might have seen something. I'll be waiting for your call."

He dialed the duty officer.

Hal walked in just as Cliff finished making the calls. "What's up, Cliff?"

"Cora's worried about Tuesday. Tuesday didn't answer her phone earlier. She would not cancel plans that she'd made with Cora and not tell her. Cora's on her way over there now."

"She could have gone out, you know. That wouldn't be unusual," Hal said.

"No, maybe not for someone else, but she was supposed to go out with Cora today. If she had changed her mind, she would have canceled. I just spoke to the officers who patrol her street and they report everything quiet. The neighbors say the same thing."

"What about the baby? Maybe she's in the hospital," Hal said. "Did you check the hospital?"

"No, but I will. She would have called me, but it's worth a try."

The second line rang while Cliff was talking to the admitting clerk at the hospital.

Hal picked up. "Sergeant Cliff Moran's office."

"Hi, this is Cora. May I speak to Cliff?"

"Hold on."

"Thanks," Cliff said and hung up the other line.

"Cora's on the phone, Cliff. She sounds worried."

"Hi, Cora. Is she there?"

"No. Cliff. I'm really worried now. Her car's not in the garage. The beds aren't made. She would not leave the beds unmade. Something's wrong. Maybe you had better get over here."

"Stay there. I'm on my way," Cliff said and replaced the phone.

"From my vantage point, sounds like she's not home," Hal said.

"We'll assume McCallister has her and Patty until we locate them," Cliff said. "We'll have Randy McCoy get a couple of his men together and go to Winding Ridge."

"Bert Howard and Randy McCoy are already in Winding Ridge investigating the whereabouts of Aubry Moats. They haven't come back yet," Hal reminded Cliff.

"They'll be in touch," Cliff said. "In addition to tracking Aubry Moats, they'll do their routine check at McCallister's cabin. That may be a break for us, if McCallister's heading there. McCoy and Howard would spot him and stop him in his tracks."

"I'll get Tuesday, Patty, and McCallister's description out on the wire," Hal said. "They could be anywhere. We'll consider him armed and dangerous."

Half an hour later, Cliff rushed into Tuesday's living room, where he found Cora frantically pacing back and forth, ringing her hands. Linda sat in front of the television and watched the Disney channel, blessedly unaware of the events unfolding around her.

"Cliff! Thank goodness you're here! Something's wrong! I know it!"

Cliff searched each room in the house. He found nothing. The house hadn't been ransacked. As he reached to open the front door, he noticed the window just over the doorknob. "Look at this, Cora. The windowpane looks as if it was recently replaced. The putty's a brighter white, although it has some gray smudges on it. Do you know anything about it?"

"No. I would think that if she needed something like that done, she would've asked your advice."

Cliff opened the door and looked at the outside of the window. "I'll send a man from the lab to dust the door for prints. Have you touched the window or the area around it?"

"No, Cliff. I just unlocked the door and came in."

"So, the door was locked?"

"Without a doubt."

"Looks like she went somewhere on her own. Her car's gone and there's no sign of forced entry. Ah, but something's not right."

Cora and Linda went back to their house just in case Tuesday tried to contact her there. Cliff promised to keep in touch, and he headed back to his office.

Hal updated Cliff. "While you met with Cora, I deployed men to knock on every door in the area with instructions to call immediately if they came up with anything. Otherwise, they'll report back when they've covered the area. Bert Howard and Randy McCoy haven't checked in, and I don't know if or when they got back from Winding Ridge. I haven't been successful in getting in touch with them."

"Great, we don't want to let the trail get cold," Cliff said. "At this point we know something unusual has occurred. I noticed that the glass on Tuesday's front door may have been tampered with and called forensics in to check it out. They agreed to give it top priority. My guess is that's how McCallister got into the house. He broke out the glass and reached inside and unlocked the door. Later he replaced the glass with a new one that he obviously had brought with him. Looks like he tried to throw us off by smudging the new putty."

"What about prints?"

"Don't know yet, but I'm sure it was McCallister. You know we don't have prints on him."

"Can't hurt to check, though. We can't leave any loose ends. It could have been someone else."

"The hell it is! Let's go to Winding Ridge. I have a gut feeling that's where he's taken them."

"Cliff, he isn't stupid, or we'd have found him by now. He would know that's the first place we'd look."

"Supposing McCallister used your line of thinking and took them there? We have to check! We can't reach McCoy and Howard by cell phone—there's no service up on the mountain—and I don't want to wait for them to get back. It's imperative to find out—as soon as possible—if McCallister's taken Tuesday and Patty to the mountain. We can leave word for the men to wait for us at Winding Ridge and warn them that McCallister may be headed for the mountain with Tuesday and Patty. Actually, if my hunch is right, he's had time to get there by now."

Cliff and Hal rented a four-wheel drive and gathered emergency supplies. They had already had a taste of climbing the snow-covered mountain trails and knew what they needed to be prepared.

As they sped west on Interstate 70, Cliff gripped the steering wheel until his knuckles turned white. "She trusted me for her safety," he said. "We've got to find her."

"Calm down. We'll find her."

The farther they drove, the worse the weather became. The weather had been clear in Wheeling, but in the last twenty minutes they had been driving deeper into a huge snowstorm. Cliff had to slow his speed. Despite the foul weather, they reached Interstate 79 and headed south.

back to the girl. The wail of the wind took her voice and made it faint.

"I'm okay," Patty sobbed. "Don't worry 'bout me. I'm just scared."

"We can't make it up this mountain, Jacob," Tuesday cried. "If you don't care about my welfare, you must care about your daughter's."

"Oh, yes, you can. I'm helping you, and Patty's used to these conditions. Both of you keep moving, unless you want to camp out in this lovely gorge until the snow melts," Jacob threatened.

"You're a pig," Tuesday said.

"Shut up, both of you," Jacob said, pulling at Tuesday's arm. "I've already warned you about calling me a pig, and if you call me a pig once more, I'll force you to climb this mountain all by yourself."

Tuesday said nothing; she knew he had the advantage. But rage grew in her heart and she vowed she would stop at nothing to see him behind bars.

"Earlier, just as we topped the hill, I saw Aunt Aggie's cabin for a second," Jacob said in the same tone of voice he would have used had they all been out on a pleasant hike. "Under the circumstances, the valley's as good a place as any to leave the truck. The road is rarely used and won't be accessible for some time."

If they had reached the crest, they would have been where the back road forked with the more often used road that dead-ended at Aunt Aggie's cabin. No one lived along the back road they were stranded on. Made by a logging company that had bought a few acres of timber from McCallister's father a few years before his death, the road was virtually unused after the logging company had taken the timber out. McCallister had used the road some when he ran moonshine, before he walked into the business of selling children, before he met George

Cunningham, and the black marketing of children grew to be much more profitable.

As Jacob climbed, he grabbed branches and rocks for support and dragged Tuesday behind him. Patty carried Summer on one arm and the shovel in the other hand as she walked directly behind Tuesday, ready to help her if she slipped backward. Tuesday was badly shaken, feeling battered and bruised after the impact of the truck hitting the huge rock buried under the snow.

Ultimately, they reached the cabin. Except for the relief from the biting wind and blinding snow, it was as cold and uncomfortable inside as it was outside.

Jacob sat Tuesday on the cot that Aggie had used for a bed. Leaving her shivering uncontrollably, he made preparations to build a fire in the stoves. "Patty," Jacob ordered, "don't just stand there. Help me gather wood and paper to get a fire going."

"Aunt Aggie always kept th' old catalogs ya brung her mostly out in the toilet. Except there's th' ones she likes to look at under th' wood box." Patty moved to the wood box that sat beside the wood-burner and picked it up. There were two catalogs. Patty set the wood box aside and handed a catalog to Jacob.

While they built a fire, Tuesday surveyed her surroundings. Forced to relive her nightmare of eight months ago, she felt as if she had been transported back in time, even though the cabin was not the same four-room cabin that Jacob had taken her to back then. She looked around the huge room. Above her was a loft that extended around the side wall, to her left, and ran the full length of the front of the room. A stepladder was propped against the outer edge of the loft near the corner.

The cot she sat on stood against the front wall. To her right sat a potbelly stove, a twin to the one in

Jacob's cabin, with two rocking chairs placed in front of it. A small square table was placed in the center of the room with two chairs, one on each side. Across from the cot, a woodburner sat below a small window.

She could smell a cat odor mixed with other scents: sweaty clothes, mildew, and old, sour cooking odors. In her condition, it didn't take much to make her nauseated.

Jacob built a fire in the woodburner. Next, he stuffed paper into the guts of the potbelly and lit a match, he waited until it caught and flames leapt out from the opening. Then he slammed the metal door shut, moved to the cot, and sat next to Tuesday.

"Are you okay?" Jacob asked, pushing Tuesday's blonde, silky hair from her face. Her skin was bright pink from the cold, biting wind. Her teeth chattered noisily as she sat and shivered.

Tuesday slapped his hand away angrily. "I'm chilled to the bone and may start an early labor from this unthinkable trip up the mountain, and you have the nerve to ask if I'm okay. You're a lunatic, Jacob, and I want nothing to do with you. Do you understand? Nothing!"

"I'm not going to take offense to what you're saying until the baby's born. I'll just mark it up to your condition and general female nonsense.

"Patty, come sit beside Tuesday," McCallister demanded, turning his attention to the girl, and marched out the back door.

"Ya okay, Tuesday?"

"Don't worry, honey. I'm okay."

"I don't think ya are. I can help, if ya tell me what ya need."

"Okay, Patty. I'm sure I've gone into labor. I know you're only a little girl. I should be taking care of you." It broke Tuesday's heart to realize that Patty—in a matter of hours—had lost the carefree attitude of a child, a disposition she had developed over the time she had lived in Wheeling with Tuesday.

"It's okay. I know more than ya think." Patty sat her doll on the end of the cot and helped Tuesday take off her coat. Then she covered her with a quilt.

After Tuesday was comfortable, Patty put her hand on her swollen stomach so she could feel Tuesday's contractions. Right away, she felt a strong one and knew instinctively that the baby was on the way.

Tuesday watched Patty's face. She noticed that Patty kept her eye on Summer. It looked as if they communicated in some strange way. *Communicating with a doll? What am I thinking? Patty has never had a doll. She has no friends so she is getting overly attached to her, that's all.* She shook her head as if to clear it, but she knew somehow that communicating was exactly what Patty and the doll were doing. *The baby's coming. That's all I can deal with now.*

Meanwhile, McCallister walked down the snow-covered path to his cabin. The snow was so deep it made walking almost impossible. Soon the insignificant cabin came into view, looking lonely, time-forgotten, and abandoned. There was no smoke coming from the chimney to give it warmth and life. The only tracks were animal.

"This is perfect," McCallister said out loud to ease the eerie silence. "I was lucky to get on the mountain in this weather. If I'd started only one hour later than I had, I wouldn't have made it myself—almost didn't, anyway. They won't think that I'm stupid enough to bring her here," he laughed. Echoes of his laughter vibrated back to him shattering the heavy stillness. "I disappeared eight months ago, and to all concerned for good!"

The snow fell thick and fast, making it hard to see. It was nine-thirty, and eight inches of new snow had fallen since six o'clock that morning. If the snow continued throughout the night, there would be four feet on the ground.

Seemingly out of nowhere, the dogs ran to Jacob, barking, jumping, and circling around his legs in wild glee. They had always feared McCallister—maybe they sensed the cruel streak in him—but in their hunger and exultation to be fed, they were happy to see him. Jacob kicked at the dog nearest to his right with his heavy boot. The dog ran howling in pain. The others backed off.

He walked to the rear of the building. The snow had piled high against the cabin and obscured the back porch, having drifted halfway up the back door. It would not close again if it were opened. The snow would drift inside the cabin without the door to hold it back. He must not leave any sign of his having been here or anywhere on the mountain. Opening the door would not only leave a clue someone had been in the cabin, but would set the time of entry to merely hours after the storm had hit. The tracks he had left as he made his way in the snow did not matter. The falling snow would swiftly cover them.

He walked around to the front of the cabin. The wind blew from the back to the front, and the snow hadn't drifted to the cabin on that side.

McCallister stepped up the one step to the porch and pushed the door open. The smell almost knocked him over as he stepped into the living room. He moved to his left through the curtained doorway that led from the living room to the bedroom, which held the four-poster bed.

The source of the foul ammonia odor, which overpowered the ever-present scent of unwashed, sweat-soaked clothing and the sour odor that came from the unwashed quilts and sheets scattered throughout the cabin, was the chamber pot. The women had left it unemptied the day they were forced to leave the cabin in the driving snow.

Cats were everywhere. Apparently, they had lived on field mice, and with no one to put them out they'd done their business throughout the cabin.

He found a change of clothes for Tuesday. Her jeans and sweaters, which had been left behind when she had gotten away from him eight months before, were still in her luggage. They would not fit her now, but would later. He found an old feedsack dress of Annabelle's. It needed washing, but it would serve Tuesday until after she gave birth. The dress had been discarded many months ago when Annabelle had made a new one.

He could not manage carrying the old, home-made crib up the mountain to Aunt Aggie's cabin. In any case, anyone checking the cabin would be suspicious if the crib was gone. Cliff Moran had been there before; he knew about the crib and the luggage.

After gathering needed clothing for Tuesday, McCallister found a dress for Patty. All either of them had with them were nightclothes and coats. He carried their things out, leaving the front door ajar to allow the cats to come and go.

While McCallister was searching his cabin for necessities for Tuesday and Patty, a few miles above him in Aunt Aggie's cabin, Tuesday's delivery time was drawing nearer. "Patty, the pains are getting closer and harder. I can't do this without a doctor."

"Try to relax, Tuesday. My mas do it without a doctor. I heared Aunt Aggie talkin' to Daisy an' th' other ones when they're birthin' an' she told'em to breathe with th' pain an' don't push."

Patty sat by Tuesday's side and held her hand, trying to be brave but looking as frightened as Tuesday did.

Tuesday was alarmed by the situation. She knew that without a doctor's care a woman could die in childbirth and that Patty would not know what to do to help if anything went wrong. She could not help remembering that Patty had confided that her mother had died while bringing her into the world.

A new contraction tore through Tuesday's abdomen and she screamed with the pain, unable to breathe as Patty had counseled her to do. She fainted.

At the sight of fresh blood staining the quilt, Patty stifled a scream of her own. "Summer, what should I do?" Patty waited a moment as if listening to the doll, and then she pulled back the quilt. "Tuesday, can you hear me?" Patty sobbed. "Ya need to wake up and tell me what to do. *Tuesday, wake up!*"

Mary Lou and Eva Belle managed to carry Rose up the ladder to the loft where the women slept. They laid her on her soggy mat. She was soaked from her fall and the driving snow. Eva Belle took Rose's wet feedsack dress off and Mary Lou put another one on her.

Rose had not regained consciousness. Eva Belle covered the unresponsive Rose with her own dry quilt, and after hanging Rose's quilt across a rafter to dry, they left her alone.

Below the loft, oblivious to Rose's condition, Joe and Frank talked. "Ya can't get off th' mountain, Frank. Snowin' hard an' it's gettin' deep," Joe said. Frank had planned to leave for Wheeling later that day.

"I can see that, damn it. I need to get away from here for a while. Babies are going to be born. I want to make the deal for their sale," Dillon said. "When is that one due to have her child?" Frank nodded toward Daisy.

"Anytime now, I heard her sayin'."

"What about that one?" Frank looked toward Annabelle.

"She's 'bout th' same time as Daisy. An' as I told you, Sara's goin' to have my baby in about seven months," Joe bragged.

Saddened by her current dilemma, Annabelle listened to Joe brag as she, Daisy, Sara, and Aunt Aggie stood around waiting to be told what to do. Annabelle perceived that Aunt Aggie was distressed about not being able to take charge. Daisy and Sara were used to being ordered about, and the change would not be quite so hard for them.

Annabelle and Aunt Aggie each were accustomed to being in charge. Although lately their lives had been totally wrapped around their battle—with each other and with Joe—for who held the authority over Rose, Daisy, and the children, suddenly being told every move they were to make still was not an easy transition.

Annabelle turned her attention to Daisy, who was watching Frank with a small smile on her face. She disapproved that Daisy looked forward to being with Frank. Annabelle believed they should stay loyal to Jacob. She wanted to comfort Sara, who looked miserable at the thought of Joe with these other girls. Before Patty had run away with Tuesday, Joe had thrived on having Sara and Patty at his beck and call, but had no compassion for Sara's feelings of jealously. Annabelle had no doubt he would continue to be unfeeling toward Sara.

McCallister was in sight of Aggie's cabin when Tuesday screamed. He tried to run the rest of the way, but the deep snow made that impossible.

Exhausted, wet, and cold, he somehow managed to continue on at a faster pace.

When at last he walked into the cabin, it was noon. It had taken him much longer to make the trip to his cabin and back than he had planned.

"What in the devil is going on?" Jacob yelled at the sight of the huge amount of blood covering Tuesday and the quilt.

Patty jumped at the unexpected demand.

"Answer me, girl!"

"I don't knowed," Patty said, crying in relief that an adult was there. It made no difference that it was her father, whom she greatly feared.

"She looks white as a ghost." There was fear in Jacob's voice.

"Ya need to do somethin'. I don't want her to die like my ma did."

"Let her sleep. As long as she's asleep, she's okay."

"How'd ya knowed that?" Patty asked.

"I just know," Jacob said. "I want you to keep your eye on her and keep her warm."

Tuesday had been quiet since she had passed out just after the frightening scream; her pains had obviously subsided. Patty sat at Tuesday's side as her father had ordered.

While they waited for another indication of trouble from Tuesday, the fire in the stove blazed brightly, sending shadows dancing across the room.

Tuesday woke with a gasp, "Patty, are you here?"

"Yeah, I'm right here." Patty took Tuesday's hand in hers.

Jacob gathered a box of chocolate and a cup. He reached for the teapot that sat on the woodburner. "A cup of hot chocolate should do the trick." He reached in his pocket and took out a white pill. He dropped it into the hot water, and spooned a generous serving of chocolate into the cup. "Rest is what you need, Tuesday. Drink this. It'll relax you," he said as he stirred the mixture.

She refused to take the cup.

"Don't try my patience. Take this and drink it."

She was drained and having no fight left, she took the cup and slowly sipped the hot liquid.

Patty, you take care of her," Jacob ordered, putting his coat back on. "And I want you to fix something to eat."

Tuesday sighed with relief when Jacob strode out the back door. She did not want him around when she gave birth. When, after only a few moments had passed, he stomped back inside the cabin leaving clumps of snow in his wake, she choked back sobs of disappointment.

"There's no use to try to dig a path to the outhouse before the snow and wind stop," he said, throwing his coat on the back of a chair. Out of doors the blizzard was assaulting the cabin and snow was falling heavily.

While Patty stood at the woodburner preparing the meal, Jacob lit the oil lamp and sat at the table, waiting for his food. Patty had never learned to cook on the woodburner. With three women in the cabin, the children had been assigned outside chores. Annabelle had done most of the cooking.

Patty now learned there was a huge difference between cooking on Tuesday's modern appliances and starting from scratch using an obsolete stove. Back in Wheeling, she'd helped Tuesday cook occasionally. They had used prepared food that made cooking simple. Patty had no idea how to make bread, or biscuits, or how to cook dry beans. It took years of practice to cook on the woodburner. The heat could not be adjusted, and burning the food was a beginner's fate. Patty fried eggs, bacon, and potatoes to a blackened crisp.

"Can't you do anything right?" The smell of the burnt food disgusted Jacob. "We can't afford to waste food. With this blizzard, we'll be mighty hungry before I get into town to restock our food supply." He shouldered Patty aside, picked up the skillet, and slid the burned food onto a tin plate. "You eat this." Jacob shoved the plate to the edge of the stove and, from a tin can on a shelf, scooped lard in the now sizzling skillet. The shelf was made from a wooden crate that was nailed to the wall beside the window over the stove. He broke two eggs into the skillet. Next, he put four strips of bacon into the skillet and cut up a potato. When the eggs were done long before the bacon and potatoes, he spooned them onto a tin plate, leaving the bacon and potatoes to sizzle.

Not wanting to draw Jabob's attention but unable to lay quiet even with the aid of the sleeping pill, Tuesday cried out as another pain ripped through her body as the baby strove to be born. She felt the wetness, as the cot was soaked once again. *Dear God*, she prayed, *please allow the baby to live and let me live to care for it. And please, I pray that Jacob will leave the cabin before I give birth. In Jesus' name I pray.*

12

*H*ALFWAY UP THE MOUNTAIN ROAD LEADING TO Winding Ridge, Cliff and Hal were detained by a snow slide that blocked the road completely. It was 4:00 P.M. and twilight had already fallen. They'd been on the road six hours. Normally the drive from Wheeling to McCallister's cabin could be made in four and a half hours. Bert Howard and Randy McCoy had not reported in, and Cliff and Hal did not know where they were now, but from the looks of things the men had turned back, as Cliff and Hal would now.

"Cliff, I hate to say I told you so, but it's obvious that since we can't get up the mountain McCallister couldn't have either."

"Don't be so sure. McCallister had a head start," Cliff said, making his case. "I talked to Tuesday shortly after Patty went to bed. Must've been around ten or eleven." Cliff held his hand up to stop Hal from commenting. "That makes it fourteen hours since anyone has talked to her. They could be on the mountain now, having arrived before the blizzard—assuming it was McCallister. I know you doubt it, but it doesn't sit right that Tuesday and Patty were living under the shadow of being taken by McCallister and out of the blue an unknown assailant breaks in and takes them!"

Angrily, Cliff turned the Blazer around. To their left, the ridge dropped sharply three hundred feet to a valley below. All of a sudden, the Blazer slid sideways into the culvert at the edge of the road. It tilted dangerously on its left wheels as it slid toward the edge of the cliff, plowing enough snow as it went to halt the skid. Brutally, the right wheels came down in a jarring landing. When the Blazer came to a sudden stop, they sat precariously on the edge of the cliff with the mountain towering high above them on their right and an endless abyss on their left.

Back in Wheeling, Tom reclined in a hospital bed, watching the door for Simon and Toby.

Simon Leonard was the only parent Tom had ever known. Simon had bought Tom when the boy was two months old; he was now five years old. Simon simply called the boy Tom, with no family name. Simon had paid extra to get a child with no birth record because there would be no one to claim such a child.

Simon bought Jeff at the age of three; he was now six years old. He called him Toby. Leonard had not known Jeff's given name. He had not encouraged the boys to learn and did not talk to them, nor did he allow his servants or guests to speak to them. As a result, Jeff had forgotten the few precious words that he had learned from his parents.

Before their rescue and their admission to the hospital, the boys spent their days in an upstairs room at Simon's mansion, except when he required them for his parties and the games he used them for.

The room was furnished with twin beds, two dressers, and a few toys.

The boys were served three meals a day. A designated servant brought their food to them and cared for their personal needs. When Simon wanted to punish the boys he did it by withholding food. He had not tolerated the normal rebelling that children went through.

Just days before the discovery that the boys were unlawfully under Leonard's care, Jeff was on his third day of punishment. Recovering from a recent bout of the flu and after being allowed only bread and water, he grew weaker. He was being disciplined for hiding in an attempt to avoid one of Leonard's parties.

A guest at the party, a new acquaintance whom Simon had invited, misjudging him as a pedophile, had taken pity on the boys. Although he was not exactly a law-abiding citizen—he was at the party for the drugs—he loathed child abuse and had tipped off the police.

The boys had developed their own language, partly vocal and partly sign. No one other than the boys could understand the unfamiliar sounds or hand signs.

Jeff was a timid boy with blonde hair and blue eyes; Tom's dark hair and brown eyes were as stark a contrast to Jeff's characteristics as his rebel nature was.

A nurse came into Tom's room. "Hi, Tom, how are you feeling today?"

Nancy had heard from the hospital staff the little they knew of Tom's background.

Tom looked at her, saying nothing. Nancy put a thermometer in Tom's mouth and took his pulse. He allowed her hand to stay on his wrist, but spit the thermometer from his mouth.

"Please keep the thermometer in your mouth," Nancy said kindly and put it back between his lips. After checking his vital signs, Nancy tried communicating with Tom, in an attempt to gather more information for the doctor, but was unsuccessful.

Allowing the thermometer in his mouth the second time, Tom looked at Nancy with curiosity in his huge brown eyes, leaving the impression that he had understood what Nancy had asked of him.

At headquarters much later that night, Cliff and Hal sat exhausted and disappointed after the near disaster that had happened on the road from Winding Ridge. After losing control of the vehicle and ending up tottering at the edge of the cliff and a sheer drop to sure death, Cliff had cautiously eased the Blazer away from the ledge to safety. He had eased forward carefully, away from the drop off, and moved slowly down the mountain road. Both men, despite the cold weather, unexpectedly had wet armpits.

"Take it easy, man," Hal had admonished Cliff, gradually releasing his death hold on the dash.

Back at the police station, Cliff and Hal sorted through their day's worth of messages. There were no new leads for them to follow-up. According to reports, neither Tuesday's neighbors nor the patrol car that cruised the street had seen or heard anything unusual the night she and Patty were taken.

"Where the hell is she?" Cliff groaned.

"Tuesday's car wasn't in the garage. If someone took her, where's her car?" Hal asked. "Damn! When I put out an all-points bulletin on the three of them, I didn't add Tuesday's car. Her car has to be somewhere."

"I'll get on it," Cliff said, picking up the phone.

As Hal left to find the detectives they had sent to Winding Ridge, Cliff spoke to the desk sergeant.

"Howard, I need you to add Tuesday Summers' car to the all-points bulletin we have on McCallister." He gave the sergeant the description of the car and said, "I'm coming down to talk to Leonard. Have him brought out to a holding room." Cliff got up and stretched, grabbing his jacket as he headed to the front desk.

"Hi, Moran. Leonard is in 2B," the desk sergeant said. "Want a cup of coffee before you go on down? You look as if you could use one."

"Thanks," Cliff said. "I could use a break. After I question Simon Leonard, I'm on my way to the hospital to speak to the boys," Cliff said.

"What's the scoop on that?" the officer asked. "From what I hear it's bizarre."

"Bizarre is an understatement. Simon Leonard got Jeff three years ago. We found out who his parents are. We know absolutely nothing about Tom or how long Leonard has had him. Can't trace him.

"While I'm speaking to Simon," Cliff asked, "will you check with someone and find out if Hal was successful in locating the officers we sent to Winding Ridge? I've got to know what they have to say."

"Sure, no problem. I'll find out and I'll be waiting when you're finished with Leonard."

"Thanks, that'll be a big help," Cliff said. He threw his Styrofoam cup into the trash.

"Man, you look exhausted. From what I hear you've had a long and miserable day," the duty officer said to Cliff as he came into the holding area. "Why don't you do yourself a favor and go home after you talk to Leonard?"

"Time's running out," Cliff said. "Got to take advantage while the trail's hot. There's not only Leonard and the kidnapping ring. You know that my finance, along with a young girl who is in her charge, is missing."

Cliff followed the officer to cell 2B, where Simon Leonard sat awaiting questioning. The officer let Cliff in and he sat across from Leonard.

Simon Leonard was a small man with straight, blonde hair and blue eyes. He was a man who was open about being gay.

"Leonard, you can save a lot of time if you tell me who you bought the boys from," Cliff warned.

Leonard crossed his legs, looking at his fingernails as if he had just discovered them. His mannerisms were feminine. "I got those boys legally. You have nothing on me." He smiled at Cliff, blowing on his fingernails as if to dry them. Behind the smile, resentment was written all over Leonard's face.

"Leonard, don't give me that load of rubbish. There's no doubt Jeff was kidnapped. You couldn't possibly have gotten him legally."

"If I answer your questions, will you give me a break? Let me off, and I'll tell you everything you want to know about how I got the boys and whom I got them from," Simon demanded.

"Leonard, the only break I'm going to give you is a broken neck, if you don't talk. I'm in no mood to play games with you." Cliff slammed his notebook on the table, causing Leonard to jump.

Leonard sat with his legs crossed, bouncing his foot up and down. "I want my lawyer. I must talk to him privately."

"Your attorney is on his way," Cliff said. "I asked the duty officer to call him."

Cliff left the holding area and went to his office to wait for a summons from the guard, who would call him after the attorney arrived and spoke to Leonard. He paced back and forth across the room.

"I've let Tuesday and Patty down," he shouted out loud, venting his frustration. "They looked to me for protection and I've failed them." He picked up a stack of papers and flung them across the room as hard as he could. While papers flew everywhere, he leaned on the desk, his hands flat on the surface, vowing that he would capture Jacob McCallister if it was the last thing he ever did.

At that very moment, Hal entered the room. He stopped abruptly, his mouth open at the sight of papers floating across the room, while Cliff, palms flat on the surface of the desk, looked as if he was waiting to be frisked.

"Cliff, what the hell . . ."

"Hal, I can't take it. I let them down. I have to do something, but what?"

"Sit down. You're not helping anyone by falling apart, talking to yourself, and throwing everything in sight. Get a grip!"

"You're right. I just had to vent a little steam." Cliff sat at his desk and raked his fingers through his hair.

"When I find them, McCallister will pay dearly," Cliff pledged. He slammed his fist on the desk. "Damn! I hate to think of the condition that I found them in, huddled in that small cave. Was it only eight months ago?"

"Yes," Hal said, "it was. What I have nightmares about are the rats they were forced to club to death. It looked like a holocaust occurred in the cellar house where they were locked up."

"I can't bear to think what McCallister has in store for them after that," Cliff said. "That's why we have to find them, and soon!"

"We're doing all we can," Hal said.

"There're no lengths McCallister wouldn't go to keep Tuesday and Patty at his mercy. But what he doesn't know is that there is no obstacle that he can put in my path to stop me from finding them."

"I can say that we've made some headway. Tuesday's car was found at the Stonewall Jackson Mall,"

Hal offered. "It was parked in the back corner. The doors were locked."

"Where is it now?" Cliff asked bolting to his feet once again.

"Relax, Cliff. There was nothing in or on the car to indicate where she is or who she's with."

"Assuming it was McCallister," Cliff said, standing, "in order to throw us off his trail, he parked his car, or truck, at the mall and walked to her house. I would guess the car was left at the mall so we would believe that an unknown captor took them from there. He walked to her house from there, knowing he would draw less attention if he stayed off the streets and walked through the backyards where he was out of reach of the light from the street lamps."

"That could have happened," Hal allowed.

"Remember we suspected that someone Tuesday did not hire had replaced the window on her front door," Cliff said. "In fact it never needed to be replaced at all. We both know if she was in need of repairs, she would have asked me to take care of it."

"I see your point," Hal said. "To believe that there was no break-in is foolish."

"Right," Cliff said, "and there is no doubt that it was replaced. The men from the lab found that the putty was so new it had not dried yet. The prints were smudged, but we know that someone got in by removing the glass and putting in a new one to throw us off."

"That sounds likely," Hal conceded. "I'm agreeing more and more with you that it must have been McCallister."

"I'm glad to hear that," Cliff said, "I need your support, and you can't give it if you don't believe in my theory."

"By the way," Hal said, "I talked to Randy McCoy and Bert Howard. They were forced to come back from Winding Ridge, not wanting to be stuck there because of the weather; McCoy felt they were needed more here. They'd called in from Fairmont to give us the road conditions, but we had already left for Winding Ridge,"

"Did they talk to the sheriff and check McCallister's cabin?" Cliff asked.

"Yes," Hal answered. "The sheriff claimed that his deputy regularly checks McCallister's cabin and McCallister had not been seen anywhere in the area. After talking to the sheriff, our men made it to McCallister's cabin. There were no signs of life there at all. They were able to make it to Aggie's cabin as well, and it was the same story there. McCoy reported that they got off the mountain only by the grace of God. It was that bad. They knew we'd never make it."

"Did they mention if there was anything out of the ordinary?"

"No. Sounds like you have something in mind, though."

"Yes, I do. Like if McCallister had been around making preparations to bring Tuesday and Patty there," Cliff said.

"What would they be? He never did anything special for the others. You saw the place yourself."

"I don't know. I just had a hunch. He could have been there, though. My bet's that McCallister could run circles around the mountain and neither the sheriff nor the deputy would notice him. I got the impression that the sheriff couldn't care less about what happened on the mountain above his town."

"Wait a minute," Cliff said. "Are you sure about both cabins having no signs of life?"

"That's what McCoy and Howard reported, and they are the most reliable men we have," Hal said.

"What do you make of that?" Cliff asked.

"I have no idea."

"Did they check it out with the sheriff?" Cliff asked.

"Yes, they did," Hal said. "You remember how the sheriff is. He ranted at them and said it wasn't against the law for people to be away from their homes and he wasn't about to conduct an investigation into the matter."

"The man is so damn uncooperative and always on the defensive," Cliff said. "Makes you wonder, doesn't it?"

"Do you think he has something to hide, or is he just bigoted and feeling self-important?"

"Maybe both," Cliff said, "but I wonder where McCallister's women are. It's not as if they can get into a car and go wherever they wish."

The ringing phone interrupted them. "Sergeant Moran here. I'll be right down. Want to come with me, Hal? Simon Leonard's attorney's here, and Leonard's ready to talk."

"Sure, let's go."

13

*A*UNT AGGIE CLIMBED DOWN THE LADDER AFTER
checking on Rose's condition. She had to
admit she didn't know what to do to help Rose.
"How's she doin?" Annabelle asked.

"She's still unconscious. I ain't never had to deal
with a doctorin' problem like this one, so I ain't.
Don't knowed what to do, so I don't," Aggie
answered.

"If she doesn't eat, she's goin' to die," Big Bessie
said with the authority of one who is regularly
sought out for other people's medical needs. Rose
had been unconscious since she had fallen the
morning before, and she'd had nothing to eat or
drink since. "Better fix her some hot soup and make
her sip on it. There's some broth in th' meat we had
for supper yesterday. Ya can heat it up for her."

For once, Aggie welcomed the advice and every
half-hour she climbed up the loft ladder, carrying a
cup of warm broth, and forced a few drops into
Rose's mouth.

While the activity was going on with Rose,
Annabelle kept her eye on Frank. She wanted noth-

ing more than for him to leave. In the over-crowded
cabin, Frank's mood was vile. Annabelle hated the
foul weather that kept him on the mountain.
Unaware of Annabelle's watchful eye, Frank and
Joe sat at the table waiting for their food. They discussed the problems the weather caused them,
ignoring the women as they scurried around.

Big Bessie gave orders in an attempt to keep the
chaos down. There was not enough room in the
world's largest kitchen for three women, yet there
they were in the world's smallest and most ill
equipped. Everything was in mass confusion, as the
women kept getting in one another's way.

Finally Frank roared, "Big Bessie, get the food on
the table, now!"

In the corner of the kitchen from where Annabelle
watched, she was forced to bite her tongue. *I sometimes thought that Jeb was unreasonable an' I got powerful mad at him,* Annabelle thought, *but I think Frank
takes th' prize in bad manners an' meanness. I never, ever
thought I could live in worse conditions than I was, but
bein' here I've discovered I was wrong.*

"How did you like Mary Lou last night, Joe?"
Frank asked.

"Humph," Annabelle couldn't hold back.

"I liked her fine," Joe answered, giving his
mother a stern look in an attempt to keep her quiet.
"Goin' to like havin' th' girls when I'm wantin'."

"Glad to hear it. You need something, just ask,"
Frank said and turned angrily toward Annabelle.
"Don't think I didn't hear your growl of disap-
proval. I'm going to let it pass for now, but you
would do well to remember that I don't tolerate dis-
obedience of any kind."

"Okay," Joe attempted to draw Frank's wrath
from his mother, "I need one thing. What do ya say
I go to Pa's cabin an' get Aggie's cats an' dogs?"

"No, boy. I don't want more mouths to feed. Aggie can do without them damn cats and dogs."

"She needs to have her snuff. Can ya get snuff for her?"

"Sure, I'll bring her snuff. Until then Big Bessie can share with her."

At Frank's show of temper, the younger women had retreated to the loft and the others gave up any attempt to talk to one another. They were quiet as they went about the clean-up chores.

Soon, the light flickered in the oil lamp as the oil burned low, and shadows skipped around the room. Dillon did not keep a large supply of oil, and to conserve their supply the women routinely retired to their beds when darkness fell. He insisted they didn't need to be up and about after dark. Dillon did the same when he was on the mountain. Wheeling was a different story. He enjoyed the city's nightlife, and while there he slept till noon on most days.

The next day, long before daylight had brightened the outdoors and filtered into the cabin window, Big Bessie quietly left the bed and Frank, who slept soundly. She had been the one chosen to warm the bed the evening before.

Expertly, she built the fires in the stoves, warming the cabin as she prepared to make breakfast. As Big Bessie scooped lard into the large skillet, Daisy's scream shattered the silent morning. Bessie hurried to the center of the room, where she could see the loft.

Startled awake by the piercing scream, Frank jumped out of the bed. "What the hell's going on here?"

"It's Rose. She's dead. She's already cold an' stiff," Annabelle cried.

"Damn it, anyway," Frank shouted. "It's too damn cold to bury anyone. Can't dig in the frozen ground if I wanted to." Hopping from foot to foot,

Frank pulled his coveralls over his long johns. "Joe," Frank yelled to be heard up on the loft, "get Rose, wrap her in her quilt, and put her on the back porch. Soon as we can dig a path to the cellar house, we'll move her in there and you can bury her when the ground thaws."

After he had climbed into his overalls and pulled on his socks and boots, Joe clambered down the ladder. "Frank, don'cha think we can leave Rose where she is 'til we can get her to th' cellar house?"

"It wouldn't matter to me one way or another," Frank said. "I don't sleep on the loft, but it's too warm in here to keep a dead body. I say you get her and put her on the back porch."

Annabelle was heartbroken, but kept her feelings to herself. She comforted Aggie, Daisy, and Sara as Joe and Frank went about the business of disposing of Rose's body. Rose had been like a sister to Annabelle and the others.

In her grief, Annabelle became all too aware of the extent of Frank's cold, uncaring nature, but she was most surprised that Joe went about the business of disposing of Rose as if it were merely another chore to take care of.

This is as bad as it gets, Annabelle thought. *Now I'm thinkin' my life with Jeb in his overcrowded cabin wasn't as bad as I'd thought. At least there I wasn't treated like a stranger or someone that wasn't welcome. I was in my own home with my own things.*

Startling Annabelle out of her thoughts, Sara and Daisy wailed, "No, no," as Joe started down the ladder with Rose wrapped in a quilt. Annabelle turned them away from the gruesome scene.

"Don't push yet, Tuesday." Patty's hand pressed on Tuesday's stomach, and she felt the next contraction begin.

Tuesday was exhausted. She had been in labor for twenty-six hours. Her pains had begun upon her arrival at Aggie's cabin. During the past eight hours, since Jacob had given her the sleeping pill, she had slept fitfully, her pains dulled by the drug. The pains now coming harder and only a few minutes apart had awakened her from an uneasy sleep.

"It won't be long now," Patty said. "Th' top of the baby's head's comin' out."

"Do something, Patty." Jacob paced back and forth. "I lost one woman in childbirth. That don't matter now, but I don't want to lose Tuesday. And I damn well can't afford to lose the baby."

McCallister's money supply was dwindling. He needed a baby broker. His longtime contact, George Cunningham, currently rotting in jail, was of no use to him any longer. From his rented room in Ten Mile Creek, Jacob had followed the news broadcasts of the trials for Cunningham and his people, and the outcome was that most of them were behind bars.

To get quick, easy money for Tuesday's child when it was born, McCallister needed a new middleman. Frank Dillon's connections were out. He would not take kindly to being approached concerning the matter, but those people who had worked for Cunningham and had escaped being brought to trial, because Cunningham was afraid to implicate anyone, were worth talking to. One of them was Aubry Moats; McCallister had attempted several times to make contact with him. Moats knew and had worked with every baby broker around the state. So far, Moats had not contacted McCallister.

Until he solved the problem of finding a market for the child, the first item on McCallister's agenda was to get Aggie from Frank Dillon. Frank had taken her only as one of McCallister's conditions when he had offered the women and children to Dillon. Aggie was of no use to Dillon; she was only another mouth for him to feed. He had Big Bessie and Joe to keep his women under control. However, for McCallister's scheme, Aunt Aggie would be a great help. She could look after Tuesday and Patty and she was tops at preparing and storing raw food. The mountain women had a knack for making a meal from the most meager ingredients.

The second step was to make a visit to Rose's father, Herman Ruble, who lived on the other side of the mountain. That was going to be a challenging task. McCallister did not have his truck to drive off the mountain to Winding Ridge and along Route Seven, where the road to Centerpoint went off to the right, running to Broad Run and Ruble's cabin. He would have to walk the ridge. The distance between Aggie's cabin and Ruble's, going across the ridge as the crow flies was much shorter, than the road.

Herman Ruble had three daughters besides Rose, whom Jacob had bought from Ruble a couple years earlier, and a son. Ruble would be happy to get his daughters, whom he could not afford to feed or clothe, off his hands for a few hundred dollars each, the same amount of money he'd paid for Rose. The girls would make a good start for him. And if Ruble was willing to part with his son, it would solve McCallister's major problem; to insure that Tuesday and Patty could not run away when he made his trips to Wheeling. Purchasing the boy would not be easy, though, since the mountain men depended upon their sons to see to the chores.

Frank and Joe dug in the snow, making progress foot by foot. They were well aware that the cellar house and outhouse were thousands of heavy, back-breaking shovels away. The snow had finally stopped coming down after dumping four feet on the ground. The snowdrifts were many and looked for all the world like a giant ice cream sundae waiting for gooey topping, nuts, and cherries.

Nearby, off to the side of the back porch, Rose lay like a discarded life-size doll to be used for a grotesque scene in a horror movie. Wrapped in her quilt, she would stay there until a path could be dug to the cellar house, where she would remain until a grave could be dug. In this grave she would be buried—without ceremony.

Annabelle watched from the kitchen window as Frank and Joe worked together. She was bent on staying out of Big Bessie's way after getting an assignment that morning better suited to the younger girls.

Annabelle, who hated for anyone to boss her around, had stewed as she had washed the clothes, thinking about the way Aggie had taken over at Jacob's cabin before. Now she was forced to do the bidding of this fat woman, whom she had swiftly learned to dislike. Annabelle knew that Big Bessie had given her the job of doing the laundry to put her in her place—as Big Bessie saw it. It hadn't taken Annabelle long to discover that keeping quiet and staying out of Big Bessie's way was the only way for a peaceful coexistence in her unwanted new home.

Annabelle could see that Aggie had no intention of adopting the same attitude. Aggie was not going to give in if she could help it. Annabelle watched as Aggie gathered a few potatoes from the crate that one of the girls had brought in at Big Bessie's request and was preparing to peel them. *Aggie's fightin' a losin' battle,* Annabelle thought. *I'm goin' to bide my time an' Big Bessie'll be sorry for what she's doin' to my family. When Frank leaves for th' city Joe'll not allow Big Bessie to treat us that a way. Aggie's too stubborn to listen to anythin' I got to say. Too stubborn to bide her time.*

"Aggie," Big Bessie said, towering over the smaller woman like a bad dream, "ya wait till I tell ya what to do. I knowed how Frank likes his food cooked. It's my job. Ya knowed to wait for me to tell you."

"Just cause ya so big an' fat, don't make ya knowed more an' me, so it don't," Aggie exploded.

Eyes blazing, Big Bessie swung her arm back and slapped Aggie.

"I wished I'd stayed in my own cabin and taken my chances on starvin', so I do," Aggie said with tears of anger and pain stinging her eyes.

"I'm sorry, Aggie, I didn't mean to lose my temper. Ya can go ahead an' peel th' taters. Jus' set yourself down at th' table," Big Bessie said.

Yeah, Annabelle thought, *she wants to ease th' pang of guilt she feels for slapping a much smaller an' older woman. Big Bessie does like Aggie, though. I can tell she likes to talk to Aggie betta than th' younger girls who're only interested in gigglin' and whisperin' to one another about Frank an' Joe. Th' only problem is, Aggie wants to be in charge an' Big Bessie's not 'bout to give up, or even to share that job with another person. That's why Bessie don't like me an' I ain't goin' to have nothin' to do with someone that wants to boss me around.*

Annabelle failed to see herself as more aggressive than Big Bessie. Because she thought she was the one who should be in charge, she was simply acting accordingly.

After dinner that evening, Frank taught Joe to play poker. Joe caught on quickly, basking in the attention of an adult male who treated him as an equal. Jacob McCallister had never treated Joe like anything except a possession. McCallister's women treated him like a child. Joe was agog with his new life as an equal to the head of the house.

Engrossed in their game, they were barely distracted by the activities of Sally Ann, Eva Belle, Mary Lou, Emma Jean, and Melverta as they prepared for bed, scurrying around the cabin and climbing up and down the ladder.

The older women sat around the potbelly stove. Big Bessie managed to engage them in affable conversation. Aggie had softened a bit since Bessie had slapped her that morning; it would behoove her to get on Bessie's good side. Daisy, who'd had no run-ins with any of Frank's women, participated in the relaxing conversation. Annabelle, still was stinging from the embarrassment of scrubbing laundry on her knees at the bidding of another when she was accustomed to giving the orders, only listened.

"Mary Lou, get in bed so it'll be warm for me when I get in," Frank bellowed and the women's chatter stopped. "You other girls get up on the loft. I'm getting tired of you all prancing back and forth."

Mary Lou ran across the room and climbed in the big bed. The other women and girls retired to their respective mats.

14

CLIFF AND HAL ENTERED THE ROOM WHERE SIMON and his lawyer waited. Simon Leonard had not moved from where he had sat earlier. Simon's lawyer paced back and forth in front of him.

"Are you ready to cooperate?" Cliff asked. He turned a chair around and sat with his legs straddling it.

"Yes," Simon Leonard answered, uncrossing his legs and folding his hands neatly in his lap.

Leonard's attorney had advised him to answer the detective's questions and to make a deal if he could because Leonard clearly had no defense. Besides that, the attorney had reminded Leonard, the detectives were aware of the details of the adoption. They knew that Steven Lloyd, who initiated Jeff's adoption for Leonard, had made a deal on the side with Leonard after the agency turned him down as an adoptive parent, proving the adoption was illegal. And Jeff's parents unquestionably had not put him up for adoption; their reporting the abduction was ample proof of that. The attorney had pointed out to Simon that in addition to all the other incriminating evidence against him, he had Tom living in his home without legal custody, or at the very least parental consent. A deal was the only thing he could hope for.

"Did you buy Tom and Jeff from the same person?" Cliff asked.

"Adopted," Simon said.

"Okay, did you get the boys from the same source?"

"Yes," Simon answered.

"Who?"

"Steven Lloyd. He works at the B. A. Parent Adoption Agency." Simon picked imaginary lint off his trousers, throwing Steven Lloyd to the dogs.

"How did you learn you could get a child through Steven Lloyd?"

"Well," Simon answered, "as far as I'm concerned I adopted legally."

"Don't give me that crap," Cliff said. "Our deal is that you open up. We all know you didn't get the boys legally."

"If you want me to talk, let me!" Leonard said. "I'm telling you the truth as I see it. You wanted information on the people I dealt with and I'm giving it. As I said, I believed I adopted legally."

"Go on," Cliff said. "It doesn't matter that we differ on that point. Who'd you deal with?"

"I went to the B. A. Parent Adoption Agency and, believe me, I applied through proper channels. I know that single people have adopted and hoped I could. We all know I have the means. But I was turned down. Can you imagine," Simon asked, pursing his lips, "saying I was of questionable character?

"A few weeks later," he went on, "Steven Lloyd, who I knew worked at the adoption agency, contacted me. Obviously, he knew of my wealth; he had access to my application. Steven told me I could have a boy, which was what I required, for sixty thousand. He told me there was no record of the boy's birth, but would not tell me any of the details, which promised to be very fascinating. I paid him sixty thousand for the boy, whom I call Tom. He was two months old at the time. Accordingly, I had to hire a nurse to take care of him."

"And Jeff?" Cliff asked, watching as Simon's lawyer continued to pace back and forth.

"Oh, my little Toby. I got him about three years later. Tom was three years old then, Toby was three as well. They were like twins. Steven told me the boy's mother could no longer care for him. The mother was unwed and had lost her job. She just wanted to see him in a good home, so she could go on with her life. I paid sixty-five thousand for him. Well, that was almost three years after I got Tom— inflation, you know."

"Although Steven Lloyd gave you adoption papers, you knew the adoption was illegal. In a legal adoption, you don't pay for the child."

"You just hold on now. I've heard of others paying for a child. Women conceive children for a fee; it's quite common these days. You hear of it all the time on the evening news," Leonard said. "They call them surrogate mothers."

"That's different, and you know it," Cliff said

"That's your opinion," Leonard said.

"Was anyone else involved in the adoption?" Cliff asked.

"Just the lawyer who drew up the papers," Simon answered. "Steven worked with him. I don't know his name."

"Was his name George Cunningham?"

"I just told you, I don't know his name." Simon straightened the crease in his well-tailored pants and looked toward his lawyer as if for support.

An officer came into the room. "Cliff, Simon Leonard's bail has just been posted. I'll take him up when you're finished with him."

"I'm finished with him for now," Cliff said disgustedly to the officer. "And, Leonard, make yourself available, or you'll be back here locked up before you can say 'legal adoption.'"

Tom's eyes followed Cliff as he came into the room and sat on the chair beside the bed.

"How do you feel today, Tom?"

No answer.

"You can trust me," Cliff encouraged. "I'm not going to hurt you. You can be a great help to me in solving a crime, if only you answer my questions. You want to see Toby, don't you?" he asked. "I bet the two of you have never been parted since you've been living with Leonard."

Tom's eyes lit up at the mention of Toby's name, but he still refused to speak. After repeated attempts to get the boy to talk about Toby or anything else, Cliff got up and patted the boy on the head. There was curiosity in the boy's eyes, but no fear.

After leaving Tom, Cliff stopped by Jeff's room. Jeff remained too ill to talk. Cliff stood beside Jeff's bed for a while, watching the boy sleep.

Finally, Cliff went back to his office to meet the Thompsons; they were waiting for him. "I know we've been through this many times before, but I need you to tell me everything you can remember of Jeff's abduction," Cliff implored as he sat at his desk.

"Well," Amy Thompson answered, "like I said before, I was ironing. I've always ironed in front of the window in the living room where I can watch Jeff as he plays in the front yard. There's a picket fence around the yard to keep him off the street. As I watched Jeff play, the phone rang and I answered it. It was just a neighbor calling to chat. I remember, as I talked, I glanced out the window every few seconds to make sure I could still see Jeff. When I couldn't see him any longer, I was certain he must have been playing in the sandbox that was at the side of the house. I couldn't see it from the window. Although I wasn't overly concerned, because the whole time I could see the front gate that opens to the street, I cut the conversation short. I hurried to the front door and saw a truck turn the corner. It came from the street to the left—we live on a corner lot—and sped past the front of the house. I was calling, 'Jeff, come play where Mother can see you.' Then, I saw him in the truck! He was standing with his nose pressed against the window.

"The kidnapper must have parked his truck in the back alley and came through the back gate," she sobbed, remembering the horrific day. "He had dark hair, brown I think, and broad shoulders. The truck was black. It had a red '4 x 4' on the side and mud flaps that had red reflector lights. I didn't get the license number. I've always felt so guilty about that. Everyone must have thought me an idiot for not thinking to get the license number, but I was panic-stricken.

"We've lived in a nightmare world ever since, and it's not over yet," Amy continued, with tears running down her face. "I want you to know," she said as she grasped her husband's hand, "that my husband and I appreciate everything you and the department have done to find our boy. Looking at our dismal faces it must seem to you that we're ungrateful, but that's not the case. On one hand we are relieved and happy to have him back, but on the other hand it's heartbreaking to learn of the abuse he suffered at the hands of that pervert! To see him lying in the big hospital bed so pale and so sick. To know we've missed those precious baby years!" She began to cry, too overcome to continue.

"I feel the same way," Ralph said. "I know how hard you all have worked to find our son. We realize that we can never repay you. All we can do is say thanks from the bottom of our hearts. Even so we are grieved at the hideous life our boy had to lead in his first, tender years."

"Believe me I understand that you have mixed emotions," Cliff said. He had been involved since shortly after Jeff was taken and had spoken to the Thompsons often, becoming an obligatory witness to their suffering.

"That's all for now. Hang in there. Jeff'll be fine." Cliff clasped Ralph's shoulder in a warm gesture, and then embraced Amy. "One more thing, Amy, I want to show you the description of the truck used in other kidnappings," Cliff said.

"Okay. Why not?" Amy said.

Cliff handed the clipping from the newspaper to Amy. She studied it and handed it back. "It definitely sounds like the truck I saw," she said with certainty.

"Hello, Amy, Ralph," Hal greeted the couple as he came into the room. He shook hands with them.

"Cliff, soon as you're finished here meet me in your office," Hal said.

"I'm ready now," Cliff said. "We're all done. Ralph, Amy, let me know if either of you remember anything more. You never know. The smallest thing can break a case," Cliff said, and the distressed couple left to visit their son.

"It looks more and more like Steven Lloyd and George Cunningham hired kidnappers to do their dirty work for them," Cliff said as he and Hal walked down the hallway toward Cliff's office.

"I'm sure Aubry Moats is one of them, and we already know that Jacob McCallister worked for Cunningham," Hal said.

"The truck Amy described to me is even more significant in light of all the others who gave the very same description of the truck over the past year as the one used in other abductions. We know that Moats and McCallister were both known to drive a truck of that same description."

Later in Cliff's office Hal called the desk sergeant. "Bring Paul Keaton up. We're ready for him."

"What's up, Hal?" Cliff asked. "We have enough on our agenda without getting involved in a new case."

"No, Cliff, it's not a new case. I have a surprise for you. You'll want to talk to the man waiting down stairs. He called in this morning and said that on the same day that our girls went missing, he saw an automobile that matched the description of Tuesday's car pull into the mall parking lot beside a truck. He watched a man get out and transfer two females to the truck and drive away, abandoning the car. He said he didn't really think much of it until he heard a woman and girl were missing, or he would have come forward sooner.

"Needless to say," Hal went on, "I told him to get here pronto. I knew you'd want to talk to this one personally."

"Damn straight, I want to talk to him. Get him in here. This is the first ray of hope since Tuesday and Patty disappeared. If this man identifies the one he saw as McCallister, or not, I'll know which course to take."

"Looks like McCallister wasn't so smart, after all," Hal said.

"He may have made his first mistake," Cliff said. "If so, we now have a lead."

*P*ATTY SAT IN THE ROCKING CHAIR, VERY SOFTLY talking to the doll in her lap. "I don't want to think about this place. If we close our eyes, we can pretend we're back in Tuesday's house. It's warm an' clean. There's food to eat. I can almost feel th' warmth. Ya can too if ya try. Ya knowed in Tuesday's house, ya don't have to be afraid like we are here."

On the cot reclining against a pile of quilts, Tuesday held her baby girl in her arms. She was glad that Jacob had not stayed in the room for the birth. Having him there was the last thing Tuesday wanted. Given Jacob's ego, being there would only have strengthened his belief that the baby was his. As far as Tuesday was concerned, it took more than a sex act to make a man a father.

Tuesday became aware that Patty was talking. *She's talking to her doll. She must be so afraid, being brought back to this place after the trauma of running away those months ago, after enjoying a normal life.* Tuesday knew Patty didn't see the life in Wheeling as normal; she saw it as a fairy tale. She had no other experiences to judge her life by, except the poverty-stricken life on the mountain and the fairy tales her Aunt Aggie had told her.

"Patty, I've decided the baby's name will be Winter Ann. Do you like it?"

"Yeah, I do," Patty said and went to the cot.

"I named your doll Summer because she was given to me on a lovely summer day," Tuesday said. "Now, I think it's appropriate that I name my child for the season she was born. Ann is for my mother."

"I wish I'd knowed my mother. It's like I never really had one until you, but now I have a sister. She is goin' to be my sister, isn't she?"

"Of course she is," Tuesday smiled.

Patty softly patted the baby on the head. "Pa's goin' to sell th' baby if we don't get away from here in time. Maybe Cliff'll come to get us, just like before."

Hope filled Tuesday's heart for the briefest second. Then she saw the pure terror in Patty's eyes and knew that Patty was only trying to comfort her. Patty did not believe Cliff was going to find them soon enough. She had lived her young life with the knowledge that Jacob sold his children shortly after they were born. Patty had been kept only because of the birthmark that disfigured her face, and she was shockingly aware of it. Making a living from his offspring was Patty's father's livelihood and was the way of life Patty had become accustomed to over the years.

Our only hope to get away is Cliff, Tuesday thought. *When the weather breaks he will come on the mountain to Jacob's cabin, and when we're not there, he will guess that Jacob took us to Aggie's cabin and come to look for us. He told me that he was in Aggie's cabin. I bet Jacob doesn't know that. That's how Cliff found Jacob's cabin—*

by following Aggie after he'd asked her questions that she found disturbing. In her undying loyalty, she made the hazardous trip, through one of the worst blizzards in years, down the mountain to let her nephew know that he was being sought.

"Tuesday, did ya hear me?" Patty asked. "Pa's goin' to sell Winter Ann if we don't get away from here."

"Yes, Patty, I heard you," Tuesday said. "We have to pray that Cliff finds us. It's too dangerous for us to run like we did last year. Winter Ann would never survive the bitter cold."

"I guess you're right," Patty sighed. "We didn't make it on our own when I knowed th' way. I'd hate to see what'd happen if we'd wander around with a tiny baby in this blizzard lost, hungry, an' freezing."

"Like we're not almost freezing now," Tuesday said.

"I'll put more wood on th' fire," Patty offered. "There's not but a few sticks left."

It was the second day in the cabin, and they were almost out of wood for the stoves. Four feet of snow made it impossible to get to the nearby forest to restock the supply.

Awakened by the soft conversation, Jacob climbed from the loft. He had slept in his clothes, so there was no need to get dressed. Throwing on his heavy coat and boots and not bothering to speak to the females, he stepped out on the back porch. Even with the roof over the porch, the snow had drifted close to the back door. Had he not shoveled the snow from the door several times since the onset of the storm, it would be impossible to open now.

The cabin stood in a clearing with the forest three hundred yards away. The face of the mountain

dropped down sharply behind the cabin. The thermometer, which hung beside the back door, read
thirty-six degrees. "Good, it's going above freezing," Jacob said out loud, still frustrated. "Some of
this damn snow's bound to melt. I sure as hell can't
shovel it all out of my way."

Jacob picked up a shovel that was propped
beside the back door. He moved to the edge of the
porch and shoveled until he had dug a hole in the
snow about four feet deep. After relieving himself,
he hurried inside, followed by the howling, frigid
wind, and found the chamber pot. He carried it out
and emptied it in the newly dug hole. He pushed
the snow in after the foul-smelling contents and carried the pot back into the cabin.

Jacob checked the wood box that sat beside the
woodburner and the one that was by the potbelly
stove. There was no wood left, but the woodburner
was burning hot enough to fix breakfast. The potbelly was burning brightly and warming the room a
little from the wood Patty had added a few minutes
before, but soon both stoves would burn out if he
did not add more wood. A trip to the woodpile the
day before had proven to be futile; it was empty. He
had no choice but to find a way to replenish the supply soon. The forest was out. Not only was the forest too far from the cabin, the wood would be too
green to burn.

"The loft. That's it!" Jacob said.

Tuesday cringed at the unexpected outburst.
*What's he talking about now? I'm not going to stand for
this much longer. I have to do something. The girls are
depending on me.*

"Patty, fix my breakfast. Then get the hammer out
of the toolbox and start dismantling the loft. In the
meantime I'm going to dig a path to the outhouse

and cellar. We need more food," he said as he slammed out the back door.

Patty set out to obey her father's orders, not daring to ask what he had in mind about the loft.

Tuesday had been watching the activity, determined that the situation was not hopeless. She was glad when Jacob left the cabin to work outdoors.

It was the worst and the best time of her life. The worst of it was that she was trapped by a madman and was responsible for two children. The best was that she had a healthy, beautiful new daughter. Sadly, that was most definitely overshadowed by the worst of it. *It feels like there's no way out!*

No way out? I'm sitting here banging my head against a brick wall, thinking there's no way out. But there must be a way to deal with the situation. I know! Disable Jacob. That's the only way.

"Patty, come over here, I need to talk to you."

"Yeah, Tuesday, what do ya want?"

"We've been thinking of running away and we know it's not possible. But we may be able to disable Jacob. I don't want to kill him unless we have to. He's your father, after all, and I don't want the murder of your own father to be on your conscience.

"How? He's so powerful an' strong."

"I don't know yet. We must both think about it. We need a weapon, and surprise is on our side."

"Yeah, but if we don't kill him, how're we goin' to keep him from killin' us. 'Cause he will for us usin' a weapon on him."

"I know, he's stronger than we are, so a weapon is not the answer. If we didn't knock him out with the first blow, we'd never get another chance." Tuesday was excited for the first time in days. "I got it, we must find the sleeping pills he's been giving me. We'll slip them in his coffee."

"We'd betta be sure he doesn't catch on, or we'll be in more trouble than we've ever been in."

"We have no choice. We have to try. I think we have a good chance of being successful. He isn't thinking we have the guts to do anything and that will be his downfall."

"I remember that there are some leg chains somewhere. Aunt Aggie had them from th' war between th' North and South. She said that there was tunnels runnin' underground from South to th' North somewhere. Might even run under this here cabin. There's no one left that knows how to get in th' tunnel that I knowed of. If Aunt Aggie don't knowed can't see how anyone'd knowed."

"I wish you knew how to get into the tunnel. We could escape without having to take a chance on infuriating Jacob," Tuesday said.

"We'd have to take the oil lamps with us, an' there's probably rats in th' tunnel too."

"We've dealt with rats before. I wouldn't let that stop us. It's a moot point anyway, I don't see how we could find the entrance to the tunnel if not even Aggie knows."

"What's moot?" Patty asked.

"Oh, it means it wouldn't help anyway to know or something like that."

"Th' pills are in Pa's pocket. We have to get them when he's asleep."

"I'll be the one to do that. I think he'd be less likely to do serious harm to me than to you."

"Okay, I'd be so afraid I'd wake him up with my shakin' hands." Patty held up her hands to show how they shook just thinking about the task of searching her father's pockets.

"Here's the plan. When he goes to sleep, I'll search his pockets for the pills. When he wakes up and you fix his breakfast, put all the pills into his coffee. I hope they won't kill him, but we have to take the chance because we need for him to be out cold so we can incapacitate him until we're rescued."

"What about when he wakes up?" Patty asked.

"There'll be plenty of time for you to go to the barn and look for the chain you talked about. If you can't find the chain, there's sure to be rope or baling twine in the barn.

Patty picked up her doll. Its expression seemed to have changed to one of sorrow. "Summer, what should we do?" Patty asked the unresponsive doll.

"Patty, have you had any dreams at all?"

"No, I haven't except for bein' pulled along on a sled an' I'm sittin' alongside Aunt Aggie, an' her dogs are following settin' up a ruckus. There's Pa an' another man walkin' alongside. It don't make any sense to me."

"I can't imagine what it could mean. Are you sure that's all there is to it?"

"Yeah, we're on a sled an' I'm sittin' beside Aunt Aggie an' you're holdin' th' baby. I'll probably have it again like I always do. I think I woke up durin' th' dream or that's all there is to it."

"It doesn't make sense. I'd think Jacob was planning on taking us to another location except for Aggie and a strange man being with us. Since Jacob's the only man and Aggie's not here, how could they be with us in your dream if it's a preview of something that's going to happen?"

Later that same day Patty was preparing a dinner that consisted of biscuits—her father had shown her how to do the simple job of mixing the flour, lard, and water—and gravy that she made from lard, flour, and water. "I hear Pa comin'. When ya goin' to get th' pills?"

"As soon as he goes to sleep. Please, act normal. We can't let him suspect anything," Tuesday whispered.

Jacob came in and he was in a foul mood. While he took off his coat, Patty scooped gravy over four biscuits and set the plate on the table for her father. She knelt next to him as soon as he took his chair and pulled his cold, wet boots from his feet.

Next, she handed Tuesday a plate of two biscuits covered with the gravy. After Tuesday was comfortable eating at the cot, Patty served her own and sat at the table with her father.

Tuesday tried to hide her excitement brought on by the anticipation of restraining Jacob. *Just as soon as he falls asleep, I'm going to search his pockets for the pills. I pray that I'm lucky enough to find them quickly. I don't have any idea of how soundly he sleeps.*

Jacob finished eating. Ignoring the others, he prepared for sleep and climbed up into the loft. Although he spent a goodly amount of time working out and was in great shape, he was not used to such physical labor in such cold temperatures and was exhausted. Soon he was snoring softly.

Tuesday heard him snoring. Leaving the baby sleeping on one end of the cot, she headed for the ladder. Slowly she climbed, determined not to make any noise and awaken Jacob. Holding her breath every time the ladder creaked, she kept going. She reached the top of the ladder and crawled into the loft. As she turned and looked down, she saw Patty standing in a circle of candlelight. The flickering firelight shining in Patty's eyes revealed pools of terror.

She turned back to Jacob who was lying on his left side with his back toward her. *Oh, please let the pills be in his right-hand pocket. If not, I can't risk turning him over.* She inched closer to Jacob and carefully reached into his pocket. She felt a small plastic pill bottle. I can't believe my luck! She pulled her hand back and there were the sleeping pills. The bottle was one-quarter full.

After she tucked the bottle into her pocket, she backed toward the ladder, afraid to take her eyes off Jacob. As she felt the edge of the loft with her toes, though, she was forced to turn around to find the top rung of the ladder. She turned back and threw her leg over the side and found a rung for her foot. She grabbed the top rung with her left hand, and before she could begin her descent down the ladder, Jacob—quick as a lightning bolt—grabbed her right arm.

16

*H*AL ESCORTED THE YOUNG MAN INTO CLIFF'S
office. "Here you are, Cliff. This young man
is Paul Keaton," Hal said, waving his arm toward
Paul. "Paul, Sergeant Cliff Moran here," he said as
he motioned toward Cliff.

Briskly, Cliff moved around his desk, holding out
his hand to Paul. Paul took Cliff's hand and shook it.

"Good to meet you, Sergeant."

"Likewise," Cliff said. "Thanks for coming forward."

"You bet," Paul said.

"Please, Paul, tell me what you saw." Cliff indicated for Paul to take a seat, and Cliff sat on the
edge of his desk.

"I was parked behind the mall sleeping in my car.
I had a few too many beers, that's why I was parked
back there. I wanted to sleep it off before driving
farther. I had been there at least four hours, I guess,
when I heard a car coming around to the back of the
lot. That was what woke me. I was cold, too. It was
dark where I was parked. The floodlights are pretty
far apart, leaving dark patches. The car pulled

beside a black truck that sat in the shadows in the far corner of the lot, but I could see the man when the dome light came on as he opened the car door. He had very dark brown hair and broad shoulders. I would say he is a little over six feet tall."

"Had you had too much to drink for your testimony to be reliable?" Cliff asked.

"Like I said, I'd been asleep for no less than four hours by then."

"Good," Hal said. "That's plenty of time to sober up."

"Go on," Cliff said.

"The man got out of the car," Keaton went on, "looked around, probably to check if he was being watched, and then he unlocked the truck. He left the door open and went back to the car and lifted a woman out. He carried her to the truck. I could see, from the dome light, her hair was blonde. She looked very pregnant. She looked to be unconscious. Next, the man reached in the car and lifted a dark-haired girl out. She was also dead to the world. After he had them in the truck, he locked the car and drove away."

"Which way did he go?" Hal asked.

"He turned right," Paul remembered.

"Hal, that's a straight shot to Interstate 70,"

"Or a thousand other places," Hal said.

Cliff turned his attention back to Paul, "Look at these photos." Cliff pulled pictures of Tuesday and Patty and a composite drawing of Jacob McCallister from an envelope.

Paul took them and looked at each one carefully. "Yes, that's the man. I'm sure as I can be. The light wasn't that good." He looked closely at the photos of Tuesday and Patty. "Sure looks like the girl and the woman. They were not as visible as the man, but I think it's them."

"Paul, this is very important. What time was it?"

"It was around three in the morning."

They excused Paul. "We may need to talk to you again," Hal admonished. "Don't leave town unless you leave a phone number where we can get in touch."

"Sure thing." Paul Keaton pumped each of their hands in a firm handshake and left.

"I was right all along. McCallister has them," Cliff said. "There's no denying it now. He took Tuesday and Patty out of Tuesday's car, but where did he take them?"

"If it was him—Paul said he was drinking that night—he could have taken them anywhere," Hal spread his hands in a wide gesture.

"Someway he got to the cabin. Paul said they looked unconscious. That would account for them not screaming when he took them out of the house. He must have drugged them," Cliff said. "That's how he took Tuesday before."

"Cliff, you know no one could have gotten up that mountain road. You saw it for yourself. Randy and Bert talked to Sheriff Moats and he said they had not seen McCallister. It would be unlikely for him to get to his cabin without being seen. Especially since the deputy checks there often."

"You know the sheriff couldn't care less about what McCallister does. I'm sure the deputy checks the cabin like he says, but all Jacob would have to do is keep his truck parked out of sight and hide when he heard the sheriff's Jeep coming. Jess Willis isn't smart enough to make a surprise visit.

"Patty dreamt her father took them back to the cabin," Cliff said. "Past experience tells me not to overlook her dreams.

"Anyway, according to Paul," Cliff went on, "they left the parking lot around 3:00 A.M. I'll check with the weather service and see what time the storm hit the Winding Ridge area. I've a hunch they had plenty of time to get to the mountain before the storm got too bad."

"Maybe," Hal said, "but for now we have the make of the truck. We'll have every police officer in the tri-state area looking for it. If he is lying low somewhere waiting for the weather to clear, we'll find him. Could be holed up in a hotel or motel. We can't overlook that possibility."

"I agree," Cliff conceded.

Simon Leonard used his time, while he was free on bail, making plans to replace the two boys he had lost with two others. He did not care how much he had to pay to get them. The next time around he would get boys who had no birth record—that had been the way it was with Tom. If Jeff had not been recognized as a missing child, Leonard would not have lost the boys. He had resigned himself to the fact that he would be tried, convicted, and sentenced to a jail term, but when it was over, he intended to have two boys awaiting his return.

Simon Leonard could kiss Steven Lloyd's help good-bye after ratting on him to the police. He was now being watched, and anyone who dealt with him would be watched as well. Having lost Lloyd as a source for getting children, Simon needed someone else to fill the void. He had a number to get in touch with Frank Dillon who, in the past, had sold children through Steven Lloyd. Simon believed Tom had come from Dillon's supply, and that qualified him as a source for a kid with no birth record.

Leonard had become aware of Dillon and his activities a few years back while he was slumming in a gay pub he often frequented in search of a new companion. In a dark booth in the back of the room sat Dillon and Lloyd, who used the tavern to meet because they believed they would be safe from the prying eyes of the law. Curious about the handsome man with Lloyd—who was to Leonard's taste—he crept to the booth behind them and eavesdropped on their conversation about where to meet beautiful women and the important topic of child trafficking. That was how he had stumbled onto the fact that Dillon was involved with Lloyd and supplied him with children. Thus, he had a more important need to get to know Dillon than meeting a new companion ever could be. Leonard became one of the few people who knew that Dillon sold children—his own.

Soon after Leonard overheard Lloyd and Dillon's conversation, with the intention of meeting Dillon, Simon threw a party with the most beautiful women and invited Lloyd and Dillon. As a result, Simon and Dillon became friends of sorts.

Now Simon's plan was that Dillon, for extra money, could be convinced to sell directly to Simon. Given the fact that Dillon's middleman, Steven Lloyd, was headed for jail, it was imperative that Dillon be warned that Steven Lloyd was being watched.

Simon made several attempts to call Dillon at his home in Wheeling, getting no answer.

The year before, George Cunningham's imprisonment had been to Steven Lloyd's advantage. Steven had cooperated with George on only one sale, a small boy. He and George had disagreed on their commission and were devout enemies afterward. Since Cunningham's arrest, some of his people, who had slipped through the cracks and were not named in the allegations that had sent George and the others to prison, had been recruited to work for Steven, providing him with the much-sought-after children. He had a longer list of hopefuls waiting to buy than to sell, and having connections with George's people, who were clever at supplying children, was like a gold mine for Lloyd.

When George Cunningham went on trial, he did not point his finger at anyone and Steven was not implicated in the black-marketing of children. George was much too frightened for his own hide. He did not want to be locked up with a man who wanted revenge. George's objective was to do his time in peace.

After Paul and Hal left his office, Cliff decided to call the West Virginia State Police to request an hourly weather report and road conditions for the Winding Ridge area for the previous thirty-six hours. As soon as it was even remotely possible, he was going to find a way to get to McCallister's cabin. All the evidence pointed to McCallister as the one who had taken Tuesday and Patty.

"Hello, Sergeant Cliff Moran here. I need a weather report for the roads between Wheeling and the town of Winding Ridge, covering the past thirty-six hours. Most important of all, I need to know what time the roads to Winding Ridge became impassable."

"Sure thing. Let me get back to you."

"I need it right away," Cliff said.

"I'll do my best," the trooper said.

17

*L*ABOR PAINS WOKE DAISY IN THE EARLY MORNING hours. "Aunt Aggie, wake up." Daisy shook Aunt Aggie, "Th' baby's comin'."

"Get off th' loft, while ya can. I'll come with you, so I will."

The clap-clap of the wobbly ladder, as it hit against the beam with each step as they climbed down, woke Big Bessie. She heaved herself up from her mat. "What ya doin'? Ain't mornin' yet." Big Bessie panted from the exertion.

"Daisy's in labor, so she is," Aunt Aggie said. "Need to get her off th' loft while I can, so I do."

"Let me check her. I'm no stranger, to birthin' babies," Big Bessie said as she pulled her sweater off the spike nail and pushed her huge arms through the sleeves.

"I'll light th' oil lamps," Big Bessie said.

The confusion woke Frank, "What the hell you women yakkin' about in the middle of the night?"

"It's most mornin', an' Daisy's goin' to drop her baby," Big Bessie declared in supremacy. The light from the oil lamp she carried lighted her face and cast shadows that made her eyes look long and catlike.

"Get up, Mary Lou, and let Daisy in the bed." Frank said, as he slapped her on the rump and got out of bed and stretched.

"Big Bessie, forget about Daisy and get the damn fires built. It's cold in here. Fix my breakfast, too. Aggie can deliver the baby. You worry about my needs."

Big Bessie went off in a huff, red-faced at being sent away unneeded.

Daisy got into the bed and Aunt Aggie sat next to her, feeling self-important. Aggie put her hand on Daisy's stomach so she could time the contractions. "Set some water to boil, Annabelle. Goin' to need it, so I am."

Big Bessie hurried with Frank's breakfast, not interfering when Annabelle set water on her stove to boil. When Frank was in a bad mood, there was no need to test his temper any further.

Above them on the loft the others had been awakened by the unusual activity. "Joe, what ya think that's for?" Sara pointed to a large dog kennel in the corner.

"Don't knowed," Joe answered. "Look's like a cage to me."

Emma Jean heard Sara's question and said, "I-it's w-w-where—"

"Emma Jean, can't ya talk without stuttering?" Melverta interrupted. "It's where Frank locks us up if we don't do as he tells us. He says that's what we need to keep us in line."

"Did he ever lock ya up?" Sara asked with fear in her eyes. Her father locked the women in the cellar house when he wanted to punish them. Experience taught there was no doubt that the cage was a real threat.

Below the loft, Frank had gone outdoors with the sound of Daisy's screams ringing in his ears. Joe sat at the table and finished his meal in a hurry. He was as unnerved by Daisy's cries of pain as Frank was, and after he cleaned his plate, he followed after him.

After only an hour of labor that had Daisy bathed in perspiration in spite of the cold room, Aunt Aggie caught the baby in her capable hands. She handed it to Annabelle. "It's a boy, so it is," Aggie said.

"I can see that," Annabelle said. "Ya thinkin' I'm blind?"

"Why's she screamin' like that?" Big Bessie asked, getting her nose back in the birthing process now that Frank was out of the cabin. "Something's wrong for her be screamin' like that after th' baby done dropped."

"She's havin' twins again, so she is," Aggie said as another dark head appeared. "Ya better take care of that one, Annabelle, an', Big Bessie, we're goin' to need ya to take care of this one comin' out, so we are."

Annabelle lay the first twin on a small baby blanket that she had ready and began bathing the child. She had a washcloth and a wash pan of hot water ready for the task. She expertly bathed the child and wrapped him in a blanket. "Here ya are, Daisy," Annabelle lay the baby in the crook of Daisy's arm. "Here's your first one."

Aggie had caught the second twin and handed it over to Big Bessie. "Okay, Daisy, it's over except for th' afterbirth. Big Bessie, ya can take this one now. It's another boy, so it is," Aggie said.

After Big Bessie cleaned the second twin, she placed him in Daisy's other arm. Mother and children looked like the perfect picture of tranquillity, as they lay bathed in the flickering light and dancing shadows cast by the oil lamp.

Annabelle cleaned up the mess and made herself scarce. She was totally consumed with waiting for Frank to leave for the city. Then she planned to show Big Bessie that she could do as she pleased. Joe was her son, after all. He would be in charge, and without Frank around there was nothing to stop Annabelle from doing as she saw fit. She seemed to forget that even before Joe had brought them to Frank's cabin, he had more and more walked in the footsteps of his father, Jacob, treating the women like they were lesser beings than men.

Later that day, worn down from digging but inspired by the arrival of twins, Frank checked the fluids in the snowmobile and, after replacing the spark plugs, started it up with a roar. There was a loud flapping noise just before the motor shuddered and fell silent.

A belt had snapped and lay like a black snake in the white snow. "I was afraid th' belts was rotten," Joe said.

"I suppose I'll have to replace all the damn belts. There's not enough daylight left. Now I'll have to wait till tomorrow to leave for Wheeling."

"I hope you're sayin' ya have extra belts," Joe said.

"They're in the barn. Go and see if you can find them. I'm anxious to get out of here. The twins Daisy birthed are going to bring big money."

"So you think you can take matters into your own hands," Jacob laughed, sending chills of fright down Tuesday's spine. "Surely you didn't think you were going to get away with taking my own pills to use on me, did you?"

"Let go of me!" Tuesday demanded and jerked her arm loose. She fell to the floor with a thud, and Patty screamed with fright. Tuesday lay still, her face as white as the cold snow that lay at their doorstep.

Jacob vaulted from the loft and stood over the unconscious Tuesday, enraged. "Don't you ever try anything like that again. Now that you've shown you can't be trusted—and for your own good—I'm going to have to keep you under lock and key."

Disregarding her father's rage and the possibility that he would turn on her, Patty ran to Tuesday to help her. Tuesday did not respond, and Patty lifted Tuesday by her shoulders. She was limp in Patty's arms.

"Damn, she's out cold," Jacob said.

"Maybe she's hurt bad," Patty sobbed. "She just gave birth an' a fall could cause her to bleed inside." Patty had heard her Aunt Aggie caution the women to stay quiet for a few weeks after giving birth.

Jacob went to the sink and dipped water from the bucket. He walked back to Tuesday and flipped the water into her face. She jerked her head to one side and opened her eyes.

"Both of you go to sleep," Jacob demanded and climbed back up on the loft. He turned his back to the others, unafraid.

The next day after a meager breakfast and after shoveling snow most of the day, Jacob finished digging the paths to the outhouse and cellar. Once again Patty had prepared a dinner of biscuits and gravy. It would not be long before they had nothing to eat.

After the meal, although exhausted from a full day of digging, Jacob helped Patty dismantle the loft. Later, Jacob ordered Patty to make a bed, on the floor in front of the potbelly stove, for the two of them. That was the warmest spot in the cabin. The loft would not safely hold their weight now that it was partially dismantled. Some of the wood they had taken from the loft was burning brightly in the potbelly stove, and the remainder was piled high against the wall beside the woodburner.

Riddled with pain, bruised, and angry that her plan had not worked, Tuesday sat on Aggie's cot with the baby. She watched Patty make the bed of mats and quilts on the floor in front of the potbelly stove. She knew that when Jacob felt she was healed from childbirth he would subject her to his sexual desires once again. *I know Jacob's a little worried that I'm badly injured. I must play on that, keeping him thinking I'm not healed inside as long as I can. Jacob wants to keep me alive, and the threat of my dying like Patty's mother will keep him at bay for a while, giving me a little time to get Patty, Winter Ann, and myself away from this horrid place, but how? We can't travel in this weather. I never saw snow this deep. Cliff, please find us, please,* she prayed. *Until then the only thing I can do is watch for the perfect time to hit him over the head and knock him unconscious long enough for me to tie him up. The problem then will be to keep him tied until the weather breaks or help comes.*

"Patty, get under the quilts. It's time to sleep," Jacob ordered, interrupting Tuesday's thoughts and bringing her to the reality of Jacob's strength versus hers. "Tomorrow, I'll try to make the trip to Frank's cabin. I need Aunt Aggie here to do the cooking. She'd say, 'It ain't fittin' that th' two of you knowed nothin' about cookin, so it ain't,'" Jacob entertained himself by convincingly imitating Aggie's speech.

The only food they'd had to eat so far was eggs, bacon, potatoes, gravy, and biscuits, and now the potatoes, eggs, and bacon were gone. With Aggie there to cook she would make use of the dry beans, lard, canned wild game, and flour for making bread, dumplings, and biscuits that were put up in the cellar house during summers past. Patty and Tuesday had no idea how to prepare the flour to mix the bread or how to cook the beans.

The next morning Jacob prepared to leave. "I have to leave for a while and I don't trust the two of you alone, so I'm going to have to chain one of you up," he said. "In this weather it would be impossible for you to go out and find your way to town, but in my experience with the two of you I can't count on you being reasonable. As a matter of fact, I may not be able to make it to where I'm going myself."

"Patty, fix my breakfast," Jacob ordered. While Patty prepared his food, he made his way to the barn and came back with a chain. It had shackles on each end. He attached one end to the potbelly stove and fit the other shackle around Tuesday's ankle. The chain was about five feet long, allowing her to reach the cot and the old homemade table. Luckily for Jacob there was still a key to lock and unlock the iron. The leg iron, a relic from slave times, had been brought to the mountain by Jacob's great grandfather, who had years ago migrated to the mountains of West Virginia from the state of Georgia.

Now I know that there really are shackles here, Tuesday thought. *I pray that somehow I'll be able to use these on Jacob—and soon. If I don't get away from him soon it will be too late for my daughter! Jacob will sell her without a thought!*

After everything was in order, Jacob walked down the mountain path toward Frank's cabin. The snow was not as deep on the steep grade, but it was treacherous climbing down the snow-covered, rocky path. Jacob used the support of shrubbery to keep his footing, but without warning, a dead branch he held onto for support broke. He slid twenty feet down the rocky slope.

He lay there swearing. Soon he got to his feet and moved on.

After hours of slipping and sliding down the steep slope, Jacob reached the clearing where Frank

Dillon and Joe were working on Dillon's snowmobile outside the shed. To the right was a freshly dug path leading from the forest to Dillon's cabin, and he walked toward it. The snow had drifted deep where the mountain face stopped at the clearing. If the path had not been there, Jacob would have used his shovel to dig his way. That would have been nothing new, since he had dug his way through a number of snowdrifts in the past few days.

"Hi there, Frank," Jacob called.

"I'll be damned. It's Jacob McCallister," Frank said to Joe. "Why the hell did he come back here?"

"When did he get back?" Joe asked, watching as his father made his way toward them.

"I have no idea," Dillon said. "Can't imagine he'd come back here when he's wanted by the law."

As McCallister drew closer to where Frank and Joe stood by the shed, he called, "Looks like you're planning to get off the mountain in that thing."

"Hell, yes. If you need to talk to me, you're none too early. How did you get down the trail, anyway?"

"Wasn't easy," Jacob said and held his shovel up. "Had to dig through some places. It's going to be murder climbing back up, though."

"Why'd you risk your neck making the trip down the mountain to talk to me?" Frank asked. "Seems to me the mountain is the last place you'd be under the circumstances. Thought you'd be smart enough to be off somewhere where no one would think to look."

"I know I can count on you to keep my whereabouts to yourself," Jacob said. "You can be sure I'm always one step ahead of the law—as I've already demonstrated by the eight months I've avoided being found," he laughed.

"Anyone asks me, I haven't seen you," Frank said. "I just think you're asking for trouble being on the mountain."

"Don't worry, I know what I'm doing. I only wanted to let you know," Jacob got to the point, "if you wanted Aunt Aggie off your hands, I can use her. I need a cook bad."

"Fine with me if you take her," Frank said with relief. "She and Big Bessie don't get along too well. She's too old to have children. Just took her because it was part of our deal."

"When I started out earlier, I'd planned to get her today. After making the trip I realize I can't get her up the mountain in this weather," Jacob said. "Don't even know if I can make it back myself. It took me two hours to get here. I just wanted to be sure to speak to you about her. I thought this blizzard might have you stuck on the mountain, too; otherwise, I wouldn't have made the miserable trip."

The trip had been a hard five-mile walk through deep snow. In good weather, Jacob could have walked the distance in about an hour and a half.

"Don't matter," Frank said. "Get her when you can. Want to go inside? You can have something to eat and get warm before you start back."

"Thanks," McCallister said, "but I've got to get back. Don't want the women to see me and put up a fuss. Anyway, they talk too much. Couldn't believe how much information the women gave those detectives when they were on my tail last year. The less those foolish women know the better. Hate to turn down the food and warmth though, but along with staying out of sight of my women, I shouldn't be away from Aggie's cabin for so long."

Dillon did not ask why that was an issue.

"By the way, you haven't seen me either, Joe." Jacob nodded to the boy. There was no need for the request; the mountain people kept to their own business.

As Jacob walked back toward the mountain trail, Frank called to him, "Jacob, if you want I'll bring Aggie by when I leave here. If you need a cook, you won't want to wait until this snow melts. That could take weeks. I was going to leave this morning, but I got more work to do on my machine than I'd thought. Otherwise, I'd run you back up the mountain. I can bring her by the first thing tomorrow, though, provided I get it running by then."

"I'd be grateful. Aggie can make a meal when you'd think there was nothing at all to fix. Sure would appreciate if you'd bring her to her own cabin. For the time I'll be staying there. And thanks."

In the cabin, Annabelle came up behind Aggie, who was standing by the window watching Jacob and Frank as they talked. It was rare that anyone other than Big Bessie was permitted to stand and look out the window. Big Bessie did not like anyone in her work space and usually would shove anyone who dared to invade it out of the way. "I pray he's come to get us, so I do," Aggie said.

She had no more than spoken, when Jacob turned and headed back up the mountain. "Don't cry, Aggie," Annabelle said, sorrowful to see Aggie hurting so much. She wanted to run out and call to him, ask him to take them all home with him, but knew that Frank would not tolerate such behavior. She was too frightened to do anything. She had seen the cage in the loft and had heard the girl tell Joe and Sara of its purpose.

Annabelle stood by feeling helpless as Aggie remained by the window, with tears streaming down her face, watching until Jacob became a mere speck in the snow and disappeared from sight. Annabelle had never seen Aunt Aggie cry before.

18

*C*LIFF WAS SHOWN INTO THE ROOM WHERE THE pediatrician sat at his desk. This doctor had often been called upon to act as a Santa Claus at Christmas time. With his white hair, reading glasses that he wore propped upon the end of his nose, and generous stomach, he was invariably a hit.

"Do you have any idea why Tom refuses to talk?" Cliff asked.

"I don't think he has been taught to talk," the doctor said. "You know the situation the boys were in. My bet is if you got Simon Leonard to open up, he'll tell you he didn't teach the boys to speak."

"That's why they don't say anything—they can't?" Cliff asked.

"That's right. There's nothing wrong with their vocal cords. There's no medical reason that I can see. They've made some sounds, which sound like gibberish, and they look frustrated when they're not understood. I think Tom and Jeff learned a language of their own in order to communicate with each other, partly vocal and partly sign language."

"That's incredible," Cliff said, "that they were isolated from others so totally that they didn't pick up even the simplest words."

"They'll have to learn to speak before they can even go to school. Jeff is lucky that he has his parents to support him. If you can't find Tom's parents, he'll have to go to a children's shelter now that his health is good, but he'll need counseling for the sexual abuse inflicted upon him."

Cliff got to his feet. "Thanks for your time, Doc. I don't think Tom has the kind of loving parents that Jeff has. If my guess is right, he was born to be sold."

A while later, in the hospital room, Jeff slept. He looked frail and pale. Cliff stood by his bed even more curious after speaking to the doctor. The nurse who was on duty came into the room and stood beside Cliff.

"How can I communicate with the boy?" Cliff asked.

"I'm sure I don't know. Everyone on staff has tried without success," Nancy said.

"Since Jeff's sleeping, do you want to go along as I check on Tom?" she asked.

Tom sat propped up in his bed; he watched the television that was suspended from the ceiling. Tom looked up as Cliff came into the room. "Toby?" Tom said, looking at Cliff with hopeful eyes.

"You want to see Toby, don't you?"

"Toby," Tom said again.

Cliff patted Tom on the head. "Did you hear him? He said Toby twice."

"Yes, I did," Nancy answered. "That was good. Now we know for sure he can speak."

"You know Toby was the name Leonard gave to Jeff," Cliff said. "It's the only thing he's said that I've understood."

"Yes, me too," Nancy said. "I've been trying to get him to say anything at all, but with no luck."

"Nurse, can we take Tom to see Jeff?" Cliff asked.

"I'll check with the doctor. I don't see why not," Nancy answered.

"Okay, I'll wait. I would like to be here when you take him to see Jeff."

The nurse left the room and came back shortly with a wheelchair.

They wheeled Tom into Jeff's room and pushed Tom's chair close to Jeff's bed. Tom reached for Jeff's hand and held it. Tom was making sounds that Cliff and Nancy could not begin to understand. Jeff opened his eyes and smiled.

"Look," Nancy said. "Jeff's responding to Tom's signs and gibberish with his own signs and gibberish. It's incredible seeing the boys communicating with each other."

"I guess the doctor's right," Cliff said. "They have developed their own language."

"We should take Tom back to his room now," Nancy said. "Jeff seems to be tiring from the excitement of Tom's visit. I'll talk to the doctor and arrange for the boys to share a room."

Nancy wheeled Tom back toward the hallway. He put up a major fuss. "He doesn't want to leave Jeff, and I don't know how to tell him he can be with him soon," Nancy worried.

"Go ahead, take him to his room," Cliff said. "He'll be okay, just get started on the move."

Back in his office, Cliff read the report faxed from the trooper he had talked to about the road conditions for the past thirty-six hours. "Damn, McCallister did have the time to get to his cabin before the roads became unpassable," Cliff mumbled to himself. "I have to admit that he scarcely had time to make it, but he has had experience with traveling the mountain trails in bad weather. He's lived on the mountain his entire life, coming and going on the inadequate roads as he pleased."

Cliff picked up the phone and dialed the West Virginia State Police. It was time to inquire about the current weather and road conditions in the Winding Ridge area.

"Sergeant Cliff Moran here. I'm calling about the current weather at Winding Ridge."

"Hello, Sergeant. You're the one who wanted the thirty-six hour report?"

"Sure am," Cliff answered. "It is important that I get accurate information."

"Wouldn't give you anything less," the trooper on the other end of the line said. "The snow has stopped falling, and the snow plows are out, but there's absolutely no traffic moving on or off the mountain. You may be able to make it to the town of Winding Ridge, but there's no way you can travel around the mountain. Except," the officer amended, "on a snowmobile."

"Of all the . . . Why didn't I think of that? I could have been on my way to Winding Ridge days ago."

"Sure you could, but that's the only way," the officer said.

"Thank you. I'll do just that." Cliff replaced the phone in its cradle.

Soon after Cliff finished his conversation with the State Police officer, Hal returned. "What's new?"

"Nothing, and I'm not going to wait around here for something to happen. I'm going to the mountain in the morning. There's nothing I can do here!"

"Cliff, you know you can't get on the mountain. We couldn't even get to Winding Ridge. How in the world do you think McCallister could have gotten there?"

"I got a road condition report from a trooper at the state police. There was a window of opportunity when McCallister could have made it to the cabin before the storm got bad. And I can make it now. I'm going to rent a snowmobile. You can keep things going here. Don't let up in case I'm wrong. But I have to do something! Tuesday's in danger. You know her baby is due any time. I hate to think of her giving birth in that time-forsaken cabin. And don't forget McCallister is in the business of selling children. I bet, due to the time he's spent in hiding, he's in desperate need of money. I have this gut feeling I can't shake that he has them back in his cabin as we speak!"

"Maybe you're right. Maybe he did get them to the cabin. Who knows, maybe he used a snowmobile to get there. I know how you feel. Go! I'll do all I can here. Keep in touch in case something happens here that you need to be made aware of," Hal finally agreed.

"Cell phones and the police radios don't work on the mountain in most places. I'll just have to go to the pay phone in town when I need to check in with you."

Tom's doctor agreed to move Tom in with Jeff after talking with the nurse. The two boys' emotional well-being was important to their physical health, and the doctor agreed with the nurse and Cliff that it would be good for them to be together.

When the boys were settled in one room together, Jeff appeared to be much more alert and contented. The boys were playing an unknown game when Jeff's parents walked into the room. The boys grew quiet as they watched the adults. Jeff had begun to form a bond with his all-but-forgotten parents, and now it was obvious that he was comfortable in their presence.

"Look at Jeff," Amy said. "He looks happy now that the other boy is here. Maybe they should be together. Tom has no parents that anyone knows of. Let's try adopting him. What do you say?"

"We need to think about such a huge step," Ralph warned. "We can't jump in without some soul searching and discussion together and with the doctor."

"Well," Amy said, "they have been raised as brothers. Why don't you talk to the doctor? He'll know what steps we'll need to take if we decide to go ahead." Ralph smiled at his wife. "I'm happy to see you look to the future again."

Ralph left to see the doctor, and Amy sat between the boys' beds. She started their first speech lesson. It would be the first of many.

CHAPTER

19

*S*LOWLY, LIGHT FILTERED THROUGH THE KITCHEN
window, announcing a new day. Big Bessie,
busy building fires in the stoves, jumped at the
sound of Frank's voice from behind her. "Fix my
breakfast, Big Bessie. I'm leaving after I eat." Normally he would not get out from under his warm
quilts until the fires had begun to warm the cabin.

"Joe," Frank bellowed, "get down here. I want to
talk to you." Joe dressed quickly in his overalls and
flannel shirt. He clambered down the ladder, making enough noise to wake the entire household, and
sat at the table where he and Frank usually talked.

Frank handed Joe a key. "This is a key to the kennel. You're sure to have seen the cage up on the loft.
No doubt the girls have told you all about it," Frank
laughed. "If any one of the women give you trouble,
lock her in. Of course, Big Bessie and Annabelle are
too fat for the kennel, but they will fit just fine in the
cellar. If you don't keep control, you're no good to
me. I'm trusting you with my livelihood. Don't disappoint me, and I won't disappoint you."

"Ya can count on me, Frank," Joe said.

"I'm anxious to make a deal for the twin boys. Your pa's misfortune is my good luck."

"Aggie, dress for outdoors and get down here," Frank yelled.

In short time Aggie was dressed and down from the loft. Eyes huge with terror, she stood before him waiting to be told what he wanted. He did not bother to tell her that he planned to take her to McCallister, knowing that was where she longed to be.

"After we eat our breakfast, you're to come with me. I'll tell you when I'm ready to go."

Aggie nodded that she understood and went to see if Big Bessie wanted her help.

"He's goin' to drop ya off th' mountain to freeze to death. He'd have one less mouth to feed," Bessie said, her face fixed into a holier-than-thou sneer.

"Shut up, Big Bessie," Annabelle demanded as she too climbed down the ladder, wanting to put the larger woman in her place with a sharp slap. She would not have the bossy woman treating Aggie with such disrespect. She feared that Big Bessie was not far from the truth, though. She could not imagine another reason Frank would want Aggie to go with him. She knew Aggie was worried. She had kept Annabelle awake with her tossing and turning throughout the night. Annabelle knew Aggie dreaded what was to come with morning. Most of all though, Annabelle knew Aggie was heavy-hearted about Jacob, whom she had raised as her own son, coming to Frank's cabin and not asking to speak to her.

Ignoring the women and their bickering, Dillon, looking delighted to be on his way at last, slapped Joe on the back good-naturedly. "I'm off to the real world," he said. "Don't let me down, Joe! Just see that you keep everything together till I get back."

"I'll do what you're wantin', Frank," Joe said. "Ya don't have to worry."

Dillon yelled for Aggie to get her coat and come with him. Without another word he left the cabin with a tearful Aggie following behind.

Dillon sat on the snowmobile and waited as Aggie clumsily stepped off the porch and, with short deliberate steps, moved toward the snowmobile. He motioned for the terrified woman to sit behind him. Without warning, he started the motor. Aggie, startled by the loud reverberation, reluctantly climbed onto the machine. Her arm crept around his waist in a mighty grip of terror. The racket of the motor seemed as deafening as the roar of an avalanche.

The snowmobile lurched forward, gliding up the mountain, with snow billowing around them. The miniature ice chips thrown by the snowmobile's passage through the snow stung their faces as they wound in and around outcropping boulders, moving swiftly as they climbed ever higher.

They passed the trail that McCallister had used as he had made his way to Dillon's cabin the day before. Neither of the passengers on the snowmobile was able to see the tracks McCallister had left in his trek to Dillon's cabin.

After forty minutes, Aggie's cabin came into view through the blinding, mini snowstorm that was created by the snowmobile's passage. "You're home, Aggie," Frank said.

At last Aggie was actually looking at her own back door. "Thanks, Frank," Aggie sobbed. "I can't believe it, so I can't. Thought ya was goin' to get rid of me cause I'm no use to ya, so I did." Tears of relief streamed down her face.

She clumsily climbed off of the unfamiliar machine. She looked away from it. "I hope I never have to get on one of them machines again, so I do,"

Aggie shouted over the roar of the engine. "I've got to thank ya, though, so I do, but ya should've told th' others. They're goin' to worry that you killed me off, so they are."

"Joe knows," Frank bellowed. "The others don't need to know."

"Please tell Annabelle. She needs to knowed, so she does," Aggie begged.

Ignoring Aggie's desperate plea, Dillon drove off with a loud roar as he gunned the motor, causing the old woman to be assaulted with a spray of snow. Quickly, Aggie turned toward her back door. "Now what's he got me into?" Aggie mumbled to herself. "Is Jeb here? I don't see no truck, so I don't. Looks like I'm th' only soul on this mountain, so it does. Not even my cats an' dogs to keep me company, so there ain't. Maybe I'm goin to starve to death after all, so I am."

Coming up the mountain, the snowmobile had stirred up so much snow the smoke going up from the chimney had not been visible as it rose into the sky. She moved toward the cabin, looking like a lost nomad destined to roam the snow-covered mountain peaks. Taking small steps to keep her footing, she determinedly made her way toward the back door. Suddenly the snow swallowed her right foot—Dillon had not given thought to where he had set the woman down. She fell head first and disappeared from sight.

Daisy and her twins were permitted to use Dillon's bed during his absence. A new mother was favored as long as her children were allowed to stay with her. Big Bessie would not assign any chores to her for a few weeks. With McCallister's women now living in the cabin, there were more women than chores, anyway.

The twin boys, one on each side of Daisy, looked much like the twins Daisy had brought into the world two years before—Tammie Sue and Jimmie Bob. She had no source to go to for suggested names, so from her own limited memory of boys' names, she called the twins Billy Bob and John Paul.

Now that Frank was gone, Big Bessie made her move to take over, ignoring the fact that Joe was now in charge. She was not one to give up her position without a fight.

Allowing Big Bessie a little rope to hang herself with, Joe put up with her rebellion for a time, and then he took a stand that put a stop to her petty insubordination. "Ya thinkin' ya can do as ya please," Joe told her. "Maybe if I lock ya up it'll put ya in your place. I knowed ya too fat for me to put ya in th' kennel, but ya can fit in th' cellar, like Frank said, just fine. Ya knowed Pa's back. Ya seen him from the window talkin' to Frank. If ya don't think I can keep ya in line, maybe I should call on Pa."

Luckily for Joe, Big Bessie had no idea that Jacob McCallister had enough troubles without someone else's. Consequently, Big Bessie backed down. Joe had won his first and most important battle.

Annabelle got an extra thrill out of the confrontation between Joe and Big Bessie. *He's just makin' my job easier. In th' morning I'm goin' to start the stoves and make breakfast. We'll just see if Big Bessie can stop me,* Annabelle contrived.

In the middle of the night Annabelle was awakened from her sleep by the first of her labor pains. Oddly, the first thing she thought of was her earlier wish of getting ahead of Big Bessie by starting the morning chores. *I suppose I won't be startin' th' break-fast this morning,* she thought. She would be in labor for the next twenty hours. She had not slept in the loft after Dillon had gone. The climb was too dangerous for her in her heavy, clumsy condition. Annabelle shared the bed with Daisy, and the twins slept in the old homemade crib that Joe had brought in from the barn.

Big Bessie had shown her displeasure that Annabelle had taken to sleeping in the bed without asking permission by pushing unwanted jobs on her, like emptying the slop jar. Pregnancy was never an acceptable excuse for the women to get out of their chores. They routinely worked up until the baby was born unless there was a serious problem, such as bleeding. Joe had intervened on Annabelle's behalf, making the women more dedicated to their attempts to undermine each other's authority.

Annabelle woke Big Bessie and Daisy. Big Bessie got up from her mat by the potbelly stove and started the fires; there would be no more sleep for anyone that night.

Aggie lay with the weight of the snow blocking out every bit of light. There was no air to breathe. She was entombed under a foot of snow that had come down on her like a small avalanche when she slipped off the edge of a rock hidden in the snow. Now she couldn't move her legs or arms.

Luckily, moments earlier from inside the cabin, McCallister had heard the engine of the snowmobile. He grabbed his coat and started outside. Watching Dillon guide the machine around his aunt and roar down the mountain, he muttered, "Good old Dillon, he kept his word and brought my aunt back." Aggie was short stepping—trying not to sink into the deep snow—toward the cabin when she dropped from sight. He jumped from the porch and ran to the spot where Aggie had disappeared. She had fallen into a trench formed by a huge rock that had been in the ground for years—the county was littered with many huge rocks that protruded from the ground, blemishing the countryside—and the wall of the cabin. When she fell, the loose snow from the wall of the path had caved in on her.

McCallister dug the snow away from his aunt and helped her to her feet. "Are you okay, Aunt Aggie?"

"Thought I was done for, so I did," Aggie said as she brushed the snow from her clothing.

"Come with me, Aunt Aggie. Let's go indoors."

Aggie followed her nephew inside the cabin. The first thing she saw was Tuesday on her cot with a baby by her side. Patty was in a rocking chair in the corner, clutching a doll. Aggie stopped in her tracks, taking in the horrific mess made by the dismantling of the loft. "What happened to th' loft? I ain't never had such a mess in my place, so I ain't."

"We needed the wood for the fires, Aggie. I had to tear it down or we would have frozen as well as starved. I need for you to fix us something to eat."

"I want ya to fix it, so I do. I don't like a mess."

"Don't worry about it, Aunt Aggie. I'll take care of it. You just worry about fixing something to eat."

"What's she doin' here? That's your baby, ain't it? Don't ya have enough trouble? I knowed th' law's lookin' for ya, so they are."

"We'll talk later, Aggie. We're hungry."

"I don't want to talk later, so I don't. I can see what's goin' on, so I can. I don't need a bunch of education to see what's goin' on. I want ya to take her home, so I do. Ya are goin' to keep on an' go to jail."

Patty left the cot to give Aggie a hand with the cooking. She gathered the bucket to go out back and draw water from the well.

"Patty, ya get out of my way. Ya never could cook, so ya couldn't," Aggie admonished the girl.

"I knowed that, but I can help ya if ya want," Patty said. "I was just goin' to fetch ya some water."

"Okay," Aggie said, "do that an' when I'm ready, ya can knead the dough for th' bread. Your hands are stronger 'an my old hands, so they are."

As Aggie prepared the meal, she banged pots and pans as if to punctuate her presence. "I want my cats and dogs, Jeb, so I do. They're goin' to die with no one to feed them, so they are."

"I'll get your cats and dogs, Aunt Aggie. They're at my cabin. They're okay for now. I was down there the other day, and they're fine."

Tuesday stared at Aunt Aggie, whom she had never met. She did know Aggie was the one who had raised Jacob. Tuesday had never known Jacob to deal with a woman quite the way he dealt with his Aunt Aggie. He had treated the women who lived with him in his cabin like so many cattle to feed and tend to. She could tell that Jacob truly cared for his aunt just by the tone of voice he used with her. He would not permit anyone else to tell him what to do, but he allowed her to say what she wanted without a hint of the irritation the others, Annabelle, Daisy, Sara, and Joe, managed to stir in him. Tuesday was sure that he would let her go only so far, though.

The petite, spunky woman with curly white hair had a sweet face, and Tuesday took a liking to her immediately. Aggie, unlike Jacob's women, did not look like life had gotten the best of her and now that she was in her own home once again, she was a ball of fire, going about the business of making a meal.

From the days of being held prisoner in McCallister's cabin only eight months earlier, Tuesday remembered Rose, who had moved from day to day, not having any interest at all in the present day nor in what the next day would bring. Also, she recalled that Daisy was totally wrapped up in her appearance in her pursuit of attracting Jacob's attention. Annabelle's main interest in life was being in charge.

Soon Aggie had the dough mixed for the bread, and Patty stood at the table kneading the mixture with her fist, folding the dough inward from side to side and inward back to front. On the stove the dry beans were bubbling in a huge pot, sending a tantalizing aroma through the cabin.

"How long before the food's ready?" Jacob asked.

"Can't ya see, I only just mixed the dough an' Patty's still kneadin' it," Aggie said. "It's goin' to be three or four hours before th' foods ready to eat, so it is. Ya was just havin' your breakfast when I came in. Ya can't be starvin' already, so ya can't."

"What we had for breakfast wasn't worth eating," Jacob said.

"You're missin' my cookin', so ya are."

"Guess I'll go after your cats and dogs if I'm going to have so long to wait until we eat." He grabbed a chunk of dough and threw it into a skillet. "Fry this, Patty."

"Ya never did listen to me, so ya didn't."

"You know I have a weakness for fried dough, Aunt Aggie."

"Ya just have a weakness for food, so ya do."

"I've already cleared the way down the trail," Jacob went on. "It won't take me long to get to my cabin and back."

Patty sat the iron skillet on the stove; the burner was already hot. Next, she scooped a chunk of lard in the pan and it immediately began to sizzle. She flattened the glob of dough and dropped it into the sizzling grease.

"After I have my dinner, I'll make plans to see Rose's father. Remember Herman Ruble, Aunt Aggie? He's the one I got Rose from. I may have to clear a bit of the trail to Herman's cabin each day until I reach it."

"Here's your fried bread, Pa," Patty said, handing a tin plate to her father. The aroma of the freshly cooked bread made Tuesday's mouth water.

"What ya goin' to see him for?" Aggie said. "If you're thinkin' what I think your thinkin', we have enough folks to feed."

"You just tend to your business, Aunt Aggie," Jacob said. He picked up the fried dough with his fingers and began eating it.

"Well, if you're goin' to listen, I was goin' to tell ya that Rose died, so I was," Aggie said.

"That's too bad," Jacob said. "Wonder why Frank didn't tell me about it?" Having no further interest in the matter, Jacob wiped his hands on a rag—its primary use was a dishtowel—grabbed his coat, and left, allowing a gust of cold air to invade the cabin before he slammed the door behind him.

Patty stopped kneading the dough. She picked up her doll and stood sobbing with it clutched in her arms.

"That was no way to break such news to a young girl," Tuesday said. "Come here, Patty." Patty moved over to the cot where Tuesday sat and she took the girl in her arms, giving Aggie a stern look.

"Suppose not," Aggie said. "Patty, I'm sorry, but there was nothing' anyone could do, so there wasn't."

"That's okay," Patty hiccuped. "I miss Rose an' Annabelle an' Sara an' Joe an' Daisy. It's sad that Rose died, but I have Tuesday an' Summer now."

"What ya talkin' about, girl? It's not summer time. It's winter, so it is."

"Aunt Aggie, Summer's my doll's name," Patty said, holding the doll toward Aggie.

"Get it outa here. I don't want to hold that thing, so I don't," Aggie said.

"Just wanted ya to see her," Patty said.

"Put th' doll down an' get back to kneadin' th' bread. I want supper to be ready when Jeb comes back, so I do."

Patty sat the doll in the corner atop the discarded mats and began kneading the dough once again.

"Bet th' two of ya are hungry for some good food, so I do," Aggie said, making conversation.

Great, Aggie's anxious to have someone to chat with. Maybe I can get some useful information out of her. "Yes, I'm very hungry, Aggie."

"Let me see th' baby. I love to hold a baby, so I do," Aggie said.

Tuesday handed the baby to Aggie.

"'Tis a pretty one, so it is. Is it a boy or a girl?" Aggie asked, holding the baby to her breast, twisting back and forth in a rocking motion and patting the baby firmly on the back.

"She's a girl, Aggie," Tuesday answered. "Her name is Winter Ann."

Tuesday pointed first to the baby and then to the doll and said, "Winter Ann Summer. The doll was a present to me on a lovely summer day so I named her Summer. Winter Ann was born on the worst of winter days so I named her Winter Ann. Now we have 'Winter Ann Summer' all the time." Aggie looked at Tuesday with a blank look in her eyes, having no idea of the play on words.

"You're Jabob's aunt, the one who raised him, aren't you?"

"Yeah, I am, so I am. Don't get too attached to this little one. Jeb's goin' to sell it, so he is," Aggie warned. "Ain't no fancy names goin' to save her, so they ain't."

Tuesday was alarmed by the calm, cruel announcement. Her fantasy of getting help from Aggie was dashed, and she reached for her child. "No, Aggie. He will not sell this child. She is my daughter and I will not allow it."

Aggie handed the baby back to Tuesday and sat beside her. "He's goin' to sell it, so he is. Ya can't stop 'im, so ya can't. Ya just have to 'cept it, so ya do."

Tuesday's spirits fell to a new low called fear. *It's so obvious that Aggie's one hundred percent loyal to her nephew,* Tuesday thought. *I guess I can kiss goodbye the idea of her helping Patty and me get out of this hellhole.*

A few hours later, Jacob opened the back door, carelessly letting it slam against the woodburner with a loud bang. The aroma of fresh baked bread and beans cooking in fatback made his mouth water, and his stomach growled in hunger.

There were six cats following him. The dogs had been allowed to follow him only as far as the back porch. "Get away from here you mangy mongrels," Jacob had shouted, and the dogs had run back a few feet and barked at him, wagging their tails. Aggie would not stand for the cats to be out in the cold, though. There would be no living with her if they were not allowed in.

"Jacob," Tuesday cried, "you can't allow those cats in here. It isn't good for the baby. They're filthy and they may carry diseases."

"When the hell did you start telling me what to do?" Jacob said in a voice that sent cold chills down Tuesday's spine. "I say what happens here. I would advise you to remember that."

"Aggie, I'm hungry," Jacob said in a completely different tone of voice. "Is the food ready? It sure smells good in here." Jacob sat on a chair at the table and held his feet out for Patty to remove his wet boots.

Tuesday was appalled by his attitude of continually expecting to be waited on. Likewise, she could not get over the rapid changes in his personality—one minute cruel and evil, the next kind and charming—depending on whom he was speaking to.

"Here ya are, Jeb. Ya can eat all ya wantin', so ya can. There's aplenty, so there is." Aggie set a bowl of beans and a large loaf of freshly baked bread in front of Jacob.

Tuesday watched as Jacob tore off chunks of the bread. He dipped them into the beans and then stuffed the dripping mixture into his mouth. By the time Jacob had finished his meal, he had polished off the entire loaf of bread.

After Jacob ate, he pulled on his coat and his boots, and without farewell, he left, not bothering to tell them where he was going or when he would be coming back.

Tuesday was aware that Aggie and Patty did not think it was unusual that he told them nothing. But she could not get used to the fact that he treated women like they were cattle that need not know anything.

"Come on, Tuesday an' Patty," Aggie said breaking into Tuesday's thoughts. "Ya sit at th' table. Ya betta eat ya food before it gets cold, so ya betta."

Patty, with Summer in her arms, and Tuesday, with Winter Ann wrapped in an old quilt that she had torn to a baby-size blanket, moved to the table. Soon they were eating the food that Aggie had set in front of them. They were hungry. Tuesday had been in labor when they had food to eat, but had not been able to eat much. Patty had served herself only small portions, leaving the larger share for her father.

Aggie sat in one of the rocking chairs to watch them eat and asked Tuesday, "What's it like in th' city? Ain't neve' been in th' city, so I ain't."

"Maybe Patty could tell you better than I."

Patty looked up from her plate and said, "Don't think I can 'splain it, but I'll try. You're goin' to have to see it to understand what it's like. Don't have to wear lots of clothes in th' house. It's always warm. There's a big white an' shiny box. Th' box is taller'n me. Ya can open th' door an' there's food a plenty. Anythin' ya wantin' to eat. There's different rooms for th' kitchen an' th' bedroom an' there's a television room. Even th' room ya eat in is a separate room. Th' floors are covered with th' softest thick cloth, like fur. Ya can even sleep on th' floor it's so soft, but th' beds have a big—" Patty held her hands six inches apart to show Aggie the depth—"mattress that's soft and firm. It's like you're in heaven sleepin' on it."

Aggie listened to Patty with huge eyes. "It sounds like a fairy tale to me, so it does. Can't have no food in a big shiny box. It won't keep, so it won't. Can't build a cabin with rooms for everythin'. Can't narry a stove keep it warm, so it can't. Why ya wantin' fur on th' floor anyways? Can't even sweep it, so ya can't. Goin' to have to show me for me to believe it, so ya are." Aggie pulled her snuffbox from her apron pocket and dipped her forfinger inside, pulling out a line of snuff. It was the last of what she had from Dillon's supply. She used her left forefinger to catch her cheek, pulling it back, exposing her teeth, and filled the pouch between her lip and gum with the snuff.

"Aggie, would you like to see my house?"

"Yea, I would," Aggie answered, "some day when I have th' time, so I would. Don't have th' time now. Jeb needs my cookin', so he does." She tucked the snuffbox neatly into her apron pocket.

The baby began to cry. Tuesday was thankful that Jacob was not in the cabin when she realized that it was time for Winter Ann to nurse. Looking at the precious face of her daughter as she hungrily suckled at her breast, she feared for their future. *Is Cliff Moran our only hope to get away from Jacob?* Tuesday asked herself.

Several hours after Jacob left, Patty finished cleaning up from their earlier supper and quietly moved to the cot, leaving Tuesday and Aggie to themselves. The light cast by the lanterns flickered, tossing shadows about the room. Except for the tragic mood and huge mess from the partially dismantled loft, the scene looked deceivingly cozy. Patty held her doll, and Tuesday fed her child. Aggie contentedly rocked in her chair beside the potbelly stove, listening to the wood crackle as it burned, sending heat and flashes of light into the room, happy to have her nephew back and, most of all, happy to be back in her own cabin, away from Big Bessie.

"I'm afraid, Summer," Patty whispered to her doll. "It was bad before when Pa wouldn't let Tuesday go an' we had to escape. Then we didn't have a tiny baby to take care of like we do now. I just don't knowed what to do. I miss our warm cheerful house in Wheelin'. It's too cold in here, an' there's nothin' to do.

"We'll get home again, I promise, an' next time Tuesday takes me to th' mall I'll take you, too." At the same time Patty talked to the doll, she was actually comforting herself. "You won't believe th' clothes, th' toys, th' food, an' th' beautiful people ya see there. I knowed before I got ya, ya had to spend most of your time in th' box in th' attic and didn't get to go nowhere. I won't let that happen again."

As Tuesday nursed her baby, she could hear Patty in the background murmuring to her doll. It worried her, although she knew having an imaginary friend wasn't unusual for a child. Tuesday felt Patty was a little too old for such a pastime.

"What ya doin' talkin' to that doll?" Aggie complained. "Ya soundin' crazy, like th' old woman that lives down by th' forest."

"Aggie, that's not an appropriate way to talk to a child," Tuesday said.

"It's true," Aggie insisted. "There's a old woman what lives down by th' forest an' everyone says she's a witch, so they do. All th' children are afraid of her, so they are."

What am I going to do? Tuesday thought. *I can't believe I'm finding myself back in "the nightmare" once again. Only this is worse. I have a newborn and a young girl in my care. But the worst of it is having to deal with the snow the raging storm left behind. I won't give up,* she vowed. *Someway we'll get out of this horrific nightmare and back home. The main thing is that I keep Jacob from selling my precious child, and I must not allow him to rape me again! As soon as Aggie's asleep, I'll find a weapon—a gun, a knife, or scissors. Anything sharp will do. I won't give up the idea of giving him the sleeping pills, either. Maybe with Aggie back, he'll drop his guard. I must not allow him to sell my child. If that happens I may never see her again.*

High above Aggie's small cabin and a few miles across the ridge, Jacob could see Herman Ruble's cabin in the distance. Normally the trip across the ridge—where there were no roads—could be made in an hour and a half on foot. Today, digging as he went, it had taken him four hours, and he was just coming in sight of Herman's cabin. At that, he was pleased that he had made the trip in the time he had. Jacob continued walking.

Jacob knocked on Herman's door and a pretty girl answered, timidly hiding herself behind the door. Visitors were not the norm.

"Herman Ruble here, girl?"

"Who are you? Why ya wantin' my pa?"

Jacob had no patience with women's questions. He pushed the girl aside and moved past her inside the cabin.

IMON LEONARD ATTEMPTED EACH DAY TO REACH Frank Dillon by phone. His goal was to make a deal with Frank for the infant boys he coveted. He would have to wait while they grew, but Dillon was the only way he knew of to get children who had no birth records. Leonard would have to spend some time in jail for illegally adopting Tom and Toby, but that time would be made easier knowing that he had a new start with babies growing into boyhood while he was there.

When Dillon finally answered the phone, Simon said, "Hi, Frank. Simon Leonard here. I've been trying to catch you for days. I need to speak to you. It's very important that I see you before you talk to anyone. Can you come by my house today?"

"Sure," Frank said. "Give me a couple hours. I just got back in town."

"That's fine. See you then." They hung up.

Simon was determined to prevent Frank Dillon from contacting Steven Lloyd. It would be Dillon's undoing to be seen talking to Lloyd; every move he made was being watched.

Later when the doorbell rang, Simon rushed to answer it. "Hi, Frank, good to see you. Come in. We can talk in the den." In the den, Simon rang for the servant. "Would you like a drink, Frank?"

"Sure. I never turn down a free drink."

The servant came into the room. "Bring us some whiskey, and leave a bucket of ice and the bottle. We don't want to be disturbed for any reason."

After the servant brought the drinks and put the ice and bottle on the bar, Simon handed Frank one and helped himself to one. "I hope you haven't talked to Steven Lloyd since you came back."

"No," Frank said and sipped his drink. "I haven't talked to anyone with the exception of you. I just got to town when you called. What the hell is up?"

"Lloyd is being watched. The law has taken my boys away, and one has been identified as a kidnap victim. The police discovered I bought Jeff through Lloyd. They'd want to question you if you were seen talking to him. I know you would not want to have to explain how you know Lloyd, or how you've earned the money to live so well in a very expensive part of town. Anyway, after this meeting we must have no contact since I've been linked with Lloyd, although, since Lloyd is known to be my supplier, I doubt if the police are concerned about whom I speak to. As far as they're concerned, it's cut and dried."

"Glad you called me," Frank said. "I'd intended to call Lloyd right away. I could have walked right into a trap that I couldn't fight my way out of. My motto is to stay away from trouble. Now that dealing with Lloyd's not safe, I'll have to find someone else to make my connections for me. I have a set of twin boys I need to sell."

"What luck! Frank, I can't believe it." Leonard delicately clapped his hands together. "That's another reason I wanted to speak with you," he said, pursing his lips. "I want two boys and was looking to talk to you about you selling direct to me. I never dreamed I'd have a chance to get twin boys. That's great, just great. You'll make more money. And with no middleman involved, who will know?" Leonard clasped his hands around his knees, wearing a pleased look on his face.

"I never deal directly with a buyer, Simon," Frank said. "There's no way. No!"

"Listen, Frank. You can't lose. Actually, I believe it's safer. Only two people will be privy to the deal. You! And me!" In a grand gesture, Simon poked his finger at Frank and then at himself as if to punctuate his statement. "Neither one of us is going to rat on the other."

"I don't know," Frank said, leaning forward and putting his glass down, "I've never sold a child directly to anyone before. Obviously I'd make more money, but I can't have a bunch of people knowing I sell children. Too risky."

"Like I said, no one will know but the two of us," Simon said. "I know we can make a bargain if the price is right. I'll make you a deal, as they say, 'one you can't refuse.'"

"What's that?" Frank asked, slowly relenting.

"I will pay you fifty grand now and fifty-five when I get them," Simon said. "You could not get more than that anywhere."

"If I do this, there's one thing," Frank said. "I will not bring the children to you. I don't want to be seen with the boys. You'll have to arrange for someone in your household to pick them up. That'll keep an outsider out of it."

"No problem. This is what I want," Simon said, leaning forward, his hands as if in prayer with his fingers lightly touching his lips. "I want you to keep the boys until they're three years old or until I get out of jail. I don't want to raise babies again. If I hire a nurse, it'll draw attention to me; the police will want to know why. They'll find out I have children and want to know where I got them. If I wait until the boys are three, my housekeeper can look after them. By that time the heat's off. I may be in jail for a while, anyway, Frank. This deal is perfect for me. And you. The cost of your women caring for the boys while I'm in prison is mere pennies compared to the price I'm paying for the boys."

"You'll pay for that care, too." Frank was weakening. The down payment was more money than he ever had, and he would have it right away. Plus, he had the balance to look forward to.

"Frank, the best part of the deal is," Simon continued to sell Frank on the idea, "how can you be charged for selling the twins when you still have them?"

"You're right about that," Frank said, "but in three years you will give me the second payment and then you will have the boys."

"Cross that bridge when we come to it," Simon said with a flip of his wrist. "I don't see any risk. With just the two of us in the deal, who's to let the cat out of the bag?" Simon spread his hands and shrugged his shoulders. "No one."

"Okay," Frank gave in. "I would be lucky to come out with twenty or thirty thousand on my own since I'd be forced to use a middleman. And it's no problem for me to keep the boys for three years. Simon, you have a deal." Frank reached out his hand.

"Deal," Simon beamed, taking Frank's extended hand.

"The more I think about the arrangement," Frank said as he shook Simon's hand, "the more I like it."

Simon let out his breath as if he had been holding it all this time. "I'll arrange to pay you the first fifty thousand in cash right away."

"We can't be seen together," Frank said. "It's too risky. I'll get a locker at the bus station on Main Street and mail you the key. After you put the money in the locker, mail the key back to me."

"Sounds like a game plan to me," Simon said. He had the biggest grin on his face.

Frank left to take care of the details.

"Hal, I'm ready to leave for Winding Ridge," Cliff said. "I have a truck loaded with a snowmobile and emergency supplies. Unlike before, I'm prepared for anything. McCallister won't slip through our fingers this time."

"By the way, have you heard? Simon Leonard had a visitor yesterday," Hal said.

"What about it?" Cliff asked.

"I'm checking out anyone who has any contact with him. I'll call downstairs and see what they have. They've had plenty of time to run a check with the D.M.V.," Hal said, as he picked up the phone.

A little later an officer knocked at the door. "Come in," Cliff said.

"Here's the information we got," the officer said. "The name, vehicle info, his record, and his address. He's driving a Blazer that he rented yesterday. We got his address from the rental agency in Center-point. He has no criminal record or even traffic violations that we've found."

"Thanks," Cliff said and the officer left the room. Cliff looked at the computer printout. It read, "Frank Dillon, General Delivery, Winding Ridge, West Virginia. "What luck," Cliff said. "Look at this, Simon Leonard is mixed up with Steven Lloyd, who is known to sell children illegally. This

man, who comes to visit Simon, has an address the
same as Jacob McCallister, who also sells children.
There's got to be a connection, Hal. What a break!
When I get to the mountain, I'll talk to Sheriff
Moats and see what information I can get on this
Frank Dillon."

"That town where the car was rented," Hal said,
"Centerpoint. I remember seeing a sign on the way
to Winding Ridge that read, 'Centerpoint ten miles.'
The arrow pointed off to our left as we passed the
turn-off. The sign was about ten or fifteen miles
before we turned off to Winding Ridge. It sounds
like there's something going on here. The man
rented the car yesterday, so he got off the mountain
as far as Centerpoint in spite of the weather. I suppose you can get up there and McCallister managed
to make it too, just like you thought."

"Get the detective who spotted Dillon at Lloyd's
house and we'll see if we can get a composite drawing of Dillon," Cliff said.

Hal picked up the phone again. "Officer Merrill
back at his desk yet?"

"No," the duty officer said.

"Find him and tell him to get Fred Warner and
come to Cliff Moran's office. We need a drawing of
Frank Dillon."

When the composite was finished, Cliff looked at
the likeness of Frank Dillon and said, "I'll be
damned. I met this man on the mountain above
Winding Ridge; his cabin is about a mile below
McCallister's. I remember him because his speech,
like McCallister's, did not have a hint of a mountain
twang like most of the people who live there. I
thought at the time something wasn't right. Not the
typical mountain man. Too refined. Look at the
drawing closely, Hal. Can you think of anyone who
resembles the man?"

"You're thinking he looks like he could be Tom's father. They do have the same features and hair coloring," Hal shrugged, "but that's too coincidental."

"I don't think it's coincidental at all. The men are kidnappers and the boy is a kidnap victim. Where's the coincidence?"

"Okay then, wishful thinking," Hal said.

"I think we need to take it seriously. It may be the case. The boy is the third child in the past year we could not trace to a missing child report. McCallister's known to sell his own children. Why not Dillon?"

"Maybe you've got something there. Check it out. I'll get the drawing copied and circulate it. When he's found, I'll put a tail on him," Hal said and slapped Cliff on the back. "Be careful. McCallister is not to be taken lightly."

21

*W*HEN JACOB PUSHED HIS WAY INTO HERMAN Ruble's cabin, he saw three young girls and a boy of about sixteen. "What's your name' boy?"

"Paul Frank," the boy answered. "Why ya wantin' to knowed?"

"I want to talk to you, and I like to know who I'm talking to. Where is your father?"

"He's dead," Paul Frank said.

"Where's your mother?"

"She's dead," Paul Frank answered, not volunteering further information.

McCallister was getting tired of the boy's short answers. "Boy, tell me what happened and when."

"Don't knowed what happened, but they died in their bed. They was sick for a couple weeks with fever, coughin', an' they was cold all th' time. Couldn't get them warm, no how. Pa died a couple days ago. Ma died just this mornin'. Can't bury 'em. Ground's too frozen. They're out in th' barn."

McCallister eyed the three girls who were in their teens, noticing they had red swollen eyes. "Sorry about that. That must be what you've been carrying on about."

The girls kept quiet.

"Do you have any other brothers and sisters?"

"They're gone'," Paul Frank answered for them. "Pa gave 'em away. He couldn't feed 'em. Said it was betta for 'em. Gave some of 'em to old man Keefover. He lives further up Broad Run. Several years ago my sister Rose was sold to a man that lives on Windin' Ridge. They needed help with their work. We're th' only ones left." McCallister did not divulge that he was that man. By keeping them ignorant, he would not have to tell them Rose had died and thereby lose their trust.

Ruble's cabin was the highest cabin on Broad Run. Below Broad Run, at the foot of the mountain's south side, lay a small town called Centerpoint, where Herman Ruble and the others on Broad Run shopped and got their mail. Winding Ridge was on the north side of the mountain, nestled in the foothills far below Jacob's and Aggie's cabins. There were no roads connecting Broad Run and Aggie's cabin except for old, grown-over logging trails, which was a shorter distance as the crow flies and the way Jacob had come walking.

"Do you have food to eat?" Jacob asked.

"Not much left," Paul Frank said. "Don't knowed what we're goin' to do."

"Paul Frank, I'm going to bring my family here, and I'll take care of you and your sisters. You'll do as I say. I'll not stand for any nonsense."

A new plan was in the making. Jacob would bring his aunt, Tuesday, the baby, and Patty to live in Ruble's cabin. The three girls and Paul Frank would be perfect for Jacob McCallister's new start.

"I'll never be traced to this place," Jacob mumbled to himself, moving around the cabin. "To get to here in a vehicle, anyone would have to drive through Main Street in Centerpoint. There's no reason for Moran or anyone to look for me here. As soon as they discover that I'm not in my own or Aunt Aggie's cabin, they'll have come to a dead end."

"Ya talkin' to yourself? Sounds like ya got someone lookin' for ya," Paul Frank said. "The militia's tryin' to get me to join them, an' it's gettin' to be a problem. Is that who you're lookin' to get shed of?"

"Sure, Paul Frank," McCallister said. The story was better than having him know the law was after him.

McCallister had met Herman Ruble and become aware of his household when he sold moonshine. When he had moonshine for Ruble, he would travel to Herman's cabin by way of Centerpoint. From his cabin above the town of Winding Ridge, he'd drive to town, and then down the mountain road to Route Seven. From the foot of the mountain it was fifteen miles to the turn-off to Centerpoint. At the turn-off, the road went winding up the mountain through Centerpoint, running along Broad Run. It dead-ended at Herman's cabin. As the crow flies, or as McCallister walked, it was only ten miles across the back of the ridge from Aggie's cabin to Herman's cabin.

"Is it Elrod Knotts, th' militia lord, who's lookin' for ya?" Paul Frank asked.

"That's none of your business. I'll ask the questions. What're the girl's names?" Jacob asked.

"That one there's Ruby. She's fifteen." Ruby, painfully shy, wore her long brown hair in braids.

"Th' next one's Ida May. She's thirteen." Ida May's hair was long and brown with natural waves. Outgoing and rebelling against authority, she had been allowed by her father to do pretty much as she pleased. He didn't have the time or energy to keep her under control.

"Th' next one is Rachel. She's eighteen." Rachel wore her brown hair cut very short. She had boyish mannerisms and liked to dress like a boy, refusing to wear the feedsack dresses like the other girls. Instead, she wore bib overalls and flannel shirts. She looked and walked more like a boy, but her figure gave away the fact that she was a girl. Their father always said, "If she want's to dress like a boy, she can do boy's work."

"I want to take care of my sisters; I'm responsible for them. I promised my pa and my ma I'd take care of them, so I got to do what I can. I can accept your help, or I could work in the coal mines, or join the militia that Elrod Knotts runs out of his store in Centerpoint." Except for the coal mines, there was no work in the area. If it were not for the responsibility of his sisters, Paul Frank would have struck out on his own.

"Guess you won't have to worry, will you? Because you are accepting my help. I won't take no for an answer. I'm moving here soon with my family. Do you have enough food for a few days?" McCallister took over.

"No," Paul Frank said. "Maybe we'd better get some supplies in before we go for your family."

"Have you ever gone to town to buy food?" Jacob asked.

"Yeah, Pa sent me all th' time. I take my sled in th' winter. In th' summer I take my wagon. I can get a right smart load on 'em an' Big Red does all th' pullin'."

"Talk about asking the right question," Jacob said in relief. "The sled and horse is the perfect way to bring the others, maybe the only way in this weather. Boy, you think you could get three people and a baby on your sled and bring them from around the other side of the mountain?"

"Sure I can," Paul Frank said, "just hook th' sled up to Big Red an' she does th' pullin'." Big Red was Herman's workhorse. She was used for transportation and plowing.

"Good. I must get my family as far away from Winding Ridge as I can. We'll bring my family here tomorrow. First, we'll bring supplies from town."

"If you're tryin' to get away from Elrod Knotts and his militiamen, my place ain't th' place to hide out," Paul Frank said. "They're always after me to join an' they've been gettin' downright insistent about it lately."

"I'm not worried about the damn militia," McCallister said. "I've had a few tangles with Billy Hazard and Stoker Beerboer. They know where I stand."

At daybreak the next morning, Paul Frank pulled his heavy coat off a spike nail where it hung by the back door. He went to the barn where he kept the sled. While Big Red had her ration of oats, he put on her harness and hooked her up to the sled.

He had the money McCallister had given him for supplies tucked in his pocket.

McCallister was waiting in front of the cabin when Paul Frank led Big Red from the barn, pulling a sled behind her. The sled was built of wood and was about four feet wide and six feet long. There were two-by-fours around all four sides, making side rails. The runners were also made of wood.

"I don't want to be seen, so I'm not going to town with you," McCallister said. "While you're gone I'm going to nose around the barn and see what tools your father had. We may need to do some repairs on my truck when we can get it from the hollow I left it in."

"I can handle gettin' th' supplies," Paul Frank said.

"Be quick then," McCallister said.

"Get up," Paul Frank ordered, flicking the reins. Big Red headed down the mountain trail.

It was lunchtime before they were ready to head for Aggie's cabin. And after a satisfying meal—good food was something McCallister had not had for some time—they headed out. When Paul Frank brought Big Red around to the front of the cabin once again, McCallister climbed into the sled and Paul Frank, walking alongside Big Red, guided the horse toward Aggie's cabin. The sled glided over the trail that McCallister had left when he made the trip to Ruble's cabin the day before.

It was widely known that the militiamen wanted possession of Ruble's cabin and were impressed with Paul Frank and wanted him to join their membership. In McCallister's new plan to get back in business, he had not taken into consideration the militia and what effect they would have on his plan if he took up permanent possession of the Ruble cabin, but McCallister had effectively handled the militia in the past.

Tuesday had fallen asleep the night before, waiting in vain for Aggie to join the others and go to sleep, leaving her to safely search for a weapon. And to Tuesday's surprise, when she awoke that morning, Aggie was at the woodburner. *Doesn't that old woman ever sleep? I'll just have to keep my eye out every minute. I can't give up. There must be a way I can get my hands on the pills or a knife.*

As she rocked her child, Tuesday watched Aggie's every move. She was relieved that Jacob stayed away the night. With his aunt to watch over her, Jacob had dispensed with the shackles. Tuesday thought of the meager avenues she had to get away from Jacob McCallister and the threat of losing her daughter, knowing she could not endanger the lives of Patty and Winter Ann in a failed attempt to run away. Her only chance was to put Jacob out with the pills or use a knife, and then she could disable him. She had convinced herself that running in the horrific weather was not the answer. Also, she knew Cliff would be searching for them, and she simply had to be patient. She had learned the hard way that had she and Patty waited it out eight months ago instead of running, they would have saved themselves much pain and suffering.

Why does Jacob seem so confident that he's safe here, she wondered? *Cliff found me before on this same mountain. Surely Jacob knows that Cliff will come looking for us. Why is he so confident?*

It was now late in the day and Tuesday had made no progress on her plan. She watched as Aggie made preparations for dinner, having no idea if her nephew would be back or not. She prepared the meal as if he would be there to eat.

"Here," Aggie said, interrupting Tuesday's thoughts, "ya can use these rags for diapers."

Tuesday had been having a problem keeping the baby dry, as well as everything else around her. She picked up a rag and said, "I need diaper pins Aggie, or it won't stay on her."

"Ya don't need anythin' fancy, so ya don't." Aggie scolded as she laid the rag out on the cot and folded it into a triangle. Removing the old quilt from around Winter Ann, she laid the baby on the rag and pulled one end between the baby's legs. She pulled the remaining two ends around the baby's waist and tied them together. "There, that should do it, so it should. We're goin' to have to wash 'em ever' mornin', so we are."

Tuesday was relieved that Aggie had solved her problem, although it was not the way she would have wished to care for her baby. She could think of no other solution. She could not help thinking of the expensive baby clothes and blankets she had bought and put away in the nursery back in Wheeling.

"I'll send Jeb to th' cabin to fetch th' baby things that's there, so I will," Aggie said. "Don't have much, but there's a few diapers an' baby things that they had for th' babies, so they did."

"Thank you, Aggie. It has been a problem not having baby clothes."

The stomping on the back porch alerted them that Jacob had returned. They were astounded as he walked in with a handsome boy following him. The boy, almost Jacob's height, had curly, black hair, a dimple in his chin, and deep green eyes. The contrast between his eyes and hair was very becoming. Jacob introduced the boy to the women, and when the boy smiled he flashed white, even teeth, an uncommon sight with the mountain people.

"We're moving out of here in the morning," Jacob said. "Each one of you can take what you can roll in a quilt. Paul Frank and I will load what food we have left on the sled. We'll not be coming back here, so don't leave anything you need."

"Ya knowed it's goin' to plague me to leave my home again, but if I must, I need to take my cats an' dogs, so I do." Disappointment at leaving her cabin rang in Aggie's voice.

"Aunt Aggie, if you can get the cats and dogs to follow us, they can go, too."

"They'll follow me alright. They're not goin' to want me to leave 'em, so they won't."

"Okay, Aunt Aggie. Do what you must."

"You like her, boy?" McCallister nodded toward Patty. Paul Frank was watching her with interest.

"Yeah, I like her."

"You can lay with her tonight if you want."

Paul Frank shrugged his shoulders.

"You ever lay with a girl, Paul Frank?"

"No, I ain't. My sisters won't let me, an' Pa said it ain't right for a brother to lay with his sister."

"Patty, make me, Aggie, Paul Frank, and yourself places to sleep after supper tonight. You sleep with Paul Frank and do as he wants. I won't put up with any trouble from you. I have more trouble than I need the way it is."

"Paul Frank, sit at the table," Jacob invited. "Aggie, me and this boy are hungry. Feed us."

Aggie scrambled to get some beans and bread for them to eat.

"Boy," Jacob said as he joined Paul Frank at the table, "I want you to do as I say. If you don't, I won't hesitate to kill you." Jacob revealed this in a deadly calm voice.

"What is it ya wantin' me to do?"

"I must be able to trust you. If you do as I say, you'll be rewarded. You can take Patty or your sisters anytime you want. Don't ever touch Tuesday. She's just for me. The women are to do as you say when I'm not around. If they don't, you're to punish them. After we get them to your cabin we will discuss how and where they are to be punished if needed." Jacob knew Tuesday and Patty were listening and the discussion would serve to keep them in line.

Living with three sisters, Paul Frank had learned at a young age that women had minds of their own. His father had never mistreated his sisters, nor had his father mistreated his mother.

"Jacob, you will not allow that boy to get near Patty! I won't stand for it! Do you hear me?"

"You're not in a position to be telling me what to do. I make the rules around here. Just like the others," Jacob gestured toward Patty and Aggie, "you would do good to remember that."

Oh, what gall. He really believes that I'm one of his foolish women. He must be insane to think he can treat me like his possession, Tuesday thought. *I will never allow myself to bend to his will like the others. I believe I could actually kill him if I had the chance, and it may come to that!*

"I know it's earlier than we usually turn in, but we have a lot to do tomorrow," Jacob announced. "After Paul Frank eats we all should get some sleep."

After the meal, Patty sat in the farthest corner, which was only about twelve feet from the others. She whispered to her doll. "I don't knowed what to do. I knowed Tuesday can't help me none. I don't want that boy to lay with me." Patty rocked the doll back and forth all the time watching Paul Frank and her father.

"I think he looks like a nice boy, though. Do you? He has kind eyes." Patty held the doll up as if she could see his face. "He's good lookin' too," Patty giggled for the first time since her father had broken into the house and forced her to drink the hot chocolate. For the briefest second she remembered she had known happiness for a while. "I wish I could be happy like I was only a week ago. Now, I'm so afraid, Summer."

Later, after everyone had settled down for the night, Patty timidly lay beside Paul Frank as she'd been told. Jacob was on a mat on one side and Aunt Aggie on a mat on the other side of them.

22

THE SUN SHONE ON THE PURE WHITE SNOW, CASTING millions of glittering diamonds across the great expanse in Cliff's line of vision. Tom's photo and the composite of Frank Dillon lay at his side. When Cliff had encountered Dillon at his mountain cabin, Dillon had been sporting a beard, but Cliff would have seen the resemblance between Tom and Dillon even if Dillon had not been clean-shaven in the drawing. Tom's distinct gray eyes, bone structure, and hair color were a duplication of Dillon's own.

Cliff and Hal had spoken of the possibility of Tom's being Dillon's child and the prospect raised many questions about known facts. Leonard got Jeff from Lloyd. Did Leonard get Tom from Lloyd or from Cunningham? Were Steven Lloyd and George Cunningham working together? It had been proven that McCallister and Cunningham were cohorts. Did McCallister sell his children exclusively to Cunningham? Maybe he worked with others as well. Maybe Dillon sold his children only to Lloyd and there were no connections with McCallister and Dillon, or Dillon and George, as far as business went, and that would explain why the investigation into George's dealings hadn't revealed Dillon's involvement.

Cliff passed the sign that announced that Centerpoint, the town where Dillon had rented a car, was to the left. He drove another ten miles to a spot off the side of the road wide enough to park. The road to Winding Ridge was up ahead and to the right about five miles. Cliff unloaded the snowmobile and started it up. After locking the truck, he climbed onto the snowmobile and with a resounding roar and spray of snow raced toward Winding Ridge. He whizzed by several cars abandoned in snowdrifts. Cliff would not rent a room in the boarding house, nor would he ask questions around town. In past experience, asking the mountain people questions had proved to be a waste of time. He headed straight for McCallister's cabin, handling the snowmobile expertly. He prayed that Tuesday had not gone into labor in the isolated cabin.

Hal sat in his office going through the records that Judy Grear had managed to smuggle from Steven Lloyd's files. Although there was a special force investigating those incriminated in the reports, he was double-checking for anything to connect McCallister, Dillon, and Lloyd. There was no mention in Steven's records of Jacob McCallister or Frank Dillon.

The phone rang, "Lieutenant Brooks here."

"Lieutenant," the officer said, "we spotted the rental vehicle that was booked in the name of Frank Dillon. It's parked at 2148 Concord Avenue. What do you want us to do?"

"Just watch him. If he leaves, follow him," Hal said. "I'll find out who owns the house." Hal sent a man to the county courthouse to find out who owned the house, which was located in an upper-class neighborhood.

Inside 2148 Concord Avenue and unaware that he was being investigated, drink in hand, Frank Dillon sat in his favorite recliner. Totally at home in his orderly living room, he was calling a few of the people he knew who worked for Steven Lloyd. He was not interested in warning anyone that Lloyd was being investigated. Dillon only sought information. Although Daisy's twins were sold to Leonard, he needed to be prepared to sell the others that were coming. Annabelle was due anytime and so were a few of the other women. On a hunch, Dillon had left a message for Aubry Moats to get in touch with him. If anyone could find Dillon a connection, it would be Aubry, who had more connections with baby brokers than anyone Dillon could think of. As a rule he stayed away from Aubry Moats, being from the same county and in the same line of work, so to speak.

Unlike McCallister's experience in trying to get in touch with Aubry Moats, Frank Dillon had no trouble. The fact that McCallister was running from the law and Dillon wasn't was what made the difference. Aubry not only returned Dillon's call, but also promised to have someone call him soon. Aubry only had a number for a voice mail to contact the man who could help Dillon in his endeavor.

A few hours later Frank got a call from a man named Marty Townsend. They made arrangements to meet in two hours at a bar and pool hall.

Townsend conducted his business in Wheeling; his home was a two-hour drive from there. The distance served well to keep his two lives separated. Marty Townsend was respected as a leading citizen and businessman in the community of Fairmont where he lived. His business had been a front to begin with, but his wife and sister-in-law had actually turned it into a profitable enterprise. Townsend was active in the community, deliberately appearing to be above reproach. There wasn't one person who'd have thought that Marty Townsend would break the law.

A couple hours after the call, Frank sat in a booth where he could see the front door, waiting for his new connection. Marty would be wearing a blue, pin-striped suit. Frank would have no trouble recognizing him; the other patrons in the bar wore faded jeans and leather jackets.

The tavern was small. A pool table occupied one corner, and several pinball machines stood around the wall to the right of the bar, which ran along the wall across from the booths. Frank entertained himself by watching the couple in the back booth. The young girl was twisting her finger in the boy's head of hair—his hair was much longer than hers—and trying to get him to kiss and make up. Without warning, the girl stood up, threw the contents of her glass into his face, and stomped off. "I never liked you anyway," she called back as she strutted off.

The door opened and Marty Townsend a tall, distinguished-looking man quietly slipped into the bar just as the angry girl was leaving. She looked Marty Townsend over. He appeared to be in his forties. "Want a date?" the girl asked, giving her newly abandoned boyfriend a backward glance.

"You're jail bait," the new arrival laughed. "Why don't you find someone your own age?" At that the girl left the bar in a huff.

Dillon stood up and Townsend walked toward him. They both sat down as a waitress came over to take their drink order.

After listening to Dillon's proposition, Townsend seemed to be uninterested. "You're going to have to tell me a hell of a lot more than that if you want my backing."

"Like what?"

"Like, everything. I never work blind. That's why I'm so successful. If you want to do business with me, start talking."

Frank Dillon never revealed his life on the mountain, how he got the babies he sold, not even—until most recently—to Simon Leonard, who knew more than most. "I'm not inclined to do that," Dillon said firmly. "The less anyone knows, the safer I am."

"Too bad," Marty Townsend got up, dropped a few dollars on the table for his drink, and turned to leave.

"Wait," Dillon blurted, "I want to make this work."

After a few seconds' hesitation, Townsend once again took his seat. "It's the only way I'll work with you. I won't take chances. I need to know how you operate. Then I'll decide if I approve. I'm doing a profitable, safe business and will continue to do fine without you."

"Okay, I see your point." Frank had no choice but to relent. "It's not my custom to be open with my middlemen. I've worked on the same premise as you, and it's kept me above suspicion when men all around me are arrested. Like you, it's safer for me to keep my business to myself. I'll tell you how and where I get the children I supply you with only if you are open with me. Where you live, who you deal with, everything."

"No!" Marty Townsend held firm to his no-exception rule of never telling his suppliers or other connections anything about himself. It was a foolproof standard that kept him safe from the law.

Frank had no choice. The man sitting before him was the route to go. Townsend was above reproach and ran his baby brokerage like a business. "I breed my own children."

Townsend downed his drink in one gulp and, in his surprise, choked. After he finished coughing, he said, "I've never worked with anyone who sold his own children. Don't sound too profitable to me. Lucky to sell one a year, aren't you?"

"You're right," Frank said in an overly smug tone, "if you only have one wife. I happen to have nine wives, and they are all under thirty. Six of them are in their teens."

"Are you serious? That's against the law," Townsend said, looking for all the world as if he had never broken the law in his entire life.

"What the hell do you think? That what you're doing is legal?" Dillon laughed. He went on, "Believe me, no one cares what's going on where I keep my women. It's the way of life there."

"Where is that?"

"On the mountain above Winding Ridge off Route Seven."

"Sounds great," Townsend said with admiration. "I'm a very careful man. I keep up a front as a solid citizen and am an asset to the community where I live. I have never been suspected of any crime or wrongdoing, and I want to keep it that way. It sounds like you have a perfect set up to me. Of course, that is, if your women don't rebel. Just how do you keep them quiet, allowing you to sell their children?"

"They were raised in a very remote area," Frank explained. "They can't read or write. They have never been anywhere except where they were raised. They don't know any other way of life. I'm their provider and their reason for living. As a matter of fact, I bought each of them from their fathers except three of them, which I got from their previous husband."

"That's quite a story," Townsend said.

"The best thing about the whole deal," Dillon elaborated, "is the children have no birth records. They were all born in the cabin. No one knows about them! No one! I'll have a child to sell every couple of months. My babies are worth more than a kidnapped child is; no one's looking for them. I bring them to you as infants, and a newborn will bring much more than an older child any day. I have every right to expect big money for my children."

"This is a good deal, Frank," Townsend said. "Remember, the phone number you have for me is voice mail, so you'll never actually get me. You're wasting your time if you keep trying. I check it twice a day. You leave a message, and I'll call you back within a day. When you call, leave a message that you're Artie Johnson and that I have the number to return your call. This way our names will not be connected. I will know to call you. I don't want you to mention my name or your own name or the subject of our business, just as a precaution in case of a phone tap. It pays to be careful.

"I can't figure why you worked with that wimp Steven Lloyd," Townsend went on. "You must have known he would get into trouble eventually. He never covered his ass."

"Here's my phone number," Dillon said. "I'll contact you as soon as a child is born." Frank Dillon put on his coat; on his face, he wore a self-satisfied, smug look. In one day he had sold the twins and made a new business connection.

Lieutenant Hal Brooks had driven across town to talk to Steven Lloyd. He stood at Lloyd's door, ringing the doorbell, one of those that made a musical chime. The chime barely drowned out the loud voices coming from the television.

Abruptly the TV went quiet, and the dead bolt turned with a loud click. The door opened as far as the security chain would allow. Steven Lloyd peered through the opening at Hal, his beady eyes barely visible through the small crack between the door and the jamb.

"Let me in, Lloyd. I want to talk to you," Hal demanded.

Lloyd unhooked the security chain and reluctantly allowed Hal into his apartment. "What do you want?" Steven Lloyd whined resentfully.

"I want to know who you got Tom from," Hal demanded. "I'm not leaving until you tell me." Hal sat on the sofa, demonstrating his intent to stay as long as it took.

"Who's Tom?" Lloyd asked in a voice filled with dread.

"You know who the hell Tom is," Hal said in exasperation. "You sold him to Simon Leonard. I want to know who you got him from."

Steven Lloyd got up and paced back and forth. Lloyd was out on bail awaiting trial; the incriminating records taken from his office by Judy Grear had indicted him. Omitted from the records was the little information Lloyd had on Frank Dillon, his name, his Wheeling phone number, and the fact that the children he brought to Lloyd for sale had no birth records.

"He was given to me to put up for adoption by his mother, as most of the kids were. She could not keep him," Steven Lloyd lied. "I really don't remember much. It has been several years, you know."

"If that's the case, why didn't you take the adoption through the agency?" Hal asked.

"Must have been a paper trail mistake," Lloyd said. "I just don't remember that far back."

"I didn't come here to hear fairy tales, Steven. I think you do remember," Hal said impatiently. "I think you got him from a man named Frank Dillon. You'd tell me because you don't mind getting Dillon into trouble. But you're afraid of what Dillon will do to you if he finds out that you gave me his name, so I'm not going to tell him. You get my drift?"

"How the hell did you come up with an idea like that?" Lloyd asked in a fear-filled voice.

Hal did not miss the dumbfounded look on Lloyd's face at the mention of Dillon's name. "So I'm right. You know Dillon."

"I don't know what you're talking about," Lloyd quivered. "There's no way you can conceivably connect me and the man."

"Why are you so upset that I believe you know Dillon?" Hal asked. "Is it that you know that knowing him could incriminate you?"

"I know nothing of the kind," Lloyd denied.

"I know the boy came to you from Dillon. I fancy Tom is Frank's son. They look alike."

Lloyd sat down hard in the chair across from Hal. "For the last time, I don't know anyone by the name of Frank Dillon. If the boy looks like someone you know, I can't help it. I told you I helped Tom's mother place him in a home."

"Don't give me that crap. If you were doing something legal you would have gone through the B. A. Parent Adoption Agency where you work. This deal was under the table. I know you got the boy from Dillon, so admit it."

"I told you," Steven repeated, "I don't know any Frank Dillon. I helped the boy's mother place him in a home because she could no longer care for him. So

I didn't go through the agency—hang me. I needed to make an extra buck."

"I thought you said it was a paper trail mistake." Hal got up and grabbed Steven by the shirt collar. "You sniveling coward. You will tell me the truth. I know you're afraid of Frank Dillon, but you'd better cooperate with me or I'll show you what fear really is."

Hal knew that he was not going to get anything out of Steven now. He let loose of Steven's shirt with a little shove and Steven fell back into his chair. "I'll be back. You can count on it, Lloyd!"

After Hal left, Lloyd got on the phone. "I got a visit from a detective. I'm worried. He questioned me about a man that I must not be connected with. I don't know what to do."

"Honey, get a hold of yourself. You're your own worst enemy, acting like a trapped rabbit."

Steven gripped the phone until his knuckles turned white. "The detective will be back and ask more questions. I must be prepared and keep my cool or I'll blow it. The man must be told about the detective's visit. I must tell him at once that I wasn't the one who mentioned his name. Oh, no, I'm a dead man. Maybe if I tell him, he will appreciate being warned that someone's throwing his name around town."

Steven Lloyd's girlfriend loved the money he made from his dubious sideline, but he was getting on her nerves more and more lately. She had told him often enough to act like a man and handle his own business without crying on her shoulder every time something went wrong. When everything was going well, he was a fun-loving, big-spending date. On the other hand, when things were not so good, he was a wimp.

"Steven, quit whining. You worry too much. From what I know you have yourself covered. How about taking me out on the town tonight? I'll wear the dress that you like so much. The night will get your mind off your troubles. We'll go shopping for new outfits. Then we'll go to a four-star restaurant and have the best wine and a meal fit for a king."

CHAPTER

23

*W*HEN CLIFF CAME IN SIGHT OF THE CABIN, THERE was no smoke coming from the chimney, a good sign that it was uninhabited. The unrelenting snow had long since erased McCallister's tracks. The snow had drifted halfway up the back door. He tried the front door, as McCallister had had to do before him.

Cliff opened the front door, and the nauseating smell hit him in the face. The cats had messed throughout the cabin. He went inside and searched each room. Tuesday's luggage was still where he had seen it before.

Cliff started the snowmobile and roared up the mountain, heading toward Aunt Aggie's cabin. With a premonition that he must hurry, he flew up the trail, leaving a thick, swirling, white mist of snow in his wake.

Tuesday's sixth day in Aunt Aggie's cabin was the last. After her concern the night before that Jacob had given Paul Frank permission to do what he wanted with Patty, she was now even more distraught at the bombshell news that they were moving to a new location. Until now she'd had hope of being found, aware that Cliff knew where Aggie's cabin was located. *Where is Jacob taking us?*

As Paul Frank and Jacob loaded the sled, Tuesday's dim ray of hope for rescue by Cliff slowly diminished. Her knowledge that Jacob didn't know that Cliff had found Aggie's cabin eight months before had been her mainstay of sanity.

Tuesday became aware of Patty sitting in the corner, talking to her doll.

"I think we're goin' to like Paul Frank, Summer," Patty whispered to her doll. She would whisper to her doll and then hold her up to her own ear as if the doll were answering. "Pa told him he could do whatever he wanted with me an' he didn't say nothin' to Pa. Maybe Paul Frank knowed it'd just get Pa rowed up an' Pa'd push for it. Paul Frank went right to sleep an' didn't bother me. I think he's nice, don't ya? Just like Cliff. If I hadn't got to knowed Cliff, I'd never believed a man would be nice to me."

I'm glad to hear he didn't touch her. I fell asleep and didn't know what happened during the night. Jacob must have been so tired from his trip on foot to Paul Frank's house he went right to sleep as well. Tuesday sighed in her relief.

After the sled was loaded Patty, Tuesday—with tears of frustration streaming down her face, the baby, and Aunt Aggie sat on the floor of the sled. Jacob and Paul Frank walked alongside and Paul Frank drove the horse. The sled slowly lurched forward.

As they were inching away from Aggie's cabin, Tuesday thought she heard the roar of an engine coming closer . . .

Sara and Mary Lou sat rocking Daisy's twins near the potbelly stove. Sara had made friends with the others and had stopped spending all her time mooning over Joe. She'd learned to enjoy having the other girls to talk to and interact with. Actually, she was happier than she had ever been, even when she'd had Joe all to herself. She had never really gotten to know her half-sister, Patty, and had not known the satisfaction of having a close girlfriend or sister. Had it not been for Sara's fear of Patty because of her phenomenal dreams, which uncannily came true, they may have formed a close bond.

"Too bad we can't keep th' babies," Sara said.

"Yeah, they're cute, ain't they?" Mary Lou said. "We can't get too attached to them, though. Frank's goin' to sell them."

Joe sat at the table as the two girls talked and rocked the twins.

Life was easier for him now that Sara was getting along so well with the others. All and all things were going smoothly, after a few run-ins with Big Bessie. So far, he was on top.

At the woodburner, Big Bessie and Annabelle were preparing the meal. "I don't want ya to start the taters yet," Big Bessie demanded. "Th' meat ain't goin' to get done at th' same time if ya start them taters now."

"Ya thinkin' I don't knowed how to cook?" Annabelle asked. "I knowed when th' meat's goin' to be done."

Big Bessie pushed Annabelle out of her way. "Told ya I don't want ya to commence cookin' th' taters yet." Big Bessie grabbed the skillet from Annabelle's hand.

"Th' taters is better when ya fry them slow an' let 'em simmer in th' fat," Annabelle said. She got another skillet from the shelf, added a scoop of lard, and set it on the burner to heat the lard. She began slicing the potatoes.

The battle of wills between Annabelle and Big Bessie was a source of entertainment for the others. Joe usually settled the disagreement by giving Annabelle her way. "Ya women shet up your arguin' an' both of ya can cook th' meal," Joe said. We're hungry an' I'm getting' tired of waitin'."

Angrily, Big Bessie browned the flour to make the gravy. "I betta get th' gravy goin' or ya goin' to take it over too."

Mary Lou was the only real problem Joe had. She constantly tested him to find out how much she could get away with. He was much more attracted to her than the others, and although he'd tried to hide his affection, she had sensed his special feelings for her. Not only was she the most attractive, she happened to be the most interesting and had a huge imagination about the world and its possibilities. He disliked the idea of locking her in the cage and perhaps breaking her spirit but simply could not take the chance of Frank finding out he allowed her to get away with conduct that Frank himself would not tolerate for a second.

Knowing of Joe's feelings for her, Mary Lou did as she wanted. She was more careful when Big Bessie was near and behaved as Big Bessie expected, as Big Bessie thought nothing of striking her across the face with her powerful, meaty hand. But Big Bessie could not be everywhere, and Mary Lou took more liberties each day. As the other girls began to notice the time together and the looks between Joe and Mary Lou, jealousy and resentment caused disagreements between Mary Lou, who had been everyone's favorite, and the other girls.

As tempers flared, it was not in Joe's best interest to ignore her behavior any longer. The day after Annabelle gave birth to her baby, Joe locked Mary Lou in the cage.

Just as Cliff broke the crest of the hill heading toward Aggie's cabin, the sled lurched over the ridge fading from sight. He never saw it. It was lightly snowing but, to be on the safe side, McCallister had Paul Frank go back and smooth over their tracks about every hundred yards. McCallister had Paul Frank repeat this process until they were half way to Herman's cabin.

"Ya hungry?" Aggie asked. She shivered as they glided along in the rough wooden sled.

"No, I'm not, Aggie," Tuesday said listlessly. "The others may be."

"Well, I brung some biscuits, so I did," Aggie said.

Aggie passed out the bread to each of them, giving Paul Frank and Jacob, who were walking most of the time, larger portions.

The cats had managed to jump into the sled earlier in the trip and at the aroma of the biscuits were aroused from their napping. They became nuisances, sniffing at the food and forcing everyone to hold it out of reach.

Tuesday nursed the baby, sheltering herself and the baby from the icy wind with the heavy quilt.

The rugged terrain made the going rough at times. Tuesday and the baby were jostled about, making it difficult to nurse. Beyond that, Tuesday was so cold that her teeth chattered. She feared that having Winter Ann out in the bitter cold air would be harmful to such a young infant. She had wrapped her in a heavy quilt and from the beginning of the journey held her close, trying to keep the cold wind from the small, fragile body. As the sled lurched along Tuesday's heart sank lower; they were obviously going much farther from civilization than Aggie's cabin was. It was apparent that there were no roads for the sled to follow.

Finally, she saw a huge, two-story cabin come into sight. With the many times the sled had become lodged on rock piles and had to be dug out, it had taken them what was left of the day to make the trip. They were wet, cold, and exhausted.

"Everyone get out," Jacob barked. They climbed from the sled. Their legs were stiff and numb from sitting so long on the splintered, cold floor of the sled.

"Paul Frank, after you rest awhile, unload the sled," Jacob called. He helped Tuesday to the door, as Patty helped her aunt. Jacob opened the door without bothering to knock, and they went inside.

The cabin was much larger than the ones Tuesday had lived in for such a short time. There was the same style woodburner for cooking, the same pot-belly stove for heating. A door led out the back way directly across from the front door where she stood. The back door was to the right of the woodburner with a small window above the stove. The potbelly stove was to her right and an interior doorway to her left. She could not see beyond the tattered curtain that hung from a wire secured by spike nails on each side. A huge wooden table in the center of the wood plank floor had a dozen chairs scattered around it. Half a dozen rocking chairs were scattered around the potbelly stove, and a sofa sat by the front wall.

Tuesday sat in one of the rocking chairs by the potbelly stove for warmth. She'd never been so cold. Angrily, she watched Aggie's mangy cats come in the front door behind Patty and Aunt Aggie. She believed the cats would follow the sled through the deep snow, but had not counted on the mangy beasts climbing inside with them.

The noise attracted Paul Frank's sisters and they came downstairs. Tuesday saw a steep, narrow stairway as they parted the curtains at the bottom and entered the room. She wondered who they were, but the most important issue on her mind was that she was cold, hungry, and tired. All she really wanted to do was eat and get some sleep. Rocking Winter Ann, she wept. She was devastated, being unable to find a way out of a hopeless situation.

After McCallister went out to help Paul Frank with the horse, Patty stood beside Tuesday and put her arm around her shoulder, lending comfort. "Do you know where we are, Patty?" Tuesday asked.

"No," Patty answered

"It would be suicide for us to attempt to make our way off the mountain, then. I suppose in this weather it doesn't matter anyway. Winter Ann would not survive the cold. Patty, have you had any dreams since Wheeling?" Tuesday asked.

"Yes," Patty said, "I don't understand it though. I dreamed about Cliff. He was goin' through th' snow fast. I don't knowed how he was goin' though."

"Maybe on a sled?" Tuesday asked.

"No, it wasn't a sled. I don't knowed what it was though."

"Patty, have you ever seen a snowmobile?"

"No, I haven't, an' I don't knowed what ya mean."

"I heard a motor as we were leaving Aggie's cabin. I bet Cliff is on a snowmobile looking for us— it would account for him moving fast in your dream—and that's what I heard. Oh, if we had been a few minutes later. I pray that he can follow our trail. Don't mention a word of this to anyone. We can't let Jacob know he's about to be caught."

"I won't. I sure hope you're right," Patty said in a wistful voice.

Cliff glided to the side of Aggie's cabin and, making a large circle in the snow, drove around to the back. There was no smoke coming from the chimney and consequently the cabin looked deserted. Except for the tell-tell mounds of snow that appeared to be man made, it looked as if the place had been long abandoned.

Cliff climbed off the snowmobile and went in the back way. The cabin was trashed. It had been fairly neat when he had sat and talked to Aggie months ago. Since his last visit, someone had wrecked the loft. The old woman could not have torn the loft down. Cliff searched the small cabin and found the stove was hot, but could not find one clue to who had torn the loft down, disturbed the snow, and built a fire in the stove.

"Whoever's been here is still around," Cliff said to himself.

CHAPTER

24

IEUTENANT HAL BROOKS HAD SENT FOR RANDY
McCoy, the detective who was in charge of
tailing Frank Dillon. He paced back and forth as he
waited. His pacing was interrupted by a knock at
the door. "Come in."

"You sent for me?" the detective asked as he
made his way to the chair in front of Hal's desk and
sat down. Randy McCoy was a pleasant man who
exuded cheerfulness. Usually wearing a smile,
McCoy was the sort of man that everyone liked. His
red hair and freckles looked great with his skin coloring. He did not have the pinkish skin tone usually
associated with red hair; his skin was more of an
olive color. His green eyes sparkled with energy.

"Yes, I want an update on Dillon," Hal said.

McCoy took his notebook from his breast pocket
and flipped through the pages. "Here it is. I think
we've made some inroads into this Frank Dillon
case. Detective John Gibson followed Dillon to a
pool hall in the not-so-good side of town. Gibson
reports that Dillon sat in a booth and ordered a

drink. Gibson also surmised that the bar, based on way the man was dressed and his overall manner, wasn't the sort of place Dillon would patronize. He simply didn't fit in. It was a strange meeting to my way of thinking. Know what I mean?"

"Sure, go on," Hal said.

"After Dillon sat there for about twenty minutes, he was joined by another man. Dillon stood when the man came in. You know, like he recognized him. The newcomer took a seat in Dillon's booth. He was dressed in a pin-stripe suit and looked very distinguished. Their conversation couldn't be overheard because of the noise created by the pool players and the jukebox."

"What is Dillon up to?" Hall asked.

"Don't have a clue," McCoy said.

"Maybe Lloyd's his broker and he realizes that he's in trouble and is feeling around for a new connection," Hal said. "I'm sure that Dillon doesn't know that he's being watched."

"Probably not," Randy said, "but if he does that'll tell us Lloyd warned him and we'll know that they have a connection. But Lloyd couldn't have warned Dillon in time, because the meeting happened shortly before you questioned Steven Lloyd."

"The meeting with Lloyd was revealing as well. I could tell that he was taken aback when I mentioned Dillon's name. He oozed fear," Hal said. "It convinced me that Lloyd has a connection with Dillon and is afraid of him for some reason."

"My question is," Randy said, "what was Dillon up to meeting Marty Townsend in that bar? It's obviously not a place either of the men would go."

"Great, we have a name," Hal said.

"Not only did we get his name," McCoy said, "we got his license number and address."

"That's more than I'd hoped for," Hal said.

McCoy referred to his notebook: "Marty Townsend, Peirpoint Road, Fairmont, West Virginia. According to folks who were questioned, he is a model citizen. I checked for any police reports on him myself. He's never been charged with a crime. The man even coaches a Little League team, is on the town council, and he does volunteer work at the community hospital. I made some calls around town, and from what I could find out, the people in the community like and respect Marty Townsend." Randy got up and paced back and forth for a minute before speaking again. "Regardless of all the praise and goodwill people have for this man, I smell a rat. And when I smell a rat, there's usually one lurking in the shadows."

Hal leaned back in his swivel chair and propped his feet on his desk. What Randy had just told him could not justify putting much-needed men out to watch Townsend. As a matter of fact, it seemed a waste of time and manpower to watch a man simply because he met a crime suspect in a bar, but he had the same gut feeling Randy had.

"Watch him," Hal said.

"You got it."

Marty Townsend sat in his office, mulling over his conversation with Frank Dillon and Dillon's set-up. There was enough money generated in the furniture business for him to live a middle-class life with his wife having almost everything she wanted, but that just was not enough for Townsend. Marty did not want almost everything; he wanted everything that money could buy, and his wife spent money like it grew on trees.

Alice, his wife, and her spinster sister ran the business very well. That allowed Townsend the free time to make what he thought of as real money.

Alice was beautiful, but she was a cold woman and Marty was greedy. He wanted more. So he kept a mistress.

Townsend picked up the phone to call her. Mandy was totally unlike his wife. She was not as beautiful as Alice was, but she had warmth and charm. She was cute and vivacious. Townsend could never talk with Alice the way he did with Mandy.

Mandy answered the phone on the first ring. She was out of excuses for not seeing Marty. Keeping up the sweet, loving girlfriend act was beginning to bore her. She was tiring of him, but his money kept her hanging on. He was tirelessly generous with her. She had a plush, high-rise apartment. He allowed her to have credit cards, and she could buy clothes and anything else that she wanted. Of course there were limits, but secretly she was impressed with the amount of money he allowed her to spend. She needed people around her, though. Most of all, she wanted her freedom and a man who would be interesting, fun, and certainly a more suitable lover.

"Hello," Mandy finally said.

"Hi, Babe," Marty cooed. "For a minute there I thought I had a dead line. What took you so long to say hello after you picked up the phone?

"Sorry, Love. I was distracted for a second," Mandy cooed back.

"Baby, I want more time with you. We never have enough," Marty said. "I miss having someone to share my problems. It's so easy to talk to you."

"Oh, Marty, I'm so glad you called. I was missing you," she lied.

"I want to see you tonight,"—her heart sank—"but I just can't,"—then soared. "I hope you're not too disappointed," he said with regret in his voice.

"I will make it up to you. Go on a shopping spree. Buy something sexy while you are at it."

"Tonight?" she asked.

"Sure. You spend so much time alone," Marty said. "You go and have fun."

She had a hard time keeping the smile out of her voice. "I was longing to see you. Will I see you tomorrow?"

"I don't know yet, Babe. I'll have to let you know. I'll call you tomorrow at noon."

She was free of him the remainder of the day and until noon tomorrow. He did not expect her to be home if she was out shopping. "I was looking forward to tonight," she purred. "I understand, though. I'll be waiting for your call tomorrow."

Mandy got her Great Dane's leash and called him for a walk. While she walked, she made plans for a good time that night. She strutted down the tree-lined street with Brute. His wagging tail mirrored her own happy feelings; his to be outdoors, hers to have the free time to do as she pleased. The air was cold, but invigorating.

She was so distracted by her plans to call her friend Dorothy and ask her to go out bar hopping that night that she walked right into something solid. Brute growled deep in his throat; she tightened her hold on his leash. She had been looking down at the sidewalk, not thinking about what was ahead of her. The something solid wore a pair of black shoes. She looked up into the face of a handsome man. Abruptly her displeasure turned to a welcoming smile. The man had been standing there quietly watching the apartment building across the street.

"I'm sorry, miss," he apologized, although it was she had who had walked into him.

"I should watch where I'm going," she blurted.

"No harm done," Frank Dillon said, as he looked her over. "I'll forgive you if you'll have dinner with me tonight."

"I would love to. I was just trying to decide what I was going to do tonight. Here's my address and phone number." Mandy handed him her card. She never played games and pretended to be Miss Goody Two-Shoes, unless of course she was after money. Tonight she was after a good time and she only had until noon the next day. There was no time for games.

"I'll pick you up at seven. That okay?"

Long after Mandy left, Frank Dillon stood and watched the apartment building across the street. Steven Lloyd lived in the building. "It looks as if I might have to get rid of the spineless wimp," Dillon said to himself, walking back toward his rental car. "I can't rely on him to keep quiet if he's taken in."

25

*A*FTER A SLICE OF STALE CORNBREAD, TUESDAY decided to skip the evening meal. McCallister had Rachel show her to the bedroom upstairs. She was so exhausted she could barely keep her eyes open.

Rachel led Tuesday, with her baby held to her breast, up the narrow stairway to the second floor, which was one huge room. In one corner sat a large bed. On all four walls were tall, narrow windows with no window covering. Mats and quilts were scattered over the remaining area.

Rachel pulled the quilt back for Tuesday and found a nightgown in a pile of clothing in the corner and gave it to Tuesday to sleep in. She took the baby from Tuesday's arms and waited.

Tuesday felt uncomfortable by the way Rachel watched as she removed the feedsack dress, almost as a man would stare.

"It's cold up here," Rachel said as she rocked the baby back and forth, "but some of th' heat from the potbelly below rises through th' cracks, so's it's warmer than outdoors."

Tuesday took the baby from Rachel and climbed into bed. She fell asleep immediately.

Below, Patty and Aggie were getting settled in. Aggie rummaged through the kitchen area, becoming familiar with the workspace and supplies, taking over the household, as was her habit.

She scurried around putting the meal together. With an old woodburner and only food to cook from scratch, cooking was a constant chore.

Ida May, the one who had been doing the cooking from the time her parents took ill, came in from the well with a bucket of water. "Woman, move out of th' way an' let me get th' bucket on th' stove to heat th' water," Ida May said.

"Don't be pert. My name's Aggie, so it is. Put th' bucket on th' back burner an' go on an' git out of my way an' I'll tell ya when I need ya to do somethin', so I will." Aggie shooed the girl away, discouraging any attempt she made to help in the kitchen.

Unmindful of the rivalry in the kitchen area, Patty sat in a rocking chair, holding Summer in her arms. "I think we're in big trouble now, Summer," Patty whispered to the doll. "I've no idea where we are."

Patty held the doll to her ear. *We can't stay here, Patty.*

Rocking her devoted confidante, apprehensive about her new surroundings, Patty waited for Aunt Aggie to call her to supper.

Rachel came downstairs and sat in the rocking chair next to Patty. "That's a nice doll," Rachel said. "My mother gave me an' my sisters a rag doll, one time. She'd made it for us outta yarn. That was when we was little, though."

"This is th' first doll I ever had in my whole life," Patty said.

"Can I see it?" Rachel asked.

Patty hesitated and handed the prized doll to Rachael. "Please, be careful with her," Patty pleaded. "She's special to me."

Rachel took the doll and looked it over from head to foot. "It's very nice. Ya are lucky to have it." She handed the doll back to Patty.

"Thank ya, besides Tuesday, an' th' baby, an' Cliff, she's all I have in th' world."

"It's just a doll," Rachel said. "People are goin' to think ya are crazy if ya don't be careful."

"I don't care what people think," Patty said. "I'm goin' to do what I'm wantin' with my doll. I told ya she's special in a way ya can't understand."

"That's spooky," Rachel said with scorn.

Patty got up from the rocking chair and went to the kitchen. "Aunt Aggie, can I help ya with supper?"

"No, I got too much help th' way it is, so I do." Aggie gave Ida May, who was stirring the gravy, a scornful look.

Later that night, Tuesday was startled awake by the creek of the bedsprings as someone settled on the edge of the bed. She opened her eyes. From the light of the oil lamp, which Jacob had lit to guide his way up the stairs, she saw him sitting on the bed, removing his boots.

Mary Lou could barely move, but worst of all she could not stretch her legs to relieve the painful cramps that had been plaguing her for three hours. She had cried for someone to let her out until her voice had become hoarse.

"Ya knowed what, Melverta? Th' day that Jeb McCallister'd come down th' mountain to visit Frank, I was inside th' outhouse where I was day-dreamin' over a catalog that was filled with beautiful models. I seen through th' crack in th' out-house wall that Jeb McCallister was out talkin' to Frank. I bet Frank took Aggie to Jeb's cabin. He don't have no stomach nor cause to do harm to th' old woman like Big Bessie's been tellin' Annabelle. Maybe when I'm let out of this cage I'll run away an' find Jeb an' Aggie. Joe'll be sorry then. Not only will he lose me forever, Frank'll be furious with him."

"Then Joe'll take it out on us," Melverta said, resting her head on her fists, her elbows propped on the rough floor of the loft.

"I can't help it, Melverta," Mary Lou said. "He's goin' to be mean no matter what I do."

"I suppose you're right 'bout that," Melverta said.

"Anyway, I seen Jeb lots of times as he'd gone by in his truck, an' he's a looker. Frank likes me best. Maybe Jeb'll like me, too, an' there's a chance that he could be persuaded to take me to th' city with him."

Melverta rolled her eyes; there was no argument about the fact that Dillon preferred Mary Lou to the others. "I don't knowed why Jeb'd want to take th' likes of ya to th' city. He'd only have use for ya in his cabin so ya'd make babies like his women always did."

"Ya don't knowed what you're talking about. Ya don't knowed how to get your way with men like I do," Mary Lou said.

"An' I suppose that's why you're in th' cage an' I'm not," Melverta said, laughing. "An' if Frank ain't ever taken ya to th' city, what makes ya think Jeb's goin' to?"

"Maybe he will an' maybe he won't, but I vow that when I'm let out of this cage, I'll leave this cabin forever," Mary Lou said. "If I have to pretend for a time that I learned my lesson, well, then I'll do it."

"You're talkin' crazy," Melverta said. "How'd ya knowed you'll find Jeb and Aggie?"

"I will," Mary Lou said. "I knowed Jeb an' Aggie's cabins are on up th' mountain."

"You're crazy if you're thinkin' of chasin' after Jeb McCallister!" Melverta said.

"Told ya, men like me," Mary Lou hissed.

"Ya might be foolin' yourself 'bout that," Melverta said and lay back on her mat.

"I'm not worried. Anything's betta than stayin' here," Mary Lou said.

"Ya can't say I didn't warn ya," Melverta said.

"Don't go an' tell th' others what I told ya or ya goin' to be sorry," Mary Lou said.

"Wouldn't tell on ya if I'm sorry or not," Melverta said. "If you're gone, there'll be more food for th' rest of us."

Later in the night, Mary Lou's confining legroom kept her from sleeping soundly. She became aware of scurrying noises. Rats were sniffing around her cage, drawn by the crumbs left from her dinner. "Melverta, are ya asleep?" Mary Lou whispered.

"Be quiet. You're goin' to wake the whole place," Melverta whispered.

"I'm afraid. If I go to sleep th' rats'll crawl inside th' cage with me."

Earlier that day she had begged Joe to let her stay out of the cage when he had walked her to the outhouse. She could barely stand on her own. Her arms and legs were so cramped she felt she would never be able to use them gracefully again.

The rats were getting braver. "Get out of here, ya vermin," she screamed, sobbing.

Joe scrambled out from under his quilt. "What's all the commotion for?" In the total darkness of the loft, he lit an oil lamp, scaring any remaining rats away. He found the key to the cage and made his way to the corner where it sat.

Mary Lou's eyes reflected the glowing light in the lamp as he made his way closer to the cage.

Joe unlocked the cage door. It opened with a loud creak, but she did not move toward the door and freedom. "Come out, Mary Lou. Ya can get out now."

"I can't move my legs. Ya goin' to have to help me," Mary Lou sobbed.

Joe sat the oil lamp down and took her hands in his. As he pulled her forward her head hit on the bar at the top of the small, square door. He pushed her head down and forward, and she fell out on the floor.

Mary Lou could not walk. Her legs had gone completely numb.

Tuesday awoke early the next morning; both the baby and Jacob slept. She had been thankful and joyously relieved that when Jacob had climbed into bed with her the night before, he had turned on his side and quickly gone to sleep. Quietly, Tuesday got out of bed, taking the baby with her. The last thing that she wanted was to wake Jacob; he could have a change of heart. As Tuesday climbed down the stairs carrying the baby, she could hear voices.

"I don't like it, him bringin' people to my house an' movin' them in," the rebellious Ida May complained. "An' mostly, I hate th' way he bosses everyone around."

"Ya wantin' to starve? We're goin' to starve if we don't have no money to buy what we need," Rachel argued, in favor of them being there.

They stopped talking as Tuesday reached the bottom of the stairs. She parted the curtain and found herself the center of attention. "Good morning," she said to be polite. Tuesday saw that Aggie had made herself at home at the woodburner. Apparently she was preparing breakfast.

Patty sat in a rocking chair beside the potbelly stove, and as it had become customary, she held the doll in her arms. Tuesday noticed that her face lit up as Paul Frank came in the back door, carrying an armload of wood. He threw the wood into the wood box that sat beside the woodburner.

"Aggie, when're we goin' to eat?" Paul Frank asked.

"Soon's Jeb comes down. Can't eat until he's had his, so we can't." As if on cue, Jacob stomped down the stairs making it known that he was starving. "I want my breakfast, Aggie. I have a lot to do today."

"Yeah, it's ready, so it is. Just sit yourself down an' I'll have it in front of ya in a jiffy, so I will."

Aggie bustled around, filling Jacob's plate with gravy, sausage patties, and biscuits. She had managed to find a jar of canned sausage in the cellar house, and she put a generous serving of everything on his plate.

"Give Paul Frank a plate, too. We're going to Centerpoint to get some supplies," Jacob ordered and wolfed down his food.

Tuesday felt a ray of hope. She knew the cabin he had kept her in before had been above the town of Winding Ridge. Now she knew that the trails leading away from Paul Frank's cabin led to Centerpoint. She would find out what she could while Jacob and Paul Frank were gone. She knew the winter storm was long over and the snow was melting. There would be snowplows out.

"Let's go, Paul Frank. You've had plenty to eat." Jacob demanded as soon as Paul Frank put the last piece of his biscuit in his mouth. They got up with a loud scrape of their chairs. After pulling their heavy coats off the spike nails, they left with the sound of the back door slamming ringing in the women's ears.

"Tuesday, ya goin' to eat?" Patty asked. "I can hold th' baby for ya." She sat the doll on the chair next to her.

"Thank you, Patty." Tuesday lay the child in Patty's capable arms.

"Hi, Winter Ann," Patty cooed to the child. "Want to meet ya sister?" Patty reached for the doll and set it on her knee. "Winter Ann Summer," she said both names, nodding to the baby and to the doll. "I believe she'll help keep us safe." Patty talked as if she believed the child and the doll understood. "Do ya notice th' doll looks like your ma?" Patty asked Winter Ann.

The doll did look like Tuesday. Her parents had ordered the doll from a company that made dolls in the likeness of the potential owner. All the doll manufacturer required for this feat was a picture of the child the doll was supposed to favor.

Tuesday sat at the table and allowed Aggie to serve her the greasy breakfast. She knew that she must keep up her strength.

"You ever been to Centerpoint, Aggie?"

"No, I ain't, so I ain't. Don't have no business in Centerpoint, so I don't."

"I have," Rachel volunteered, wanting to win Tuesday's affection and dependence, and not having a clue she was thinking of getting away.

"How far is it?" Tuesday asked.

"In good weather it takes 'bout an hour to make it there on foot," Rachel answered.

"How do you get there?" Tuesday asked, encouraged by Rachel's willingness to answer her questions.

"Jus' 'bout any path ya take gets ya there. Ya jus' start down th' mount—."

"Shet up, Rachel. Ya talk too much, so ya do. Jeb won't like ya tellin' Tuesday everythin' ya knowed, so he won't."

"I don't have to listen to ya," Rachel said. "You're just a selfish, bossy, old woman, only wantin' what Jeb's a'wantin'. He's not th' only person in th' world, in case ya hadn't noticed it."

Aggie had never encountered such insolence from a child. She was at a loss for words.

26

ARKNESS HAD FALLEN, AND CLIFF SETTLED DOWN in his sleeping bag in front of the potbelly stove, where he'd built a blazing fire. After not finding McCallister and his captives in either cabin, Cliff was at a loss. "Maybe Hal was right," Cliff said aloud to himself just to break the uncanny silence. "McCallister could not get on the mountain. A snowmobile is the only way, and would it be conceivable to carry an unwilling, pregnant woman and child behind him? Still, he may have made it before the worst of the snowstorm. There was a window of opportunity from the last time there was contact with Tuesday until the blizzard started. No! I don't think McCallister was the one who dismantled the loft or the one who built a fire in the stove. It seems obvious, if he had gone to the trouble to bring Tuesday and Patty here through all the obstacles, he would still be here. I'll have to ask the sheriff if he has much trouble with vagabonds around here."

Worn down from his long trip, Cliff fell asleep. As he slept the fire grew dimmer, the wood slowly burning to ashes.

Cliff awoke to a cold, bitter morning. He was hungry, and he was stiff and cramped. He walked and stretched, trying to loosen his muscles. Using all the wood that was left in the wood box, he built a fire in each stove.

Having a breakfast of canned Spam, a can of orange juice, and four slices of bread, he warmed beside the potbelly stove. The road to Aggie's cabin dead-ended and there were no other homes farther up the mountain. "Nowhere to go but down," Cliff said aloud. "Now's a good time to stop by Dillon's cabin. My next stop is Sheriff Moats' office. It ought to be interesting to hear what Sheriff Moats has to say on the subject of Dillon's being a waste of time or not. The sheriff must know about the new turn of events.

"Now I'm talking to myself." Cliff shoveled ashes over the fire to extinguish it in preparation of leaving the cabin.

A short time later, Cliff wound down the mountain, heading in the back way to Dillon's cabin to avoid the swinging bridge. He ran the snowmobile close to the back door and climbed off. Cliff knocked on the door and a huge woman, whom he had encountered on his previous trip to the mountain eight months earlier, answered the door. As before, she reminded him of a porcupine with her homemade haircut and huge, round face. Before she could react, he walked past.

Joe sat in a rocking chair beside the potbelly stove. He stood as soon as he recognized Cliff as the detective who was responsible for his father's disappearance. "What ya wantin'?" Joe asked.

"Where's Frank Dillon?" Cliff demanded, knowing the boy expected him to ask about McCallister.

"What ya wantin' with Frank?" The boy looked dumfounded.

"I need to talk to him. I'm not going to hurt anyone," Cliff tried to reassure the boy.

"He's not here. I'm in charge, so if ya wantin' somethin' ya hav' to ask me."

The women, except for Mary Lou and Melverta, who listened from the loft, were huddled around the potbelly in their rocking chairs.

"I know you three are from McCallister's cabin," Cliff pointed to Daisy, Annabelle, and Sara. "Where are the others?" Cliff demanded. "Why are you all here?'

Joe did not answer, and with a harsh look kept the others quiet. "Boy, I want you to answer my questions. First, why are you and McCallister's women here?"

"It's not your business," Joe announced in an inflexible voice of conclusion.

"Do you know why your Aunt Aggie's cabin has been trashed and the loft dismantled?"

Joe looked genuinely surprised, but did not respond to the question. As it was obvious the boy would not answer questions in the absence of force and probably knew nothing, Cliff turned and left. For Cliff, the fact that McCallister's women lived at Dillon's cabin only confirmed that McCallister was still on the run.

The snowmobile moved swiftly down the mountain as Annabelle watched from the window. It's roaring whine grew dimmer as it gradually became a speck in the snow. She had no doubt that she had not seen the end of the detective. Knowing that Frank was about the same business that Jeb was, she believed that Frank was on his way to the same end. "I can't say as I'm sorry to see Frank in trouble with th' law. I just don't like th' man," Annabelle said.

"How can ya be so ungrateful?" Big Bessie demanded. "My man gives ya a place to live and takes care of ya and ya have th' nerve to wish bad on him."

"Ma, ya don't knowed what you're talkin' about," Joe said. "We need Frank right now. When I'm old enough I can take care of ya, but now we need Frank."

"My bet is that ain't goin' to happen," Annabelle predicted. "When th' law gets after ya, that's it. They take ya away."

Meanwhile, Cliff pulled up in front of the jailhouse. He eased down on the throttle and came to a stop behind the sheriff's Jeep. Before the echo of the roar of the snowmobile had died down, Cliff was standing in front of the sheriff's desk. "Afternoon, Sheriff," Cliff greeted the sheriff while he hurriedly whisked his magazine out of sight.

"What you wantin'? Can't get shed of you city detectives even with the damnedest blizzard in a hundred years," Ozzie bemoaned, putting his cupped hand up to his mouth. When his hand came away, it held a wad of soggy tobacco. Carelessly, Ozzie tossed it into his spittoon. "Two of your sidekicks ran off the mountain just ahead of the big storm like a cat with a jigger in its paw. Now you're here like it ain't nothin' to mosey up an impassable road," Sheriff Moats complained.

He opened his drawer and pulled out a fresh pouch of tobacco. "How'd you get here, anyway?" he asked.

"Snowmobile," Cliff answered.

"If you're willin' to come here on that insane snow machine," Ozzie complained, "you must be goin' to stir up more trouble. You're already responsible for stirring up more than I got the stomach for.

Are ya ever goin' to stop plaguing me?" With a loud
whack, Ozzie slammed his drawer shut.

"Just calm down, Sheriff! I have some questions."
Cliff pulled a chair up to Ozzie's desk. He turned
the chair to face him and sat straddling the seat.
"Tell me about Frank Dillon."

"What's to know about him?" Ozzie looked genuinely surprised.

"That's for you to tell me."

"How the hell you know about the likes of Dillon?" Moats asked.

"I ran into him when I was here 'plaguing' you
eight months ago," Cliff said in sarcasm. "You must
remember—one of the times when I couldn't get
your cooperation. In any case, when I stopped by
his cabin looking for McCallister's, I ran into him
just as I was leaving after trying to talk to his
women. They wouldn't answer my questions, and
besides they would only talk to me from behind a
crack in the door. I thought it was strange that there
were several women living in his cabin. In addition
to that, the man was too polished in comparison to
the other people living on the mountain."

"That don't tell me why you'd want to know
about him," Ozzie declared. "Anyway, ain't nothin'
to tell 'bout him except he lives on the mountain.
Spends most of his time in the city, though."

"I'm sure he's tied into the kidnapping ring that
McCallister's involved in. I'm here looking for
McCallister, though. He's thought to be hiding out
after abducting two females. While I'm here, I'm
checking Dillon out, too.

"I want you to step up your watch," Cliff continued. "I've already checked McCallister's and
Aggie's cabins. No one's in either one, but somehow I think McCallister will bring them here when

the weather permits. We can't allow him to get away this time."

"He won't be back," Ozzie predicted. "Men don't return to the mountain once they get away from it, but I'll do my best, keepin' on th, lookout," the sheriff promised. "I suppose it's what I got to do to keep you from plaguin' me."

"You see that you do that," Cliff said and moved toward the door.

"By the way, Sheriff, you should know there was vandalism in Aggie's cabin. The loft has been partly dismantled. Looks as if someone holed up there for a while and left."

"I'll look into it," Ozzie said.

"Do you have much trouble with vagrants?" Cliff asked.

"Can't say that I do."

"Hear from your brother?" Cliff quickly changed the subject, throwing the sheriff off guard.

"Why do you want to know about Aubry?" Ozzie was visibly shaken by the question. "Ain't none of your business if I hear from my brother or not."

Leaving the sheriff to his seductive magazine, Cliff headed home to expand his search for Tuesday. On his way out, he made a mental note of the fact that the sheriff was overly defensive when it came to Aubry Moats.

27

$\mathcal{T}$HE LOUD BANGING AT THE DOOR WOKE STEVEN Lloyd. The lighted digital clock on his night-stand read 2:05 A.M. "Who the hell!" Lloyd threw back the covers and swung his legs out over the edge of the bed. He pulled on his robe as he went, tripping over the coffee table as he hurried to the door in the dark. "Damn it, anyway. Hold your pants on. I'm coming." Lloyd hobbled to the door, favoring his sore knee.

"Dillon! What's up? Why the hell are you here in the middle of the night?" Alarm was written in Lloyd's eyes as he faced Frank Dillon, who was fully dressed, while Steven stood there looking fool-ish in his silk robe and pajamas.

Dillon pushed past Lloyd and walked into his liv-ing room. "You asked me over."

"Sorry if I don't remember asking you over, but I surely didn't ask you to come calling in the mid-dle of the night," Lloyd said, his normal compo-sure shaken.

"Oh, yes you did. When you opened your big mouth to the detectives, you were begging me to

end your miserable life. What did you tell them?"
Dillon shouted.

"I haven't told them anything," Lloyd grumbled.
"I only told you I thought you should know that
one of them mentioned your name. They think Tom
is your boy. The boy looks like you, you know."

"That's absurd. How could they possibly know
what I look like or anything else about me? Unless
you told them," Dillon demanded, shoving Lloyd
into the coffee table.

"I didn't tell anyone anything about you. I have
no idea how they came up with your name," Lloyd
said as he caught his balance. "Only that they did! I
swear I don't. If you insist on believing that it's me
who told, you're not going to have a chance in hell
of finding out how they really got your name."

"No one knows about me!" Dillon grabbed the
smaller man by the lapel of his silk robe. "Explain
why the detectives are interested in me if you didn't
talk."

"Think! Frank, they could have been following
you. Who've you been talking to? You know that
they were on the mountain looking for Jacob
McCallister. Did they see you there?"

"I remember one man." Dillon released Lloyd
with a shove. "He was looking for McCallister. He
stopped by my cabin. I told him nothing. I hadn't
given it much thought, but I suppose he'd remember me."

"That's it, then," Lloyd said. "He'd remember
you for sure. You're too polished. You don't fit in
with the mountain people like Aubry Moats. No!
He didn't forget your face. And when he saw Tom,
he saw the resemblance."

"There's more to this than the detective seeing a
resemblance between a small boy and me. Without
another party, namely you, a connection between

me and the boy, well, it's simply not feasible. The chance meeting between me and the detective could not have been the only ground for his suspicions, or for him mentioning my name to you."

He laughed at Lloyd as he fidgeted while he awaited his fate. "I'm not going to take you out now, but if I find out you mentioned my name, or my dealings with you, you're done for!" Dillon slammed out of Lloyds's apartment. The crack of the slamming door rang in the air long after he was gone.

Still dressed in his snowmobile clothes, Cliff appeared in Hal's office. "I'm back. I don't know any more than I did when I left. They were not in either cabin," Cliff said. "McCallister's cabin was the same as it was when we were there, but Aggie's cabin has been trashed."

"Do you have an idea what happened?" Hal asked. "Was the old woman harmed?"

"She wasn't there. It was the same at McCallister's cabin. The women that I remember who lived in his cabin were gone, but I found them at Dillon's cabin. Three of McCallister's women and children are living in his cabin now. It's obvious that they feel that they couldn't take care of themselves, so by some arrangement they wound up in Dillon's cabin."

"On one hand I don't think the women living with another mountain man is unusual, but on the other hand, Frank doesn't appear to be a man who would take on that many people out of the goodness of his heart."

"It makes sense if Dillon is in the same business as McCallister," Cliff said.

"Why do you think someone would trash Aggie's cabin?" Hal asked. "There's nothing of value to steal. If someone was only looking for a hideout they'd have no reason, that I can see, to vandalize it."

"I have no idea," Cliff answered. "I wouldn't think that there would be homeless people in that isolated place, where they would have no chance of getting handouts. The wood from the loft must've been used for firewood."

"It's a piece of the puzzle, though," Hal said. "When we fit the pieces together, we'll find Tuesday."

"Did Randy McCoy or Bart Howard say if the cabin had been disturbed?"

"No, they didn't. If it had been, they would have said so. They were told to check if there was anything unusual going on in the cabin, like if McCallister was getting the place ready for taking someone to it."

"You have anything new?" Cliff asked.

"I've been gathering information on Dillon, and the fact that he has taken McCallister's women in only implicates him further. We all know that Dillon didn't take the women in out of the goodness of his heart. Selling his own children is the only explanation for Dillon's taking McCallister's women," Hal said. "It explains everything we've found out so far—he's involved in selling children and wants to increase his breeding stock."

"You're right," Cliff offered. "The set up is identical. The cabin's too small for all those people to live in."

"The fact is, Dillon's lifestyle is similar to McCallister's. Hell, he's doing a much better business than McCallister was. He owns a large, expensive house in the upper-class section here in Wheeling," Hal updated Cliff.

"I'm not surprised after what I saw in his cabin. There were three babies, two of McCallister's women, and his two children were there. I didn't see Aggie or the sickly one. There were several young girls who were pregnant. A huge woman they refer to as Big Bessie, I'd met before. I can't help wondering where Aggie and the sickly one are. The cabin is small, but I suppose that they could have been in the loft."

"Randy McCoy and his men are watching Dillon," Hal said. "McCoy witnessed a meeting Dillon had with a Marty Townsend. McCoy thought that the meeting was suspicious. They met in a dive in the slum area. You know the sort of bar where the low-life hang out. Randy said that both of them looked out of place in their business suits having a drink and conversation among the junkies and winos that patronize the place.

"Marty's apparently an upstanding citizen in his hometown, Fairmont. My guess is," Hal continued, "Dillon is selling his own children. And I bet my bottom dollar that Tom is Dillon's son."

"It's like McCallister's twins all over again," Cliff said. "At first I suspected that Tom could be McCallister's until I saw the photo of Frank and realized he was the man on the mountain I ran into. Then seeing Dillon without the straggly growth of beard drove home the resemblance."

"I'll call Randy McCoy, we'll update him on your trip to the mountain. He may have something new as well." Hal lifted the receiver from its cradle and dialed McCoy's office.

"McCoy, how soon can you get to my office? Cliff is back from Winding Ridge and I want you be in on our conversation."

"I'll be right up."

Fifteen minutes later Randy McCoy joined Hal and Cliff. "Glad to see you back." Randy McCoy slapped Cliff on the back.

"Let's get at it," Cliff said. "First off, do either of you think Dillon is connected with Jacob in Tuesday's disappearance or had knowledge of McCallister's whereabouts since he left the mountain?"

"No," Hal said, "there's nothing to support that."

"I don't think so either," McCoy said. "We've been watching Dillon and it's only speculation, but he's been seen in contact with people who are under investigation in our kidnapping case and making moves like he's looking for a new broker."

"Like you said, Cliff, Dillon has three babies that he's keeping in his cabin. He just doesn't come across as a proud papa to me."

"After visiting the cabin, I can attest to that. You say he has a sizeable home in Wheeling. No proud father would allow his children to live in the squalor I saw them in if he owned an expensive home where they could live a decent life."

"Knowing that fits what I have on him," Randy said. "My men and I have found out quite a lot in a short time. I'm sure, Hal, you filled Cliff in on the meeting with Marty Townsend."

Hal nodded. "Go on."

"These facts on Dillon connect him with Steven Lloyd. He met a young woman early yesterday afternoon. He had been standing across from the apartment building where Steven Lloyd lives. We don't know why, but think he's worried that Lloyd will talk, and Dillon wants to know who's coming and going. The meeting with the woman may or may not have been a coincidence in that she is Marty Townsend's mistress. Apparently she was walking her Great Dane when she walked right into

Dillon as he stood watching Steven's apartment building. They had dinner together that night; Dillon picked her up at her apartment. I would think she would be careful giving out her address to another man, since Marty Townsend pays her bills.

"After Dillon took the woman back to her apartment he stayed a couple of hours and left at approximately 1:30 A.M. He went straight to Steven Lloyd's apartment and arrived there at 2:05 A.M. He left Steven's apartment at 2:38 A.M. and drove to his home on Concord."

"What about Marty Townsend?" Cliff asked. "Do you have anything on him?"

"The latest scoop is the mistress. He's very generous, and he could not afford her on the earnings from his furniture business. We're digging for any other legal income he may have. If there's anything to find, we'll find it."

"I want you to keep a tail on Marty twenty-four hours a day," Hal ordered. "I think we're on to something big.

"In addition," Hal said, "something has to be decided about Dillon. If Steven told him we were asking questions about him, when he made his middle-of-the-night visit, Dillon may run. He'll realize that we're on to him. He'll remember Cliff's visit to his mountain cabin last year and tie his present problems to McCallister's old ones.

"I questioned Lloyd about the resemblance between Tom and Dillon, and Lloyd may have told Dillon. If he figures that we know too much, I have no doubt that he'll run."

"In my opinion," Cliff said, "we arrest him. We can't risk him taking off on us. The three infants and five girls, two of whom were pregnant, living in his cabin, plus what Randy dug up, is all the evidence we need for taking him into custody. As soon as possible, we bring his family to town and they'll talk."

After he left Steven Lloyd's apartment in the early morning hours, Dillon drove across town, heading home. He fumbled for the lock with his key; he finally pushed his front door inward as the key released the bolt. He went straight to his bedroom and undressed. He would sleep and make his decision in the morning as to what he would do.

For the first time in a lifetime of oppressing others, Dillon knew gut-wrenching fear. Throughout the night, he tossed and turned, plagued with his worst nightmares.

28

*A*S THE WEATHER WARMED, THE SNOW GRADUALLY melted. Jacob McCallister waited for the chance to get his truck from the valley and to get off the mountain for a few days. He and Paul Frank had worked with the horse and homemade snow-plow to clear the road leading off the mountain for the four-wheel-drive to make the trip from Herman's cabin to Route Seven, where the county plow would have cleared the road.

During the past eight months, when McCallister had kept out of sight by living in Ten Mile Creek, he had met a woman through Aubry Moats who was the head nurse at a clinic. Olene Ryder was extremely attracted to McCallister, and he took advantage of the situation because Olene arranged illegal adoptions for a fee.

Working in the clinic, she had the opportunity to meet the couples who were seeking help to become parents—the last resort before they tried adoption, a process that could be long and futile.

She charged the couples outrageous prices for caring for and taking into her home young girls

who'd found themselves in unwanted pregnancies.
Over the years Olene had made a nice profit arrang-
ing adoptions for the pregnant girls who wanted to
keep their pregnancies from their parents, and the
couples who were unwilling to go through all the
red tape or had been turned down as adoptive parents. She had teamed up with an attorney who drew
up the adoption papers, and they both made a very
tidy sum of money.

On occasion over the years, she used Aubry
Moats when she had more want-to-be parents than
pregnant girls willing to give up their new infants.
As word got around that she had the resources to
provide childless couples with anything from a
newborn infant to an older child, she gradually
built a large clientele. As a result of the demand,
McCallister's arrival in her life was an additional
way for her to supply the want-to-be parents with a
newborn infant.

Now at McCallister's low point in his life, he
was short on money and needed to make a sale to
keep him going until he had other children ready
to sell. The black marketers in Wheeling would
pay him a much larger amount for a child than
Olene Ryder paid, but in his present misfortune he
had to take what he could get. He was in no position to contact a broker in Wheeling now that he
was a wanted man.

Patty sat in a corner away from the others, holding
Summer. Her father sat by the potbelly stove doing
nothing. His foul mood made everyone nervous.

"Do ya think I should tell Tuesday about my
dream last night?" Patty asked the doll, holding her
up to her face.

With vacant, bright blue, marble eyes, the doll
stared into Patty's eyes. "Ya don't," Patty said. "Ya
think it'd scare her?"

Lost in her own thoughts, Patty jumped at her father's loud voice.

"Paul Frank, get down here. I want you to go with me."

"Sure, Jacob," Paul Frank called out from the upstairs. He ran, clambering down the stairs, and grabbed his jacket off the spike nail on the wall.

They slammed out the back, leaving a cold gust of wind to chill the cabin. "Let's see if we can get my truck out of the hollow below Aggie's cabin. The snow's melted enough for us to ride the horse. In the places that are bad, we can walk her."

"We got two horses. Don't need to take only th' one," Paul Frank said. "Pa tried to make a livin' from farmin'. Had to if we was goin' to eat."

They harnessed and saddled the horses. When they were ready, they headed toward the logging road, where Jacob had abandoned the truck to the blizzard. In the early afternoon they spotted the truck as the sun reflected on the exposed chrome, casting brilliant light back into their eyes.

"You know, Paul Frank, if we can get the truck up to Aggie's cabin, I can drive it down the main road to Winding Ridge. It'll be in better condition than the logging road. It's my experience that the mountain men will have been out scraping the roads in hopes of getting off the mountain and away from their nagging and complaining wives," McCallister laughed. "I bet you I'll have no trouble getting up to Centerpoint and back to Broad Run."

"What ya wantin' me to do?" Paul Frank asked.

"Hitch the horses to the bumper and help me dig the truck out. Better pray it starts. Been setting for days now."

Jacob got a shovel from the bed of the truck, and Paul Frank used the one they carried with them. After they dug what snow they could from around and in front of the wheels, Jacob climbed in the driver's side and tried to start the truck. The engine whined but did not fire. "Damn, it's not going to start," McCallister said. "Paul Frank, maybe the horses can pull the truck up the hill and I can jump-start the engine by coasting down the road to Winding Ridge."

"Don't think th' horses can pull th' truck if we can't start it," Paul Frank said. "Th' snow's too deep for th' horses' feet to get traction enough to carry that much weight."

McCallister climbed from the truck and opened the hood. "I'll pour gas right into the carburetor. Maybe it's not getting enough gas." He poured a small amount into the carburetor and tried again, and the engine started with a roar.

Paul Frank took the horses' reins and commanded, "Get up, Big Red! Get up, Buck!" Obeying the command, the horses lurched forward, pulling as one.

Jacob had put the truck in four-wheel drive. It slowly inched forward as the horses and truck pulled together. The truck fish tailed, and the muscular horses dug their hooves in the deep snow. Leaping forward one hurdle at a time, their muscles quivering as they strained against their load, the horses pulled the truck up the old logging road.

"Hot damn!" Jacob yelled as the truck topped the hill. "We made it!"

"Ya want me to take th' horses back?" Paul Frank asked.

"You think they're going to go back all by themselves? Of course I want you to take them back. Hurry now. It's getting dark."

Paul Frank climbed onto Big Red. He leaned over the side and grabbed Buck's reins. They plodded back toward Herman's cabin while Jacob turned the

truck around and drove down the logging trail
toward Winding Ridge.

It was growing dark when Aggie, standing at the
kitchen window, watched Paul Frank, sitting on one
horse and leading another, ride toward the barn.
When the horses saw the barn, they picked up their
speed, heading for food and rest from their trek
over the rocky mountain terrain.

Paul Frank jumped off Big Red and led her and
Buck into the barn.

"There's Paul Frank. Jeb'll not be far behind, so he
won't," Aggie said to the others. She set the beans
back on the stove and put the cornbread back into
the oven. They would be starved. They had taken
only a few biscuits with them for their lunch.

A short time later, the roar of the truck engine
announced McCallister's arrival. He had driven
down the old logging road below Aggie's cabin to
Winding Ridge. From there, he had traveled the fifteen miles along Route Seven, turned off to the
right, and driven up the road to Centerpoint. After
speeding through the town, he had headed up
Broad Run directly to Herman Ruble's cabin.

Paul Frank was in the barn taking care of the
horses. Jacob called him out. "Come here, boy. I
want to talk to you before we go into the cabin. I'm
going to take the baby and leave here as soon as I
eat. I want you to watch the women. Don't take
your eyes off Tuesday. If she's not here when I get
back, you're a dead man. Do you understand? If
you have to tie her up to keep her here, do it."

Jacob went into the cabin to eat. He would eat
then get the baby and go. "Where's Tuesday?" he
asked.

"She's sleepin', so she is. Sleeps a lot, so she does.
Ya wantin' me to wake her?"

"No, Aunt Aggie. I just want to know where she is."

While they talked, Aggie filled a plate for Jacob and set it in front of him. He sat down and wolfed his food as if there was someone ready to take it from him.

As Jacob ate, he told Aggie of his plans. "I'm going to take the baby to sell. The roads are in pretty good shape. The farmers have been out plowing around town, up Broad Run, and down to Route Seven. I can make good time with a four-wheel drive. Have one of the girls go get the baby. Tell her to be extra careful not to wake Tuesday. It will be a more pleasant experience for all of us if Tuesday doesn't know what I'm doing."

"Ruby, ya heard 'im, so ya did. Go on an' fetch th' baby."

As Ruby came back down the stairs with the child clutched in her arms, Jacob put his heavy coat on. He took Winter Ann and headed out the back door. With a roar of his engine, Jacob was gone in a cloud of snow.

Mary Lou and Melverta had been listening the day Cliff Moran was visiting the cabin, questioning Joe about Jacob McCallister. It was obvious that Moran was surprised that Joe was there. He had questioned him at length about Joe and the others living in Frank's cabin. Also, Mary Lou was in the outhouse the day Jacob had paid Dillon a visit and had learned that he was back on the mountain after almost a year of running from the law.

"I'm glad that Joe didn't tell th' man that was here where Jeb is, cause I'm goin' to leave tonight an' find Jeb an' Aggie," Mary Lou said as she lay on a mat, finally free from the cramped confines of the cage. "I don't want no one knowin' where to look for me an' I'll show Joe he can't treat me like an old dog an' lock me up in a cage. He's goin' to be sorry when he can't find me. When Frank comes back an' sees I'm gone, he's goin' to show Joe he ain't so smart after all. Yeah, Frank's not goin' to like it when he sees I'm gone."

Below the loft, Big Bessie had prepared Mary Lou's tray and called on Emma Jean to carry the meal to Mary Lou. "After bein' cramped in th' kennel for days, she's too weak to climb down the ladder just yet," Big Bessie said.

"O-o-okay, B-b-big B-bessie, I can take th' tray to her," Emma Jean stuttered. She awkwardly climbed the ladder, holding the tray in one hand as she clutched the ladder with the other. She carefully made her way up on the loft and to Mary Lou with the food still on the tray.

"Thank ya, Emma Jean," Mary Lou said and took the tray from the girl.

While Mary Lou ate, hungrily cleaning up her plate, Emma Jean climbed back down the ladder.

As soon as Emma Jean was back down below and Mary Lou had finished her food, she continued telling Melverta her plans. "I have no idea when my next meal's goin' to be, Melverta. I'm scared. Ya want to come with me?"

"No," Melverta said. "I don't have no desire to starve or to freeze to death."

"Ya can live ya life in this hellhole, but I'm not," Mary Lou said. "I'm goin' to pretended to sleep till everyone else is asleep, so don't talk to me anymore tonight."

After all activity had finally ceased, everyone had settled down for the night, and everything was quiet, Mary Lou waited another hour before she crawled out from under her quilt. Holding her breath, she felt around in the dark and found a pair of Joe's overalls and one of his flannel shirts. The heavier material would keep her much warmer than her feedsack dress. With her bundle secure under her arm, she climbed down the ladder.

She stood quietly by the woodburning stove where there was little warmth from the dying fire. It would be the end of her plans for good if she were to wake Daisy and Annabelle, who slept in the four-poster, or Big Bessie who slept across the room beside the potbelly stove on her mat.

Quickly, she dressed. Joe's clothes were several sizes too large, but she rolled up the sleeves of the flannel shirt and tied knots in the straps of the over-alls, so they would fit more snugly to her body.

Quietly, she moved to the wooden crate they used for a breadbox and found half a dozen biscuits. She laid an old bread cloth on the top of the stove, took the day-old biscuits from the crate, and set them on the cloth. She tied the ends of the cloth together, and then she tied the cloth to the belt loop in the overalls.

Finally Mary Lou was ready for a coat, but she did not own one. When the girls went outside to the outhouse or to the cellar house, they wore an old coat of Frank's that hung on a nail beside the back door. Instead of leaving the girls without a coat, she took Joe's coat, leaving him to find an old coat of Frank's.

She opened the back door as quietly as she could and slipped out.

She had never been to Jacob's cabin, which was located much farther up the mountain, as was Aggie's.

Leaving the back porch, she began her long jour-ney by walking toward the trail that led higher up the mountain. The memory of being trapped in the kennel, driving the hungry rats away, and fighting mind-numbing fear drove her on.

Tuesday woke and reached for her child. The baby was not there. She sat up in a panic. *The others know better than take Winter Ann without my consent.* Tuesday jumped from the bed. "Where's Winter Ann? Where's my baby?" Tuesday screamed as she stumbled down the stairway.

Tuesday burst through the curtain and realized at once that the baby was not in the room. "Where is my baby?" Tuesday demanded as fear clutched at her heart. No one had the heart to tell her that her child was gone.

"What's wrong with ya, girl? There's no reason to scream, so there's not."

Patty sat holding her doll. "I couldn't do nothin' to stop him," Patty sobbed.

"Sit ya self down an' be quiet," Aggie said. "I'm goin' to tell ya, so I am."

Tuesday sat down, terrified. She knew that she was not going to like what Aggie was about to tell her, but she knew that she must hear it.

Aggie knelt at Tuesday's feet and said, "Jacob needed the money and he's took the baby to sell, so he has. Ain't nothin' to do for it, so they ain't. We need to eat, so we do."

"You silly old woman," Tuesday screamed. She felt the room spin and fought to remain in control. She had to reach down to the depth of her soul to keep from losing her sanity. "People don't sell children to pay for their food. They work. It's against the law to sell children. How long ago did he leave?"

"Tuesday," Paul Frank said, "we can't do nothin' about it. Ya knowed that Jacob's goin' to do what he wants, an' we have to accept it."

"No, we don't, Paul Frank! Don't you understand? People just don't live like this. I will not accept this. I'm going to leave here right now and I will find my child. I will not sit still for this. If I have to, I will kill the bastard for taking my child."

"Tuesday, ya can't leave here," Paul Frank said. "Jacob'll kill me when he comes back. I'm sure he wouldn't think twice about killin' ya, either. He took his gun with him. He takes it wherever he goes."

"Then go with me. You need to learn a better way to live. You'll end up like Jacob if you stay here."

"Yeah, Paul Frank," Patty said, jumping from the rocking chair. "Come with us, please. We need ya."

"We'll have a better chance of getting away if you help us. "Please, Paul Frank," Tuesday pleaded. "We may not make it otherwise."

"I knowed Jacob'll kill me when he gets back an' found ya an' Patty are gone," Paul Frank said. "But I'll not stop ya from leaving."

"Go with them," Rachel said. "It's th' only way. To stay here would only mean death for ya."

"I can't leave ya," Paul Frank said, "I promised Pa I'd take care of ya."

"Don't make no sense to stay," Rachel said, "cause Jeb's goin' to kill ya, and either way we'd have to make do without ya."

"Yeah," Patty said, "I've had dreams 'bout gettin' away from here an' ya was with Tuesday and me."

"Why didn't you tell me?" Tuesday said, alarmed that Patty had kept something so important to herself.

"Winter Ann wasn't with us an' I couldn't tell ya," Patty sobbed.

Tuesday took Patty in her arms and comforted her. "It's okay, Patty, don't cry. But please don't keep anything away from me again."

"If I'd told ya before," Patty hiccuped, "maybe we could have stopped Pa from takin' Winter Ann."

"Maybe, but I doubt it. Patty, Jacob is much stronger than we are and he only took her while I was sleeping so there would be no fuss. We can't do anything about that now. I do wish you had told me, though. Remember what Cliff said, 'Your dreams are a warning and if we heed them they can be useful.'"

"I'm so sorry," Patty sobbed, hugging Tuesday as if she would never let go.

"Are you with us?" Tuesday asked Paul Frank.

"Yeah, I'll go with you." Paul Frank made up his mind. "Let's get started. Th' sooner we get away from here th' betta."

They each gathered warm clothing to wear. Patty and Tuesday wore overalls that had belonged to Paul Frank's father. Ruble was a smaller man than Paul Frank was. Paul Frank's mother wore only feedsack dresses, but there were heavy coats that had belonged to her for Patty and Tuesday.

"Are you ready, Patty?" Tuesday asked.

"Yeah, as ready as I can be."

"Don't sound so glum. We made it before when we had no idea what we were getting into. Now we're prepared. We learned a great deal from our escape down the mountain last year."

"Yeah," Patty said, "an' th' best thin' is we have Paul Frank to help."

"Ya can't go no where's, so ya can't," Aggie demanded. "Jeb's not goin' to stand for it, so he's not. Y'all just sit down an' Aggie's goin' to fix ya somethin' to eat, so I am."

Aggie was totally ignored while Rachel, Ruby, and Ida May helped the other three prepare for their trip off the mountain. His sisters were taking a chance on facing McCallister's wrath, but it was Paul Frank that he would hold accountable.

Finally, Aggie sat in a rocking chair, defeated. She could not keep them there. She was a small woman, and there was no way for her to stop them. "Ya knowed Jeb's countin' on me to keep ya here, so he is. What ya think he's goin' to do to me when he sees that ya are gone?"

"Aggie, I'm sorry for you," Tuesday said, "but you brought your troubles upon yourself. It looks like to me that you have condoned your nephew's behavior all his life."

They were warmly dressed and ready to leave. Each of them carried an extra change of clothing wrapped in a quilt, which they had tied on their backs with bailing twine. Each of them had a stash of biscuits and cornbread. The food had been placed in the center of a large cloth and each corner was tied securely together and tucked into their belt loops.

To Aggie's dismay Tuesday, Patty, and Paul Frank actually walked out the back door. She got up from the rocking chair and watched out the back window as they walked from sight, the moon lighting their way.

29

THE LATE-MORNING SUNLIGHT SHINING IN THE window of Dillon's bedroom woke him. He sat up in bed as if he were a Jack-in-the-box. Spurred on by the events of the night before, he threw back his covers and got out of bed.

Dillon had no choice. He would run. Simon Leonard would help, if for no other reason than that he would want to protect his access to the twin boys.

He retrieved his suitcase from the closet and started packing. He got the eighty thousand dollars from his safe in the kitchen and put it on the table. He never kept his money in banks, nor did he pay taxes. The Internal Revenue Service would not take kindly to his source of income.

Unexpectedly, there was a loud knock on the door.

"Who the hell!" He spread the newspaper over the money and went to the door.

"We have a warrant for your arrest, Frank Dillon. You have the right to remain silent. You have the right to an attorney. If you can't afford an attorney, one will be appointed for you. Anything you say may be held against you in a court of law. Do you understand your rights?" Cliff read him his rights while the uniformed officer handcuffed Frank's hands behind his back.

The officer gathered Frank's luggage, and as Cliff walked over to the opened safe, Hal removed the newspaper revealing the cash. "Look at this loot," Hal said. "Dillon has a great deal of explaining to do. We know he's not employed, so how did he get this pile of money?"

"I'm sure you're thinking the same thing that I am. He got this money from selling his own children," Cliff said. "And it's obvious that he was getting ready to run."

At the station Frank Dillon was told that he would be allowed to make one phone call. He called Simon Leonard. "Simon, call an attorney for me. Pay him what you have to. Take it from what you owe me. If you want me to honor our deal, you'd better get me the best. Don't mess up, Leonard, understand?"

"I will take care of it right away, Frank. But you know it won't help your case if anyone discovers you know me."

"I know that. You're the only one I know who could help me in this situation. The cops don't know who I'm calling. This will be our last contact until you get me out of this mess."

"I understand," Leonard assured Dillon. "I'll get right on it. Don't worry."

"I won't worry," Dillon said. "You have as much at stake in this as I do."

A couple of hours later, the fingerprinting and the mug shot were done. Dillon was led to his cell, where he was allowed to see the attorney who, at Simon's bidding, already waited there for him.

"Frank, I'm your attorney, James Maxwell. Sit down and we'll get on with it."

"I want out of here," Frank said with steel in his voice. "If you can get me out I'll see that you're well paid."

"Are you guilty of the charges against you?" James Maxwell asked Frank, watching Frank's face closely to determine weather he was lying. "Please tell the truth."

"Hell, no, I'm not guilty. And I don't belong here. The way I see it, you're being paid big money to get me out. The question is, can you?"

"I don't know yet. I have a lot of questions to ask you. Tell me the truth. If you don't, then I can't help you. If you want my help, give me the facts."

After James Maxwell left, Frank lay on the cot in his cell. "You didn't tell your lawyer the truth, did you?" Dillon's cellmate gloated. "I never heard such a cock-and-bull story."

"What the hell's it to you?" Dillon asked. "I didn't come in here to neighbor."

"From the sound of it, if you get out on bond, you had better run," the inmate said, ignoring the fact that Dillon was not interested in talking. "Sounds to me like you're headed for the pen, and they don't like child abusers there."

"He was getting ready to run," Cliff said. "He had his luggage out and had taken his money from his safe. We got to him just in time. If we can't hold him, he's gone. I'd bet the farm that he won't sit around waiting for a trial. It'll be the same as Jacob McCallister all over again. It's like McCallister disappeared from the face of the earth."

"We'll move fast," Hal said. "We'll meet with Mascara and ask him to get the judge to deny bail. The fact that he was getting ready to run and the seriousness of his crimes against children will be enough to get his bail denied."

"I hope you're right," Cliff said. "He must be held without bail until trial. We need time to gather enough evidence to have him indicted by the Grand Jury."

"First, we get a DNA test on Dillon and Tom to establish that Dillon is Tom's father," Hal said. "Second, we'll send McCoy and Howard to Dillon's cabin to get the women and children for questioning."

"Great," Cliff said. "They know the mountain, and I can direct them to Dillon's cabin. While you're rounding up McCoy and his men, I'll arrange for the hospital to get a sample from Tom. We'll need to get a court order for Dillon's sample. I'm sure he won't consent to it. I'll have a lab technician on standby to get the sample."

"Establishing that Tom is Dillon's son is the key to locking him up for a very long time," Hal said.

Later, McCoy and Howard left for the mountain, and Cliff called the prosecuting attorney. "I need to talk to you," Cliff said to Ron Mascara.

"I'm free first thing in the morning. What's up?"

"Remember McCallister? We got another one who's cut from the same cloth," Cliff answered. "I intend to keep history from repeating itself."

W-w-w-where's M-m-mary L-lou?" Emma Jean asked Melverta when she awoke and saw that Mary Lou's mat was empty. Mary Lou never got out from under her warm quilt until she was practically thrown out.

"Leave me alone. She's probably gone to th' outhouse," Melverta said.

"I t-think w-w-we should l-l-look," Emma Jean said. "I h-heard y-ya all t-talkin' about r-r-runin' a-a-away."

Melverta and Emma Jean crawled from under their quilts and climbed down the ladder to check whether Mary Lou had already gone down to the kitchen. There was no one but Big Bessie, Annabelle, Daisy, and the three infants below the loft.

"What's th' commotion about?" Annabelle asked.

"Mary Lou's gone," Melverta answered.

"Maybe she's only gone outdoors," Big Bessie said, "except I ain't seen her go out, an' she never goes out before daylight. I've been up doin' my chores long before that. Ya betta get Joe," Big Bessie smirked. "He's th' one in charge."

"Ya'd like nothin' betta than gettin' Joe in trouble with Frank," Annabelle said. "Ya'd do anythin' to be in charge again."

"I ain't goin' to squabble with ya," Big Bessie said. "Melverta, get Joe."

Melverta climbed back onto the loft and faced Joe. "Mary Lou's gone, Joe," Melverta said.

"What do ya mean Mary Lou's gone. She don't have nowhere to go." Joe reached for the overalls he had taken off the night before. They were not there, although he had left them in arm's reach.

"Melverta, look an' see if ya can find my overalls. I can't find 'em.

"I don't see 'em. Ain't nowhere else to look."

"They have to be here," Joe yelled at Melverta, impatient with her inactivity. "Overall's just don't get up an' walk away by their selves."

Emma Jean climbed back up the ladder, "Y-y-your c-coat's g-g-gone, J-J-Joe. I c-c-can't f-find your boots n-n-neither."

Joe was well aware that if something happened to Mary Lou, Dillon would kill him. Mary Lou was Dillon's favorite. "All of you look for her. Look in the outhouse an' th' barn. She's probably just gone out to th' outhouse. Hurry."

Joe rummaged around for his extra pair of overalls and a flannel shirt, but he did not own a second pair of boots. Barefoot, he climbed down the ladder intending to wear the boots that the girls wore when they went to the outhouse. They were not there.

Joe sat at the table. "I can't believe that she'd run away. Where would she go? She don't have nowhere to go. She's never been off th' mountain. I'm sure that on her own she's never been further than a'hundred yards from this cabin."

The door opened with a bang. It was Melverta coming back from her search. "Didn't find hide nor hair of her, I didn't."

"What 'bout tracks?" Joe asked. "She must have left tracks."

"Didn't pay no attention," Melverta said.

"Ya ain't goin' to find her," Big Bessie smirked. She had begun her morning chores.

"Maybe ya want locked in th' kennel," Joe said to Big Bessie. "Maybe I should just backhand ya, goin' about your business, startin' th' fires in the stoves an' preparin' breakfast with that self-important look on your face. Thinkin' Frank's goin' to see how much he needs ya."

"No ones ever run away when I'm th' one in charge," Big Bessie said with a sneer on her face.

Annabelle sat quietly in a rocking chair, taking all the activity in. *Ya only helpin' me out, Big Bessie, ya goin' too far talkin' to Joe that a way*, Annabelle thought. *Keep makin' Joe mad an' I won't have to worry 'bout ya plaguin' me no more.*

"Give me them boots an' some socks, Melverta. If I wasn't so mad, it'd be funny—Mary Lou tryin' to run away. I don't knowed what she's thinkin' of, she must knowed I can track her. She's goin' to be lost an' confused tryin' to find her way in th' blindin', white snow where after a while ya don't knowed which way to go. She won't be far an', I'm goin' to find her. This time she'll stay in th' kennel until she remembers who's th' boss." After Joe pulled the old, oversized boots on his feet, he slammed out the back door.

Joe didn't see any fresh tracks going down the mountain toward town, but he did see new ones leading into the forest, going across the path that McCallister had made the day he came calling on Dillon. Joe followed the new tracks, grateful that a light skiff of new snow had fallen through the night.

Just as Joe was leaving the cabin to find Mary Lou, two snowmobiles moved swiftly up the road to Winding Ridge. Randy McCoy was in the lead and Bert Howard brought up the rear. They had learned the roads to and from McCallister's cabin, and Cliff had made them a diagram that showed the location of Dillon's place, a rectangular cabin halfway between McCallister's and town. The map Cliff had drawn showed a road that branched off the main trail leading to the back of the cabin. Also off the main trail, a swinging bridge crossed over the creek to the front of the cabin. Dillon's cabin was larger than the others along the way.

McCoy and Howard reached the town and raced down Main Street. After finding the road they wanted, they roared up the mountain. Howard saw the larger cabin come into view. He signaled to Randy, "That's it." Since the only way to get to the front entrance to the house was a swinging bridge, they continued past Dillon's cabin and used a road that veered off to the right. They drove past the tracks Dillon's snowmobile had made as he drove down the mountain after taking Aggie to McCallister. The tracks went from the road behind Dillon's cabin to the right and ran up the mountain.

After passing the swinging bridge, they made the first right and crossed the log-bridge. They maneuvered the snowmobiles quickly toward Dillon's back porch, where the trail dead-ended. There was no one in sight. The only sign of life was the smoke coming from the chimney.

"Did you notice the tracks?" McCoy asked. "They ran down the trail to the left as we were coming up. It looks like a snowmobile left Dillon's cabin, went further up the mountain and back down this trail bypassing the cabin to head for town."

"That's most likely how Dillon got off the mountain," Howard noted. "No surprise there."

"Yes," McCoy said, "or they could be Cliff's tracks from when he was here. It hasn't snowed enough to have covered them."

The women were watching from the window as the men climbed from the snowmobiles and headed for the cabin.

"Wish Joe was here," Annabelle said. "He'd run them men off."

"They're not th' same ones that came to our cabin when they was huntin' Pa," Sara said.

"It's not th' detective that'd come here a couple of days ago either," Annabelle said.

Unafraid, never having gone through the experience that McCallister's women had, Big Bessie opened the door. "What ya wantin' here?"

McCoy and Howard pushed past Big Bessie and walked into the cabin.

"We're taking you in for questioning," McCoy said.

"Who?" Annabelle asked alarmed.

"All of you." McCoy answered.

"Ya mean to th' big city?" Annabelle asked, hoping that was not what the detective meant.

"I'm afraid so," Randy said. "It's necessary, or we wouldn't trouble you with going."

"Why, we can't go to th' city," Big Bessie said. "We have no call to go anywhere. We have to be here when Frank comes home. I'm not goin' anywhere with th' likes of ya."

"Where's the boy?" Randy McCoy asked.

"What ya wantin' my boy for?" Annabelle asked more alarmed than ever. "He ain't done anythin'. He ain't been nowhere but on this mountain his entire life." Annabelle was not aware of Joe's affiliation with the militia and the assignments they occasionally gave him. The women had no idea that Joe had taken possession of the truck that McCallister had abandoned—upon Aggie's advice—when he walked off the mountain eight months ago.

"Don't worry. The boy is not accused of anything," Randy said. "Like we told you, we want all of you for questioning. If the boy hasn't gone away, get him and the others together."

"What others?" Big Bessie asked.

"There's one called Aggie and besides Joe there should be another female and three babies."

"How ya knowed so much?" Annabelle asked.

"You must remember that Detective Cliff Moran was here a short time ago," Randy said. "He counted the women and children, and there are two women missing."

"Ain't goin'," Big Bessie said.

"I for one would love to go to th' big city," Daisy said.

"Ya shut ya mouth," Big Bessie said. "All of us're stayin' here just like Frank wants. Ya men can go back to where ya come from."

"Sorry, we have a warrant. You have no choice," Howard said, holding out the papers.

"Ya knowed we can't read," Annabelle said. "Anyway Joe's not here an' we can't go anywhere without him."

"If I was you," Big Bessie warned the men, "I'd get out'a here 'fore he gets back. I wouldn't want to see any shootin'."

"Are you saying that Joe's armed?" Randy asked.

"Don't knowed what y'all're talkin' about, but if I was you I wouldn't want to tangle with th' likes of him."

Annabelle knew that Big Bessie was trying to scare the men off, but did not like her putting her son in a bad light. Before Annabelle could say anything in Joe's defense, she heard him clomping across the back porch heading for the door.

Please don't let Joe have his huntin' rifle with him, Annabelle prayed, knowing he took it with him even when he was not on a hunting jaunt. Joe never went far from the cabin without his rifle. There was always the chance of running across game, and they were always in need of food. *Don't want no fightin' or killin'.* She steeled herself for trouble as the door opened.

Cliff and Hal waited outside his office to speak to Ronald Mascara, the prosecuting attorney. "He'll see you now," the secretary said, nodding toward the door to Mascara's office.

The detectives entered Mascara's office. "Have a seat," Mascara offered. "What's up?"

"We arrested a man yesterday who we're certain is involved in selling his own children," Hal said. "We want to keep him in jail. He's from the remote mountain wilderness and has had the cunning to hide from us for years. We have good reason to believe that he'll run."

"Do you have enough evidence to indict him, other than what you believe?" the prosecutor asked as he made notes. "You know as well as I do that we can't hold him without hard evidence."

"We have a boy who was sold as an infant and believed to be the man's son. We're having DNA tests done on the boy," Cliff explained. "We need a court order allowing us to get DNA samples from Dillon. We need it fast. We're bringing in three infants and the women he keeps as his wives for questioning. Our men are picking them up today."

"Another thing," Hal said, "there was eighty thousand dollars in cash lying on his table when we arrested him. Looks like he was also packing to run. The man has no known employment to account for that great amount of money."

"He could have inherited the money," Mascara offered.

"In a cat's ass," Cliff said. "It also could be a pay-off for his children.

"I know that we're right on this, Ron," Cliff continued. "We can prove it, too. But if he's let out of jail we'll never find him. Remember Jacob McCallister. He has evaded capture for months now, and he's on the run again after abducting the very same females he had held hostage on the mountain in a miserable cellar house last year.

"I'm on to this case because I have a gut feeling it'll lead me to Tuesday and Patty," Cliff went on. "I made a promise to keep them safe, and I intend to do just that."

"Let's not make the same mistake this time," Hal said. "We'll take this one before the Grand Jury and indict him. His women will be all the testimony we need."

"We should've brought McCallister's women in last year," Cliff said. "We may have learned something that would have been useful in protecting Tuesday from McCallister. This time the expense can be no deterrent. We're onto something big. Seems like the further we dig, the more illegal child trafficking we uncover."

"I'll see what I can do," Mascara agreed. "I'll set the ball in motion and speed things up as fast as I can."

Cliff and Hal left Mascara and went directly to Cliff's office.

"We need to contact a social worker to take care of the women's needs," Hal said.

"I had one in mind," Cliff said.

"Melinda Scott?" Hal guessed.

"Yes, I believe she is best for the job. I'd like to talk to her and fill her in on the women and how they live."

"That's an excellent idea," Hal said. "As far as we know, the women have never been away from the mountain and are going to be ill equipped to handle being in the city."

"I'd be surprised if they knew what a phone was," Cliff said as he picked up the phone.

"Melinda, can you come to my office?" Cliff asked. "We have a situation and need your help."

"You're in luck," Melinda said. "Today I handed over a double case load to two new social workers. Except for needing a little supervision from time to time, they're doing great. I'll be right there."

Half an hour later, Melinda knocked on Cliff's office door.

"Glad you could come right over," Hal said as he shook her hand. She was as tall as Hal, who was of average height for a man. Big boned, she was attractive in an unusual way, but her features were too large for her to be considered pretty.

"What's up?" Melinda asked. "It sounded important."

"We have a situation," Hal answered. "Randy McCoy and Bert Howard are on their way here with women and children who have never been to the city. They were raised in a remote mountain area. They've lived with no electric, no plumbing, no heat except for woodburning stoves, and no phone service."

"You want me to play mother hen to them," Melinda laughed.

"I guess you could say that," Cliff grinned.

"How many are there?"

"We're not sure," Cliff said. "There may be eight or more women, one young man, and three infants."

"Sounds interesting," Melinda said. "What do you want me to do?"

"After we question them," Hal said, "we need you to set them up in a hotel. I'm sure they'll need instruction and guidance in the niceties of hotel living."

"Like helping them order from room service?"

"Among other things," Cliff answered. "You'll have to remember that what we take for granted, they don't have a clue about."

"That's for sure," Hal threw up his hands. "They won't be in the hotel forever. With Dillon on his way to the pen, they'll need direction in living in the modern world, period."

"You'll need to arrange for them to stay in a home for abused women as soon as possible," Cliff said. "They need counseling in abuse."

"It's going to be tough," Hal said. "They don't even know that they were being abused."

"Sounds like this is going to be a challenge," Melinda said. "Not to mention very interesting. Getting someone into a shelter for abused women takes time. They're all full and there's always a waiting list. Getting that many women placed will be tough and time consuming."

"They can stay in the hotel as long as needed," Hal said.

"In the meantime, we can question them together and separately," Cliff said. "It's crucial that we get as much information as possible. Now that we know that Dillon and McCallister are in the same business, I have every expectation that the women may know something that can lead us to McCallister's whereabouts."

"You're right, Cliff," Hal said, "and wherever he's taken Tuesday and Patty, he has selling Tuesday's child in mind. So if we can find out about Dillon's activities, it may very well lead us to McCallister."

"Can you clear your schedule, Melinda?" Cliff asked. "I'm afraid that this case is going to eat into your time."

"It could be a problem," Melinda said. "But after all, there are two new workers in the office, and this assignment sounds like one I would enjoy for a change. Yes, I'll make time. I'm eager to get started."

Visitors were becoming a sign of bad trouble, and Joe had seen the snowmobiles as he came in sight of the cabin. "Damn, I don't have my gun with me," he mumbled. "Hope there's one of Frank's in th' barn."

Joe searched the barn and found no weapon of any kind. Having no choice, he boldly walked to the back door, ready to fight if necessary.

"What ya doin' in my place?" Joe asked. "Ya don't have no call to be here botherin' my women."

"Good day, Joe," Randy McCoy said. "Seems like you crop up every time we have to come to the mountain to investigate child abuse. You living here now?"

"What's it to ya?" Joe asked.

"You know that selling children is a crime," Bert Howard said. "If nothing else, you saw what happened to your father."

"What ya wantin' here?" Joe demanded. "We're mindin' our own business an' I ain't sellin' children."

"We have reason to believe that Frank Dillon is, and we have come to take you all in for questioning."

"I'm not goin' anywhere an' ya aren't takin' th women anywhere, either," Joe said.

"You have no choice," McCoy said. "We have a subpoena from the court to bring you all in."

"I don't knowed what that is," Joe said.

While Randy had talked to the others, Howard had gone through the cabin and loft looking for guns. He found three rifles under the four-poster bed and took them to the snowmobile in case Joe got any ideas about using one to prevent the detectives from taking the group in.

"If we go, are ya goin' to bring us back?" Annabelle asked.

"Of course, we have to bring you back," McCoy answered. "Unless you decide that you want to stay in the city."

"I've a mind to go," Big Bessie said. "Since it seems we have no choice, it might be fun to see th' city. That is if ya goin' to take care of us like Frank does. We expect to have a place to sleep an' food."

"We'll take proper care of you," Howard said. "You don't have to worry about that."

"I'm so wantin' to go to th' city," Daisy said. "Can we go today?"

"Gather what you think you'll need," Randy said.

The others, resigned to having to take the trip, scurried around gathering a change of clothes and rolling their stashes in their mats and quilt, while Daisy spent her time combing her hair.

"Please," Randy said, "you don't need to take any bedding. All that will be provided."

"What if there ain't enough for all of us?" Annabelle asked.

"There will be. Don't worry about that," Howard said.

From the time Joe had come into the cabin refusing to cooperate, he had sat at the table not saying anything more.

"Joe, get your things together," Randy McCoy said.

"Mary Lou took my spare change of clothes an' ya took th' guns. I don't have nothin' else to get together."

"Who is Mary Lou?" Howard asked.

"She's one of Frank's women an' she ran away day before yesterday. When I came in an' found ya here, I was comin' back from lookin' for her. I've been tryin' to find her since she ran cause she'll surely freeze to death. There's not much chance she's going' to find shelter. She doesn't know her way around th' mountain. An' in this weather ya could go around in circles an' not knowed it."

"She'll be back when she finds she has no better place to go," Big Bessie said. "There's food enough for her an' wood to build a warming fire."

"Why'd she run?" McCoy asked.

"How'd I knowed?" Joe said.

"What'd you do to her?" Randy asked.

"I ain't done nothin' to her," Joe said. "She's just a hard-headed female who don't knowed her place."

"Boy, do you have a lot to learn," Bert Howard said.

Mary Lou walked blindly. Joe had come within fifty yards of her as he called her name, but the gusting wind had carried his voice away long before it could reach her ears.

She had passed her destination of McCallister's cabin shortly after Joe had missed spotting her in the cover of blowing snow. Everywhere she looked was the purest white. The brightness was blinding her. Mary Lou was hopelessly lost. And she was cold, tired, and hungry. Eight hours had passed since she'd left the cabin and safety. She found a cave to take a rest from the biting wind, and she finished the last of her biscuits. Not wanting to waste the little daylight remaining, she left the cave and started walking once again.

"I wish Joe'd find me," Mary Lou shouted aloud, stumbling along in the too-quiet expanse of frozen land. "I don't knowed where I am. I'm hungry an' I ain't seen another cabin since I left Frank's." She sat down in the snow, a lonely lost figure; her need for revenge was long gone. To her right, the face of the mountain rose majestically, towering into the sky. To her left, the mountain gently sloped down and in places dropped sharply to yet another plateau.

Mary Lou cupped her hands around her face, shielding her eyes from the sun. She looked for a cave or a cabin. Seeing nothing but the blinding whiteness of the snow, She gave up hope of finding a shelter. She dug a hole in a snow bank where she could rest concealed from the wind. Soon she was asleep.

Only twenty minutes away from Ruble's cabin, Tuesday still had hopes of finding the way into Centerpoint without mishap.

Having no idea when to expect McCallister to return, she, Paul Frank, and Patty were following a walking trail to avoid the road that led from Center-point up to Broad Run. Paul Frank had grown to know a number of paths as he traveled over the mountain, going hunting, fishing, or shopping for food. He was accustomed to being out in harsh weather. He knew, almost without thinking, which direction to go.

As they followed Paul Frank, Tuesday could not push away the memory of the time she and Patty had attempted unsuccessfully to make their way to Winding Ridge after escaping from McCallister's cabin. One big difference this time was that Jacob was not one step behind, hunting them down like dogs. Instead, he was on his way to sell Winter Ann.

Tuesday was numb. Her dear friend, Cora, had gone through the same horror over two years before, and with the help of Cliff Moran, had found her daughter again. *And so will I,* Tuesday thought. *There is no time to cry, no time for weakness, and no time for me to feel sorry for myself. I know I have to be strong if I ever hope to see my daughter again.* It was all Tuesday could do to keep herself from panicking.

"Wait," Paul Frank commanded. "Look. Do ya see somethin'?"

"What, Paul Frank?" Tuesday asked alarmed. "What do you see?"

"I don't knowed. Looks like someone lyin' in that snow bank."

They walked closer, not sure whether what they saw was an animal or a person. Patty was the first to get close enough to see. "It's a girl. She's sleepin'," Patty called back to Tuesday and Paul Frank.

Tuesday watched Patty go to the girl, who awoke at the sound of their voices. Patty placed a hand on her shoulder. "Get up," Patty whispered. "Ya goin' to freeze layin' here in th' snow."

"Who're you?" Mary Lou asked.

"We're mountain folk, except for Tuesday here," Patty explained. "She's a city woman, but she's okay."

"I'm hungry an' so cold," Mary Lou complained. "I haven't had anythin' to eat except biscuits."

Tuesday untied her ragbag from her waist and got a biscuit for the girl. "What's your name?" Tuesday asked as she handed her the biscuit.

"My name's Mary Lou. I'm one of Frank Dillon's wives. I've run away. Frank's taken Jacob McCallister's women and children in with us an' Joe locked me in a cage, and when he let me out, I took his clothes an' ran. I'm tryin' to find Jeb and Aggie. I'm wantin' to stay with them."

"Who's Frank Dillon?" Tuesday asked.

"He lives on th' Windin' Ridge side of th' mountain," Paul Frank answered. "I think he lives in a cabin below Jeb. Th' militia's tryin' to get me, McCallister, and Dillon to join them, but none of us never wanted in."

"I've wondered how Jacob's women were," Tuesday said. "Are they alright?"

"Yeah, but they can't get along with Big Bessie," Mary Lou said. "Everybody wants to be boss."

Tuesday said sorrowfully, "I bet they can't," she said. She remembered all too well how Annabelle gloried in taking charge when Jacob was away from the cabin.

Tuesday sat in the snow beside Mary Lou. "We're going back to the city. You can go with us. You wouldn't like it any better living with Jacob than you did living with Frank."

"I've always wanted to go to th' city," Mary Lou sobbed. "I can't believe it. I get myself in th' worst trouble of my life and it turns out to be my dream come true."

"You can stay with me and go to school until we find you a home," Tuesday said to comfort the girl.

"I always wanted to go to th' city, but I never thought it'd really happen."

"Mary Lou, why did you run in the worst blizzard in years?" Tuesday asked. "Why not wait until good weather?"

"Couldn't take it anymore since Jeb's family came to live with us. Joe's so mean. He locked me up in a cage cause I didn't do what he wanted."

"I don't understand that," Patty said, looking much younger than she was, standing there holding her doll. "Joe's never been mean to me or Sara."

"How come ya ran away from 'im then?" Mary Lou asked.

"I didn't run away from Joe. I ran away from my pa an' my life on th' mountain. I always wanted to go to th' city an' live." Patty shifted her doll to her other arm.

"That sounds like a smart girl, wantin' to be in th' city an' have a life, but if you're so smart, what ya doin' with a doll an' actin' like a baby?" Mary Lou asked. "It's hard enough getting' around with two hands to help in climbin' cross some of th' gullies."

"It ain't none of your business if I have a doll," Patty said unashamed. "She's my friend, an' ya can't understand 'bout us, so ya don't need to make fun of me."

"I'm sorry. I didn't mean to make fun of ya," Mary Lou apologized. "Ya just seem too old to be carryin' a doll around."

Patty turned around and started walking again.

"It's not unusual in her case," Tuesday explained. "We'll tell you about it sometime. "It's okay, Patty. Wait for us."

Mary Lou finished her biscuit and stood on wobbly legs. "Okay, I'm ready. Let's go to th' city. An', Patty, I'm sorry, I didn't mean anythin'," she called to Patty's retreating back.

"I'm pretty sure we're close to Centerpoint now," Paul Frank announced.

"Wait, Paul Frank. You mentioned the militia. Do they pose a danger for us?"

"Yeah, they could, but they're tryin' to get me to join, so I don't think they're goin' to bother ya," Paul Frank said. "At this point they're tryin' to get on my good side."

"Why is that?" Tuesday asked with raised eyebrows, wondering if there was something she should know about Paul Frank.

Paul Frank saw the inquisitive look and grinned. "Don't worry, it's not my criminal mind that they want. It's my farm."

30

*M*ARTY TOWNSEND PICKED UP HIS PHONE TO CHECK his private voice mail before joining his wife for breakfast. He had not heard from Frank Dillon since they had met in the bar two weeks before. Dillon had said there was a baby due anytime.

Marty's wife, Alice, called him to breakfast. "I'm coming. I'll be right down," Marty yelled with his hand cupped over the mouthpiece of the phone, although there was no one on the other end to hear him. There were no messages on his voice mail.

By the time Marty had finished his phone call, Alice was at the table drinking her morning coffee and reading the paper.

"Good morning, dear," she greeted him as he hurried down the stairs, a frown wrinkling his forehead.

"Did you have a good night?" Marty asked, taking a seat.

"I slept very well, thank you." She did not look up when he spoke to her. She was engrossed in what she was reading.

"What's so interesting in the paper?" Marty asked.

"A bizarre story of a man in Wheeling who's been arrested for selling his own children," Alice said. "Can you imagine someone selling his own children?"

"Let me see the paper," Marty said nervously. "I'm in a hurry this morning. Do you mind?"

She handed him the paper. "I'll get your breakfast. I guess I can relax with the paper after you leave for the office."

As Marty read, his face flushed and sweat broke out on his forehead. The story was of Dillon's arrest. The police had discovered that a boy who had been sold on the black market was believed to be Dillon's son. Also, they were investigating the fact that Dillon may have had several wives. It was believed that the women were kept in his mountain cabin located in the wilderness.

Marty went to the phone and dialed a number. "Hi, Fred. Marty here. I need a favor." Fred Lawson was Marty's attorney. "I just read a story in the paper this morning about a man who sells his children." Marty kept his voice down so Alice couldn't hear his conversation. "I want you to see if you can find out what's going on. I had some dealings with the man on another matter," Marty lied. "After reading the story, I have no doubt that the man's in deep trouble. From what I know about him, the story was right on the money. My problem is if the man's desperate for financial help, he may threaten to implicate me as blackmail to get that help."

"Marty, is there more to this than you're telling me?" Fred asked.

"You know better than to ask me that," Marty said. "I always tell you what you need to know. Just do as I ask and nothing more. That's what I pay you big bucks for.

"I need you to take care of the matter. Whatever it takes," Marty continued. "I can't talk to Dillon. I'd be putting myself in the position of having to explain my connection with him. That's not acceptable. I simply can't stay out of it and hope for the best. If I don't act, I'm afraid he'll try to blackmail me for help. I feel it would be much better if you contacted him than for him to contact me."

"You're right about that. If he goes looking for you, he'll leave a trail straight to you. Being in jail doesn't allow a man any privacy. Let me look into it and I'll get back to you," Fred said. "Although, I hope you're not asking for trouble. I would advise you to stay out of it unless you're positive that he'll try to get in touch with you."

"I told you. I have no choice," Marty said. "I'm not taking a chance. Clean it up!"

"Okay, Marty. I'll do what you want. I'll hire him a lawyer if he doesn't have one. We can't have him connected with me since I'm your personal attorney. I'll pay the one I hire and you can reimburse me. That way there's no connection to you."

"Even if he has an attorney maybe you should get one to take over so we'll know what's going down."

"I'll take care of it, Marty," Fred said. "Don't worry, it'll be on the QT."

"See that you make it your top priority," Marty said. "The thing is to keep my name out of it. And, Fred, keep me posted."

"What was that all about?" Alice asked when Marty came back into the room. "You sounded stressed.

"Nothing," Marty answered. "Just a business matter."

After he finished his breakfast, Marty left for the office. He was anxious to call Marcie. Under no circumstances did he ever take the risk of calling her from home.

The attorney who was hired by Simon Leonard was escorted to Dillon's cell for the second time in as many days. "Okay, Dillon, let's get down to brass tacks," James Maxwell said. "Sit down and quit pacing. I can't think if you're going to walk back and forth passing me every few seconds."

"I'm going to go crazy if I don't get out of this place soon," Dillon said.

"Please, sit down," Maxwell said.

"Okay, I'm sitting. What do you want to know?"

"Your hearing will be sooner than I had expected. We need more time, but we're not going to get it. The prosecuting attorney wants your ass. I would like to postpone the indictment, but apparently the prosecutor thinks he has enough evidence to indict you. I'm going to tell you what I know they have on you, and I want you to tell me that it's not true and why. Can you handle that?"

"Ask away," Frank said with confidence.

"How many wives do you have?"

"None," Frank answered. "Why'd you ask me a question like that? Who the hell you been talking to?"

"Why do you suppose that the prosecutor thinks you have several wives?"

"How the hell would I know what the prosecutor thinks. I've never been married." It was true that Frank had never been formally married.

"Where do you live?" James asked.

"You know where I live. You said we didn't have much time, so why are you asking questions that you know the answers to?"

"Look, Dillon, I know that you have a cabin in the mountains. I know that you're not telling me the truth. I told you that I can't help you if you don't tell me the truth. Now, for the last time, tell the truth!"

"Okay, Maxwell, so I haven't been telling you straight. The truth is so close to what they think that I've been afraid that the telling would implicate me. The prosecutor will try to twist it to conform to his own game plan. So you had better listen close."

In desperation, Frank began telling James Maxwell the tallest tale that he'd ever told.

Main Street came into view. "We've made it," Tuesday said. "We're almost there."

"Yeah, that's it," Paul Frank said. "Centerpoint."

As they walked along the street, a truck pulled up beside them. Tuesday's heart went to her throat when the dirty black truck stopped.

"You're a pretty one," the boy called out his window to Tuesday.

She was relieved to see that it was not Jacob, but the relief was short lived. The driver looked every bit as menacing as Jacob, and fear once again settled in her stomach.

"Ya get outta here an' leave us alone," Patty screamed.

Ignoring Patty, the boy continued to leer at Tuesday. He whistled a wolf whistle and banged on the side of his truck with a balled up fist.

"You're mighty brave sittin' in your truck makin' rude noises, Walt. I want ya to get out of here," Paul Frank said and kicked the truck. "We don't want to be bothered by the likes of you."

A mean, angry look replaced the leer on Walt's face. "Us town boys have a hard time toleratin' our possessions bein' trashed by mountain riffraff,"

Walt sneered. He opened the door to get out. "I'm goin' to kick some respect into ya, Paul Frank," Walt said.

Paul Frank took a chance that Walt had heard of Jacob McCallister from his moonshine days and warned, "She's McCallister's woman. Ya knowed he's goin' to kill ya if ya bother her. I'm takin' care of her, to get to th' grocery store."

Walt had heard of McCallister and like anybody else was not willing to get into a position to tangle with the notorious man, but after all, rumor had it that McCallister was gone from the mountain for good and temptation was too great. Walt stepped out of the truck and walked toward Tuesday. "Like I said, you're a pretty one." Walt reached out to touch Tuesday's silky blond hair.

Without warning and to Tuesday's horror, Paul Frank stepped forward and threw a powerful left jab into Walt's stomach, leaving him breathless. Before Walt could recover, Paul Frank landed a powerful punch into Walt's face. Walt staggered backward, then caught his balance. He immediately lunged at Paul Frank and landed a blow sharply to his jaw. Paul Frank stumbled backward, and Tuesday caught his arm and broke his fall. Regaining his balance, he shoved her safely out of the way. Then quickly he lunged forward. With his left arm he grabbed Walt around the neck, getting him in a hammerlock and putting painful pressure on his neck and arm. "Ya think ya can tangle with me? You're wrong! I'm responsible for these women an' you're dead meat if you think you're goin' to get away with anythin' with them. Say you'll get out'a here an' I'll let ya go." Paul Frank jerked Walt's arm for emphasis.

"I'm gone," Walt said, his face turning bright red in embarrassment.

Paul Frank released Walt with a shove. Scrambling to get his footing, Walt ran back to his truck and jumped in. With tires spinning in the melting snow, the truck swerved from side to side as it was driven away, splattering slush over the cars parked at the side of the street.

"Thank you, Paul Frank. I don't know what we would've done if not for you. I feel bad jeopardizing your life, but we must find my daughter. Anyway, this could be a new beginning for you. I promise I'll help you start your new life and later to send for your sisters."

"It's nothin'. We need to find Winter Ann. Besides, I don't want nothin' to happen to ya, an' Patty, an' Mary Lou."

When the fight began, Patty had backed out of the way holding tight to her doll. "He's so strong an' handsome, Summer. He fought Walt an' wasn't afraid. Th' more I get to knowed him, th' more I like him. When he first come to Aggie's cabin with Pa, I thought he was mean just like Pa, ya knowed like Joe was gettin' to be—wantin' to be like Pa. It's goin' to be so good to have Paul Frank in th' city with us. We can go to school together an' I can have a real friend, besides ya of course."

After Walt was gone, Tuesday turned to Paul Frank. "What do we do now? It looks as if the town people are not so friendly."

"We don't need th' town people. There's a bus to someplace—I don't knowed where, but if ya have th' money we can get away from here."

"Great," Tuesday said. "Let's go to the bus depot then, and find out the bus schedule."

"Come on an' follow me," Paul Frank offered and started walking down the street.

As they headed toward the bus station, Patty made sure she walked alongside Paul Frank.

They discovered that there was a bus going out at 5:00 P.M. that would get them to Wheeling at 10:30 P.M. They had five hours to wait and were hungry. Tuesday suddenly realized that she had no money with her.

Tuesday found a payphone beside the ladies room. "What ya doin', Tuesday?" Paul Frank asked.

"I'm calling Cliff. He'll wire money for our food and bus tickets, or come for us. He's the man who rescued Patty and me when Jacob had us held captive. He knows how to get here."

Tuesday had Cliff's private number and crossed her fingers that he was in and would answer the phone himself. *Please be there, Cliff. There's no time to waste*, Tuesday thought while the phone rang.

"Sergeant Cliff Moran here," Cliff's voice answered.

"I have a collect call from Tuesday Summers. Will you accept the charges?" the operator inquired of Cliff. Relief, fear—not knowing made him light-headed.

"Yes, of course, I'll accept the charges," Cliff shouted into the phone.

"Go ahead, please."

"Tuesday, please tell me you're okay."

She could not believe her luck; he was in his office. "Physically, yes."

"Where are you? What do you mean?" He could not believe that he was actually hearing Tuesday's voice.

"We're okay," Tuesday could scarcely keep the sob out of her voice. "Jacob broke into my house and brought us back to the mountain. I should have paid more attention to Patty's dreams. We knew that they always came true. It happened too many times to ignore. Now it's too late."

"I was right. I knew it was McCallister. But I don't understand—I was at McCallister and Aggie's cabins four days ago and they were abandoned. And what do you mean it's too late?"

"He took the baby," Tuesday sobbed and realized that he said he'd been to the cabin. "You were at the cabin four days ago?"

"Yes. What about the baby?"

"Oh, no! You would have just missed us," Tuesday cried, knowing that had Cliff arrived earlier or they had left later she would not have suffered the loss of her daughter. *I must pull myself together or he can't help me.* Tuesday gathered all the self-control she could muster from her very soul. "I think it was four days ago that he took us by sled to a cabin across the mountain ridge," Tuesday explained. "As we left Aggie's, I thought I heard the whine of an engine coming up the mountain. Now I think it was you, but I'll tell you all about that later. Jacob left the mountain yesterday with my baby. He intends to sell her. I've managed to get to the bus depot in Centerpoint with Patty, Mary Lou, and Paul Frank, who lived in the cabin that Jacob took us to. I have no money with me, nor my credit cards. I have no idea what that bastard did with my purse. We're hungry, too."

"How long is it before the bus leaves there?" Cliff asked.

"Five hours, and it will arrive in Wheeling at 10:30 P.M. They say most of the roads are passable now."

"That would be eleven and half hours without food when you're already hungry; otherwise I'd get tickets with my credit card. I'll come for you; I'll bring food. Centerpoint is half an hour closer than Winding Ridge. I can get to you in four hours and have you home by eight o'clock. Do you have a safe place to wait?"

"Just a minute." Tuesday turned to Paul Frank. "Is there a safe place for us to wait? He can be here in four or five hours."

"I guess th' bus depot's th' safest place to wait, if Jacob don't come an' start lookin' for us."

Tuesday relayed this to Cliff.

"McCallister could come back. We don't know where he took the baby. Don't take the chance. The bus depot would be the first place he'd look when he discovers you're gone. Ask Paul Frank if there's anywhere else to stay," Cliff said.

She turned to Paul Frank again, "He doesn't think it would be safe to stay here. Is there somewhere else we can go?"

"Yeah, we can go to old man Clouser's," Paul Frank answered. "I used to go to his house and play kick th' can with his boys, Orly an' Orne an' Everett. They live in th' first house comin' up th' mountain road to Centerpoint after leaving Route Seven."

"Cliff, he said we can wait at the house that sits on the road as you come up to Centerpoint after leaving Route Seven. It's the first one you'll come to. The man's last name is Clouser."

"Hurry and go there now. Don't take any chances. Jacob could come back at any time. If you can get there without walking the road, do it. I'll be there as soon as possible. I'll pick up some sandwiches."

"Hurry! And, Cliff, be careful Jacob's carrying a gun. I must get my baby. It's all that matters right now."

"We'll get the baby, but you must be strong and stay clear-headed. Get to the Clouser home as quickly as possible," Cliff pleaded. "Wait, if by some chance you can't stay in Clouser's house go back to where you're calling from and call me on my cell phone so I'll know where you are. My cell phone will be in range for at least the next two or three hours. Once I get near the mountain range, there are no towers. I won't have service."

"Hurry!" Tuesday pleaded.

"Patty, who's Tuesday talkin' to on that thing?" Mary Lou asked.

"It's a phone," Patty said. "I never saw one till I went to live with Tuesday either. Ya can talk to anyone that has a phone too. An' in th' city everyone has a phone."

"I can't imagine."

"Just wait till ya an' Paul Frank get to th' city," Patty said, smiling from ear to ear. "There's so much to see ya won't believe your eyes. I'm goin' to show ya everythin'."

Paul Frank listened to the girls talk as they lagged behind. The trip would be exciting if Tuesday's fear did not hang over them like an evil cloud. "Come on, girls. We have to remember th' most important thin' is to find the baby."

"I knowed," Patty said. "Cliff'll find her. I knowed he will." The fact that Patty had not revealed a dream in which Winter Ann was found remained unspoken.

31

A T THE SAME TIME THAT CLIFF TOOK THE URGENT call from Centerpoint and rushed from his office, unwilling to take precious time to let someone know where he was going, Hal got a call from Randy McCoy. He was at home for lunch indulging himself in extra time with the twins and his wife.

"Hal, its Randy McCoy. Howard and I are at the station with Dillon's women and children. What do you want us to do now?"

"How many are there?" Hal asked.

"You're not going to believe this, but there are eight women, one boy, and three infants."

"Call Cliff and have him meet me in the office as soon as he can," Hal instructed. "Tell him that I'm on my way."

"Sure thing, I'll take care of it now. We'll stay with Dillon's women until one of you gets here."

"Thanks, Randy. You and your men have done a great job."

Hal hung up the phone with triumph. He kissed his wife and foster children and rushed back to his office, excited about having Dillon's own women to implicate the man.

McCoy arranged for folding chairs to be brought to Hal's office. Next, he tried to find Cliff, who had left after receiving the call from Tuesday without taking time to let anyone know where he could be reached. Finally, after getting no answer in Cliff's office and finding no one who knew where to reach him, Randy reached Cliff on his cell phone.

Hal walked in just behind the men with the folding chairs. Randy was waiting to tell Hal the good news. "Hal, Cliff got a call from Tuesday. She and Patty are safe. He doesn't know much yet, but McCallister is the one who abducted them. Apparently she and Patty were able to escape from him."

"That's great!" Hal said.

"Not totally. McCallister has Tuesday's baby," McCoy said. "Cliff didn't know anything else. He'll call us when he does. He wants us to be on alert to go after McCallister as soon as he gets to Tuesday and learns what happened."

"What time did he leave?" Hal asked.

"About an hour ago," Randy answered.

"Get Bert Howard to gather the men we used last year and have them wait for word from Cliff," Hal said. "Time is going to be essential, and those men already have an understanding of the way McCallister is and how he might think."

They were interrupted by the arrival of McCallister's and Dillon's families. Hal recognized Joe, Annabelle, Sara, and Daisy from McCallister's cabin the previous winter.

"How in the devil did you get them all here?" Hal asked.

"We had to take them off the mountain on the snowmobiles, each of us taking one at a time to wait at Higgins' Garage, where we rented a station wagon. With the Bronco we had used to get the snowmobiles to Centerpoint in the first place, we loaded everybody up, and here we are."

A court recorder was present to take the deposition.

Hal sat at his desk hardly knowing where to start. "Dillon's in jail. Do any of you know where jail is?"

"That's where ya want to send my pa," Joe answered.

"I don't knowed what jail is," Big Bessie said.

"It's where people go when they don't obey the law," Hal explained. "In jail, you would lose your freedom to come and go as you please."

They were not paying much attention to what was being said. The women gawked—their huge eyes taking in everything. They had never been in a place like this building. And in contrast to the surroundings, they looked as if they had been zapped there from a forgotten time.

"Dillon broke the law when he sold your children."

All Hal got when he paused for comments were blank looks. "It would be easier if you'd tell me your names. Will each of you tell me your name, so I can ask you individual questions?"

Hal started from the right side of the room with the women. As he nodded to each one she cooperated and gave her name. As each spoke her name, Hal matched it and the face in his mind. When he finished with the women, he nodded toward Joe.

"My name's Joe McCallister an' I don't want to be here. I have nothin' to say to th' likes of ya."

"That's too bad," Randy McCoy said. "You could be locked up if you refuse to cooperate."

At McCoy's remark, Annabelle gave up trying to take in her strange surroundings and got ready to fight on her son's behalf. "Ya don't have to threaten

Joe. We'll tell ya what ya want." Annabelle gave Joe a stern look. "Joe, I knowed ya don't think ya have to listen to a woman, but I'm your ma an' I'm goin' to tell ya what to do anyway. Answer th' questions. If ya don't, we're never goin' to get back home."

"All right," Joe said. "I'll answer th' questions. What do ya want to knowed?"

"First, where is the woman who was sickly?" Hal asked.

"She's dead," Joe said. "She fell comin' down th' mountain to Frank's cabin. After she fell, she got sick and died."

"Bessie, how long have you been Frank Dillon's wife?" Hal asked.

Big Bessie would never do anything to get Frank in trouble, but she did not know that her answers to the questions would do harm. She answered with pride, "Don't keep track of time, but I've had seven of his youngins. Been with 'im since I was just a girl."

"Where are your children now, Bessie?" Hal asked.

"Don't knowed where they are," Big Bessie answered. "Ya have to ask Frank that question."

"Bessie, did your husband sell your children?" Hal asked.

"Yeah."

"Melverta, has Frank Dillon sold any of your children?" Hal asked.

"Yeah, he did," Melverta answered and stared out the huge window. The lights outside mesmerized her.

"How many of your children has he sold, Melverta?" Hal asked.

"Jus' four. Th' others died as soon as they was born," Melverta answered.

"Eva Belle, how many of your children has he sold?" Hal asked.

"Sold two of my children," Eva Belle answered. "Two was all I ever had."

Sally Ann and Emma Jean had not borne children yet, but verified that Frank had sold the children born to Frank's women.

"Joe, what have you got to say? Why are you, Sara, Annabelle, and Daisy living in Frank Dillon's cabin?" Hal asked.

"Frank would've killed Joe if ya hadn't taken us from Frank's cabin today," Sara butted in without being asked. "He was bound to kill 'im for allowin' Mary Lou to run away."

"Shut up, Sara," Joe said. "I can answer th' questions."

"Well, Joe, why were you and the others there?" Hal asked again.

"Pa told Frank to take us in an' he did. He needed me to keep control of th' women when he wasn't there. Frank don't like to stay in th' cabin all th' time, so he needs me to be there. Ya knowed a woman needs a man to take care of her. Ain't nothin' wrong with that."

"Boy, you're in for a rude awakening," Howard laughed. "In my experience it's best to let a woman have her way."

"Okay, Joe," Hal continued. "Do you have an understanding of why your father left the mountain and gave his women to Frank Dillon?"

"Because ya an' th' other ones came to th' mountain. I'm not sure why, except 'cause of him sellin' th' babies an' ya say it's not right. Ya were goin' to put him in jail. Ya goin' to put us in jail?"

"We'll see. The women haven't done anything wrong. For you it may be as simple as counseling. The main thing is we want to stop Dillon and McCallister from selling children. It's against the law. Do you know where your father is now?" Hal asked.

"No, but he was on th' mountain a couple of days ago. I didn't get to talk to 'im. Don't knowed where he went from there." There was no alternative for Joe but to answer the questions flung at him.

"How long ago was he on the mountain?"

"Don't knowed exactly. Three, four, five days maybe." Joe shrugged his shoulders. "Just saw him th' one time."

"By the way, Sara, who's Mary Lou?" Hal asked.

"She's one of Frank's wives. She ran away a couple days ago."

"Where would she go?" Hal asked puzzled. "You've had the worst blizzard in years."

"Don't knowed," Sara said, "but there's no place to run."

"You all look tired, and so are we," Hal said.

"Randy, we'll get something sent in to eat. After that, call Melinda Scott and have her to come in. She can get them settled in a hotel later. They must want to get some rest. I bet they're hungry too."

"Yeah, we're hungry," Big Bessie interrupted. "Ain't had nothin' to eat since th' men came an' took us."

"I have a lot more questions, so after you eat, expect to have another session. McCoy, I bet they would like pizza."

He looked at Howard. "By the way, do you have the men ready to go when we hear from Cliff?"

"They're ready and waiting," Howard said.

Forty minutes later, Joe and each of the women were enjoying the pizza with gusto, a food they had neither eaten nor heard of. They ate until they were stuffed.

Hal picked up the phone to make a call.

"Joe, what's he's doin' puttin' that thing up to his ear?" Annabelle asked. "Don't seem like he's talkin' to us."

"It's a telephone," Joe said. Joe had seen the phone that was at the gas station in Winding Ridge and knew what it was for. It meant nothing to him. He did not have anyone to call, nor did he have the money required for a pay phone.

"Why's he talkin' to it?" Annabelle asked.

"He's not talkin' to th' telephone. He's talkin' to someone who has a telephone too," Joe said.

Smiling at their obvious confusion, Bert explained what was going on.

"Is th' room we're goin' to be stayin' in as good as this one?" Big Bessie asked.

"What do you mean?" Bert Howard asked. "It'll have beds instead of desks and chairs."

"Ya mean everyone's goin' to have a bed?" Sara asked.

"Sure, maybe two of you will have to double up, but no more than two," Hal said. "Joe will get his own room since he's the only male."

"That's good havin' a bed to sleep in, but I meant is it goin' to be warm in th' room we're stayin' in, like this one, even when there's no stove ya have to hunker around?"

"Oh yes, most people don't heat with wood anymore," Bert explained. "They have electric or gas instead of wood for fuel. The lights use electricity," Bert said, pointed to the florescent lights. "Also, there's a furnace that heats the entire building."

"I knowed about some of the light an' heat," Annabelle said. "Before we had to go live in Frank's cabin, we went to town an' to church sometimes. I always noticed it was warm in th' church but I couldn't see no potbelly stove."

"Th' school was like this with th' lights above an' it was warm with no stove or wood box sittin' around," Sara said.

"Frank never wanted us to be mixin' with th'

town folk, he said it'd only cause trouble," Big Bessie said. "An' I can see that he was right. Just look where it got ya." She stared at Annabelle as if her present troubles were Annabelle's doing. "You're th' one's been mixin' with them towns folk, not us."

"Ya don't knowed what you're talkin' about," Annabelle hissed. "Ya silly hillbilly, Jeb and Frank are th' ones what's got us in this mess."

"Okay, ladies, let's not fight. As soon as we take a break, Hal has more questions for you," Bert said.

"I'm powerful tired," Big Bessie said. "I don't never stay up till all hours. It's time for bed."

"I know it's getting late, but we're finding a place for you to stay," Bert said. "As soon as Melinda Scott arrives she'll take you to your rooms. You'll be okay."

"Can we get to the house if we stay off the road?" Tuesday asked Paul Frank. They walked toward the back of the bus depot as they talked.

"We can go down this path an' there's a clearin' that we can cross," Paul Frank answered.

"It's too steep to climb down," Mary Lou complained.

"Ya can climb down," Patty said. "Just hold on to th' limbs that's a growin' out of th' rocks."

"I'll help you," Paul Frank offered. He took Mary Lou's hand and helped her first. "Wait where ya are, Patty an' Tuesday. I'll come back an' help ya down."

Finally, they made their way to the Clouser house and knocked on the door.

The old woman who answered the door looked like Olive Oyl, wearing a faded feedsack dress that hung loosely on her skinny body.

She recognized Paul Frank and let them in. "Who ya got with you?"

"They're my friends. We need a place to stay for a few hours. We ain't had nothin' to eat for two days.

I knowed that ya don't have much, but can ya spare some bread for us?"

"Jus' sit yourself down an' I'll do th' best I can. Ain't never turned away narry a hungry soul. I guess this old woman can fix ya all a bite to eat."

Mary Lou fell to the floor; she had fainted. She was exhausted and chilled to the bone. She had been exposed to the harsh weather much longer than the others had.

While the woman tended to Mary Lou by putting her to bed, covering her with two quilts, spooning a cup of warm soup between her lips, and forcing her to swallow it, the others sat at the large table in the huge, homey kitchen.

Turning her attention to the needs of the others, the woman scurried between the table and stove preparing a meal for them with what she had. The "bite to eat" turned out to be enough food for twice the people sitting at the table. She had taken freshly baked cornbread from the oven, and she served beans with ham and boiled potatoes. After the plainness of the food Aunt Aggie had prepared with the meager ingredients that were available to her, Tuesday could not believe she was being fed a meal like this.

As they ate, Tuesday noted that the old woman wore a look of pride as she sat watching them. It was obvious that she enjoyed cooking for others. They all ate until they thought they would burst.

"It's too bad that Mary Lou missed th' meal," Patty said. "It was one of th' best meals I ever had, Mrs. Clouser."

"I'm glad ya liked it," the old woman said. "An' ya have a mighty fine doll there. Guess I ain't never seen one like that."

"She's my friend," Patty said.

"I want to thank you, too," Tuesday said. "Your hospitality is rare to see these days."

"You're welcome," the woman said. "It ain't often I get to see such a pretty one."

"There's goin' to be someone come for us in 'bout two, three hours," Paul Frank said. "We need to sleep for a couple hours. Ya mind puttin' us up?"

"Ain't no bother," the old woman answered. "The boys and Pa are out huntin' an' won't be back for a while. There's no one to trouble ya a tal'." She showed them to the bedrooms on the second floor.

There were three beds covered with feather ticks; Mary Lou was sleeping in one of them. "Paul Frank, ya can sleep in that one in th' corner, an' Tuesday an' Patty, ya can sleep in th' one next to Mary Lou," the old woman said, remembering everyone's names. "I left a plate of food for th' girl for when she wakes up."

"If nobody's here when ya wake up, just make yourselves at home," she went on. "We're goin' to th' indoor fair at th' community building over at Centerpoint this evenin'. Won't be back til' late."

"Thank ya," Paul Frank said. "We appreciate all ya have done for us."

"Now, don't ya forget to have th' girl to eat. She's already weak and she needs some nourishment."

As the woman left, the three climbed into bed and immediately fell asleep.

A short time later, Tuesday heard the men come in from hunting. The activity woke Paul Frank up, too, although the men soon were quiet when the old woman told them that they had guests who were sleeping. Tuesday noticed that Paul Frank was awake. "Why don't you go see your friends? You said you used to visit them."

"I don't want to wake th' others. They need their sleep; I ain't goin' to disturb them."

A little later, both Tuesday and Paul Frank fell back to sleep, but Paul Frank was awake again long before Cliff had pulled up out front. When he became aware that an automobile had pulled up and heard the sound of an engine idling in front of the cabin, he got out of bed quietly and looked out the window. A Blazer sat near the front door. There was one lone man in the vehicle. Paul Frank waved for him to come in.

"Tuesday, get up. Cliff's here," Paul Frank whispered.

Tuesday sat up and shook Patty and Mary Lou. "It's time to go, girls. Wake up."

Tuesday, with the others following behind, went downstairs and opened the door. Cliff was already out of the Blazer. He rushed to her side. She could not hold back her tears.

"Thank God you're safe," Cliff said. "Don't cry. I promise we'll find the baby."

"She's gone, and I can't bear it." Tuesday sobbed and clung to Cliff, finally breaking down under the fear and stress. "Find her, please."

"We'll find her," Cliff held her close to him. "I won't rest until I do, I promise you. And believe me, Jacob will end up behind bars. He's going to be stopped."

Tuesday wept, her head resting against his shoulder.

Paul Frank helped Mary Lou down the stairs and led her to the kitchen. "Sit down here. Ya need to eat so we can go," Paul Frank said, putting a plate in front of her.

Aggie was traumatized by what had happened. Tuesday, Patty, and Paul Frank were gone. She lived for her nephew, and there was no way of knowing what his reaction to the recent events was going to be. She continued her regular routine of cooking, keeping the fires going, and tending to her cats. She had become friendly with Ida May, Rachel, and Ruby. They were slowly warming up to the sweet-faced, elderly woman. They enjoyed the way she could entertain them with the stories she told, half true and half made up.

Out of Aggie's hearing, they discussed the situation. "I hope Tuesday an' Patty get where they want to go safely," Ruby said.

"I'm afraid for Paul Frank," Rachel said. "Jeb threatened to kill him if he didn't do as Jeb wanted, an' Jeb wanted 'im to keep Tuesday here."

"Jeb'll go after them," Ida May said. "If he finds them, he'll make good his threat."

"That's why I called ya together," Rachel said. "We have to protect Paul Frank. We need to think of somethin' to tell Jacob when he comes back. I'm sure Aggie will go along with it. She's scared he's goin' to be mad at her 'cause they're gone."

"What can we tell 'im, Rachel?" Ruby asked. "Don't knowed how we can pull this off. He's goin' to know Paul Frank went with them no matter what we're goin' to tell 'im."

"We have to try," Rachel said.

"If we make up a story an' he don't believe us, he's goin' to turn his anger on us," Ida May said. "If we get caught makin' stuff up, we're just flirtin' with disaster."

"I agree with Ida May," Ruby said. "All we can do for Paul Frank is pray."

The humming of Jacob's engine could be heard coming closer in the distance. The time to invent a story was suddenly gone. They went downstairs to support Aggie. "Don't be afraid, Aggie, he needs ya more than ya need him," Ruby said.

"I remember when Tuesday ran away from 'im before, so I do," Aggie said, "He was violent with his wrath, so he was." Aggie squared her shoulders and watched out the window, as the black truck rolled through the white snow, growing larger as it neared the cabin.

Jacob was obviously in a good mood as he swung down from the driver's seat of the truck. Reaching into the back, he pulled out two bags filled to the top with food. He headed toward the back door of the cabin, carrying the bags as if they were weightless. Aunt Aggie moved forward and opened the door for him.

"Hi, Aunt Aggie. I'm sure glad to be back. Made more money than I'd hoped. Brought you some snuff."

"Thank ya. I'm down to lickin' my empty can, so I am."

"What's the problem?" Jacob asked. "You look like you're about to jump out of your skin."

"Tuesday an' Patty's run away, so they did. That no-good Paul Frank couldn't stop them, so he's gone with them, so he did."

Jacob slammed the bags he'd been carrying on the table. "I ought to throw you out in the cold," he said. "Can't anyone do anything I ask?"

"How ya expect her to stop anyone from doin' anything?" Rachel asked. "She's just an old woman ya keep around to wait on ya hand an' foot."

"Girl, if you know what's good for you, you'll keep your mouth shut. If I want your advice, I'll ask for it." He kicked a chair out of his way.

"The one I counted on as ironclad security against Tuesday running away was her safe ticket back home," Jacob said.

"I suppose it never occurred to ya that Paul Frank wouldn't do as ya say," Rachel said. "He don't think th' way ya do."

"You're really asking for it," McCallister said to the rebellious girl. "I've worked too hard to make this happen. I'll not let her get away that easy." He kicked the offending chair across the room. With a loud snap it fell over as one leg buckled. "How long have they been gone?"

"Left just after you, so they did." Aggie refused to cower.

"Damn, they had time to get to Centerpoint and find a ride to Wheeling." He pounded his fist on the table.

"What ya goin' to do?" Aggie asked, tempting his rage.

"I don't know," McCallister said. "I suppose I should start by flogging the four of you."

Frustrated, McCallister sent the chair crashing across the room, with a mighty kick. Terrified, Ruby recoiled to the rocking chair. She huddled there shaking. Finally intimidated by McCallister's great strength and unreasonable rage, Rachel and Ida May retreated to the relative safety of the pot-belly stove.

The girls' father, Herman Ruble, never spoke to them the cruel way Jacob McCallister did, and they didn't know what to do. He was wearing down their armor of courage.

Following suit, Aunt Aggie's show of bravery crumbled, and she stood by the woodburner with tears of frustration and sadness running down her face.

32

*J*OE, BIG BESSIE, MELVERTA, EVA BELLE, SALLY ANN, Emma Jean, Annabelle and her new baby, Sara, and Daisy and her new twins were still in Hal's office when Cliff came rushing in, at 10:00 P.M.

After Cliff had taken Tuesday, Patty, Mary Lou, and Paul Frank to Tuesday's house, he'd called for Hal at home and found that he was doing a late night at the office. But he had definitely not expected the bizarre scene he found. Howard and McCoy, back from Winding Ridge, were picking up empty pizza boxes that were scattered over the room with McCallister's and Dillon's households in attendance.

"Glad you're back," Hal said. "Dillon's women have been a great help. We're getting the information we need to keep Dillon in jail without bond until trial."

"Talk about being blindsided. I'm so bent on initiating the search for Tuesday's baby that I hadn't thought any further about the trip you made to pick up Dillon's women."

Cliff needed to see Hal, but Tuesday had absolutely refused to let Cliff put her and the children up in a secure location to protect her from McCallister, leaving him with no alternative but to post men to guard the house night and day.

"What's going on?" Cliff asked, looking around at the now-familiar faces.

"We're getting the answers we thought we would," Hal said.

"Hal, I need to talk to you. Will you come to my office where it's quiet?"

"Sure, let's go."

Cliff turned toward his office and hurried down the hallway with Hal at his heels. Meanwhile, Joe and the women sat and waited, along with McCoy and Howard, to be told what to do next.

"Hal, McCallister's taken Tuesday's baby. It was born in Aggie's mountain cabin. Tuesday called around noon today from a pay phone in Centerpoint, asking me to come for them. That's why I've been out of the office."

"Damn, with the baby born in the wilderness, there's no picture, no footprint I.D. It's going to be tough," Hal said.

"If we don't find her while the trail's hot we may never find her. Hal, I just can't let that happen!"

"Settle down," Hal said. "We'll find her."

"I pray that you're right," Cliff said.

"How did you miss them? You were in both cabins only four days ago."

"They were not at Jacob's or Aggie's cabin because McCallister had moved them to a mountain cabin above Centerpoint. According to Tuesday I probably missed them by mere minutes. I could tell someone had been there by an irregular area in the midst of undisturbed snow cover, but someone had spent time attempting to erase the telltale tracks.

"At first, I didn't think it was McCallister. His taking them to Aggie's cabin under such harsh conditions in the first place and then leaving again in the same circumstances didn't make sense," Cliff explained. "But then I learned he took them by horse and sled across the ridge to Broad Run, leaving us to think he hadn't gone to the mountain after all. He knew I had no reason to look in Broad Run for them, and that makes me wonder if that was his plan all along. Had Tuesday not gotten away and let me know where she was, we never would have found them."

"Do you know whose cabin it was or why he was able to walk in and take over?" Hal asked. "Maybe he owned both cabins and it's a second set-up."

"No, he didn't. Herman Ruble and his wife who died the day before McCallister moved in owned the cabin. Their deaths were an opportunity for him to use the cabin for himself. With the adults dead, the children had no choice. Anyway, Herman and his wife are in the barn since it's too cold for a burial—ground's too frozen to bury them now. Herman's son, Paul Frank, helped Tuesday and Patty get away."

"Joe filled us in on the story of McCallister's women," Hal said.

"We can't let McCallister's trail get cold. We need Randy McCoy and Bert Howard on this one. They're the best men for the job. They've been chasing McCallister as long as we have."

"I've had Bert assign whatever men you need to get the job done," Hal said. "Let's get them on it."

"That's what I say. Do you want me to have Mary Lou brought in for questioning?" Cliff asked.

"Yes, later. We have more than enough on Dillon, but let's not get too sure of ourselves. Can't get too much evidence. But all in all we'll have no problem keeping him behind bars. This is where it all starts, with the men who supply the baby brokers."

Hal went back to McCallister's and Dillon's women and children. Cliff's job was getting Tuesday's baby back. He paced the floor while he waited for Randy McCoy.

"Here I am, ready to go, Sergeant," Randy McCoy said as he walked into Cliff's office.

"We have our work cut out for us this time, Randy," Cliff said.

"If we find out where McCallister hid out during the last eight months, we'll find Tuesday's baby, I'm sure of it."

"I got two men on it," McCoy said.

"You know," Cliff said, "it just dawned on me. McCallister would go back to Herman Ruble's cabin after he attended his business, and with no reason to think otherwise, he would expect Tuesday to be there. We can't afford to lose time," Cliff said as he stood. "We'll have to move fast."

"My men are standing by," Randy McCoy said. "We're ready for whatever it takes."

"We can't afford to lose a second," Cliff said. "We'll take our men and head for Centerpoint. I can assume that Bert Howard and John Gibson are going along with us; they've been in this from the beginning and know the score."

"Hal made it clear that you would want Howard and Gibson," Randy said.

"Good. We'll take snowmobiles in case we have to use them in some of the more remote areas. We'll send Howard and Gibson to Winding Ridge to talk to Sheriff Moats. He can get dogs ready for our disposal. We may need them."

"You don't think he has the baby hidden on the mountain somewhere, do you?"

"Anything is possible," Cliff said. "We can't assume anything. Every possible lead must be checked."

"You're right about that," Randy said. "We need to talk to anyone he has been in contact with. Go back over everywhere he's been."

"Until McCallister comes back to Ruble's cabin, he doesn't know Tuesday got away. So he may come back to Broad Run for Tuesday, or maybe he has already came back for her. We'll station two men to patrol the foot of the mountain at Winding Ridge and at Centerpoint," Cliff said.

"If McCallister comes off the mountain—and we've learned he can come off either way—he'll have no chance of slipping through our fingers. Howard and Gibson can go on the Winding Ridge side of the mountain, stopping at the sheriff's office, then to Dillon's cabin, and on to McCallister's cabin. Next, they'll go on to Aggie's cabin and if they haven't found McCallister yet, they'll go over the ridge to Herman Ruble's cabin. That's where Tuesday said he'd finally taken her. Tell your men that if McCallister's found anywhere along the way, they should take him to the sheriff's office. Hog-tie him if they must.

"I had thought about having Paul Frank go along with Howard and Gibson since he knows his way around the mountain, but I feel better about Paul Frank being in the house with Tuesday, Patty, and Mary Lou. With the guard outside and Paul Frank inside, it's not likely that McCallister's going to get to them.

"With the Winding Ridge side taken care of, you and I can go directly up to Herman's cabin from Centerpoint," Cliff said. "We'll need two men to patrol the road that leads from Centerpoint at Route Seven and two men to patrol the road that leads from Route Seven to Winding Ridge. If McCallister's on the mountain, he'll not get away this time.

Get your men squared away and meet me ba
in thirty minutes."

"Sure thing," McCoy said.

"I'm going to the FBI headquarters," Cliff said as
he picked up his coat. "I have a composite of McCallister. They can get involved now. Kidnapping is a
federal offense, and at this point there's no doubt
that there was a kidnapping. They'll send out news
bulletins and circulate McCallister's composite
around to all police departments. McCallister must
have left a trail from Centerpoint to where he took
the baby—and back."

"Someone will have seen him," Randy said.
"He's had to have made a few stops along the way.
See you in thirty minutes." Randy left to get his men
on the move.

Down the hall in Hal's office, the interrogation
was finished. The answers Hal had gotten from
questioning Joe and the women were similar. There
was no question about Dillon's and McCallister's
activities in the illegal trafficking of children.

There would be a hearing, and Joe would be
charged as an accessory to Dillon's crimes. Melinda
Scott, the social worker, would request that Joe be
assigned to a counselor and be confined to a rehabilitation center. Joe had already shown, by his
treatment of Mary Lou, that he could be as cruel as
McCallister and was heading down the same
road—unless there was some sort of intervention.

Emma Jean, with much stuttering, had told the
story of how Joe had locked Mary Lou in the dog
kennel for days, not allowing her out for any reason.

As soon as Melinda could arrange it, the women
would be taken from the hotel and put in a shelter
for abused women, a place equipped to teach the
women a skill that would make them employable

in the area of housekeeping, child care, sewing, or other work that would make them self-reliant. They would also receive help finding permanent housing.

When Melinda Scott finally escorted Joe, the women, and three babies to a hotel, they made a spectacle walking into the lobby. Melinda was dressed in a navy blue suit and matching pumps. She looked very much a successful businesswoman. But the patrons in the hotel lobby stared as eight ragged women and one teenage boy followed her. Three of the women carried babies in their arms. Their boots were ill fitting and laced with baling twine. Except for Daisy, each woman's hair was in total disarray.

Rather than having the women and boy clomping through the lobby behind her, the social worker asked them to sit and wait on the sofa and chairs provided for the hotel's customers.

At the check-in desk, Melinda rented five rooms, which would put two women, and in three cases a baby, in each of four rooms and Joe in a room of his own.

"Okay, ladies. Follow me," Melinda said.

The women were not paying attention to her. They had gone bug-eyed at the reception area. The twelve-foot-high ceilings, the chandeliers, the plush furnishings, and the multi-colored carpet were incomprehensible to them.

"I never seen a place such as this," Daisy said.

"It's beautiful," Sara said.

"Are we stayin' here with all these people?" Big Bessie asked. "I don't think I can get any rest here a'tall. I don't see anyone layin' down to sleep an' it's long past my bedtime an' my poor old feet ain't used to these heavy boots on my feet all day."

"We got our slippers and nightdresses," Annabelle said.

"We can't change our clothes here with all these people around," Big Bessie said.

"Oh, no," Melinda said. "You're not staying here. This is the lobby. It's a public place. Follow me. I'm taking you to your rooms."

Melinda found an elevator and pushed the up button.

The women had been on an elevator at the police station, but it didn't have a glass window looking out over the grounds like the one they found themselves in now. Sara grabbed Annabelle's hand.

"Well 'pon my soul, I don't believe what I'm seeing," Annabelle said. *This's like bein' in a dream world. What am I goin' to do here?* Annabelle did not know what to think. Everything was so far removed from her home in the mountain cabin.

"I'd call it magic," Sara said. "Th' kids at school always said th' old woman that lives down by th' forest can do magic."

"That's nonsense," Big Bessie said.

"For once I'd have to agree with Big Bessie," Annabelle said. "There ain't no such nonsense as magic, Sara. You're soundin' like Patty talkin' crazy like she's always talkin' 'bout knowin' somethin' from her dreams."

"It's not magic," Melinda intervened. "You've been in a car or truck, right? They're run by a motor just like this elevator is. This elevator, like a car, has been designed with the motor hidden out of sight."

The elevator came to an abrupt stop on the eighth floor.

"What's goin' on?" Big Bessie said as the doors opened.

"It's okay," Melinda said. "Just a sudden stop."

"Oh, my word," Annabelle said, astonished at the long row of doors leading down a hallway longer than any house she could imagine in her wildest dreams.

I feel like I'm dreamin' and can't wake up, Annabelle thought. *I don't even knowed if I want to wake up. Ain't no wonder Jeb's always wantin' to be in the city. Havin' all th' food he's wantin'. I sure loved every bite of that pizza pie. Th' best thing is it's freezin' cold outdoors an' I'm warm as toast indoors an' don't have to huddle around a stove.*

One by one the women and boy stepped from the elevator.

Frank lay in his cell staring at the ceiling. A key fumbled in the lock. "You have company," the guard said and slid the cell door open.

"Who are you?" Frank asked the visitor.

"I've been sent to help you," he said, shutting the cell door with a clang.

"I hate the clanging of that damn door with a passion! At night the CLANG . . . CLANG . . . CLANG . . . CLANG down the row of cells rattles my nerves until they're raw. During my whole life I've come and gone as I please."

"Yes," the visitor said in sarcasm. "Master of your fate as well as master of the women in your life."

"I don't know who you are," Dillon said, "but if you came to harass me you can get the hell out of here."

Frank stood and the man placed his briefcase on Dillon's cot.

The visitor waited until the guard had left before he spoke again. "Dillon, I've been sent by Marty Townsend and his attorney. Mr. Townsend wanted me to find out if you have an attorney and what the situation is."

"I'll be damned. Good old Marty. I have an attorney, but he doesn't believe a damn thing I say. If he represents me, I'm a dead man."

"Are you guilty of the crime that you have been arrested for?"

The man's eyes reveled that he knew that Dillon was indeed guilty. Marty lived beyond the law, and this man and Townsend's attorney doubtless knew that he did. "You can give me an honest answer. My intentions are to help you regardless of your innocence or guilt."

"Yes." Frank finally told the truth. "I sell my children. They are mine to do as I please."

"Sit down, Frank. I don't want to hear you say that again. Although if you had lied I'd have felt differently. Whenever my representative or I ask you a question, you must tell the truth. I don't want any surprises. As far as I'm concerned, you're innocent. I was told to help you if I can. You're not to mention Marty's name again. He does not want his name connected to you. Do you understand?"

"Yes," Frank answered and sat on his bunk waiting to hear what the attorney had to say.

"I'm not here to represent you."

"What the hell you doing here if you're not going to represent me? Piss me off?"

"I'm here to make sure you get the help you need. Marty doesn't want his name to come up in the trial. I'm here to see to that."

"I need a new attorney, is what I need."

"Get rid of the one you have now and I'll hire someone else. The new attorney will be in to see you in the morning. You can count on him, but remember that you must do as he says."

Fred Lawson had hired a showy lawyer to keep Dillon confident of his release; he was a man who won cases that others were sure would fail. Lose or win, it was important that Dillon believe Marty was on his side and thus keep his mouth shut throughout his trial about his short affiliation with Marty. If Marty's lawyer failed to get Dillon off, he would be safely tucked in a prison cell where no one would listen to him for a very long time.

Hal stepped into Cliff's office. "Ready to go?"

"Yes, we're out of here," Cliff answered. "We'll get there early in the morning."

"I need a minute with McCoy before you go. It's important," Hal said.

"What's up?" McCoy said.

"McCoy, what have you come up with on Marty Townsend?"

"Not much more than we've already talked about. I have Detective Sines tailing him."

"Send him to my office before you leave."

Later, there was a short rap on Hal's door. "Come in."

"Lieutenant, I'm Detective Robert Sines. You wanted to see me?"

"Yes. Update me on Marty Townsend," Hal said.

"Something just happened that I think is of utmost importance," the detective said.

"What is it?"

"I got word from the desk sergeant that Dillon just had a visitor. The visitor is a close associate of Fred Lawson; Lawson's the same attorney who works for Marty Townsend. We picked up that bit of information in the initial investigation into Townsend's background. I'm sure Marty's attorney sent him to help Dillon."

"Townsend must feel confident that he's above suspicion to take that chance," Hal said. "Of course he couldn't have known he was being watched when he met with Dillon at the bar or that we got practically his life history from the D.M.V."

"Obviously," Sines said, "Marty Townsend's running scared that Dillon will talk if forced to flounder without help."

"Keep a tail on him," Hal said.

"Sure thing," Sines agreed.

"People like Dillon and McCallister are the backbone of this baby selling scheme," Hal said. "The baby brokers, George Cunningham and Sam Johnson, who pay people to kidnap children, would not have a business without people like Lloyd, Moats, Leonard, Dillon, and McCallister. The fact that Marty Townsend met with Frank Dillon—whom he has nothing, except child trafficking, in common with—in an out-of-the-way dive makes me believe that Marty is very likely a baby broker. We don't want him to get suspicious, or he'll lay low. It's to our advantage that he has no idea he screwed up by meeting Dillon that one short time."

"He has no reason whatsoever to think he's under suspicion," Sines said. "McCoy has seen to that. We're extremely careful that it stays that way. That's why we haven't questioned Marty's mistress yet. McCoy feels it's better not to take the chance that she'd tip Townsend off."

"I agree with Randy. Stay away from her for now. Keep me informed."

"You bet," Sines said.

33

*M*ARY LOU WALKED AROUND TUESDAY'S HOUSE looking at and touching everything. "I can't believe what I'm seein'. Wish th' others livin' in Frank's cabin could be here and see your house. They wouldn't believe how soft an' thick this carpet is under my feet. It's amazin', an' look at th' windows. I've never seen anythin' like it. Th' windows in th' cabin I lived in were dirty an' ya couldn't hardly see through them."

"Before I came here, I never thought much about pretty windows," Patty said. "Th' glass in these windows is sparkly clean an' th' pretty curtains are somethin' that I only saw from th' outside of th' houses in Windin' Ridge when I was goin' to school, but seein' them from th' inside is betta."

"Paul Frank, you look worried. What's bothering you?" Tuesday asked, noticing that he was very quiet.

"I was just wonderin' what's goin' to happen to me now, an' I'm worried about my sisters. Ya knowed I worry about them being left at Jacob's mercy. Can't help but to worry about it."

"After Jacob's found and locked up in jail, you can go back there if you want to. Cliff will see that you get back. I'd hoped you'd consider staying here in town."

"I don't knowed how I could do that. I don't have a place to stay. My place is on th' mountain."

"That's not necessarily true. Paul Frank, you can live here and go to school. You can get a job and have a much better life."

"Then who would take care of my sisters? There's no way I can stay here."

"If you like it here, you can. We'll think of something. There are people who take in foster children and help them get a start in life. You know without your parents there's nothing left for you and your sisters on the mountain."

"I'd like to stay in th' city. I knowed a few people who'd left th' mountain an' never came back. Now I knowed why, but I'll stay only after I make a place for my sisters. They won't survive alone on th' mountain."

"I'm happy to be back," Patty said. "I'd die if I had to go back to mountain life after living with Tuesday."

"Patty, why don't you show Paul Frank and Mary Lou around?" Tuesday asked. "I need to make some calls. I don't want to keep Cora waiting any longer than necessary. I know she has been worried about us."

Patty took Paul Frank and Mary Lou through the house. She showed them where the bathroom was and how to flush the commode. She took them to the kitchen and opened the refrigerator. "Look, there's plenty of food. Ya can have anythin' ya want to eat. I'm goin' to give ya some ice cream. Have ya ever had ice cream?"

"Don't even knowed what ice cream is," Mary Lou said.

Paul Frank and Mary Lou marveled at the creamy, sweet taste.

"This is th' best stuff I've ever eaten," Paul Frank said. "I never had any food that was cold an' tasted good too."

"It's 'posed to be cold," Patty laughed. "It's ice cream."

"It's so good, whatever it's 'posed to be," Paul Frank offered.

"I'm glad I ran away from th' mountain," Mary Lou said. It's been my lifelong dream to leave th' mountain an' live in th' city. I'd sit in the outhouse by th' hour an' look at th' catalogs with the pretty women with th' pretty clothes."

"Me too, Mary Lou. Ya share my dream. I've always wanted to leave th' mountain an' wondered why the others never even thought about it."

"That's th' way it was with me," Mary Lou said. "Th' other women couldn't care less about leavin' th' mountain. Sometimes it made me wonder if I was crazy thinkin' how wonderful it'd be an' th' others not carin' at all."

"I want to tell you, I'm surprised that Joe locked ya in th' dog kennel, Mary Lou. He was fond of me and Sara an' we always had fun together, but the older he got the more he's wantin' to be like Pa."

"I'm not goin' to think about that no more," Mary Lou said. "I have a new life now that Tuesday's goin' to help me."

"Okay then, how 'bout I show ya where ya goin to sleep," Patty said. "Ya won't believe th' beds. After sleepin' on mats on th' floor with cracks lettin' th' freezin' air in, th' bed is like sleepin' on a cloud.

Did ya ever lay in th' ground an' wish ya could get up in th' sky an' snuggle on th' clouds?" They giggled a silly laugh, a sound that would have been foreign in the mountain cabin.

Patty took Mary Lou upstairs to the room they would share. It was the room that Tuesday's mother and father had shared before they died.

"O-o-o-oh," Mary Lou said. "Look at th' bed. It's bigger than th' table back at th' cabin." She ran and jumped on the bed. "Which side do I get, Patty?"

"I sleep on th' side close to th' window where Summer's layin'," Patty said. "Ya can have th' other side. Th' bed's so big, I always feel lost when I'm goin' to sleep. It'll be nice havin' ya here," Patty smiled.

Mary Lou stretched out on her side of the bed, wearing a huge grin on her face. "I'm in heaven. I never knowed there was beds like this. I just can't believe it." She looked at Patty and Paul Frank, who were also grinning from ear to ear. "Am I dreamin'? Just hours ago I was takin' my life in my hands by runnin' away an' havin' no idea where I was goin'."

"No, you're not dreamin'," Paul Frank laughed, "but you could have been attacked by a mountain lion or a militiaman."

Downstairs Tuesday heard the laughter and it almost warmed her heart to hear them behaving like normal children. *I can only imagine what it's like for the three of them after living in the worst conditions I can imagine,* she thought. *I can't help them now, though. My heart feels as if it's breaking in two. I must find my daughter. I must!*

Jacob sat at the table after sending the girls upstairs. "Don't know how you stand their incessant chatter, Aunt Aggie. It gets on my nerves and it's distracting. I need to determine my next move."

"Ya must knowed that Tuesday, Patty, an' Paul Frank has had plenty of time to make it to th' city by now," Aggie warned. "Them detectives could be on their way to the mountain with men and dogs like they came after ya before, so they could."

"Since you know it all old woman," McCallister said, "which way will they come up the mountain?"

"Them detectives are goin' to knowed by now that ya are holed up in Herman Ruble's cabin, so they will," Aggie warned. "Surely, they'll come up the road to Centerpoint."

"I'll go across the mountain ridge and drive down the road from Winding Ridge," McCallister said.

"How ya goin' to get ya truck across th' ridge? We had to get here by sled. Ya can't drive your truck that a way, so ya can't. Ya'd get stuck, so ya would."

He stood up and shouted, "Shut up, old woman. I can't just sit here. I must do something fast."

"Can I give you advice?" Aunt Aggie asked, not one to stand by and keep her opinion to herself. "I'm not just a stump a sittin' in this rockin' chair, so I'm not."

"Just what advice can you give me? You don't know nothing. You've never been off the mountain."

"Well I knowed that ya goin' to run into th' law if ya go down th' road to Centerpoint, so ya are. Ya can bet th' detective's not sittin' scratchin' his butt, so he ain't. He's on his way to th' mountain, and he knows you're in Herman Ruble's cabin like Tuesday's done told him, so he does. Ya can't get th' truck across th' moutain to Windin' Ridge, so ya can't. So ya goin' to have to walk off th' mountain, so ya are."

"How the hell am I going to make any time walking? If I walk I'm going to be a sitting duck. They brought dogs the last time they came for me. They will again. I can't be out taking a stroll."

"Ya just wastin' time thinkin' about takin' th' truck, so ya are. There ain't no way, so they ain't. Just take time an' listen to your old aunt. They could be comin' up th' mountain road right now, so they could. If ya walk to th' old loggin' road ya can make your way to Higgins' Garage, so ya can. They're goin' to be lookin' for ya truck, so they are. Go along th' ridge like ya headin' for Windin' Ridge and make a turn at the old mines. There's a loggin' road that goes straight down to th' road that comes off Route Seven, so there is. Ya can walk th' creek bottom so's they can't see you. Th' creek bottom follows Route Seven, so it does. In 'bout five miles ya will be in back of Higgins' Garage, so ya will."

"How the hell do you know all this, old woman? I'm getting fidgety setting here doing nothing. I can imagine the detectives surrounding the cabin and charging through the doors. I need to be doing something other than listening to a silly old woman."

"I knowed ya should. That's what I'm tryin' to tell ya. One time I took it in my head to run away from th' old man my pa sold me to, so I did. I didn't knowed what to call it then, but I was livin' right here on Broad Run. I can look out of th' window in th' kitchen an' see th' road what goes to th' old cabin, so it does. Anyway, after I'd run away an' I was walkin' up th' mountain, tryin' to find my way back to my own cabin, I came on to th' old mine, so I did. I found the loggin' road and stayed on it until I came to th' Higgins' car place. I was dumbfounded, so I was. Just didn't knowed where I was. I turned and walked back th' same way I'd come, so I did. I knowed then, I couldn't find my own cabin so I went back and fixed supper just like I was supposed to, so I did. I can't tell ya how to get on it from here, so I can't. Ya knowed th' road if ya take th' time to think it out, so ya do. This ain't th' time to go off half cocked, so it ain't."

Jacob sat down. "I know the road your talking about. I'd forgotten about that road, Aunt Aggie. I've been on it many times when I used to sell moonshine. Walking the road, I'd be out of sight on a road almost forgotten by most mountain folk. Certainly the detectives won't find it. I'm sure to avoid anyone looking for me. I can get a car from Higgins' Garage.

"Do you want to go with me? You'll starve if I leave you here."

"No, Jeb. I'll stay with th' girls. We'll make do. Maybe someday ya can come back an' see me, so ya can. I'll not leave th' mountain, not while I still have breath in this old body, so I'll not."

"Here's five hundred dollars. This will keep you for a long time if you're careful. The girls know the way to town to shop. They've gone with Paul Frank and their father." The five hundred dollars—and the money he had used to buy the supplies that they needed—was a small part of the money he'd made from the sale of Winter Ann.

It would take him most of what was left of the evening to make his way to Higgins' Garage.

"Ya goin' to rent a car at Higgins' Garage?" Aggie asked.

"Renting a car is a sure way to leave a trail," Jacob said. "Stealing a vehicle is the way to go since car theft isn't my M. O. I guess it doesn't matter if I'm suspected of stealing anyhow, might as well take what I need and increase my chances of getting away. I don't think that the big-feeling Detective Cliff Moran would look at car theft as nearly the crime as selling children."

"I always told ya that you're goin' to get in trouble for sellin' your youngins, so I did," Aggie said.

"Shut up, old woman. How many times have I told you I don't want to hear it? This sure as hell isn't the time to get into I told you so's."

"I'm your aunt an' I raised ya like my own son, so I did. I'm just tryin' to help ya. Ya don't need to be so harsh with your old aunt, so ya don't."

"I'm sorry Aunt Aggie, I'm just worried. I won't feel secure until I put miles between this cabin and me. I can't shake the feeling I have of Moran crashing into the cabin. It's almost too real."

"Then ya best be getting' out of here, so ya had. I'm goin' to miss ya, though. It plagues my soul to knowed ya are in trouble, so it does."

"I'm sorry about that and I'm sorry to leave you alone, but when things cool down I'll try to check on you. Now I must go. When I get to Higgins' Garage, I'll steal a car and abandon it when I feel I'm far enough away to be safe."

"Ya'd betta be careful drivin' around in a stolen car, so ya had," Aggie warned.

"I won't keep it long. There's enough cash to buy a truck when I'm ready. Aunt Aggie, you can bet I'll not leave a trail for the law to follow. I've no intention of rotting in jail. I'm not done with Tuesday, either. I've gotten away from the law before and I can do it now."

Jacob put on his heavy coat, picked up his shotgun, and left. He carried no baggage.

Looking like the characteristic mountain man, floundering down the rocky mountain with his shotgun across his shoulder, Jacob moved as fast as conditions allowed. Often he stepped out and his leg disappeared in the snow up to his thigh. Swearing, Jacob stabilized his footing. He was disoriented because the snow cover hid crucial landmarks, and it had been a long time since he had used the logging road. It would be all too easy to choose the wrong way, and if he did, it would be a costly mistake.

"I'm an idiot," Jacob said aloud in his frustration. "Why didn't I ride one of the horses? It would have been a hell of a lot faster. Maybe I should go back and get one."

As McCallister debated the idea of going back for the horse, he kept walking. Just before he turned around to go back he saw smoke coming from a chimney in the distance.

He tried to run and fell headfirst down a sudden drop off. He lay at the foot of the unseen rock, cursing Tuesday aloud for disobeying him. He shouted to the heavens above him, "She don't know when she has it so good. When I get her back, I guarantee that she'll wish she had never disobeyed me."

There was a loud cracking noise followed by clucking, cackling, and squawking. Looking into a pair of bright, beady eyes, Jacob turned white as a ghost.

Tuesday felt as if she would lose her sanity if her baby was not found soon. She felt sorrow such as she had never felt. I must do something. She picked up the phone and called Cliff's office. There was no answer. She dialed Hal's office, and Hal answered on the second ring.

"Lieutenant Brooks speaking."

"Hal, where's Cliff?"

"He's over at the F.B.I. office. He's due back in fifteen minutes to meet Randy McCoy."

"It dawned on me that Jacob would go back to the mountain," Tuesday said. "He has no way of knowing that we got away. Is Cliff going back there in case Jacob returns for me?"

"As a matter of fact, he is. He's leaving as soon as he gets back here and hooks up with McCoy."

"I'll be there in ten minutes. I want to go with them."

"Tuesday, that's not a good idea. Cliff will not allow you to go. You could get hurt."

"I cannot just sit and do nothing. I'll go crazy. I must find my daughter. I'll be there in ten minutes. Don't let Cliff leave without me or I'll go alone." She hung up the phone.

"Paul Frank, I need to leave. I'm going with Cliff to the mountain. I'm counting on you to take care of the girls. Don't leave the house or let anyone except Cora in, Patty knows who she is. I'll call her and see if she can come over to check on you and the girls a couple times a day while I'm gone. I have no idea how long it'll be. I'm counting on you."

Tuesday opened her garage door with the remote and backed across the driveway. The officer, who was there on guard, blocked her way and when she stopped he came around and motioned for her to open her window. "Where are you going?"

"I'm going to meet Sergeant Moran and if you need to confirm it call Lieutenant Brooks, he knows I'm coming."

"I'm here to protect you," the officer said. "I can't do that if you're out in your car and the children are in the house."

"I'm going to meet Cliff Moran. Please stay and keep watch over the house."

"Wait, I'll radio in for instructions," the officer said and walked over to his squad car.

Tuesday sped from the driveway, leaving the officer holding his radio. His face wore a look of dismay.

After Tuesday left, Patty showed Paul Frank and Mary Lou the basement where the laundry area was located, and she gathered the towels from the laundry bag.

"What are those for?" Mary Lou asked.

"They're towels. They're for when ya take a bath or shower. Ya can dry yourself off."

Mary Lou touched the towels and rubbed one against her arm. "I never felt cloth so soft."

"When I first came here I had trouble learnin' how to use everythin' an' thought I would never learn," Patty said. "So don't ya worry. Ya'll catch on."

"I want to learn so bad," Mary Lou said. "I can never go back to th' mountain after bein' in this house. Livin' here must be what bein' in heaven's like."

"I'm hungry. Let's make somethin' to eat." Patty put the towels in the washer and then added soap and turned it on.

"I knowed ya have never had sandwiches like I'm goin' to fix for ya," Patty said. "Let's go to th' kitchen."

After Patty got the bread from the breadbox, she opened the refrigerator and chose a package of lunchmeat and presliced longhorn cheese. Passing over the mustard, she got out the Miracle Whip, which was her favorite.

"Can I help ya?" Mary Lou asked.

"Yeah, I'm goin' to lay out th' bread an' ya can put th' meat an' cheese on it an' I'll go behind ya and spread the Miracle Whip."

"I never ate anythin' like this," Paul Frank said. "It smells good, though."

"Wait," Patty said. "I forgot the lettuce. That's what makes th' ham an' cheese sandwich so good."

Patty opened the refrigerator door and along with the lettuce, found three cherry sodas. After opening the sodas, she handed one to each of the others. "Ya'll love these. They're my favorite. Taste it," Patty offered.

"Wow, it's good." Paul Frank held the bottle in front of him and said, "It's cold and it bubbles in your throat. I always get a soda when I go to Th' General Store in Centerpoint, but I never had this kind."

"It's sweet too, I never had anythin' sweet very often till I came here. Sometimes Pa would bring candy when he came from th' city."

The sandwiches were ready and the girls waited for Paul Frank to take the first bite. "I have never had a sandwich like this," Paul Frank said. "I saw bread like this in th' store, but Ma always made her own. Pa said it was cheaper."

"Some say th' bread ya bake yourself is betta if ya have th' right ingredients, which we never seemed to have at th' cabin, but I like to buy it in th' store," Patty said. "I told ya you're goin' to be surprised at all th' food you've never tasted."

"Where do ya get all this stuff?" Paul Frank said. "Back home we don't have lettuce in th' winter time."

"At th' mall an' th' grocery store," Patty proudly shared her newfound knowledge. "It's not like The General Store at Windin' Ridge, no way. In th' grocery store there's rows and rows of food ya never even imagined. It doesn't matter what time of th' year it is, ya can get fresh vegetables and fruit. In th' mall there's endless stores an' ya go from one to another without ever goin' outdoors. When Tuesday comes back she'll take us. I promise ya'll love it."

"Ya knowed," Mary Lou said, "this is the best time I ever had."

"Wait until ya taste some of th' different ways to make food," Patty said. "Italian food is my favorite."

"What's Italian food?" Paul Frank asked.

"It's pasta an' lasagna an' there's so many different kinds of sauces. Even some of th' food ya had in th' mountain is betta here. I don't knowed about ya, but we never had fancy things when I lived on th' mountain in th' tiny cabin with so many people. We only had th' necessities. Like Pa was sayin' that's all we needed was th' necessities."

The doorbell rang and Patty ran to answer it. Cora stood there. "Hi, Cora, is somethin' wrong?" Patty asked, knowing it was too late for a visit. "Where's Linda?"

"It's late and Linda is home asleep. Bill's with her. Can I come in?"

"I'm sorry," Patty blushed. She moved back and allowed Cora to come in.

"Tuesday asked me to check on you. When I drove up all the lights were on, and I knew you must be awake," Cora said. "Is everything okay?"

"Yeah, Cora. I was showin' Paul Frank and Mary Lou around th' house an' we were havin' somethin' to eat."

"It's late and from the looks of it, you all need a bath," Cora smiled. "With Tuesday so worried about her baby, I see that she didn't take the time to get her guests settled properly."

With Cora's help, the kitchen was put back in order and Paul Frank was sent to the downstairs bathroom for a shower. Patty happily showed him how to use the shower fixtures while Cora got Mary Lou started. In short time the three youngsters were clean and ready for bed.

After the good-nights were all said and the lights were off, Cora left, with the promise that she would come back the next day and take the three of them shopping for the clothing they badly needed. During the time that Tuesday was gone Cora would spend as much time as necessary helping Paul Frank and Mary Lou to get settled.

"Hold on, Cliff," Hal answered the phone. "Lieutenant Brooks here." Hal listened as the officer told him that Tuesday had left in her car, against his advice, saying she was coming in to see Sergeant Moran.

"Continue your stakeout at the house and look after the children. We'll take care of Tuesday." Hal put the phone back in its cradle.

"What's up?" Cliff asked.

"That was the officer who's guarding Tuesday's house," Hal said. "He said Tuesday is on her way here. She intends to go with you."

"I don't like the sound of that," Cliff said, "but I don't know what I can do. She's stubborn and when she makes up her mind, you can't change it."

"You better," Hal said, "I think its going to be too dangerous to have her with you. McCallister could fool himself that it was okay to sell his own children, but any fool knows it's against the law to kidnap a child and sell it. And he is going to be dangerous when confronted."

"I should have anticipated that Tuesday would insist she go on the hunt for McCallister," Cliff said. "He's running scared now. There's no telling what he'll do. He's carrying a gun and if we back him in a corner he'll use it. It's too dangerous."

"I tried to tell her," Hal said. "She said she had to do something or go crazy. I tell you, we need her to stay put here. You're her fiancé. You should have some influence over her."

"I'll do what I can," Cliff said.

"Maybe you could convince her it's better for the child if she stays home," Hal said. "She will slow you down in that wilderness trying to get around on the rugged terrain."

Before Cliff could react, Tuesday dashed into Hal's office, wearing jeans, ankle-high boots and a heavy coat. "I'm ready to go."

"Tuesday, please stay at the house. McCallister is dangerous. He must be feeling like a trapped animal by now. If he's back, he knows you got to me and that we know he sold your daughter. In that case, he knows that he has no chance of beating any charges against him. He'll act in desperation, and desperate people can't be predicted. He will do anything to avoid capture—including murder."

"I can't sit and wait! I'm desperate too! You know the kinds of lives the children are sold into. The longer it takes, the slimmer our chances will be of finding Winter Ann."

"Tuesday," Cliff pleaded, "please stay here. For you to go is a mistake. How can I stop you?"

"I'm going. This is not debatable."

"Tuesday, you'll slow us down, and I'll have to concentrate on keeping you safe," Cliff said.

"Tuesday," Hal said, "I'm not trying to be cruel, but you'll only hinder the search. I know it's hard for you staying behind and feeling helpless, but you must stay here. Go home and go to bed."

"No! Hal, I will not stay! I'm going and that's that. If Cliff won't take me with him, I'll go alone."

"I guess she goes then, Hal. She'll do just as she said. I think her hideous experiences with McCallister showed her that she could meet any challenge head on. She'll be safer with Randy and me. I'm going to have to allow her to go along."

"I give up," Hal said. "I'm going home. I've had a long day and it's late."

Joe and the eight women with three babies walked down the long hallway with Melinda in the lead. Coming to room 225, she inserted a card into the lock mechanism and when the light blinked, she opened the door.

"This room connects to the rooms on each side of this one," Melinda said. "The two rooms across the hall are connecting rooms as well. That makes it easy for you to visit one another."

Melinda crossed the room and opened the door leading into room 227. Crossing the room to the other side, she opened the door to room 223. "You all can decide which room each of you wants and who's staying with whom."

The women were barely paying attention to Melinda as they touched, gawked, and bounced on the beds trying them out. "Please," Melinda pounded her car keys on the dresser, "It's late and we need to get everyone settled and—"

"Miss, where do you want these baby beds?" Three men were lined up outside the door and each of them had a crib.

"Put one in this room and the other two in the adjoining room," Melinda said.

Daisy's twins had been fussing for a while and at the latest commotion began crying loudly. Soon Annabelle's baby joined in.

"Okay, everyone gather around me," Melinda ordered sternly. "We'll never get out of here if we don't get organized."

The women, tired and cranky, gathered around the social worker.

Melinda turned down the nearest bed to them. "Each of you will have a bed, and there's a bathroom in each bedroom. Follow me. I know most of you haven't seen a bathroom."

In the bathroom, Melinda turned on the water. "This knob is for hot water and the one on the right is cold water. You can bathe or shower, whichever you prefer." Melinda demonstrated how to use the shower and the bath. "Some of you have used the toilet facilities back at the station, but in case you don't know, after you use the toilet, push down on this handle and flush." Melinda pushed the handle and the others watched as the water swirled out of sight, only to fill the bowl again.

"Well-l-l-l, 'pon my soul," Big Bessie said. "I ain't never seen such as that. I don't knowed if I can get my big bottom over that little hole."

"Don't be such a hillbilly," Annabelle said. "Th' hole ain't no smaller than th' one cut in your outhouse for sittin' on. An' it sure is betta than th' slop jar we use when we can't get to th' outhouse."

"Okay, ladies," Melinda said. "It's late. Please get ready for bed. I'll take Joe, Eva Belle, and Sara across the hall. You have twenty minutes to ask questions before I leave, so start getting ready for bed so you'll know if you have any."

34

*A*FTER DRIVING THROUGH THE NIGHT, CLIFF MORAN, Alex Parker, and Ned Dugan unloaded the snowmobiles at the intersection of Route Seven and the mountain road leading up to Centerpoint. "Remember, men," Cliff said, "McCallister is a strikingly handsome man. He has dark brown eyes and dark hair that looks salon styled. He is tall and muscular. His clothing could either be the average mountain garb or suit and tie. Hell, he could be dressed for the city or for the country. You can't judge by his clothes, so don't be fooled by that. You have the composite drawing. Be sure you're familiar with it."

"Got it," Alex nodded. "It's right here handy." He pointed to the front windshield where he had taped the likeness.

The Centerpoint side of the mountain taken care of, Detective Corporal Randy McCoy, Tuesday Summers, and Sergeant Cliff Moran drove to the foot of the road to Winding Ridge, followed by Bert Howard, Rex Tripp, Walter Wildman, and John Gibson. They left the trucks and unloaded their snowmobiles. Bert Howard and Rex Tripp were assigned to patrol the intersection to Winding Ridge. Walter Wildman and John Gibson were assigned to scour the area in hopes of finding McCallister. Randy McCoy and Cliff Moran, with Tuesday clutching his waist, headed back toward Centerpoint and Herman Ruble's cabin on their snowmobiles, leaving a spray of snow behind them.

The sheriff's office was Wildman's and Gibson's first destination. "The sheriff and his deputy must be in. The Jeep is here," Wildman shouted, as they cut their motors in front of the building.

"Hope so. We don't have time to waste."

Sheriff Ozzie Moats looked up as the two detectives from the city walked into his office. They weren't strangers anymore. "Getting' so you make up part of the town population," the sheriff said. "I'm sick of you city detectives comin' to my town, but I might add your number to the population sign what stands outside town. What you wantin' here now?" the sheriff asked. "Seems like someone must've built a freeway from the city to my front door."

"Don't get smart with us, Sheriff. We're looking for Jacob McCallister. You know that it's serious business. Have you seen him?" Gibson asked.

"No, we haven't. You know we've been keepin' an eye out for him. My deputy goes up on the mountain a couple times a week. Ain't seen hide nor hair of him. I told that other detective, what comes here from your big city, that McCallister won't take the chance on comin' back here. I'm in charge on this mountain and I don't understand why you city detectives don't listen to me. I knowed what I'm talkin' about. McCallister ain't about to come back here once he gets a taste for the city."

"Well, you're wrong on all counts," Wildman said. "McCallister was here. He took over Herman

Ruble's cabin above Centerpoint at Broad Run after living in his aunt's cabin for a few days. He's been charged with kidnapping, child endangerment, and bigamy. We consider him to be armed and dangerous. I find it hard to believe that a man can get away with all those crimes and go undetected by the sheriff's department for so many years."

Deputy Jess Willis came out from the back when he heard voices. "What's goin' on out here, Sheriff?"

"Nothin', Jess. These men from the city are sufferin' from delusions. They say McCallister's gotten himself in trouble over in Doddridge County, over at Broad Run. They're not smart enough to know that our jurisdiction only extends throughout this county."

"There's no need to be on the defensive, Sheriff," Gibson said. "McCallister was in the county for weeks. He's believed to have holed up in his aunt's cabin at least twice—the first time, to get it ready for his hostages, and the second, to hold them there. I don't believe that you've cooperated with our department at all, Sheriff, but that's water under the bridge. We just wanted to check out all possibilities. Wildman and I are going on the mountain. We've reason to believe he's still there somewhere."

"How do we get to Herman Ruble's cabin from Aggie's?" Gibson demanded.

"Jess, you've been on the mountain more than me," Sheriff Ozzie Moats said. "Give them directions."

"Well, it's hard to say," Willis began. "I mean there's no landmarks to mark your way. Best I can tell you is when you leave Aggie's cabin, go south, follow the ridge, zig zag as you go, 'cause if they camouflaged their tracks, I doubt they would have kept it up long and you'll find them again."

"You want dogs?" Ozzie asked, picking up his spittoon and spitting a brown glob into it. "Old man Keefover's got the best," he set the spittoon back in it's place and rubbed the back of his hand across his chin.

"No," Gibson answered, "the snowmobiles would scare them. We're going to have to do without. For now."

The fall was hard and put McCallister in a vulnerable position. The clucking, cackling, and squawking above his head grew louder. The fretting cackles, accompanied by huge, flapping wings from three large wild turkeys, kept McCallister from gaining his footing. The turkeys had been roosting in a tree, and McCallister's fall had greatly disturbed them.

Suddenly, the birds' maddening clamor was interrupted by an earsplitting, sharp crack. A huge branch—weighted down by the heavy snow—fell atop of McCallister, creating a whirlwind of snow and sharp twigs. The birds retreated, and an eerie quiet followed the uproar over the noise of the breaking branch. Without warning, and to his horror, two huge birds that looked to weigh thirty or forty pounds took wing and descended upon him. With a wild flapping of wings that scattered dead leaves and icy snow, the birds' sharp claws found his chest and began pecking at McCallister's face. Unable to get away, he covered his face with his arms.

Mustering all the strength he had, he elbowed the birds with a powerful swing of his upper right arm, using his cupped left hand over his right fist to drive more power to the blow. Frightened, the turkeys leapt away, leaving McCallister to suffer the sting of the flurry of feathers as they fled in their fear.

He picked himself up and brushed the snow from his coat at the back of his neck. He broke a limb

from the branch that had fallen and swung at the
three turkeys that were by now long gone, more
startled by McCallister than he was by them.

"If it ain't just a flock of turkeys," he said aloud,
just to hear the sound of a human voice. "Thought I
was a dead man. I guess I've heard too many of Aunt
Aggie's outrageous stories. Damn I'm cold. At least I
think I know where I am now. Look's like Higgins'
Garage up ahead. If I don't steal a car soon it'll be
unnecessary, since I'll be frozen stiff. A car heater
sounds like heaven just about now, but soon as I'm
warm and dry I'll dump it and grab another one."

Fifteen minutes later, he came to the wooded area
that sloped down behind Higgins' Garage. He
stopped, scanning the trees for any surprises. Finding none, he entered the parking lot from the
wooded area in the back of the building. There were
half a dozen cars parked there.

He checked to see if anyone was watching and
looked inside each car to see if the keys were in the
ignition. Keys were in all of them. It was a matter of
choosing the vehicle he wanted. A few of the cars
were for sale, and others were parked there for ser-
vicing. He couldn't afford to take one that would
quit on him a few miles down the road.

He found a late model front-wheel-drive with an
invoice tucked behind the sun visor. "Perfect,"
Jacob said aloud, breaking the unnerving silence
once again. "It's repaired, and the front-wheel-drive
will be the next best thing to a four-wheel-drive.
Luck's with me. From here it'll be a piece of cake.
I'm just half a mile from Route Seven."

"Thank you, Mr. Higgins. The keys are very help-
ful," Jacob mockingly thanked the absentee garage
owner, starting the car. He headed down the back
road that intersected with the road that began at
Route Seven and ran through Centerpoint continu-

ing up the mountain through Broad Run. That road and the back road that he traveled on now intersected about a hundred yards above the intersection at Route Seven, which was now to his left. McCallister stopped. There were two snowmobiles sitting at the intersection at Route Seven.

He wasn't close enough to recognize who the men were. "That looks like a roadblock. . . Can't take a chance," McCallister worried aloud. "Have to assume it's what it looks like. Moran's handy work, no doubt. What the hell am I going to do now? If I make a U-turn and go back the way I came, or even turn right from so close to the roadblock and head back up the mountain, it'll spook them, arousing their suspicions, and they'll follow me for sure. Do I go back up? Or"—he put his hand on his shotgun—"speed through shooting?"

One of Corporal Randy McCoy's men, Officer Bob Murdock, was on lookout at a school bus stop. A school bus driver, who had noticed a man in a black truck hanging around the bus stop a few days prior and the day that Ashley Blake was kidnapped a few months back, reported that an identical truck was lingering at his stop once again. It had been there on Monday morning and each day afterward. It fit the description of the truck involved in the kidnapping of Todd eight months ago.

At his post on Friday, Murdock was patiently watching when the man in the truck made his move. As the children scattered to their various homes, the man jumped from the truck and grabbed a young boy who walked alone. The man pulled a rag from his back pocket and forced it into the boy's mouth, cutting off his cries. He ran with the boy, and with him slung over his hip, opened the truck door and threw the boy inside.

Just as the man was hooking the seat belt around the boy, Murdock quietly stepped up behind him and held a gun to his back. "You're under arrest. Put your hands behind your back."

The man obeyed. He was caught in the act. There was no way to explain the boy with the gag in his mouth buckled into the seat belt of his truck. "Keep ya mouth shut an' I'll pay ya big money. I got th' cash. Just let me go," the man whined.

"Stop your blubbering. I'm not interested." After cuffing him, Murdock forced the man to the ground, face down, and took the dirty rag from the boy's mouth.

"What's your name?" Murdock asked the boy.

"Robbie Hudson," the boy sobbed. "I want my mom."

"Can you tell me her name and your phone number?" Murdock asked.

"Yes."

"Tell you what, let's go to the station and call her." Murdock lifted the boy in his strong arms and grabbed the man by the scruff of the neck and jerked him to his feet. "My car's over there," Bob Murdock said, nodding toward a blue Chevrolet halfway up the block.

The man stumbled toward the car as Murdock read him his rights.

"I don't want no attorney," the man said. "Just let me make a phone call."

Hal took the message that Murdock radioed in and hurried down to wait with the desk sergeant. With the evidence that he had gathered up to this point and along with what this latest arrest could uncover, Hal had no doubt that Frank Dillon and Jacob McCallister were destined to spend the greatest part of their lives in prison. The DNA test had come back and showed that there was a ninety-nine point nine percent chance that Dillon was Tom's father. Still, the most damaging evidence was what the women had revealed about the many children that Dillon had sold.

Also, Dillon and Marty Townsend had been tied together. Marty had been cunning in his criminal activities, but had indeed made a big mistake when he had used the bad judgment of having his personal attorney deal with Frank Dillon.

Now Hal waited with the desk sergeant in the squad room for Murdock to arrive with the man who drove the kidnap truck. There was hope that if the man talked, his testimony could tie many loose ends together.

Soon after Hal got the message and came downstairs, Murdock came into the busy reception room, carrying the small boy in his arms. Murdock pushed the handcuffed man—Robbie Hudson's would-be kidnapper—in front of them.

"Someone watch this pervert while I talk to the lieutenant," Bob nodded to a uniformed officer nearby. "Caught the scumbag red-handed," Murdock said. "He picked up this boy at his school bus stop, he gagged him, and threw him into his truck."

"I could hardly believe it when you radioed in," Hal raved, slapping Bob Murdock on the back. "Go ahead and take the boy to the lunch room while the desk sergeant locates his family."

"Here's his phone number, and the parents' names, Sergeant." Murdock tore a page from his notepad and handed it to the desk sergeant.

"I'll take our 'catch of the day' to the interrogation room and see if I can find out who he is and who he works for," Hal said with glee in his voice.

"Hey, I'm allowed a phone call. I have my rights," the would-be kidnapper said. He would call his brother, knowing his partners in crime, Simon

Leonard, Marty Townsend, Steven Lloyd, and George Cunningham, would all turn their backs on him now.

"You'll get your phone call after you tell us who you are," Hal said. He led the man down the hall. "Go in and take a seat. I'll be right back." Hal gave the man a little shove and he lurched into the room. Hal closed the door, locking it.

Hal went back to the desk sergeant. "I'd like to have the prosecutor, Ron Mascara, in on the questioning. Think you can get him for me? In the meantime, our man can stew. Maybe he'll be more willing to talk after being shut in a windowless room."

"Works a lot of the time," the desk sergeant commented. "Are you going to book him?"

"Damn right," Hal said. "Hell, he was caught in the act."

"When you're ready, bring him back around here for his mug shots and finger printing. I'll have Chuck rounded up and waiting for him."

In the small, bare, stuffy room the man sat at the table. "What now? I'm in deep shit now for sure," the man complained out loud. Having no friends or close family around him, he often talked to himself. "Do I talk or do I clam up? Guess it makes no difference, caught me fair an' square. My brother'll get me out of this; he ain't no sheriff for nothin'. Can't tell him I'm a big executive in a fancy office now, not after havin' to go crawlin' an' beggin' for his help.

"When's that city slicker detective comin' back? I've a right to my phone call. Can't stand bein' shut in a room with no windows. Ain't no air to breathe."

The door opened and Hal came in with another man following behind. "I hear it's not a good sign to be talking to yourself," Hal said.

Aubry did not respond.

Hal and Mascara sat, one at each end of the table. The two men watched the man, waiting to see what he would say on his own.

"What ya lookin' at. I got a booger on my nose or somethin'?" the man asked. "I told ya before I need to make a phone call."

"Soon as we have your name, address, and where you were taking the boy. After that you can make your call," Hal said.

"Name's Aubry Moats." Aubry wanted to laugh at the look of surprise on the detective's face. "I must be a celebrity. Ya all look like ya got a big one this time."

"Damn, I should've guessed from your mountain brogue who you are. You're the man in the truck! And you're Sheriff Ozzie Moats' brother, aren't you?"

"One and th' same. What's your name? Like to knowed th' name of th' people I associate with, even if they're arrestin' me."

"I'm Lieutenant Hal Brooks. This man is Ron Mascara, the prosecuting attorney. I imagine you'll be seeing a great deal of him in the near future.

"Ron," Hal said, "I guess this explains Sheriff Ozzie Moats' bad manners when Cliff and his men asked questions about the sheriff's brother."

"He must have had knowledge or at the least suspicions that his brother was involved in criminal activities," Mascara said.

"Well, Aubry Moats, you've been pretty busy since you've left the mountain," Hal said. "We've been following your trail of abducted children for a couple of years. Where've you been living since you gave up mountain life?" Hal asked.

"Ten Mile Creek."

"I heard Jacob McCallister lived there during the past year," Hal said on an impulse, having no idea, whatsoever, where McCallister had been. He knew, though, that the fact that Moats had the identical truck McCallister drove eight months ago and came from the same mountain wasn't a coincidence.

"Yeah, but before his trouble, he wouldn't socialize with th' likes of me. Afterward I don't mix with th' likes of him. Show him who's important now," Aubry bragged.

"That's interesting. What trouble?" Hal asked, hardly containing the excitement in his voice at discovering where McCallister had been the past eight months. The information was absolutely imperative to the rescue of Tuesday's baby.

"Told ya, after my name and address, I ain't talkin' no more 'til I get to make my call."

"You'd better be calling an attorney like Murdock told you. You're going to need one."

"Don't want no damn attorney takin' my money," Aubry said. "When it comes to money, I don't trust anyone 'cept myself."

"Make your call. We have all the time in the world," Hal said, "but I want to know where you were taking the boy first."

"That's easy. I was takin' him to Steven Lloyd."

"Ron, Cliff must know immediately that Aubry Moats was apprehended and he gave us McCallister's whereabouts for the past eight months. McCallister may have taken Tuesday's baby there; he'd feel safe enough. He lived there eight months without having the law come knocking at his door. Will you get someone to round up Murdock and send him to me? I'll see that this scumbag makes his call."

"Damned right," Mascara said, "and it's time we bring Steven Lloyd in. I'd say with Moats' testimony and the documentation we have from Judy Grear we have more than enough on him to put him behind bars."

Hal led Aubry out to the phone and unlocked the cuffs.

The phone on the other end rang six times, and Aubry was ready to give up when Jess Willis picked up. "Deputy Jess Willis."

"Hey, old buddy, how ya doin'? I need to talk to my brother. He there?"

"He's in the back. Wait and I'll get him," Jess said.

"What ya think I'm goin' to do, hang up cause he ain't sit'n at th' phone waitin' for my call?" Aubry asked. "I ain't talked to my brother or ya for a couple years."

"Same old troublemaker," Willis said. "Hold your water and I'll get him."

"Sheriff, you'll never guess who's on the phone," Willis yelled.

"Suppose I shouldn't have to guess since I've got you to answer the phone and tell me what's goin' on," Ozzie spat. "Can't you take care of it?" he asked. "I'm already put out by them big-feelin' city detectives roaring up to my door on their hideous snow machines and interrogatin' me like I'm a lowlife criminal. It gets a man in a ill-tempered mood."

"I think you'll want to take care of this one," Jess smirked. "It's your long-lost brother."

Sheriff Ozzie turned as pale as his white shirt. "Gimme that phone," he ordered. "Why didn't you tell me?"

"What the hell you wantin', Aubry?" Ozzie shouted in Aubry's ear. "You're in trouble, aren't you?"

"Yeah, ya got that right, Brother! I need ya to get me a fancy lawyer. Th' cops here are tellin' me to get one, but I don't trust them here. I need ya to get me one we can trust. And I resent your attitude. Ya always did expect me to get in trouble. Ya should be happy now."

"What you need a lawyer for?" Ozzie asked.

"Told ya, Big Brother. I'm in trouble. Been charged with kidnappin'."

"Damn you, Aubry. I knowed you'd come to a no-good end."

"I ain't at a no-good end if ya get me that lawyer. If I let them city cops get me one, he'll be on their side. I can tell 'cause they keep askin' to get me one. I keep thinkin', why they care? Ya do this an' when I get out I'll see that ya get paid handsomely."

"You always were an idiot, Aubry. They have to offer you legal counsel. Otherwise you can get off on some technicality."

"Don't trust 'em. Ya get me one. I'm in th' city jail in Wheelin'." Aubry hung up. He knew Ozzie would do as he had asked him. Mountain blood ran thick from brother to brother.

35

*M*AKING A CALL TO PLAY IT COOL, MCCALLISTER dropped the shotgun at his side. Taking a chance that the patrol would think nothing of a car coming from the back road to continue up the mountain, he took the road to the right. There was no warning shot from the roadblock, no officer jumping on a snowmobile to chase after him. As a matter of fact, the reflection in the rearview mirror revealed that no one at the intersection was paying any attention whatsoever to him. Keeping his hand on the gun at his side, he moved slowly from their sight as he continued up the road at a slow pace. As the road ran up the mountain to Centerpoint, it wound past single houses that were widely spaced, the very places where he had sold moonshine in the past.

Well out of sight of the roadblock, he pulled the car off the road and sat with the heater full blast, warming him and drying his wet clothing.

"I must keep calm and think," McCallister whispered aloud just to hear the sound of his own voice. The quiet and feeling of aloneness were getting to him. "The men on snowmobiles at the foot of the mountain could only mean that Moran found out about Herman Ruble's cabin on Broad Run." McCallister pounded on the dash, a sharp blow that sent pain up his arm.

"So Tuesday, Patty, and Paul Frank have reached Tuesday's home in Wheeling and spilled their guts. The men patrolling will know what I look like and they'll be looking for my kisser, and my truck as described to them by my little family. Well, they aren't looking for this car, or a bald farmer. And the only thing that I need to become a bald farmer is a razor."

Jacob pulled back on the road and casually headed into the town of Centerpoint, which lay ahead about a quarter of a mile. There was no snow-mobile following behind him. Apparently—when he had turned right as he left Higgins' Garage—it had not looked as if he had had a change of heart about his direction only after spotting the road-block. He pulled in front of The General Store and scanned the area for any unusual activity or strangers. Except for the many cars and trucks that were parked at the community building, all was normal and no one was in sight. It was the same typical, sleepy, nowhere town from Jacob's moon-shine days. Hurrying, he entered the store.

"What can I do for ya today?" Elrod Knotts, the proprietor asked.

McCallister did not recognize the man. "I need a straight razor, shaving cream, and aftershave—Old Spice, if you've got it."

While the clerk gathered McCallister's purchases, he browsed around looking at the limited supply of clothing on display. He picked up a plaid, flannel shirt and a pair of khaki pants and had the clerk add them to his purchases. This was not the first time McCallister had used this same disguise. When he had relocated to Ten Mile Creek he used the photo, taken in the guise, on the fake license he now carried.

"That'll be forty-six dollars," Elrod Knotts said.

McCallister paid, hurried from the store, got in the car, and headed in the opposite direction from Route Seven where he had first spotted the men on snowmobiles.

It was late afternoon, and there was a county fair going on in Centerpoint's community building. Folks had brought in the canned goods they'd put up the summer before—home grown—straight from their own gardens. Some had brought their homemade pies, cakes, bread, and casseroles, too. Others brought crafts made of wood.

Booths and tables were set up, displaying homemade quilts and knick-knacks. For the hungry there were hot dogs, hamburgers, pepperoni buns, meats, potatoes, pies, cakes, and soft drinks. Moonshine was kept out of sight, but the ones looking for the brew knew whom to ask for it. All were offered for sale or trade. For show, the men and boys brought in the blue-ribbon livestock they'd raised. A lean-to attached to the community building was used as a barn. Because of the recent snowstorm, hauling the animals a great distance was not possible, and the barn was not nearly filled to its capacity.

There were game booths with various games where prizes ranged from homemade stuffed bears, homemade dolls, hand-whittled wooden toys, and handmade items for the adult winner.

Over the entire expanse of the building, various singsong voices could be heard calling, "Hot dogs, one dollar an' fifteen cents, get'm here," or, "The finest pepperoni buns what're made right in Opal's kitchen, only one dollar an' thirty cents apiece. Ya can get'm right here at Ronnie Mack's booth." The calls from the game booths promised that prizes would be won every five minutes.

With not much to do in the winter months, nine-tenths of the population attended the indoor fair. Likewise, many people from Winding Ridge attended the fair annually, although the winter fair in Winding Ridge was larger and grander. The fairs, along with the movie theaters, were the only enter-tainment available to the mountain folk, and every-one wanted to go. Of course, neither McCallister nor Dillon had ever allowed his family to attend either fairs or movies.

To avoid coming in sight of the patrol once again, McCallister continued on through town, passing the community building, and took a left. There were a few houses along the dirt road that dead-ended a half mile out. Finding a house on the lane with no one home was more than likely since the inhabi-tants would be at the fair. He picked one with no vehicles around. No smoke came from the chimney, indicating that the fire was banked to hold until the family's return.

Parking the car close to the front door, he got out, gathered his bags, and walked inside like he lived there. First he used a poker in the woodburner to get the fire burning again. He added more wood and set a pan of water on the burner. Next, he set out his razor, aftershave, and shaving cream. He pulled the pins and cardboard from the shirt and threw them back into the bag.

When the water was hot, he set the pan on the side table that was used for washing hands and shaving. His face looked back at him from the mir-ror, which hung above the side table. The unkempt look of the two-day-old growth of beard looked the way it did in the photo on his fake license, so he dis-pensed with a facial shave. Using the straight razor, he cut his hair as close to his scalp as possible. Then he squirted a generous amount of the shaving cream into his palm and rubbed it over his head. With the blade firmly between his fingers, he shaved a swipe from his front hairline to the nape of his neck. After each pass with the razor, he rinsed it in the hot water. When all the hair had been removed, he rinsed his bald head.

In the cloudy mirror that hung over the sink, McCallister saw a new man, he would no doubt blend in with other mountain folk. "Damn, it's amazing how a haircut can change a man's appearance," he said to his reflection and laughed. "Aunt Aggie wouldn't even recognize me if she was at the roadblock and I passed by her in a car."

After cleaning the hair and soap from the top of the table and rinsing the pan he had used, McCallister changed his clothes and put his old ones in the bag along with the hair he'd swept up. Checking to make sure he had not left anything that he'd brought with him, he smiled a self-satisfied smirk that he'd pulled it off. There was no doubt that he looked like the typical mountain man. The suave Jacob McCallister was gone.

He was too wound up, and it was too risky, to sleep for a few hours. He banked the fire, left the house the way he had found it, and got into the car. With the fair still going strong, the car most likely had not been reported stolen. The owner of the car and Higgins, the garage owner, would be at the community building enjoying the festivities with the others.

Before starting the car, McCallister removed the partial plate from his mouth and slipped it into his pocket. He smiled at himself in the rearview mirror. His pink gums, where his front teeth should have been, were not a pretty sight; a bald, unshaven mountain man with a snaggle-toothed grin stared back at him from the mirror.

McCallister drove down the lane and onto the main road past the community building through Centerpoint and headed toward Route Seven. Soon, at the foot of the mountain where Route Seven intersects, the snowmobiles came into sight. The men patrolling were obviously alert and ready for action.

McCallister came to a stop next to Alex Parker.

"See your license and registration please?" Alex asked, not really interested since the man bore no resemblance to McCallister. He was obliged to go through the procedure just the same.

McCallister reached into the glove compartment and found the registration and removed his license from his wallet. He handed both to Alex with a big smile.

Alex looked at the photo. It was obviously the same bald man, with the broad gap in his front teeth, who sat in the car.

"Who ya lookin' for? Never had to show my ID to get off th' mountain before," Jacob said in his best mountain brogue.

"We're looking for Jacob McCallister. Have you seen him?" Alex asked.

"Can't say as I have. Don't believe I knowed him," Jacob answered, relaxing as it became obvious the detective had no suspicions about his identity.

"Whose car you driving? Driver's license shows your name's Victor Newman. Registration's not in your name. How do you do account for that?"

"It's my neighbor, Jim Fetty. He's usin' my truck today to haul his livestock to th' fair." Jacob had remembered the name on the bill of sale he'd seen when he stole the car from Higgins' Garage.

"Why doesn't a man with livestock have a truck of his own?" Alex asked, not really suspicious.

"His truck's on th' blink."

"He's okay. The name on the registration's James Fetty." Dugan said. He had radioed in to the D.M.V. for a license check while Alex questioned the man. "Car's not hot."

"You're free to go, Mr. Newman." Alex waived McCallister on.

With a final grin to the detectives, McCallister turned right on Route Seven, with sweat forming in his armpits even though the temperature inside the car wasn't much warmer than outside.

CHAPTER

36

*A*FTER CHECKING WITH ALEX PARKER AND NED Dugan to see if they had anything to report Tuesday, Cliff, and Randy McCoy left the men patrolling the intersection below Centerpoint and sailed up the mountain road on their snowmobiles. As they came in sight of the town, Tuesday noticed that there were dozens of cars and trucks parked around a huge rectangular building. Along the lone street, designated "Main Street" by the sign at the beginning of the cobblestones that made up the length of the street, vehicles lined each side. The town was nearly a twin to Winding Ridge.

Cliff pulled up in front of The General Store and climbed off the snowmobile. He helped Tuesday, whose skin was blood red from the cold wind hitting her face beneath the helmet.

"Why are we stopping here, Cliff?" Tuesday asked. "I'm sure this road will take us to Herman Ruble's cabin. There's no need to waste time asking."

"Just want to ask a few questions," Cliff said. "Maybe we'll learn something useful. Never hurts to ask. We could use a hot cup of coffee, too. Hard to tell when we'll get our next one."

Randy came up behind Tuesday and Cliff. "I'm all for that." They entered the country store with a bang of the screen door that had not been removed as summer ended and winter came on.

"What can I do for ya today?" The clerk asked his usual question.

"We're in dire need of a hot cup of coffee and a place to warm up," Cliff said.

Tuesday prayed they would get a lead on Jacob in the bargain.

"You've come to th' right place. I've got both. Just take a rocking chair by th' potbelly stove an I'll fetch ya a cup of coffee right away."

There were a dozen chairs arranged around the potbelly stove. Ashtrays were at hand near the chairs and were filled with smelly cigar butts and ashes from well-used pipes. The three of them chose chairs nearest the stove and warmed themselves in the heat that radiated from it.

"Thanks," Tuesday said taking the mug of coffee the clerk handed her.

After serving each one of them and pointing out the arrangement of snack foods they could choose from, the clerk, happy for the company, joined them around the potbelly stove. "Glad to have ya. Durin' th' week of th' winter fair what's held in the community building ain't much business for me. Might just as well close up an' go to th' fair myself."

"I was going to ask why there were so many cars and trucks lining the street and around the community building," Cliff said.

Tuesday sat savoring the hot coffee and the warmth from the stove in spite of her urgency to get to her daughter before it was too late.

"Had any customers at all today?" Cliff asked.

"Except for y'all, just a pitiful few," the proprietor offered.

"Any strangers been around last few days?" Cliff inquired.

"Don't believe there've been strangers, just people from Windin' Ridge and th' mountain folks from both sides of th' mountain come in for th' fair. There was old man Kenney, Hilda Grottendieck, Elsie Oney, and a few from th' surroundin' areas that I ain't got their names fixed in my head. Just knowed their faces an' that they're mountain folk. Why ya wantin' to knowed who'd been in my store?"

"We're detectives from Wheeling. I'm Sergeant Cliff Moran." Cliff shook the clerk's hand. "This is Corporal Randy McCoy, and Tuesday Summers. We're looking for Jacob McCallister."

"Pleased to meet ya," Elrod was visibly relieved that they were not here about the militia that met in his back room each month. "I'm Elrod Knotts, th' sole proprietor of this here establishment. What ya wantin' McCallister for?"

"He's wanted on kidnapping charges."

"I heard of 'im. Think he ran moonshine at one time. Ain't heard of 'im for years now. He's from th' mountain above Windin' Ridge. Don't knowed that I ever met 'im though. I ain't one for drinkin'." Elrod rambled, not willing to give strangers information on a fellow mountain man, even though he and McCallister had a standing dispute about the local mountaineer militia, and McCallister's unwillingness to join or support the movement.

"Here's a likeness of him." Cliff handed the composite drawing to Elrod.

"Could be th' man who'd come in here maybe ten, twenty minutes ago. Looks like 'im. Ain't it always th' way; ya miss everythin' by th' tiniest of minutes." Elrod held out his tobacco-stained thumb and forefinger to measure the amount.

Tuesday and the others stood. "He's still on the mountain and we have him trapped," Tuesday said, her voice quivering with fear. "We can't make a mistake. Winter Ann's future depends on it."

"What did he want?" Cliff asked, hoping to get information that would indicate his next move.

"Let me think. My memory ain't what it use to be. Ya can just ask my wife on that subject. Except she's at th' fair," Elrod laughed.

Knowing that Elrod had gotten side tracked and was thinking of his wife and simply enjoying the conversation, Tuesday asked the question again. "What did he want? Please try to remember."

"Well, he didn't say much, wasn't a talker a'tall, like some comin' in. They like to take time an' visit a spell while they sit around th' stove. Not him though, just browsed around, an' findin' what he wanted he left. Didn't warm his self a'tall."

"Think," Cliff prodded. "Start from him walking through the door."

Elrod got a faraway look in his eyes, rubbing the stubble on his jowls; he ran McCallister's movements through his mind. "Got it! He was askin' for shavin' stuff. Said he wanted Old Spice if I got it, an' he wanted a straight razor. He'd ask special for it, and th' shaving cream. While I gathered his shavin' stuff, he looked at th' men's clothin'. He picked a plaid, flannel shirt and khaki pants. There ya are, I got it. It'd make my wife proud." Elrod wore a self-satisfied smile.

"What do you make of those purchases, Sergeant?" Randy asked.

"Damned if I know. Elrod, do you sell many straight razors?" Cliff asked.

"Yeah, I do. It's what we shave with around here. Men ain't got th' knack for th' fancy ones."

"It sounds like the beginnings of a disguise to me," Randy offered.

"Except that Jacob is usually clean shaven and living on the mountain there's nothing unusual about the straight razor," Tuesday said. "I am wondering where he went to shave and change, though."

"Can you tell us anything more?" Cliff asked.

"Nope. That's it, sweet and simple."

"What was he driving?"

"Don't knowed what he was drivin'. Can't see out the front unless I get to th' porch and look out. Th' windows are about useless to look out of with all th' uncrated merchandise stacked everywhere coverin' them."

"Damn, you can't know which way he went either," Cliff swore.

"Yeah, I do," Elrod said. "I could hear th' tires spinnin' an th' engine whinin' as he spun his way up th' road. That's all I knowed, though, 'cause I could hear th' car's engine."

"I bet he was heading toward Ruble's cabin," McCoy said.

"Jacob bought a razor, shaving cream, and fresh clothing. That means he needs a place to shave and change," Tuesday reasoned. "Only makes sense he'd go back to Ruble's cabin."

"She's right," Randy said. "Can't shave without water. Sounds like he intends to clean up for some reason."

"Let's go. We've taken enough time." Tuesday said glad that Cliff had insisted on stopping by The General Store. It was gratifying to know they were on the right track.

Warmed from the cozy fire and strong hot coffee,

they mounted their snowmobiles and raced up the mountain toward Herman Ruble's cabin.

To let Cliff know they were nearing the cabin, Tuesday poked Cliff in the ribs. He slowed as she pointed to the cabin coming into view. He held up his arm to get McCoy's attention and pointed toward the cabin, indicating they were at their destination.

After Cliff jumped off the snowmobile and helped Tuesday dismount, they surveyed their surroundings. Disappointment swelled in Tuesday's heart when she realized that McCallister's truck was not there. "Maybe Jacob's truck is hidden out of sight or in the barn."

"McCoy, check around for McCallister's truck," Cliff said.

"The Ruble cabin is much larger than I've come across so far," Cliff noted. Like the other cabins on the mountain, Ruble's cabin was in dire need of paint. The rustic cabin stood a thousand yards below the very top of the mountain. The view was spectacular. The mountain towered over the two-story cabin, the barn, cellar house, and outhouse, leaving them in shadow. The scene from the front porch spiraled downward and was breathtaking. The sheer drop to the left of the cabin would try the courage of even the bravest risk-taker of a skier. To the right was the road they had used to get to the cabin.

At Cliff's knock, Aggie came to the door. "It's you again, so it is. Ya goin' to plague me all my life cause I was kind enough to talk to ya an' invite ya in my cabin out of th' cold th' one time?"

"I guess it goes without saying that we're looking for Jacob McCallister."

"Don't knowed where he's off to, so I don't. Men don't bother with tellin' womenfolk their business, so they don't."

"Let us in out of the cold," Cliff commanded. His voice was short, interrupting her chatter.

Aggie stood back. "Can't stop th' likes of you, so I can't."

Inside, Cliff and Tuesday separated to search the cabin. Cliff parted the ragged curtain covering the doorway to the stairs. "Tuesday, wait here and I'll look around up stairs."

"Told ya he ain't here," Aggie said. "Ain't seen him since before Tuesday here left with Paul Frank and Patty," she lied.

"Aggie, the proprietor of The General Store said that Jacob was there about half an hour ago," Tuesday asked. "Where is he?"

"He ain't been here, so he ain't," Aggie said. "He must be mistaken, so he must."

Cliff came back downstairs. There was no McCallister, no straight razor, no plaid shirt, no new slacks on either floor. It looked as if McCallister had not come back to Ruble's cabin with his purchases.

"Cliff, where could he be?" Tuesday said.

"Maybe he's in the barn," Cliff said. "McCoy will be here in a minute."

Tuesday went to look from the window.

"Aggie, who are these girls?" Cliff asked.

"They're Herman Ruble's daughters, so they are. I'm not apt to tell ya everythin' that I knowed like Annabelle an' Daisy did when ya was makin' trouble before when ya caused Jeb to go away, so I'm not. Don't knowed why ya don't leave us alone. There ain't nothin' for me to tell anyways, so there ain't."

"Where's McCallister?" Cliff barked.

"There's no need to get ya back up, so they ain't. I don't knowed, so I don't. Wouldn't tell the likes of ya if I did, so I wouldn't"

Cliff nodded to the girls, "Where's McCallister? You'd better tell me what you know or you'll be charged with obstructing justice."

"We don't knowed where he is," Rachel answered. "Tuesday, ya knowed we'd tell ya if we knowed where he is."

"That's right," Ida May said, "When he came back for ya from sellin' th' baby an' when ya wasn't here, he left again."

"How long ago was that?" Cliff asked.

"Don't knowed exactly," Rachel said. "It's been hours, I guess."

"You're sure Jacob didn't come back here in the last hour?" Tuesday asked.

"We're sure," Rachel said.

Tuesday soon realized they knew nothing that would be of help to them. They were merely victims of Jacob McCallister's crimes.

When Randy returned from the out buildings, Cliff and Tuesday were discussing what to do next.

"Truck's in the barn," Randy said.

"That's strange," Cliff said. "He's obviously not here."

"Aggie, please tell us how Jacob left, and we need to know why McCallister bought the razor and shaving supplies," Tuesday said. "Please tell us what you know."

"Told ya I don't know anythin', so I don't," Aggie said.

"He left walkin'" Rachel said, "an' I didn't see him shavin'. He didn't even take a bath."

"He didn't have anythin' with 'im except his gun," Ida May said.

"He left walking," Cliff repeated. "That doesn't make sense. The proprietor at The General Store said he spun his wheels as he drove up the mountain. He got transportation somewhere."

"Okay," Tuesday said, "now we know he has a vehicle and he felt it was important to go shopping when he was being hunted for a serious crime. Cliff, going shopping at a time like this doesn't make any more sense than taking off walking in this weather when he had a four-wheel-drive truck in the barn."

"Right," Cliff said, "not with the law breathing down his neck."

"Maybe his purchases were for his change to the city look," Randy said. "Didn't he dress totally different when he was in the city than when on the mountain?"

"Yes, but I don't think that's it," Cliff said, "If that were true, why the plaid, flannel shirt. Did he wear flannel shirts in Wheeling?"

"No," Tuesday answered, "he mostly wore suits and ties, or sports jackets and button-down shirt with Levi's."

"Disguise." Randy said. "That's the only thing that fits."

"How would he disguise himself with the items he bought?" Tuesday asked.

"I don't know," Randy said, "but that has to be it."

"When we had him cornered before, his instinct told him to run, not to go shopping so that he'd be clean shaven and well dressed," Cliff remembered. "He just took off with the clothing on his back."

"We didn't have a roadblock set up when he ran eight months ago," Randy offered. "He saw the roadblock and realized his only option was to change his appearance."

"If that's true, we must have been in rock-throwing distance from him when we got our snowmobiles off the truck and set up the roadblock," Cliff said. "Elrod said he was in the store only ten or twenty minutes before we got there. So he must still be on the mountain."

"The men will not let anyone through without ID, and McCallister couldn't buy anything in The General Store to disguise his driver's license. I can't imagine what good the disguise would do unless he wanted to come and go around the mountain without being recognized."

"Unless he had fake ID," Cliff said. "After all, he's been a fugitive for the past eight months."

Aggie had been preparing the evening meal before they'd arrived at the doorstep. "Do ya want somethin' to eat? Don't approve of ya chasin' after Jeb, so I don't. But it ain't no call for ya to starve, so it ain't."

"We would love a hot meal, Aggie," Cliff answered for all of them.

37

*I*KNEW ALL ALONG THAT MY GOOD-FOR-NOTHIN' brother would one day ruin the good name of Moats and cost me money in the process," Ozzie complained as he slammed the phone back in its cradle. "I don't have a king's ransom, but I sure do have a hefty nest egg. Looks like Aubry's bound and determined to get me shed of it. Ain't no reason he can't use a court-appointed lawyer. Never could tell him nothin'." Ozzie picked up his spittoon and spit a brown glob out between his front teeth.

"What's the problem with your brother now, Sheriff?" Jess Willis asked.

"Ain't heard from Aubry for nearly two years, and you act like he calls every day with a problem. Ain't none of your business anyway, Jess," Ozzie said and sat the spittoon back on the floor beside his desk.

"Sorry," Jess shrugged, "but it seemed to me when you hung up the phone you were tellin' me all about your brother and his problems and I was just seein' if I could help."

"Yes, you can help, Jess. You're goin' to have to take charge for a while. Don't screw up and disappoint me," Ozzie demanded. "I'm goin' to the city. Surely you can take care of matters here until I get back." The overweight sheriff held his hand up to his mouth and allowed his wad of well-chewed tobacco to fall onto his palm. He leaned over and dropped the soggy glob into his spittoon, wiping his hand on his trouser leg.

"You're goin' to help that no-good Aubry?" Jess asked.

It was not like the sheriff to go out of his way for another; and he never traveled to the city. He was more bigoted about the big city people than he was the mountain folk.

"Don't you be callin' my brother no good. The Moats family takes care of its own. Besides, can't let my brother ruin my good name. Furthermore, it ain't none of your business what I do. You'd do well to mind your own."

"I'll be here just like I always am," Jess said. "You don't have to have a disagreeable attitude about everythin'. Guess I heard you call your brother no good about a million times."

"Just keep your opinions to yourself. I just want you to take care of things while I'm gone, not reinvent the place like you're apt to do. Take me over to my place for my truck. I'll pack and be on my way."

"You're in luck. Some of the farmers got out and plowed the snow from off the road down to Route Seven," Jess said.

"See to it that you keep up your weekly run up to McCallister's cabin like I've told you," Ozzie said. "I don't want them big-feelin' detectives from the big city on my back."

When Aubry had finished his phone call, Hal escorted him back to the interrogation room. With a small shove toward the chair Aubry had sat in earlier, Hal indicated for him to sit at the table once again.

"I'm not talkin' till my brother, Ozzie, comes with a lawyer," Aubry announced, sitting in the chair.

"Thought you didn't want a lawyer," Hal said.

"Just don't want ya city people to get me one," Aubry said.

"That's your right. I'll see if they're ready for you outside." Hal left Aubry to stew alone in the windowless room and went looking for Ron Mascara and Bob Murdock.

He found them in the day room with the boy Moats had tried to kidnap. They were eating ice cream and entertaining him while he waited for his parents. "Where'd you get the ice cream?" Hal asked in an attempt to take his mind off his ordeal and erase the fear from his eyes.

"Ah, guess you didn't know. We keep ice cream in the freezer special for our young visitors," Murdock said, playing along.

"Talk to you in the hall for a minute?" Hal asked Murdock.

"What's up?" Murdock stood just outside the door to the day room while Mascara stayed with the boy.

"Did you get in touch with Cliff?" Hal asked.

"I had the desk sergeant radio for Moran to call in," Murdock said."

"Guess all I can do is wait," Hal said.

"I think the information is the break of the century," Murdock said.

"You're right about that," Hal said. "It's important to get word to him as soon as possible."

"I'd love to be the one to fill him in about Aubry Moats giving us the name of the town where McCallister's been these past months," Murdock said.

"Moats didn't bat an eyelash when he spilled the beans on McCallister, telling us he's been living at Ten Mile Creek for the past year," Hal said.

"You know, Ten Mile Creek's near Summersville, and Cliff and Randy McCoy are four hours closer to Summersville at Centerpoint than we are," Murdock said.

"Yes, I do. That's why I want to get the information to Cliff right away. He'll want to get on it. Catching Aubry Moats and getting him to talk sure was a milestone," Hal said. "I can't wait to give Cliff the news. Our only hope of finding Tuesday's baby is to act fast."

Tuesday was the first to hear the roar of the snowmobile coming fast up the hill. She jumped from her chair and rushed to the door. She stood with the icy air blowing inside and saw one of the men they had left to patrol at the intersection speeding toward the cabin. *Please dear, God, let it be good news. In Jesus' name I pray.*

Cliff came up behind her.

"What is it?" he asked.

"It's John Gibson." She recognized him as he slowed at the front of the cabin and cut the motor.

"What's up, Gibson?" Cliff asked, stepping onto the front porch.

"Lieutenant Hal Brooks radioed me a while ago. He wants you to call in as soon as possible. He says he has Aubry Moats in custody. He was caught in the act of abducting a small boy. Aubry Moats has been living in Ten Mile Creek, and the good news is that Moats let the cat out of the bag that McCallister has spent the last eight months living there, too."

"Cliff, there's a pay phone at the bus depot," Tuesday offered.

"Thanks, Gibson. Go on back to Dugan and Parker," Cliff said. "Tell one of them to keep up the patrol alone for a while. Have the other one get some shut-eye for the nightshift. Do the same with Bert Howard and Rex Tripp at Winding Ridge."

"I think that's a good move," Gibson said. "What do you want the other men to do?"

"Find Wildman," Cliff said, "and the two of you can conduct a house-to-house search for McCallister. He hasn't come back here to Ruble's cabin like we'd hoped. From what we found out at The General Store, he may be in disguise."

"You suppose he's gotten through?" Gibson asked.

"I doubt that," Cliff said. "The men are asking for licenses and ID. We can't mess up! There's too much at stake."

"Altogether," Gibson said, "including myself, you, and McCoy, we have nine men between Centerpoint and Winding Ridge. There'll be one man on patrol at each intersection going off of Route Seven, leaving two men off duty to take the nightshift. Wildman and I will do the house-to-house. There'll be one man to stake out the fair at the community building. McCallister could be mixing in with the mountain folk."

"Okay," Cliff said. "Unless you find something, meet us in the morning. There's a boarding house across from The General Store. We'll stay there."

Gibson hustled off to get the search started.

"Cliff, why don't we just go to Ten Mile Creek?" Tuesday asked. "It makes sense that that's where Jacob has gone."

"That's what I intend to do," Cliff said, "but we can't go while we have reason to believe McCallister's still on the mountain."

"I don't know why, but I think he's no longer on the mountain," Tuesday said.

"I don't think so," Cliff said. "He couldn't have gotten past the patrol, and there's no other way off the mountain."

"What if you're wrong?" Tuesday said.

"If I'm wrong, we'll head to Ten Mile Creek," Cliff said, "but it'd be a mistake if we go and he's still on the mountain."

"How's that?" Tuesday asked.

"If he's still on the mountain, the baby may be as well," Cliff said, "and he'll have the time to go north to Wheeling while we're out of the way in Ten Mile Creek."

"That makes sense," Tuesday said. "I suppose I should leave the detective work to you."

"We're going to find your daughter," Cliff promised. "Our knowing where McCallister was during his retreat from the law is going to be his ultimate downfall."

Tuesday, Cliff, and Randy McCoy left to make the call.

"There's the phone," Tuesday pointed out.

Cliff got through to Hal right away. "What's up, Hal?"

"Murdock picked up Aubry Moats," Hal said. "Remember the truck McCallister had in the beginning? Well, Aubry Moats' truck is identical."

"Last year when I first met Tuesday at Cora's house, McCallister was there. Cora told me that McCallister had an identical truck to the one identified in the latest kidnapping," Cliff said.

"Right, I remember McCallister's truck was what first made you suspicious of him," Hal said

"As it turned out rightly so," Cliff said, "although, he was not the one doing the kidnapping, he was selling his own children."

"Aubry Moats makes his home in a small town near Southern Arthurdale. It's called Ten Mile Creek.

He says that McCallister rents a room in a boarding house in the same town. I believe that's where he took Tuesday's baby. That's where he's been holed up making his plans to kidnap Tuesday and Patty."

"What a break!" Cliff said. "We need to hurry now. My bet is he has a plan already in place to sell the baby."

"Absolutely, timing is important now," Hal said, "but what's happened since you left here with Tuesday and McCoy? I know you believed he may go back to the cabin for Tuesday after selling the child."

"Not much, but we just know he's around. He came back from wherever he took Tuesday's baby. Naturally, he thought Tuesday and Patty were still in Ruble's cabin. Since then, I don't think he's been able to get off the mountain," Cliff said. "The only two avenues off the mountain are patrolled by our men, and we found out, from a clerk at The General Store in Centerpoint, that McCallister was in the store making purchases about twenty minutes ahead of our arrival. That means he was still on the mountain when we set up the patrols and he's still there."

"The fact that McCallister's still on the mountain may be to your advantage," Hal said. "He has no way of knowing you have enough information to locate Tuesday's daughter. You have the element of surprise on your side. I'm going to stay here and coordinate the evidence coming in. You and your men concentrate on finding the baby. Since time is of the essence, your group is the obvious choice for going to Ten Mile Creek."

"I agree, and Tuesday would have it no other way," Cliff said, "but we'll need to sleep for a couple of hours."

"I insist on that," Hal said.

"I'll leave Bert Howard and Walter Wildman to patrol the exits off Winding Ridge and Centerpoint. Rex Tripp and Ned Dugan will continue the house-to-house search for McCallister."

"Sounds like a plan," Hal said. "That'll leave you, Randy McCoy, John Gibson, and Alex Parker to help out in Ten Mile Creek."

"I'll keep in touch, Hal," Cliff said. "We're tired and are going to check into the boarding house for a couple hours' sleep."

In spite of the late hour, checking into the boarding house was pretty simple. They paid in advance and were given keys to their rooms.

After they were shown to their rooms, the proprietor graciously laid out a simple meal of potato salad, sliced ham, baked beans, and homemade applesauce. Since they had not eaten since Aggie had prepared their late lunch, they were hungry. After finishing the meal they separated, agreeing to meet at 6:00 A.M. for breakfast. According to the proprietor, the meal was served at six o'clock on the dot. Gibson was to meet them at breakfast with a report on the progress of the house-to-house search, which had begun more than an hour earlier and would continue as long as it was feasible. The fair had been closed for at least two hours, and most had had time to reach their respective homes.

Cliff was removing his boots when there was a knock at his bedroom door. "Come in."

"Sergeant," John Gibson said as he came into the room, "I have reason to believe McCallister got past our patrol."

"How could that happen?" Cliff yelled.

"Calm down and hear me out," Gibson said. "I started my door-to-door search at the intersection of Route Seven and the road to Centerpoint. I was knocking on doors at the houses on the road off to the left after passing the community building. I questioned the family in the third house and they said they found tracks on the kitchen floor that were not they're when they left that afternoon. Upon further inspection they found dark brown hair in a bucket that's used for heating water. The hair was stuck around the inside and it was still wet. The hair was several inches long. The family hadn't done any hair cutting recently, and they've never used the bucket for cutting hair or shaving. It was solely used for heating water."

"So you're saying someone was there for a hair cut," Cliff asked, "while the family attended the fair?"

"Looks like it," Gibson said. "McCallister has dark brown hair. He must have shaved his head. I hate to put someone on the hot seat, but I'm sure the patrol let him pass early today."

"How the hell could they let that happen?" Cliff bellowed. "They know how important it is that we find him soon."

"From what Parker and Dugan tell me, the man was bald, virtually toothless and as Parker said if he wasn't the typical mountain dude, he don't know who was."

"Did they remember what he wore?" Cliff resigned himself to the fact that McCallister may have gotten past the patrol.

"A plaid shirt stuck out from the opening of his denim coat," Gibson said. "Here are the notes Parker gave me."

"Must be McCallister. Everything ties in with his purchases." Cliff read the notes. The license was in the name of Victor Newman. According to Parker's notes the photo on the driver's license matched the bald man with the toothless grin. The car was registered to Jim Fetty, and the bald man's explanation was that the car was a neighbor's who had borrowed his truck for the fair, leaving him with the neighbor's car.

"The car was reported stolen about two hours ago and that was hours after the bald guy drove through the roadblock," Gibson said. "Jim Fetty was at the fair and didn't know it was missing until he went to Higgins' Garage to pick it up late tonight."

"What do you make of the missing teeth?" Cliff asked.

"Must have a partial plate," Gibson said. "Parker was sure that they weren't blacked out with any theatrical makeup or anything like that."

"It's too late to go after him tonight. Put out an all-points bulletin on the car and a description of his disguise," Cliff ordered. "He's heading for Ten Mile Creek. Call the police department there so they'll be on the lookout for him. If nothing happens during the night, meet us back here at 6:00 A.M. If Tuesday weren't with us I'd be tempted to go now, except he'll most likely hole up for the night."

"Getting a few hours shut-eye's the best thing. Can't do a job if we're not alert," Gibson said. "McCallister surely won't be going without sleep."

McCallister drove through the first town to the south that he'd come to after leaving Centerpoint, looking for an isolated place to ditch the car, somewhere that it could go unnoticed for a very long time. When it was found, the car would leave a trail. A river or pond would be perfect. He could push the car into one, but they were frozen over this time of year. He passed the Big Otter bus depot. The Big Otter high school was to his right. He drove around the back and found a larger lot next to the football field. McCallister parked the car, and after tossing the keys into the trunk, he locked the doors. He walked back toward the bus depot, carrying the bag with his shaving cream, after shave, straight razor, and the hair he'd cleaned up, plastic wrappers, and pins from the purchase he'd made in Centerpoint.

Inside the depot was a huge trash container where McCallister deposited the bag. Next, he found a bulletin board with various bus schedules posted. Studying them, he found what he wanted. About halfway to its destination, the bus going to Bluefield went through Ten Mile Creek, where he would actually get off. On the off chance it'd be discovered that he had abandoned the stolen car at the Big Otter High School and purchased a ticket to Bluefield, Bluefield would then be where the police would look for him.

"Need a ticket to Bluefield," McCallister said as he took out his wallet.

"That'll be sixty dollars." The clerk took the money. "Your luggage?" The clerk asked surprised at not seeing any bags with a one-way ticket purchase.

"I'm traveling light," McCallister said. "Emergency trip. What time does the bus leave?"

"Twenty minutes," the clerk answered. "There's a snack bar over there. You have time to grab a bite."

McCallister went to the snack bar and chose a ham sandwich for a dollar fifty from a vending machine. He got a soft drink and a bag of chips.

When the departure announcement came over the loud speaker, McCallister was already standing at the one and only gate to the loading area where the bus waited.

The door opened and the bus driver stood, hand out. "Tickets, please."

McCallister went straight to the back where the seat stretched across the width of the bus. It was as good as any place to sleep. According to the bus schedule, he would be in Ten Mile Creek—the halfway point—in three hours. The bus would wind through the back roads, stopping at each town along the way. Had he driven Interstate 79, he could have been there from Big Otter in an hour and half.

The hum of the bus lulled him to sleep.

Tuesday was the first one down for breakfast. Her eyes were red and swollen from crying. She had been too nervous to sleep. She sat at the table and was served a cup of steaming hot coffee.

"Good morning." Cliff came up behind her and gave her a quick kiss as she turned to greet him.

"Cliff, let's hurry. I can't bear the thought of never finding Winter Ann. Time is critical."

Cliff sat beside Tuesday and McCoy joined them. "Morning," he greeted them. "Saw Gibson out the window snowmobiling up the road last night."

"Gibson brought us crucial information." Cliff updated Tuesday and Randy on the visit from John Gibson the night before. "McCallister got through the roadblock and I'm sure he's headed for Ten Mile Creek, where he was holed up the past eight months."

Tuesday could hardly believe her ears. "How could that be? I don't understand how he could get through the roadblock. Cliff, he knows we're after him. We can't waste any time. We've got to get to Winter Ann."

Gibson came in, stomping the snow from his boots, and joined the others at the table.

"Soon as we eat, the three of us will load the snowmobiles into our trucks and head for Ten Mile Creek. Gibson, get the others and catch up with us. We'll need your help. There's no need to keep a patrol here now that McCallister's gotten through."

38

*T*HE BABY WAS A PERFECT LITTLE DOLL. OLENE HAD made a profitable deal for Winter Ann with a couple who had agreed to pay fifty thousand dollars for her. The peace of mind they would have, getting a baby without a birth record, was worth the money to the couple. She had only paid Victor Newman a five-thousand-dollar retainer, and he was to get another five thousand when the couple paid her.

The most recent houseguest, who was not due to give birth for four months, cared for the baby while Olene worked. The baby had been with Olene for four days now. The new parents were due to come for the baby anytime. It would be good for Olene when the baby was out of the house and she had the cash. The baby was a disruption, especially at night.

Olene was in her nurse's uniform ready to leave for work when the doorbell rang. She opened the door. "May I help you?" She asked, not recognizing Jacob McCallister, whom she knew only as Victor Newman.

"Hi, doll. Don't recognize me, do you?" McCallister laughed.

"Victor, I can't believe my eyes. "What happened to your hair?" He had put his partial plate back in as soon as he had driven through the road block at the foot of Centerpoint road.

"Long story. Can I come in?"

"Of course, Victor. I'm always delighted to see you."

"I need to get lost for a while. Think you can help me?"

"I don't know. Do you have a destination in mind?"

"I was hoping that you would."

"I suppose your bald head has something to do with all this."

"It'll grow back."

"I have a friend who has a chalet at Crystal Lake. She has been trying to sell it. I'm sure she would let you stay there. I have a key. It's a pretty nice get-away, but Crystal Lake is pretty dead. They get no tourists anymore, it's run down, and there's nothing much to do, but there is a fairly large town close by."

"I don't want to leave a trail," McCallister said. "Who knows you have a friend who owns a chalet in Crystal Lake?"

"I'm sure no one does," Olene said. "You know I keep my personal life private. I confide in no one. When you're in a business like mine, you can't have any friends. I guarantee that we won't be traced."

"Crystal Lake sounds good," McCallister said. "A dead town is what I'm looking for. I had to leave my truck behind and ride the bus here. I'll need your help to gather my belongings from the rooming house and drive me to Crystal Lake."

"I'd love to, but I have to go to work first," Olene

said, anxious to be with him for any reason. "Make yourself comfortable and I'll be back around three-thirty this afternoon."

"Report in sick," McCallister said. "I can't wait until this evening."

"Okay, Victor. I'll see what I can do."

Olene reported in sick and went to change.

McCallister picked up the remote and turned to a news channel. There was no mention of his getaway or the baby.

Olene came back into the room dressed in jeans and a violet wool sweater. "I'm ready. Let me tell Mary I'm leaving."

McCallister got up, and before he could turn off the TV an announcement came on:

At three o'clock yesterday afternoon a man named Aubry Moats was apprehended in the act of abducting a young boy from his school bus stop. The boy's name has not been released at this time. It is believed that Aubry Moats is the man who was responsible for at least three other abductions in the past year. We will broadcast any further details as they become available.

"Damn, this is bad news. Aubry doesn't have a brain in his head. He runs his mouth just to hear his own voice. That settles it. I can't stay around here."

"What?" Olene called. He didn't answer. "What's wrong, Victor? I heard you say something," she yelled louder. Still not getting an answer, Olene walked back to the living room. "Somebody walk across your grave? You look as if you've been hit in the gut."

"Let's go," McCallister said. "I don't know how much time I have. Aubry Moats was picked up. He may have talked, and Moran could be on his way here by now. We'll talk on the way. He could have implicated you as well as me."

"I don't think he's going to say anything about me," Olene said. "If he does, they can't prove anything."

"I wouldn't be so sure. I've found it's amazing how that detective finds out so much once he gets on your trail. After we get me settled, I want you to take a leave of absence and pack your things and join me. It's too risky for you to stay in your house while you may be under suspicion. You'll be a sitting duck."

"Tell you what. I'll take you to get your things and then I'll take you to Crystal Lake. I'll go back to my house, take care of business, and after the couple picks up the baby, I'll join you."

"Good thinking," Jacob said. "We'll need the money. How much you getting for the baby?" McCallister asked.

"Now wait a minute. You got your five thousand dollars up front. When I get paid you get the other five. I don't know what makes you think that we're sharing the fifty thousand dollars that I'm getting for the child," Olene said.

"Look, we're in this together, now. If you want to stay with me, you'll hand over the money. Understand?" Jacob said.

"Okay, but I want a wedding ring," Olene demanded.

"We'll see." Jacob gripped her arm, giving her a menacing look.

"Okay."

"That's my girl. With that amount of money we can arrange to leave the country. Looks like I've done it again. It's getting to be a habit, me getting the better of the big Detective Cliff Moran." Jacob laughed a sound of pure joy.

Olene grabbed her coat from the hall closet, and

they went through the kitchen to the garage. They would clear out McCallister's room and be at Crystal Lake in an hour.

Ozzie came into the station dressed in his best sheriff's uniform. He huffed and puffed his way to the desk sergeant. "I'm here to see Aubry Moats. Where you holdin' him?"

"Who are you?"

"I'm Sheriff Ozzie Moats, and I'm here to see that my brother has legal counsel."

"Sheriff, if you'd take a seat over there, I'll get someone to help you," the sergeant said.

As soon as Hal got the call that Ozzie was downstairs, he went to see what it was all about.

"What you think your doin' lockin' up my brother? As one law man to another, I can vouch for him. He ain't done nothin'."

"I beg to differ," Hal said. "Your brother was caught in the act. He's been booked and is being held without bail."

"I need to get him a lawyer. You're goin' to have to help me. I've never been to the city before. Tell me where to go."

"Come to my office." Hal suddenly felt embarrassed for the sheriff, who was obviously out of his element here. "I'll get you a phone book and let you use my phone. Should be able to find someone who can come down right away and help you."

Ozzie followed Hal to the elevator. Finally, in Hal's office Ozzie took the large phone book. It was a hundred times the size of the one for Winding Ridge. Hal had turned to the listings for lawyers.

Ozzie hadn't expected so many names to choose from. There were several pages listing the lawyers' names.

"There are ads listing the areas the attorneys specialize in," Hal explained. "You want a criminal lawyer."

Ozzie frowned. "My brother needs a criminal lawyer? Don't knowed where to start."

"Best I can tell you," Hal advised, "is to call until you find one who can get here today."

Ozzie sat and dialed the first number on the list. The lawyer was too busy. So was the second, and the third, and so on until at last on the eleventh call he got a yes answer. Sam Welsh would meet him in Aubry's cell in half an hour.

"Can I see my brother?" Ozzie asked.

"Sure. I'll take you there."

Ozzie followed Hal down the hall to Aubry's cell. "Why in the world do you need such a huge buildin' for your office and the jail?"

"This is a big city, and there's a lot of crime," Hal said. "Here's your brother's cell. I'll come back later and get you myself." Hal left Ozzie and Aubry alone and went back to his office.

"Hi, Aubry. Here I am. I got you the best lawyer money can buy," Ozzie said.

"Ya betta have," Aubry said. "I can't stand it locked in this little bitty cage. It ain't fittin' for a man to be locked up like this."

Keys clanged and an officer appeared with a man in a business suit at his side.

"Good evening, gentleman," Welsh said. "I'm the attorney you called."

Ozzie reached out his hand to the attorney. "I'm Ozzie Moats and this is my brother, Aubry Moats."

"Let's get down to business," Welsh said.

After only a half an hour, Sam Welsh advised Aubry to cut the best deal that he could. He really had no choice, having been caught in the act. "Aubry, you'll be a wealth of information for the prosecution, and they know it. That's the best advice I can give you." Aubry agreed.

Ozzie couldn't argue with the facts. He went along with Sam Welsh. So Aubry talked. He told all he knew about Simon Leonard, Jacob McCallister, Frank Dillon, Steven Lloyd, George Cunningham, Doc Johnson, Molly Anderson, and Olene Ryder. He did all he could to lay blame on all the others, and painted a softer picture of his own activities. All the information was given for a promise that the prosecution would go easier on him—by giving him the minimum sentence possible for his crimes.

Alex Parker got a phone message from Hal, just before he left the boarding house, that Aubry had revealed McCallister's and Olene Ryder's addresses. Alex Parker, John Gibson, Bert Howard, Rex Tripp, Walter Wildman, and Ned Dougan were leaving Centerpoint in three trucks with the snow-mobiles in the back on their way to Ten Mile Creek. Every so often Alex tried to reach Cliff by radio to give him the information. They were on the road only a few hours behind Cliff and his group.

After a short stop in Big Otter, Tuesday and the others climbed back into the truck armed with directions to Ten Mile Creek. A call was coming in on the radio. It was Alex Parker with McCallister's address, the name of the woman to whom Aubry Moats on occasion sold his young victims, and her address. She would be the link for the sale of Winter Ann. They would go to McCallister's address first. Alex and his group would catch up with them as quickly as possible.

Shortly after the call they came to the city limits of Ten Mile Creek, Cliff drove past the rooming house where McCallister lived and parked half a block away. "Tuesday, stay in the truck," Cliff demanded.

"No. I'm going with you and don't bother to argue with me. You know how stubborn I can be," she said. Although her spirits had lifted a little with the new information, a heavy lump of dark fear invaded her stomach.

They walked back to the rooming house. Randy and Tuesday stood back as Cliff knocked on the door. A woman peered out and then opened the door. "Lookin' for a room?" she asked.

"We're looking for Jacob McCallister or Victor Newman," Cliff said. "Does anyone by either of those names live here?"

"Why do you want to know?" the woman asked, seemingly afraid to give out any information.

Cliff held up his ID and said, "He's wanted for kidnapping."

"He? You asked for two men," the woman said.

"Newman is an alias," Cliff said. "When he's on the run he uses a fake ID."

The woman needed no further encouragement, "Yes. Victor Newman lives here. He was here about forty-five minutes ago with his friend, Olene Ryder, carrying things out. They were in a big hurry."

"Thank you," Cliff said to the woman. "Can we see his room?"

"I suppose it's okay. It's up the stairs. The second room to the right. I'll unlock it for you."

They followed the woman up the stairs and down the hall to McCallister's room. She unlocked the dead bolt and opened the door to a disheveled room. The dresser drawers were open and most were empty, with unwanted clothing spilling from a tilted drawer here and there.

"He's gone," Tuesday cried.

"Let's go," Cliff could find nothing of any significance in the abandoned room.

They found Olene's house and stopped half a

block away. "I'll go to the door and ask for Olene. I'll say I'm there about the baby," Cliff said. "It's a long shot, but we've not lost anything if I don't get anywhere."

Cliff walked to the front door and a young, pregnant girl answered. "I'm here to see Olene Ryder," Cliff said.

"She's gone out. Didn't say when she'd be back."

"I'm here about the baby."

"I don't have nothing to do about that. You'll have to come back when Olene's here," the girl said.

Cliff went back to the truck and told Tuesday and Randy what the girl had said. "When I told her that I was there about the baby, she said she had nothing to do with it. Sounds like Winter Ann is there now!"

Together, Tuesday, Cliff, and Randy went back to the house and rang the doorbell. The girl, looking uneasy, opened the door.

"We're here for the baby," Cliff showed her his identification. "I'm Sergeant Cliff Moran and you're under arrest for kidnapping."

The girl turned pale and started crying. "Please, I'm going to have a baby. Why would I take one from someone else?"

"Who are you?" Cliff asked

"I'm Mary Anderson."

"Why are you in Olene's house?"

"Olene is taking care of me until my baby is born. I can't let my parents find out. They'll be heartsick."

"What happens to the baby after it's born?"

"Olene finds adoptive parents and arranges the adoption. She's been an angel. I don't know what would have happened to me without her."

"Hate to burst your bubble, but she sells the babies for profit," Tuesday said. "I believe she has my child here now."

"We want to see the baby," Cliff said and moved forward. Mary stepped aside. Tears ran down her face, and she shivered as if she were cold. They spread out, going into each room. Tuesday was the one to find Winter Ann. "Cliff, she's here. We've found her." Holding her daughter tightly to her breast, she slumped to the floor sobbing in relief and joy.

Cliff ran into the room, he lowered himself to the floor, his legs straddling Tuesday, with his arms around her and the baby. They stayed that way until Tuesday's tears subsided. As she quieted, he helped her to her feet. Still holding her beloved child, she grabbed a diaper bag and filled it with diapers and a couple changes of clothes.

As they were leaving the house, Alex Parker and his group pulled up outside. They saw Tuesday with the baby and cheered. Mary Anderson was taken to the county sheriff's office and turned over to the sheriff. Her parents would be notified. Cliff assigned Rex Tripp the job of transporting Tuesday and Winter Ann back to Wheeling while they continued the search for Olene and McCallister.

When Olene returned to her house, she didn't notice the truck with two snowmobiles parked at the curb up the block. As she turned her key in the lock two men came up to her with badges identifying themselves as detectives of the Wheeling police department.

"What do you want?" Olene asked, alarmed.

"You are under arrest for child endangerment, suspicion of kidnapping, and harboring a fugitive."

"Who is the fugitive I'm supposed to be hiding?" she asked.

"Jacob McCallister."

"I don't know anyone by that name."

"How about Victor Newman?" Randy asked.

Her eyes darkened, but she shook her head indicating she did not recognize that name, either.

The detectives read her her rights, and Cliff took her to the county jail, where they turned her over to the sheriff with the understanding that Sergeant Cliff Moran and anyone from the prosecuting attorney's office in Wheeling would have access to her for questioning, as needed for her testimony. Then Cliff enlisted the help of the sheriff's department to go after McCallister, alias Victor Newman.

While the sheriff called on his two deputies, Cliff questioned Olene about McCallister's whereabouts. Finally, after extensive interrogation, Olene admitted to knowing McCallister as Newman. "You know there are witnesses who will testify that you were seen in his company on many occasions," Cliff said. "Your determination to protect McCallister proves that you're emotionally involved with him. If you continue to withhold information, you'll be charged as an accessory to his crimes and your prison time will run accordingly. Without the charge of accessory, your prison term will be shorter and maybe the prosecuting attorney will cut you a break."

The fact that there was no future for Olene and Victor, now that he was in big trouble with the law, plus the fact that she was scared for her own hide, was enough to loosen her tongue. "Promise me no jail time and I'll talk."

"I can't do that. I don't have the authority, and besides you're going to get some time. You must know that what you have been involved in is serious."

"Look," Olene said. "I had the parent's permission in every case. I kept the mother until birth and found a home for her child. What's illegal about that?"

"My bet is the mother was under age in most cases," Cliff said. "It's obvious that Mary Anderson is."

"Alright, cut me a deal and I'll talk," Olene said.

"I can promise that I'll do all I can to persuade the prosecutor to cut you a deal for the minimum sentence. I believe he will do it on my recommendation. You've never been in trouble before."

About two hours after Cliff and Randy got all the information from Olene that they could, they set out for Crystal Lake, with the others following behind.

As Cliff Moran led the manhunt toward Crystal Lake, McCallister paced back and forth, looking at his watch every few seconds. "Where is she?" McCallister mumbled. "I expected her back by now. Something is seriously wrong."

Not one to take chances, he grabbed his jacket and headed for the front door. He was not going to let fifty thousand dollars, which Olene would collect when the couple came for Tuesday's child, get in the way of freedom.

Cora and Linda were at the house when Tuesday came home with her child safely in her arms. "Oh, Cora, I'm so glad that you're here," Tuesday said. "I have my daughter back, but I'll never have a moment's peace until Jacob is put behind bars."

"Don't worry. They'll get him," Cora said.

"I can't be so sure," Tuesday said. "He seems to stay one step ahead of the law."

"Hi, Tuesday," Patty said as she, Paul Frank, and Mary Lou came into the room. "I'm so glad you're back with Winter Ann." Tears of joy ran down her cheeks.

"Patty, have you had any dreams?" Tuesday asked. Patty hung her head and shuffled her feet. "Please tell me you haven't."

"I had some dreams about Pa," Patty said, with tears in her eyes. "He was laughin' 'bout Cliff."

"What else?" Tuesday asked.

"Let me put the baby down for you," Cora said. "I haven't gotten to see her yet."

"Okay, Cora," Tuesday said, handing over her precious daughter. "Patty, go on."

"When I have th' dream, I get so scared I wake up," Patty sobbed.

"Don't cry," Tuesday said. "Just tell me what you can."

"Seems like Pa'd gotten away from Cliff," Patty said. "I don't knowed for sure, but he's happy an' plannin' to spend th' money someone owes him. It's lots of money."

"That doesn't seem so scary," Tuesday said.

"He's plannin' on comin' for us an' takin' us again."

"I promise you that won't happen," Tuesday said. "I will never take anything for granted again. Anyway, Cliff and I are getting married right away. He will be living here."

"I'm scared," Patty said.

"You know, Cliff may already have your father in custody," Tuesday said.

Cora came back into the room. "Paul Frank, why don't you take Tuesday's car and take the girls to the mall?" Cora asked.

Paul Frank had quickly found his way around the city with Patty's help. She had learned her way the past eight months, and Cora had encouraged the three of them to discover all they could about Wheeling. Paul Frank and Mary Lou were having the time of their lives exploring the city.

The day before, McCallister's and Dillon's families had been taken to various shelters. Just before they left the hotel, Paul Frank, Mary Lou, and Patty had visited them in their rooms. Annabelle and Big Bessie were still fighting for control. They fought over which one of them would ring up room service, who got to take a bath first—anything they could think of.

"Patty, you're welcome to come back to th' cabin to live. That's what I'm goin' to do," Annabelle said. "I don't like th' city, an' I want to go home."

"No, I want to stay here," Patty said.

"I want to stay here, too," Daisy said. "I love th' city and th' pretty clothes."

"Ya look nice in th' jeans an' sweater ya have on," Patty said.

"Tuesday got them for me," Daisy said. "She's goin' to help me stay in th' city if she can. Even if I have to go back to th' mountain for a while, she's goin' to find a way for me to move to th' city."

"Sara an' me are goin' back to th' mountain," Joe said. "I don't like th' city, neither. There're too many laws. I like doin' what I want."

"I'm goin' back, too," Big Bessie said. "Frank'll expect us to be there when he comes home. Mary Lou, you otta come, too. Ya knowed Frank'll not like it if ya don't come home."

"There's no way I'm goin' back to th' mountain," Mary Lou said. "No way. How can ya want to go back? Look around ya. Ya have all th' comforts ya can ever want. All th' food ya want an' you're warm an' safe."

Melverta, Sally Ann, Emma Jean, and Eva Belle listened, not joining in on the conversation. Each of them was overwhelmed by the city but secretly wanted to stay.

"I want to stay close to my twins," Daisy said. "They're bein' adopted by Lieutenant Hal Brooks an' his wife, but I can see them anytime I want. I can't do that if I'm on th' mountain."

"I have to go back an' take care of my sisters," Paul Frank said. "I'd like to stay if it weren't for that."

"I'll never go back," Patty said. "Never!"

With Cliff Moran and Randy McCoy in the lead, the three vehicles moved along old Route 19. They had turned off the new four-lane highway at a sign marking old Route 19 South and a second sign, standing behind it, that read "Crystal Lake 10 miles."

"I'm getting nervous," McCoy said. "If McCallister was waiting for Olene to come back, we could have spooked him by holding her. If that's the case, he ran."

"I pray that you're wrong," Cliff said. "We can't let him get away again. It's obvious he's not going to leave Tuesday alone unless we stop him by putting him behind bars."

"There's the cottage we're looking for," McCoy said. "Number 33. Pull over so he won't hear the engines."

Cliff puled over motioning for the men behind to do the same. "I hate to say it, but this place looks deserted," he said.

The men came from the vehicles behind and gathered around Cliff and Randy.

"Are you wearing bulletproof vests?" Cliff asked the men.

"We are," Wildman said. "I handed them out myself."

"How do you want to proceed?" McCoy asked.

"Let's assume he's in there and try taking him by surprise."

Cliff gave instructions and the men fanned out. Cliff and Randy headed for the front of the chalet. Alex Parker and Ned Dugan headed for the rear. Walter Wildman and John Gibson went around the side. Bert Howard and Robert Sines stayed behind Cliff and Randy as back-ups.

Too late, Jacob saw the men coming to the front door. He had been about to open the back door to leave. Quickly he moved so he would be safely hidden behind the door when it opened. He was fully dressed and had his shotgun in hand.

Suddenly the door burst open with a resounding crash, and a split second later, the front door slammed open with a snap of cracking wood. The door hit McCallister and bounced forward again. Instantaneously, men carrying guns and wearing bulletproof vests who had charged in from the front and the back surrounded him.

"Drop the gun," Cliff ordered. "You're under arrest. McCoy, handcuff the bastard and read him his rights."

At long last, Cliff and the others had broken through a ring of kidnappers, baby brokers, and their sources of illegal adoption. With so many to question, the testimony would lead to others involved, creating a domino effect.

And at long last, Jacob McCallister and Cliff Moran looked at each other eye to eye. Cliff savored the victory of having cuffed McCallister, who was now at his mercy.

"McCallister," Cliff said, "you will pay for every minute that you terrified Tuesday. I promise you that. You don't look so much like the man around town with that bald head and your hands cuffed behind your back."

"Sergeant Cliff Moran," Jacob McCallister said, "you had better watch your back. Don't let up for a minute, because I promise you, this is not the end."

*A*SHLEY BLAKE WAS RETURNED TO HER FAMILY SIX months after her abduction at the hands of Aubry Moats. Ashley is now back in school and is currently under the care of a counselor to help her deal with her experience.

Jacob McCallister and Frank Dillon's trial lasted three months. They were convicted of child endangerment, selling minors on the black market, and polygamy. Both were sentenced to twenty years to life in the state penitentiary.

Aubry Moats, Marty Townsend, Steven Lloyd, and Simon Leonard were also sentenced to twenty years to life. Aubry was not given leniency for turning state's evidence due to the nature of his crime.

Olene Ryder was sentenced to ten to twenty years.

When the Thompsons were made aware that Tom's father was the one who had offered him for sale and there would be no claim on him, Amy and Ralph Thompson made a decision to begin adoption proceedings. In the meantime, they have arranged to act as his foster parents.

The Thompsons could not have another child and this was the best, and maybe the only way, to get a brother for Jeff. He was already emotionally attached to Tom and had improved rapidly after Tom had been put in the bed next to him. The Thompsons took both boys to their home upon their release from the hospital. The boys are receiving special tutoring in order for them to be prepared for school. As a courtesy, Dillon's women were told about Tom. As they could not care for him and did not know which of them was the mother, they offered no objection to the prospective adoption.

Hal has taken Daisy to his home, allowing her time to decide whether or not to return to the mountain. Hal believes she deserves to see her twins. Although there is no way Daisy could raise the children, he wants them to have a relationship with their birth mother.

Tuesday, happy with the return of her child, has taken Daisy under her wing, giving her make-up and clothing.

With the exception of Daisy, McCallister's and Dillon's women remain in a shelter for abused women. They are cared for in return for their participation in the daily running of the shelter. While in the shelter they will be trained according to their abilities for employment and eventual self-reliance. The babies are in foster homes waiting for their mothers to complete their training and finally be brought together in their own homes. Annabelle agreed to stay on in the city until Joe is released from the rehabilitation center for troubled boys, where he is serving a two-year sentence.

Sara, Sally Ann, Emma Jean, and Eva Belle are in temporary foster homes.

C. J. HENDERSON WAS BORN ON CHRISTMAS DAY. Her father, a coal miner, was a storyteller who kept his listeners spellbound. Raised on stories about C. C. Camp, Ponds murder farm, and other fearsome tales that came straight from her father's mind, C. J. began telling her friends stories of her own, often-times getting into trouble for frightening the other children.

After high school C. J. married and became the mother of two sons. During the marriage she attended college, and at her father's urging, studied real estate and became an agent. The knowledge gained from her real estate career led to a position with a utility company in which she leased property. That work took her into the remote mountainous areas of West Virginia, where she met many colorful characters. Often C. J. had to wait in her car for property owners to show up for appointments. As she waited, appointment by appointment, her first novel, *The Cabin: Misery on the Mountain,* came alive on her legal pad.

C. J. is now a real estate broker operating her own company and working on more novels.

Purchase Autographed Copies

The Cabin: Misery on the Mountain
Cabin II: Return to Winding Ridge

Name: _____

Address: _____

_____

_____ Copy(ies) of *The Cabin*	$7.99 ea.	$_____
_____ Copy(ies) of *Cabin II*	$7.99 ea.	$_____
WV sales tax (if resident) 6%		$_____
Shipping & handling (first book) $2.49		$_____
S&H (each additional book) $1.13		$_____
Total enclosed		$_____

Method of Payment

☐ Check or money order enclosed.
   Make payable to: Michael Publishing Co.
   PO Box 778
   Fairmont, WV 26555-0778

☐ Charge it to:
   ☐ Master Card   ☐ Visa
   ☐ American Express   ☐ Discover

Card Number: _____

Expiration Date: _____

Signature: _____

Note: Canadian price is $9.99.
Ask for copies at your local bookstore.

Thank you for your order.

Coming Soon!
Cabin III: Unlawful Assembly at Winding Ridge